A NOVEL

Lost Children
of the
Prophet

Angelique Conger

Southwest of Zion Publishing / LAS VEGAS

Angelique Conger/Southwest of Zion Publishing
7401 W Washington Ave
Las Vegas, NV 89128
www.AngeliqueCongerAuthor.com

Publisher's Note: This is a work of fiction. Names, characters, places, and incidents are a product of the author's imagination. Locales and public names are sometimes used for atmospheric purposes. Any resemblance to actual people, living or dead, or to businesses, companies, events, institutions, or locales is completely coincidental.

Book Layout © 2014 BookDesignTemplates.com

Lost Children of the Prophet/Angelique Conger. -- 1st ed.
ISBN **978-1-946550-09-5**

For my family,
Whom I love

CONTENTS

CHAPTER 1

Memories

If she understood the effects of a man desiring her, Ziva may have never dreamed about the coming day when her father would choose a mate for her. As she did not …

Ziva hurried down the long hall to join her father for dinner, her pale blue silk dress brushing softly against her legs. Why did I lose track of time in the bath? I did not need to dream of the man father will choose for my mate. Tall and handsome will be nice, like those boys Tawna and Kara gush about. I wouldn't know. I will go to the market with Tawna and Kara tomorrow. I do so want to have a look at those boys. How will I convince Father?

Ziva slipped into her seat at the small table in their private dining room, breathing a sigh of relief. Father had not yet arrived. She sat with her back straight, legs crossed at the ankle, her right foot bouncing as she waited.

Orak, her father, joined her soon after. "I'm sorry to be late, Ziv." He strode into the room and took his seat. "Bram kept me late, discussing problems with distribution."

"It is fine, Father. I only just arrived." Ziva smiled. "What problems are you having with distribution now?"

"The city leaders want to tax our sales. Nothing for you to worry about. I'll handle it."

Servants unobtrusively served the meal. Ziva glanced up and nodded her thanks to the man who sat her plate in front of her, then picked up her spoon to eat.

"Tax the sales? Are they not taxing each step of production? How greedy can they get?"

"I do not know, my dear. Korm's girl, Tawna, asked about you." Orak nodded to the servants and spooned soup into his mouth.

"Tawna? I haven't seen her for some time. Was she at Korm's shop?" Ziv glanced up from her food.

"Tawna came to encourage Korm to hurry home. I was glad of it, for I knew you waited for me. She is growing into a pretty young woman."

The two then lapsed into silence as they focused on eating. Ziva thought about her friend. Though they once lived in houses near each other and spent much time together, they did not visit as often, now. When Orak and Ziva moved to this bigger house, the girls were separated. They shared messages through the day, making plans for a visit to the markets, which was much easier for Tawna and Kara, who were not protected as closely as Ziva.

"We have been invited to a party at Roven's house next week." Orak interrupted Ziva's contemplation.

"A party? At Roven's? And I have been invited? Do you think Tawna and Kara will be attending?" Ziva tilted her head to the side as she peppered her father with questions.

"I believe they will," Orak said. "Bram mentioned he and his family would be going."

"I feel uncomfortable at those things, especially when I don't know anyone there."

"Of course you do, Ziv. No one likes to be in a large group of strangers. I will be there, too. You will not be alone."

Ziva noticed the kind look in his deep brown eyes and remembered how he had taken her to other parties and stayed close, unlike some other fathers. Most of them left their families at the edge of the party to seek out business cronies and city leaders. Orak did not. He held Ziva's small hand in his big paw as they walked through the crowd, stopping occasionally to visit with other merchants until they found Tawna with her mother and sisters. Ziva begged to be allowed to stay awhile with them. Orak bent to kiss her on the cheek and reluctantly left her with her friends. He then returned soon to reclaim her hand and walked with her to find food.

Ziva often wondered what it would be like to have so many sisters. It must be nice to have a sister to share secrets with, but Tawna had other opinions about sisters who were always there, listening, and crowding her. Ziva supposed it was both bad and good. She would never know. She had no mother, no brothers, and no sisters.

She looked up at her father and smiled. "You are right, Father. You are always there for me."

He beamed at her, his dark eyes shone from his dark mahogany face. She looked at his dark hands and arms, then down at her pale pink arms. His eyes were dark, while hers were blue. His hair in tight curls, dark brown; she wore hers in soft honey colored waves across her shoulders.

For the thousandth time, she wondered why she looked so different from her father. But, now was not the time to ask. She had tried before, but Orak became somber and melancholic at the question. Ziva tried to stay away from that subject in happy times. But, someday … someday, she would get her answer.

Ziva glanced at her father. "I look forward to joining my friends at the party. May I join Tawna at Bram's shop tomorrow? She can help me purchase fabric for a new dress to wear to the party."

Orak looked up, his bushy eyebrows lowered. "And how will Tawna know to meet you there?"

Ziva's cheeks warmed as she stared at the table in front of her. "She sent me a message." She lifted her eyes and rushed on. "I will be careful. If we are going to a party, I do need a dress."

"The seamstress can bring fabric for you to choose from."

"I know that, but, Father, please. I do so want to go to the market and visit with my friends. Please." She stared up at him through her long, light brown eyelashes.

Orak returned her stare, thinking. At last he replied. "I suppose I can do without Com for a span or two. Would you promise to listen to him, follow his orders?"

Ziva pouted.

"You know the market is dangerous for young women, especially for young women whose fathers are wealthy."

She breathed heavily through her nose and flicked her eyes away. "If I must."

"You must, if you are to go at all." Orak smiled.

"You will let me go? Thank you, Father." She leaped from her seat and threw her arms around his neck.

Orak gathered her close. "You may go, but you must listen to Com."

"I will. I promise I will."

~ ~ ~

At the back of the house, buried in a huge copper kettle, Nat wiped sweat from his face with the back of his hand, then grabbed more cleansing sand and continued to scour the burnt vegetables from the surface of the kettle. Cleaning pots gave him time to think, and to remember.

Five years earlier, Nat became part of Qinten's household. The scullery needed a boy small enough to crawl into the smaller kettles. He had been small and skinny then. In the years since coming to the priest's home, he had grown taller and stronger, now able only to crawl into the biggest kettles.

Part of his strength came from wrestling the heavy kettles. The rest came from Kenji. Nat remembered how the older scullery boys kept the younger, smaller boys in place by beating on them. Kenji took an instant and personal interest in Nat.

On his first day in the kitchens, Nat had not expected a foot to be thrust in his path, and he tumbled to the hard, stone floor.

"Get up scrawny," Kenji had jeered.

Nat had been warned when he arrived in Qinten's kitchen. "Beware of the older boys. They think they own the place," one of the young men who brought him to the kitchen had hissed. Nat wondered what he meant. Now, he knew.

Nat had been carrying his kettle toward the place designated for cleaning. A hand in his back pushed. He stumbled. Fighting back would not help this situation. Much as he disliked giving in, he hated battles even worse. This was one battle he feared would be forced on him. He turned toward his tormentor. A bigger boy, covered with the grime of working in the scullery, stood glaring at him.

"Hi. I'm Nat. And you are?" he said.

"Bigger and better than you." The boy shoved at the kettle held in Nat's arms, knocking him off balance.

Nat regained his balance easily enough. His last owner had been a drum maker and Nat had plenty of practice in balancing large, awkward objects of every size.

"I see. You are bigger than me. Better? I doubt that." Nat turned to move in the proper direction when a foot reached out to knock his feet out from under him and sending him sprawling, the kettle banging across the floor.

"I was told you could manage kettles," a big voice proclaimed, reaching down to pull Nat up by the back of his thin garment. "Falling does not show that ability."

A red-faced man, obviously someone who mattered in this kitchen, pulled him to his feet and bent to stare into his eyes. He wondered about telling the real reason for his fall for half a breath.

"I usually can manage larger kettles, sir." He lowered his eyes. "I am unfamiliar with this floor and must have tripped on a rough spot. It will not happen again."

"Rough spot? On my floor?" the man roared.

"Or something?" Nat whispered.

"Yes, something." The man softened. "Pick up that kettle and get it cleaned."

"Yes, sir." Nat quickly retrieved the offending kettle and hurried toward the cleaning grounds.

Nat had been inside the kettle, scrubbing for a short time, when he felt a tug on his foot. Thinking it may be the red-faced man, he quickly backed out, to see his tormentor.

"If you think you can avoid a beating by sucking up to Gowdy, you are mistaken," the bigger boy had hissed and ran off.

Nat shook his head and crawled back into the kettle. In the short confrontation, he had learned two important things. He knew the name of the red-faced man and he knew he needed to protect himself from the bigger boy.

Over the next few days, Nat learned the most vicious bully of the scullery boys had a name, Kenji. Kenji decided Nat was his personal "project." The next morning, Kenji waited for him at breakfast. Before Nat knew what was coming, he had swatted Nat's bowl of food off the table onto the floor. Nat quietly found a rag and cleaned up the mess, earning a smile from Liana, the girl who had dished up the meal. He received nothing else, only the smile.

"Food is not to be wasted. You get only one bowl of breakfast," Gowdy had growled. "What you do with it is up to you. If you want to feed the floor, that is your choice. You will wait until the next meal for more food."

Nat left the table area and walked to the scullery, found a dirty kettle, and began to clean it. Later, he watched Kenji walk through the scullery. Kenji's more frequent assignment was the task of turning the spit. When he was there, Nat felt safer traversing the kitchen. He had managed to avoid Kenji for two days. Then, while Nat sat with the other boys outside the cleaning space behind the kitchen one evening, Kenji stood over him.

"Think you can avoid me?" Kenji sneered.

"It was worth trying." Nat looked away from him.

"You are wrong. I'm here and you will not hide from me."

"Why? I do not like fighting." Nat glanced up at the bigger boy.

"Because you are smaller and deserve a beating?"

"From you?" Nat voiced his lack of concern with a shrug. Inside he prepared himself. Would it be better to allow the beating, or fight back? He had seen other, smaller boys, cowed by this bully. They gave him their food and did his bidding. Nat refused to do that. He needed his food to grow. He may be a slave, but that was all the degradation he needed. No more. He would fight.

Kenji must have believed Nat would sit and take his beating. He stepped forward as Nat punched him in the stomach. Kenji's eyes widened as he fell back. Nat stood, legs apart and ready. Kenji regained his balance and began to rain blows on Nat. For a time, Nat managed blow for blow. However, because he was smaller and weaker, it was not long before he found himself on the ground, curled in a ball, arms protecting his head. Eventually, the beating ended.

Nat had never received another beating from Kenji, he remembered with satisfaction. Though his bruises did not lighten for many days and he limped a bit longer than that. Gowdy gave instructions to the young men to be watchful of Nat. He was needed to clean the kettles and no one molested him while he healed. He could not depend on the young men to protect him all the time. It was up to him to protect himself.

He watched the other younger boys. Some wanted to be like Kenji and did all they could to move closer into his circle. These boys watched the other little boys and ran to tell Kenji whenever the others did something Kenji didn't like. Nat marked these boys, making certain they didn't know his plans.

As he healed, he spoke quietly with other younger boys. These boys saw him as a hero. He stood up to Kenji. No one else had. Alain was first to come, slipping to his side while he cleaned, whispering encouragement. Other boys found their way to tell him they were glad he stood up for himself. Nat considered two plans of attack, while watching Kenji bully and beat on other boys. He thought of leading a small group of younger boys in the fight back, but he feared if he did that, he would be perceived as a bully, as much as Kenji.

Rather than involve the other boys, Nat decided he could handle Kenji on his own. He smiled at the other boys when they offered to help him "take down that bully, Kenji" and shook his head. No. He would do this on his own.

He found a heavy, knotted stick and used it as a crutch, leaning on it when walking. He hobbled around the scullery and into the boys' dormitory, as though he were weak and hurt. He had dealt with bullies before. He knew to be prepared. It wasn't long before Kenji found him alone.

"Thought you could hide from me inside your kettle all the time, did you?" Kenji snarled. "No kettle here. Where will you hide now?"

As Nat had expected, Kenji brought his buddies to back him up. Bullies rarely went anywhere alone.

"And you came with your girl friends," he taunted.

Kenji's face reddened beneath the grime. "I beat you to nothin' before. I can do it again."

"Sure you can, with your back up choir." Nat worked to ensure Kenji was angry, so angry he lost control. He continued, "You beat me before. I'm just a little guy. You think you can take me on any time you want. Of course, you have to bring along the choir, just to be sure I don't beat you up."

"Nah. I don't need my boys to help beat you up. You're just a scrawny bit of nothin'." Kenji's anger began to show and the volume of his voice lifted. "I'll show you. Min, Drak, stay back." Kenji waved them back. "I can beat up this little piece of nothin' on my own."

"You sure?" Drak glanced between Kenji and Nat.

"Of course, I'm sure. Stay back. I'm goin' to stop the mouth of this little boy."

Min and Drak stepped back. "If you say so, Kenji. We won't join in the fun."

'Good. That leaves only Kenji to deal with.' Nat watched Kenji ball his hands into fists and move forward, balancing on the balls of his feet. No, not mad enough.

"Sure you can take care of this little boy, all alone?" Nat taunted. "I am such a little thing. You are sure you can handle me on your own?"

"Enough!" Kenji bellowed and rush forward, fists ready to pound Nat down.

Nat leaned on his stick until he felt Kenji's hot breath on his face, then swung it out, crashing it into Kenji's body with a resounding "Oof" and a crash.

Kenji looked surprised, sucked in his breath, then lifted his fists once more to beat on Nat. But Nat gave Kenji no opportunity to hit him, knocking his hands back with the club. Kenji ducked his head, obviously determined to hit Nat in the stomach with it. Nat swept Kenji's feet from under him with his club. Kenji fell with a yell and a thud.

Nat glanced quickly toward where Drak and Min stood. They had disappeared. He spun around, checking to be sure they were gone. Drak had disappeared, but Min was trying to sneak up on him.

Nat lifted his club and swept it toward Min, knocking him in the head with a satisfying thunk. Min fell to the ground, making no more noise. Nat allowed the club to continue swinging him around, hitting Kenji again as he rose, prepared to attack from behind.

The club caught Kenji across the arm. Nat heard a loud crack, Kenji dropped to the ground with a scream and cradled his arm. Nat turned to be certain Min was still down. When he was certain no danger threatened him, he walked to his dorm.

Kenji returned to the kitchen two days later. A rag tied around his neck supported the arm, tied between two sticks. There was little he could do in the busy kitchen to stay out of the way. Gowdy gave him the chore of toting buckets of cleaning sand to the boys who cleaned the kettles.

Min spent several days in bed before he finally returned to the kitchen. Drak slipped into the background, staying far away from the trouble makers. Within two weeks, Kenji and Min were sold at the slave market.

Now, Nat felt someone pulling on his legs. "What now?" he muttered, tensing as he backed out of the huge kettle. When he realized he had been stuck in memories, he relaxed a little.

"Relax, boy," Gowdy said. "Cook wants to see you."

"Cook? See me?" Confusion filled Nat. "Why would Cook want to see me?"

"Don't know, but you'd better hurry in to the kitchen."

Chapter 2

Was It Only a Boy?

The next morning, Ziva stepped into a small carriage. Com helped her tuck her skirts around her feet.

"You remember what your father said, don't you? You will listen to me. If I say we must leave now, do not argue. My job is to keep you safe."

Com stared at her until she nodded her head. "Yes, Com, I will listen."

"Be certain you do," he huffed as he closed the carriage door.

I have to listen, if I want to do this again. I hope we have no problems. Ziva scooted close to the window and gazed out at the trees and walls that surrounded the houses lining the streets, hoping to keep out those who would rob and steal. She wondered why people would want to steal from others.

They passed out of the wealthy section of the city where she lived into other sections with smaller, houses without walls, and on into the market. The road became busier, full of other carriages, people on horseback, and others wending their way between horses and wheeled vehicles, as they moved closer to the market.

Finally, the carriage slowed and stopped. Ziva knew better than to leap from within its sanctuary. She leaned back in the seat, her hands folded in her lap. Only the tiny movement of a bouncing foot betrayed her impatience.

The carriage door opened and Com held out his hand to help her step from its depths. They had reached the door to Korm's fabric shop and Tawna stood in the doorway.

Before Ziva could scurry to greet her, Com grasped the hand he held and pulled her close. "Remember, I am here to ensure your safety. Do not do anything rash." The cold in his dark eyes caused her to shiver.

"No, Com. I will listen to you."

With that, he released her hand and she hurried to her friend's side. Tawna embraced her briefly and the two young women entered the shop as the carriage rolled away from the entrance. Com followed her inside and stood watching from beside the door.

"I never believed your father would allow you out of your house," Tawna said. "How did you manage?"

"I told him I need a new dress for Roven's party. He knows I hate parties. I told him I'd go without complaint if he let me come here today. He was happy to allow me to choose fabric for a new dress."

Tawna raised her eyebrows. "Your father was happy to let you come here?"

Ziva twisted her mouth to the side. "Well, not happy. I had to bring Com," her eyes darted toward the quiet man by the door, "and listen to everything he tells me. Father sees danger for me everywhere."

"Your father is overprotective. There is no danger in my father's shop."

"I know. Which fabric should I choose?" Ziva moved to the stacks of beautiful fabric.

The girls wandered around the shop. Tawna pointed out fabrics she thought would look good on her friend, while Ziva fingered them and pulled a few from the shelf. Some she brought to her face to feel the soft texture.

A bell above the door tinkled and the girls looked up to see their other friend, Kara, breeze through the entrance. Tawna rushed to greet her while Ziva carefully set her armload of fabrics on top of the others before turning to her friend.

"How ever did you manage to escape the close watch of Orak?" Kara gushed. "I have not seen you outside that big, beautiful home since you moved in."

"I begged. I cried. I pouted."

"You?" Tawna and Kara chorused, their eyes wide.

"Not really," Ziva laughed. "But I did beg. I must have said something right, for I am here."

"With your watchdog," Tawna murmured, her eyes darting to Com.

"If he had not come with me, I would not be here. I'm happy he would come." Ziva turned back to the pile of fabrics. "Which one should I buy?"

The girls wandered through the stacks of beautiful fabrics, laughing and gossiping. Kara suggested a bright orange, but Ziva shook her head. Tawna pointed to a deep burgundy. After a heartbeat of thought, Ziva shrugged it away. After looking at all the lovely, soft fabrics, Ziva had reduced the stack to four: a dark golden fabric with swirls patterning across it in lighter shades, a light orchid covered with diamonds of deeper purple, a pale green, and a dark blue.

"Which looks best?" Ziva held each fabric near her face.

Tawna gazed into her face. "They are all lovely against your pale skin and blond hair."

"I like the green. It contrasts with your eyes," Kara said.

"It is pretty. The gold looks nice with your hair, too," Tawna said.

"I am wearing a bright yellow. Shall we dress in similar colors?" Kara spun a long curl around her finger.

"My dress is orange," Tawna said.

"Then, no. We should choose our own colors. Look different." Ziva returned to her decision. She set the gold aside. The orchid soon joined it. "Green or blue? Hmmm. Com?" Ziva turned toward the man towering beside the door. "Which would you choose? Green or blue?"

"Me? You want me to give my opinion? About fabric? Never," the big man growled and folded his arms across his chest.

16

The girls tittered. Ziva held the last two against her face. "I think I like the blue. My eyes are blue. And, I like the feel of it better."

"That dark blue?" Kara gasped. "It is so sedate, almost matronly. No young man will look at you in that."

"Then it is the fabric for me. Tawna, will you help me with the purchase?"

Tawna took the bolt of fabric from her friend and carried it to the back room. When she returned, she carried a bag, heavy with the fabric. "I will have one of the boys take it to your carriage."

"Thank you." Ziva ducked her head. "I do not know if I brought enough coin."

"My father put it on your father's account. Do not worry. We will be paid." Tawna touched her friend on the arm. "You don't do this often, do you?"

"No." Ziva brushed away the sparkling tears from her eyes.

"Let's go into the market, now," Kara whined. "I want a treat."

Ziva looked to Com. "May I?"

The big, dark man drew his eyebrows close. "Wait here, I will check the streets."

The girls watched him slip out the door.

Com returned and signaled. "You may go, but listen to me. If I say we must leave, we must leave immediately."

Ziva glanced into his eyes and saw his concern. "Yes, Com, I will."

The girls left the shop and walked, with arms linked, into the market, gossiping about the party, and other things.

"Mmm, nice looking man there," Kara ogled.

"Where?" Ziva asked. She followed Kara's eyes to see a slave, wearing only a thin rag wrapped around his waist. "Oh." She felt her face redden.

"He is not for us," Tawna said, pulling them along. "Now, he is."

"Which one?" Ziva asked.

"The gentleman standing by the jewelers stand."

The tall, well-dressed man bent over a necklace, dangling with jewels and reflecting the light.

"Yum." Kara licked her lips.

The girls giggled and continued on. A vendor passed carrying meat pies. Kara stopped him and purchased three, handing one to each of her friends. They ate the pies as they walked, laughing and talking.

A shout from the crowd caused them to look around. A boy pushed through the crowd with a man chasing him. The boy shoved himself between the girls and raced on through the crowd.

Suddenly, Com stood beside Ziva. "We must go. Now." Ziva looked into his eyes and saw danger.

She grabbed Tawna by the arm. "Come with us."

"No. We are safe. You go," Tawna said, pushing her away.

Com grabbed her by the elbow and rushed her around a corner, down a busy street, and around several other corners and down streets until they arrived at the place where their carriage stood behind Korm's shop. Ziva bent to set her hands on her knees and sucked in huge, gasping breaths. Com's breath seemed normal.

"Get in, quickly," Com ordered.

Ziva stumbled as she stepped into the carriage, falling onto the seat as the carriage moved. In no time, they were racing down the street and out of the market. The driver shouted and cursed as people rushed to get out of the way of the thundering horses hooves. Ziva held on to the strap on the side, trying to stay upright.

Eventually, they slowed, though the carriage did not return to the leisurely pace of their ride to the market. Soon, it drew to a stop in front of Ziva's door.

Ziva brushed her hair back into place with her hands. When Com opened her door, she asked, "What was that about? It was only a boy."

"The boy was a distraction. You did not see the men chasing us. They wanted to take you."

"Take me? Why?"

"Your father would pay them a hefty price to free you, or so they think."

Ziva brought her hand to her mouth to cover her gasp. "Oh. I didn't know. Thank you for saving me."

Com nodded and ushered her inside. "Perhaps you will be happy now to stay here, in the safety of your father's house."

Ziva nodded.

~ ~ ~

Nat stepped into the pantry, searching for ginger root. He stretched his back. Cook's helper seemed to be a big promotion, but it wasn't as wonderful as he had dreamed. Released earlier from the work, he rested in the evenings and no longer crawled into the huge kettles to scrub them clean.

Freedom to rest at the end of the day was counterbalanced by the requirement to wake early in the morning, for Cook prepared all the meals, including the morning meal. He required Nat's assistance—mostly for running back and forth to the pantry, like now, to retrieve ingredients for the many dishes presented to Qinten each meal. Thankfully, he was not also required to run for Baker. He'd never stop if he had to run for both of them.

By now, the pantry had become familiar. Nat found most of the required ingredients with little effort. Ginger root was new. He looked on the bottom shelf and found the tangy smelling root in a basket. Cook needed three. He found the best looking three in the basket and hurried back to the kitchen. Cook directed him to wash and peel the funny looking roots, then chop them for the dish he was making.

Nat found a small, sharp knife and began to work on the ginger. He knew he would need to work quickly, for Cook would need the ginger soon, and would think of something new to send him for.

Nat had been surprised that first day—was it only a month ago? — when Gowdy sent him from the cleaning scullery to the kitchen. Cook had simply said, "I need a new helper. You will do as I say."

Nat had nodded and was immediately put to work running to the pantry for vegetables, fruits, and any other ingredient Cook decided he needed. Additionally, he helped peel, cut, and chop, as he did now with the ginger. Nat was careful and quick and Cook was pleased with his work. Cook didn't say much to him, beyond short instructions: "Ginger, wash, peel, and chop finely."

He was used to working without extra instructions. He had been expected to speedily understand and complete his assignments without asking many questions by all his previous owners. Of course, he was required to ask questions in the beginning, but he learned easily and soon discerned many of Cook's needs before he uttered a request. Cook was learning to depend on Nat, and Nat liked that trust.

The ginger was finely chopped and passed on to Cook, who nodded, too busy for further interactions. Nat hurried to the pantry for the carrots and celery Cook would need next.

Drak stepped from behind the door, blocking Nat's way.

"Hello, Drak. Haven't seen you for a while."

"No? I've been here, turning the spit at the fire," Drak said in a surly voice.

"I have not been near the spit. Cook keeps me busy elsewhere." Nat kept his voice carefully neutral.

"Kenji and Min are gone. Sold to a slaver."

"I am sorry, Drak. They were your friends." Nat tried to sound more concerned than he was.

Drak rubbed his forehead. "Kenji never was beat like that before. How did you do it?"

"Got me an equalizer. I was smaller than Kenji. Knew he would hurt me bad if he could. So I got a walking stick and equalized things between us."

"Yeah, you sure did. Guess I'm glad you did." Drak stepped aside to allow Nat passage through the door and into the pantry, following him in.

"Glad? How so?" Nat frowned.

"Less trouble with Cook. I'm where I belong, not runnin' after Kenji."

Nat felt a bit of a smile attach itself to his face. "You aren't angry?"

"Nah." Drak stuck his hand out.

Nat slowly put his now larger hand into Drak's.

"Thanks," Drak said.

Nat's smile grew. "Do you need something from the pantry, too?"

"A side of beef. Sounds like there will be extras for dinner tonight. Unexpected, so I have to get it ready fast." Drak walked to the cooler back of the pantry where the meat was kept. Nat heard him lift a good-sized slab off the hook and sling it over his shoulder.

He reached into the baskets and grabbed his needed vegetables, holding the door and following Drak from the pantry. Nat noticed raised eyebrows and open mouths from other kitchen workers.

"Did they expect us to fight?" he quietly asked Drak.

Drak looked around. "Must have. Disappointed them, huh?" A broad smile crossed his face, then he laughed. Nat joined in, surprising the others who expected a war from them.

Chapter 3

Bait for a Man

Ziva stood in her room staring into the mirror. Her maid, Ana, had painted her face. She wanted to use a bold, bright red on her lips and cheeks. Ziva had refused. Ana gave in to her reserved nature and painted her lips a light pink and her cheeks only a shade darker.

Ana had argued for brighter colors on her eyelids. "At least, a peacock blue to highlight your eyes?" she had said.

Tigre, her yellow and black cat, stared up at her and emitted a single yowl.

"Tigre is right. Peacock is too bright. It makes my eyes fade. Do you have a blue closer to the color of my eyes?" Ziva compromised on this one point.

Ana had smiled and dug through her paints until she found the shade that matched Ziva's eyes. She had wanted to use a similar color to paint her fingernails, but Ziva insisted on a light pink.

"I am still a young girl. I am not yet ready to paint myself so brightly. I do not want that kind of attention." Tigre jumped on Ziva's lap, kneaded her gently with his front paws, then curled up to sleep.

Ana had nodded and stopped pushing.

At fifteen, Ziva felt much too young to try to appeal to men in that way. She enjoyed the feel of Ana brushing her long hair that looked like spun honey. Ana had carefully dressed her hair, placing a beautiful pin to hold the curls back from her face.

Ziva had set Tigre on the floor and stood while a long, filmy dark blue dress, created from the fabric she had purchased at Bram's shop, had been pulled over her head and tied with braided fabric matching the dress.

Now, she stood staring at her reflection. "I guess this will work," she murmured, half to herself.

"It works. You look lovely, my dear." Orak's deep voice startled her.

She glanced toward the door and smiled. "I don't look too … too grown up, do I? I am not ready to leave you."

Orak pulled her into a bear hug, careful not to disturb her hair or mar the face paint. His love radiated through the hug and warm smile. She stood on her toes and kissed him on the cheek. Orak stepped back, spinning Ziva around.

"Uhm hmmm. You do look good. Almost like a grown woman." He held up his hands to stop her flurry of words. "Not a grown woman, but almost. I know you are not ready, but it will be hard to hide your beauty for much longer."

Ziva felt the bright red of embarrassment color her face. "Oh, Father."

"I do not lie, Ziva. You know my honor."

"I do, but I do not like what you say. I do not want some man to claim me. Is there not a better way?" Great tears welled up inside her eyes.

"Be careful of your face paint," Orak warned. "We do not have time for Ana to redo it."

Ziva sniffed and regained control of her emotions, smiled, and reached over to pet her cat's back. "Bye, Tigre. Be good now." She took her father's hand.

"I'm ready. Will you stay with me awhile when we get there?"

Orak nodded and smiled down on her as they left her suite. She felt comfort in his loving presence.

When they arrived at Roven's home, she descended from the light carriage holding Orak's hand. She looked around, noting the other conveyances moving to the side of the residence. The numbers indicated neither a small party nor an enormous one. It appeared to be large enough she could stay out of the line of attention, yet small enough to find her friends. It should be a nice evening.

Orak clasped her hand, as promised, as they walked through the doors and into the large public parlor. They nodded to other guests and wandered through the crowd. He seemed to be happy to be seen with his beautiful daughter, not interested in discussing the cares of the merchant world this evening.

"You did come!" Kara squealed when she caught sight of Ziva. "Mother said all the eligible girls and their families were invited to this party. Bede had to stay home. She is too young. I was not certain you would come."

"Oh? That kind of party?" Ziva stared at Orak. "Father?"

"Roven agreed to sponsor a party to help some of the men who need a mate. It is difficult for them to meet young women." Even beneath his dark skin, Ziva saw red tinting his neck and cheeks.

"Why didn't you tell me? I would not have come." She allowed the frustration to tinge her whisper.

"I know. That is why I didn't tell you." Orak smiled. "You cannot remain in my home forever, though I would love for you to do that. You know our customs. Girls need to be mated."

"You know how I feel about that," she said between her teeth while smiling to her friend. "We will talk of this later."

Orak sighed, though he did not lose his smile. "Make the best of this. Enjoy."

Ziva lifted her head, placed an elegant smile on her face, and slipped her hand into Orak's. "I will. I'll find you later, Kara."

Ziva and her father strolled through the crowd, her eyes searching for Tawna. She had supposed Tawna would arrive earlier, but from behind, she heard her friend's voice calling. She turned in time to catch her friend's gentle hug. Now she felt she could enjoy this party, with Orak and Tawna's help.

When Orak slipped away, flashing a smile in her direction, Ziva wondered briefly about his business. Then, Tawna pulled her along and they began to stroll, arm in arm, around the room.

"Your dress is beautiful," Ziva said. "That color suits you. I can never wear that shade of orange. It makes me look yellow."

"And your dress matches your eyes. What is this party all about? All the available girls our age are here."

"Father says Roven offered to have this party to show off the eligible girls for the men. Too many young men are unmated. I suppose we are here as bait."

Tawna raised her lovely eyebrows. "Bait? Rather harsh, isn't it?"

"Yeah, I suppose. You know how I feel about all this." She felt her smile falling and purposefully reset it.

"I know. Maybe the man who chooses you will be kind."

"You jest! These men believe we are beneath them. Female mates are property to be brought out and shown off, like prized baubles." Ziva covered her contempt with a smile. Anyone looking their way would never guess. Tawna heard it and frowned.

"Do not think about that now. Dinner will be served soon. What do you think it will be? Where is Kara?"

The girls strolled through the crowds, greeting friends, and discussing inconsequential things. Kara joined them, her voice adding to the general noise of the occasion.

"Who is that?" Ziva whispered, her eyes pointed toward a man standing on the edge of the crowd. "I feel his stares."

"Who? Oh, Qinten. He is a priest of Lorca. One of the unmated."

"He is dark. No, no." Ziva blocked the protests of her companions. "Not his color, though it is dark. I feel a darkness in his soul."

"His soul?" Tawna's eyebrows arched high once more. "Do men have souls?"

"Everyone has a soul. And his is dark," Ziva replied with a sigh.

"Then you must hope he does not decide he wants you as his mate." Kara laughed and patted the back of Ziva's hand.

"Truly. I pray Orak is strong, and refuses." Arm in arm, the three girls swished their skirts and moved on.

~ ~ ~

Ziva felt Qinten's eyes brush across her several times that evening as she, Tawna, and Kara strolled about the room. She knew her trio of friends were contrasting in looks and behavior. Her modest dark blue dress matched her eyes and showed off her pale skin, honey-colored hair, and her quiet demeanor. The only jewelry she wore was seven black, tan, and orange clay beads.

She had long ago grown out of the length of hemp they had been originally strung on. Orak had found her crying when she was about seven. The hemp had shredded and the beads scattered. He helped her gather them from the floor, placing them in a small cup. Later he presented her with a fine gold chain and helped her string the beads on it. She wore it all the time. For some reason, it gave her comfort.

Tawna, taller and more outgoing than Ziva, wore a burnt orange dress, with a deeper neckline than Ziva would ever wear, that complemented her dusky brown skin and green eyes. A single strand of pearls surrounded her neck.

Shorter than either of her friends, Kara wore a bright yellow dress, matching her outgoing nature and highlighting her raisin-colored skin and amber eyes. The neck of her dress, too, dipped much lower than Ziva's, while her skirt daringly opened on the side, hand spans above her knees. Chains of gold encircled her neck and arms.

A servant announced dinner and directed the crowd to a large dining room. Orak appeared out of the crowd and escorted Ziva toward the dining area, while her friends found their families. She and Orak chose a table near the edge of the room. Soon, Tawna arrived with her parents, brothers, and sisters, sitting on both sides of the table, nearly filling it.

"Look." Ziva nudged her friend with her elbow. "Qinten thinks he will sit with us."

"I doubt he will find room." Tawna directed her friend's attention to Kara's family who was bearing down on the table. 'Kara and her sisters will fill the table."

Kara sat with her parents and sisters across from Ziva. Bram greeted both Orak and Korm before he sat between his wife and Kara. Qinten sauntered past, staring at Ziva, Tawna and Kara. Ziva saw a dark look pass through his eyes as he saw there would not be room for him. He glided past to a seat.

The noise in the room dropped significantly when servers brought each table food. Still, Ziva was aware of Qinten, sitting nearby at a table of boisterous young men who seemed not to care if the girls, and their fathers, heard their ribald remarks. She knew Orak would not give her to any of these vile men. Qinten, however, sat apart from them, choosing not to participate in their jests. She felt his gaze roam across her and studiously avoided glancing in his direction.

Ziva enjoyed the food almost as much as the company. No cost had been avoided in its preparation, and the cool peach ice desert washed away the heaviness of the other courses. Happy the meal had ended, she rose and linked arms with her friends.

"We are going to the facilities, Father. Do enjoy yourself." Ziva flashed a smile in Orak's direction as they left.

"Great dinner, but I'm glad it's over." She sighed and rubbed her stomach.

"Yes, too long sitting. I hope we can dance. I love dancing." Kara's eyes sparkled at the thought. "Will you join us tonight, Ziv?"

Ziva enjoyed watching her dance, from the sidelines. "Maybe, if the music isn't too wild. I don't want to shake my brains out."

"I don't care what they play. I'm ready to dance!" Kara let go of Ziva's arm and twirled around.

"Not me, Kara. I don't want to shiver and shake everything off. I don't care what the 'men' say." Tawna shook her head as they entered the ladies room, lining up behind others with the same idea.

When they finally managed to leave, the girls promenaded toward the ball room. The music jangled against Ziva's ears, but Kara giggled and entered the dance alone to spin and dance. Soon, a young man bowed and spun her away. Ziva could hear her laughter in the quiet spaces of the music.

She and Tawna found seats along the wall to watch. Several of the foul-mouthed men from the table nearby asked them to dance. Both Ziva and Tawna shook their heads. Not this music. Not those men.

When the tempo changed to something more moderate, Tawna accepted the invitation of a young man to dance. Ziva watched until another man offered her his hand. At least, he's not one of those foul-mouthed men.

"My name is Crites," he said as he took her by the hand.

She stood and whirled away with him onto the dance floor. They laughed and visited through the song and another, then the music increased in tempo and she had him return her to her seat, with a promise to return for another dance.

The wild music brought out the shaking and shivering she refused to participate in. Tawna's escort swirled her to her seat, with a promise of drinks. The girls watched the gyrations of the dance as they visited.

The music slowed and Kara dropped into a chair on the other side of Tawna. "I need a break."

A servant offered them drinks. "Orange juice for me," Tawna declared. "I need to clear out my throat."

"I'm going to try the …" Kara glanced at the faces of her friends, and her hand moved from the wine to an apricot juice. "… one of these."

Ziva asked for a glass of cool water. "The sweetness of juice is cloying," she said with a shrug.

The tempo of the music picked up, and soon Kara danced out onto the floor with yet another partner. Tawna and Ziva accepted a dance with different men, and joined the mass of dancers. When the tune ended, Ziva made an excuse and returned to a chair. She did not want to be pawed by eager young men.

Several dances later, Ziva noticed Qinten amble toward Bram. They spoke with heads together to hear above the music. The song ended and Bram signaled to Kara with a nod of his head.

Kara joined the men and, after a brief discussion, sauntered to the drinks table with Qinten. Ziva allowed a small growl to escape before planting a smile back on her face. Not her business.

Later, when dancing with yet another man, she noticed Kara speaking even louder than usual, her motions exaggerated. Qinten had long since given her to another. Not good for Kara.

After the dance, Ziva accepted another glass of water and joined Tawna in watching a slow, groping dance. Over Tawna's shoulder, she saw Qinten staring at them.

Chapter 4

Never Interfere

Ziva watched Kara dance with drama and flair. She did not approve of her allowing the young men to touch her so intimately. Does she know she will lose standing with the better young men, those who will treat her better? Ziva shook her head. No, Kara rarely thinks about how her actions affect her.

The music changed again, to a faster beat. Ziva's foot bounced to the cheerful music. Tawna nodded to her partner and sat beside Ziva, fanning herself with a fan she produced from a hidden pocket. A servant appeared, offering refreshments.

"Oh, the orange juice is so refreshing." Tawna smiled at the young woman as she took a glass off the tray.

"Is there any water? It solves my thirst." Ziva looked up at the girl who shook her head. "Could you please bring me a glass of water?" She added a smile with the request.

The girl nodded and slipped away.

"Water, again?" Tawna playfully tapped her arm. "Only water? I have seen you drink juices. Why only water tonight?"

"I feel safer with water. Little can be added that I cannot see or smell."

"Silly girl," Tawna laughed. "Who would put anything in our drinks?"

Ziva shrugged.

"Would you join me in this dance?" Crites stood before Ziva holding out his hand. The music lilted, enticing. She took his hand and moved with him to the dance floor

"I'm glad you found me, again," Ziva said as he whirled her out.

"I promised you another dance."

The music encouraged movement without the "shiver and shaking" Ziva abhorred. Crites kept his hands away from intimate touching. His friendly manner enticed Ziva. A definite positive among so many negatives. They shared small talk, and when the music changed, he led her back to her seat. He bowed, as she sat, asking, "Could we do this again?"

"Certainly," she replied and watched him walk away.

Tawna raised her eyebrows and Ziva shrugged.

Kara joined them. "The musicians say they need a break. How can they need a break? They strum a lute or bang on a drum, maybe blow on a pipe?"

"The answer to your question, Kara." Tawna pointed to the musicians who left their instruments and trouped to the refreshment table. "They must believe they need a rest, a drink, and something to eat. They'll be back."

They were interrupted by a young man, offering sweets. Each girl chose one, then helped herself to a drink from another tray, produced by another young man who even had water for Ziva. She and Tawna sat back and listened as Kara bubbled about all the dancing and the young men.

The refreshed musicians resumed their seats and struck up a loud, fast tune. Kara was swept onto the dance floor with yet another partner. A different man drew Tawna out to dance. Ziva sat alone watching. The priest, Qinten, who she had seen following them off and on during the evening came forward.

"Would you like to dance?"

"No, I think not. This music is much too fast," she replied.

"I agree. May I join you?"

Ziva glanced around the room and saw Orak. "I am sorry, but my father is beckoning. I must leave." She stood and hurried to where he stood, watching the dancing.

"You don't want to dance with Qinten? He will be powerful someday."

"Who is he? He has been following us around all evening. He gives me the creeps." Ziva shivered involuntarily.

"Creeps?" Orak chuckled. "Pretty strong. He is a priest of Lorca, on his way to becoming their Hight Priest. Powerful."

"I don't care. There is a darkness within him. Power and wealth are for men, not me." Ziva shook her curls and stamped her foot.

Orak shook his head. He knew well his daughter's stance on this issue. They stood together for a short time until Orak signaled a servant. "Please have my carriage brought around."

Together, Orak and Ziva found Roven and thanked him for the party, then slipped out the door. Their carriage and driver were waiting.

"No interest in any of those young men, Ziva?" Orak asked as they rode through the quiet streets toward home."

"None. Well, one. Crites asked me to dance, twice. He was respectful. He said he'd come back for another dance, but—"

"—you left before he could return?" Orak finished.

"Probably. I do not like parties like these. I do not like to be on display, as one of the 'goods for sale,' much like a side of beef in your market"

"It must feel like that to a young woman of your sensibilities."

"Promise me one thing?" Ziva stared into Orak's eyes.

"What? You know I will give you whatever I can."

"Do not sell me to that Qinten. He is dark inside."

"Not even for money and power?" Orak teased.

"Especially not for the money and power."

~ ~ ~

Shouting and yelling woke Nat in the middle of the night. He tried to close his ears to it, but the sound came close to the dorm room where he lay, before receding. He pulled his thin blanket over his ears to dampen any further noise. It was a temporary solution.

Just as he felt himself drowsing into sleep, he was jolted awake. A whip lash sizzled through the air and onto the victim's back. The poor man screamed.

Nat moved, thinking to fling the blanket back. Drak snaked his hand out from his nearby cot and latched on to Nat's wrist.

"Don't," Drak breathed.

"Don't what?" Nat responded, his voice no louder than Drak's.

"You can do nothing to help that poor man. We have heard it before. Remember? The Master must be angry."

Nat lay listening to the lash striking the unfortunate slave's back, his terrified screams, their anguish. It was not the first time he woke to such screams. He learned early to lie still, hold himself separate, away from the sound.

Shortly after he arrived in Qinten's home, Nat had been wakened by this same noise. The sound drew him up from sleep and he sat horrified, listening to it.

Another boy, not much older than him could not contain his fears. He jumped from his mat and ran out to see what caused the turbulence in their kettle cleaning grounds. Nat heard the boy's shout, followed by a short silence. The boy screamed. The whistle of the lash returned. The boy's screams echoed through the garden. At last they stilled.

The boys in the dorm lay on their mats, fearing to utter a sound, lest they, too, should be found and receive the same treatment. Nat had shuddered through the remainder of the night. His body eventually relaxed into sleep as the sun peeped through the window, the signal for the boys to rise and prepare for another day of work.

Exhausted, Nat shuffled toward the cleaning scullery, eyes half open. The boy in front of him stopped suddenly. Nat bumped into his back.

"Sorry," he mumbled.

Rather than the usual growl and slap, the boy he had bumped into said nothing. He only pointed. Nat's eyes opened wide as he followed the pointing finger. The boy who had left the dorm lay on the ground, his back bloodied and bruised. A boy near Nat ran to the bushes lining the cleaning ground and vomited. Nat fought his stomach, refusing to be one who showed such weakness. Not with Kenji watching.

One of the bigger boys threw his shoulders back and marched over to the boy on the ground. He touched the beaten boy's neck and shook his head.

"I expect Gowdy needs to know," the boy said, looking up from the broken body.

"I'll tell him." Another larger boy stepped away from the mob of staring boys and sped toward the kitchens.

Not many breaths later, the boy returned with Gowdy following close behind.

"Move on," Gowdy growled. "There is nothing to see here. You have things to be doing. Do them."

Nat shook himself and moved to join the lines at the latrines.

Later that evening as the boys gathered on the grass, after working all day, Gowdy strolled from the kitchen and stood in front of them.

"Kai did not survive the lashing," Gowdy said. "You must learn now that your lives are important to the Master only when you do as he demands. Do nothing to make him angry. Do not interfere with the Master's punishments of another. If you do, you will receive a greater punishment. Kai interfered. He no longer lives."

Gowdy stared into the faces of the boys sitting in the grass in front of him. "Never, ever interfere. We need you healthy and in the kitchen." He allowed the sound of his voice to drop on the boys, before turning on his heel and leaving them.

Now, Nat remembered those words. Never interfere. It hurt him to lay in silence and listen to another be punished. He had learned over the years that many times the punishment was undeserved. Qinten had a vile temper and when things outside his domain went poorly, a slave took the punishment.

Nat sighed and nodded. Drak released his wrist. Nat clenched his jaws and dug his fingernails into the palms of his hands, trying not to hear. It did not help. The Master must be angry indeed, for the lashing seemed to go on forever.

Finally, it ended. Nat heard the slave's quiet sobs. In the silence of the room, the others hardly breathed. Nat promised himself he would never be the one Qinten chose to expend his anger on. If that happened, Nat promised himself he would not scream. He would not give the Master the pleasure of his screams.

Chapter 5

Dark Soul

Three days after the party at Rowen's, Ziva had spent the morning studying with her tutor. For a time in the afternoon, she sat with Ana and Vita, learning to paint a picture with thread on fabric. Tawna and Kara came, and spent the last of the afternoon gossiping about the party and all the men they danced with, or rather, Tawna and Ziva spent the time listening to Kara gush about all the men with whom she danced. Tigre curled in Ziva's lap and she absently stroked his yellow and black fur.

"The Lorcan Priest, Qinten, danced with me twice. He is such a good man. Didn't try to touch me inappropriately and is a good dancer. It doesn't hurt that he is handsome."

"Qinten?" Tawna and Ziva chorused.

"He is handsome," Tawna said, "but a good man hardly describes that man. Why did you leave the party early, Ziv?"

Ziva thought about it briefly then shook her head. "I was tired."

"No, you weren't. I saw what happened."

Ziva raised her eyebrows high and crossed her feet at the ankles, resettling the cat and allowing her right foot to bounce. "What makes you so sure?"

"I was there. Remember? I walked toward you with Ti'ras when Qinten approached you. You almost ran away from him. Besides, your foot is bouncing so fast, if you don't slow it down it will bounce off your leg."

Tigre dug his claws into Ziva's leg and jumped off her lap, then curled up beside her chair, safely out of reach of her moving foot. Ziva looked down at her bouncing foot and laughed. "I give in. You are right. Qinten tried to talk with me, but my innards quiver when I am near him. His soul is dark. I see no good in him." Ziva uncrossed her feet and set them firmly on the floor. Tigre stood and stretched, then lay curled with his tail wrapped around him in the sunshine near her feet.

"I saw you walk away from him. Didn't you want to dance?" Kara teased.

"No. Nor did I want to share anything from the refreshment table. Besides, Father was ready to leave." Ziva bent over, picked up her cat, and hugged him to her chest.

"You said that during the party. What do you mean—his soul is dark?" Tawna stared at her friend.

"I am not really certain. He … feels dark when I am near him. I can't explain it, not even to myself. I just feel darkness when he is near."

"But what is a soul?" Tawna's eyes crunched together. "You speak of souls and I am lost. What are souls?"

"The part of each of us that is spiritual, eternal. I have always known about souls. And when a soul is dark, I tremble." Ziva wrapped her arms about herself, shivering at the memory.

"I don't understand, Ziv," Kara pouted. "All this talk about dark souls. Are they also light?"

"Why, yes. Especially the soul of a little child. I remember when your brother was born, Kara. When I visited and saw him for the first time, I felt incredible light and brightness around him. Other souls are not nearly so bright, but I often feel the lightness, or darkness, of a soul." Ziva's foot had stilled while she spoke and now sat quietly beside the other. Tigre lay purring in her lap.

"And Qinten's soul is dark?" Tawna leaned toward her friend.

"Black. He acts like a good man, I saw him at dinner. He did not join the ribald jokes directed at the girls, seeming even to disapprove of their behavior. But his soul is black as the crow sitting out there on the tree branch."

Tawna shivered and leaned back into her chair. "He seems so nice. He spoke to father and asked to be introduced. We even danced—and he kept his hands to himself, unlike some of the others. No grasping or groping. It was a pleasure to dance without all that. And you say his soul is black?"

"It's a show." Ziva leaned back, her foot slipped across the other and began to bounce and Tigre leaped off her lap once more. He stalked away to find a circle of sunshine to sleep in.

Ziva watched him go before going on. "He wants something and acts that way to conceal his real intentions. I fear him."

"Well, I like him. If he asked Father, I would happily mate with him." Kara folded her arms, turned away, and pouted.

"You would mate with him? Our servants have shared stories of his poor behavior." Tawna stared at their friend. "You must be jesting."

"What sort of poor behavior?" Kara turned back to face the other girls.

"He, well, he forces women to ... to ... to have relations with him." Red crept up Tawna's dusky neck.

"I don't care. He is rich and powerful. Father says he will be the next High Priest of Lorca."

"You are welcome to him." Ziva set her foot on the floor to stop its rapid bounce.

Ziva heard a door slam and horses leaving. She glanced out her window and watched Orak and Lib, his assistant, race away. Why would they do that? She shook her head and her foot began to tap.

"How did you get your father to leave early? My father would never leave that early. He has an image to portray. We must look happy at parties, even when we're miserable." Tawna frowned.

"I asked to leave. Orak isn't as dependent on others' perceptions. They know him to be independent. Otherwise, we would have had to stay." Ziva's foot stopped bouncing for a breath, then beat up and down as if to the beat of a rapid tune.

"We left later than you, Ziva. I complained when Bram insisted it was time to leave. I wish I could convince my father to do my will as easily as you do." Kara fluffed her skirts and pulled her legs beneath her.

"Father made us stay until late. We were not the last to leave, for that is as bad as leaving first, but we were far behind you." Tawna reached up to her long dark hair, began a plait, then brushed it out. "I heard Qinten growl. I suspect there was a disagreeable curse under his breath as well."

Ziva's eyebrows crawled like dainty caterpillars up her face. "And you wonder about his black soul?"

Tawna rubbed her arms, as though trying to warm them, even though the servants fanned them to cool the room.

"Have you looked at Qinten?" Kara said. "He is a good-looking man."

Tawna and Ziva laughed.

"He is handsome and he will have power one day. He will be High Priest of Lorca sooner rather than later." Kara said with a pout.

"I don't doubt that. Qinten is driven. He wants power. Perhaps that is why his soul is black." Ziva sat still for many heartbeats.

"Desiring success isn't all that bad. Bram, and even Korm and Orak, are successful. They are not bad men. They work to be the best in their business." Kara leaned forward and set her feet on the floor.

"Desiring success and seeking to be best in your field doesn't make your soul dark. It is the things you do or are willing to do that color it. Our fathers are good men. I have seen them all give to the poor on the street. They help when they can. I would hate to see how Qinten treated his servants on his return from the party.

"Perhaps. Perhaps not." Kara refused to give in.

~ ~ ~

Orak sat in his office thinking. He liked having this home with space for him to work. He occasionally found it necessary to visit his markets, granaries, and slaughter houses. He also found time to tour his farms away from the city, inspecting cattle ranches and the farms growing the grains the citizens and the many priests of Nod required. He depended on the managers of each of these places to follow his orders and do what was needed to increase profits.

Today, though, his thoughts focused not on any of his many businesses, but on Ziva. She was such a beauty and so determined.

He had promised to protect her, and already Qinten had asked. For now, he could put the decision off. But he didn't want animosity between himself and a priest of Lorca, his major customer.

The priests required many animals and much grain to offer to their god each festival day. His business would suffer if he found himself in disfavor with them, especially Lorca. But how much would it suffer? Could he survive without their purchases?

Life would be less pleasant if he were at odds with his daughter. She would not be happy. In fact, she would be hurt if he gave her to Qinten, hurt emotionally and physically. Qinten had pushed the issue. He wanted to meet with Ziva in the next week. He wanted to be her mate. Orak understood Ziva's revulsion. Qinten was dark. He had heard of his dabbling with wives of other men and his cruelty. He did not want this for his beautiful daughter. Why did that man want his daughter? Orak shook his head. It did not matter why. Qinten wanted her.

How would he avoid the trap being set for him by Qinten? He felt the danger, poised and waiting for him. His daughter or his business? He must find a way to keep both free of Qinten's grasping hands. If he allowed Qinten to have his daughter, Orak would lose her. If he did not, he could lose both his daughter and his business.

Orak let his head fall into his hands. How did this mess happen? He was certain deep thought would help him discover a way out.

Much later, a noise interrupted his reverie. Lib, his manager responsible for his city enterprises, entered, breathing heavily.

"I expect you are disturbing me for a good reason." Orak lifted his head from his hands with a growl.

Lib bent over, his hands on his knees, as he regained his breath. "A fire!" he panted. "A fire in a granary."

Orak grabbed his cloak and threw it across his shoulders as he hurried from the room. He mounted the horse that always stood waiting at the door during the day, and waited for Lib to wearily climbed into his saddle.

As they raced down the road, Lib directed him toward the commercial district. There, they found people running for the safety of doors and alleys along the streets. Their horses skidded to a stop a distance from the blaze, rearing and snorting at the smoke.

Orak and Lib jumped off, stumbling, before regaining their balance. Orak stood distracted by the smoke. This was his largest granary, filled with amaranth. Much of his supply burned within, the heat of burning grain added to the inferno.

A man appeared from the smoke offering to take the horses away to a safer place. Orak nodded and handed him the reins. Lib handed his reins to the man, then stood beside Orak, staring. Orak took in the scene, determining what he could do to help.

The men he paid to guard the granary and fight against any danger stood in bucket lines, passing buckets of water to be thrown as a cupful of moisture to be splashed on the raging blaze. Orak joined the lines, as did Lib, passing bucket after bucket toward the edges of the devouring flames, in an attempt to prevent its spread into the city.

Fire began to lick at the small shacks occupied by the poor who were employed in the nearby granaries. Many of the men Orak employed in his granary lived in these hovels. Little children, loved by these men fighting his fire, lived within those huts. The granary was lost. There was no need to lose homes if they could be saved. He directed the lines of buckets toward the small homes, hoping to save most of them.

Hours later, black smudged men fell to the ground, exhausted. The granary lay in ashes, all the amaranth lost. The men struggled to their feet to offer words of thanks to Orak, knowing he was responsible for the preservation of their small homes. He grasped each man by the forearm, though his strength was nearly gone.

Some of his wealth lay in ashes at his feet. He breathed a sigh of relief, only one granary burned. The others, and his cold meat lockers, were safely scattered in distant locations around the city. He confused his competitors, keeping none of them close together.

One bright thought in all the blackness of soot, his wealth had been reduced. Qinten may be less interested in Ziva, now. Maybe the fire was a gift in disguise?

Chapter 6

Slave Market

"Orak, please?" Ziva begged a week later. "Others talk about the slave market. I want to go with Tawna and Kara. I want to see what happens there. We'll stay near the edge. Please? I want to know. I want to see it."

"Absolutely not!" Orak roared. "Slave markets are not places for young women. I do not like to go there, myself. Too many men are wicked. Those who gather around the slave market are not the kind of men you have known, especially in the way they behave toward women. You will not go."

His declaration should have been the end of the discussion, but Ziva plunged forward. "Can I not take Com? He is a big man, big enough to frighten those wicked men. Com will protect me. I listened to him before."

"Why would you want to go to such an awful place? Men and women are degraded there. There is nothing there for you. We do not purchase slaves."

"I do not want to purchase a slave, and I don't know why I feel I should go, for sure. I only know I feel I should go. The others are going. Please?"

Ziva managed to bring tears to her eyes, aware Orak could seldom deny her requests when she used tears. She did not know why she was drawn to the slave market, only that she was. "Something important is there. Please let me go."

Orak had been touchy in the days since the fire at the granary. The timing was not good. Or, maybe it was better to ask now, when he wasn't at his best, or he would never allow a visit.

"You will stay back, away from the slaves?"

"Yes, Father, I will."

"And, you will take Com? Listen to him? Return home when he says?"

"You will let me go? Yes, I will listen to Com. Thank you!" Ziva hugged her father, covering his face with kisses. He returned the embrace, his dark arms encircling her tiny waist.

"I fear for your safety. Be extra careful—and listen to Com."

Ziva kissed his cheek and forehead once more, then ran from his office to her apartment. Orak bellowed for Com as she left, and she knew he would be there with her on the excursion the next day. She briefly sensed the unfairness of abusing Orak's love, especially during this time of his loss, then brushed away the thought. Though she rarely abused his love, she was drawn to make this trip. For some reason, it seemed important.

She sat at her desk and reached for vellum, pen, and ink. After quickly sketching out messages to her friends, and sealing them, she called the messenger to carry her notes.

Early the next morning, Com escorted Ziva to a large covered carriage, where she found Kara and Tawna waiting. Com clamored up to the front seat next to the driver, Kara's escort. Tawna's stood on the back.

"I'm surprised Orak let you come with us." Tawna made space for Ziva.

"I cried. That always works, but I don't use that weapon often. I keep tears for special occasions, such as this." Ziva sat back and straightened her skirts.

The carriage jolted forward and moved through the city toward the slave market. A thrill zipped down Ziva's spine. She had not traveled about the city so alone before. Orak had only the one time allowed her to travel into the city without him, when she met with her friends at Korm's fabric shop before Roven's party.

Her friends loved to tease her about his over-protectiveness. Although, on most days she appreciated his concern, lately she felt a chafing at the restraint. Today's outing with her friends, without Orak, caused her to be glad of Com's presence as her escort.

A big, sooty-gray man, tall and strong, Com allayed any concerns she or Orak may have had. Orak paid him well to protect his home. As a free man, Ziva trusted him. He had been a part of her life throughout her memory.

The girls chatted gaily, enjoying the company and freedom of a day out together. This was a first for Tawna, too.

"I have gold. I plan to buy a maid to help me," Kara announced.

Tawna and Ziva expressed surprise and gabbled like geese for many long heartbeats.

"Why would you need another slave?" Tawna's voice rose higher and louder than usual.

"I want one. Must I have a reason to need one?" Kara flounced her skirts.

"What will you ask her to do for you? Surely, you will buy a female to be your maid?" A quiver rippled through Ziva's stomach. She did not understand the nausea it created.

"Of course. I am not shameless enough to buy a male slave for my apartments." Kara reached out and fluffed up her full skirts. "I'm looking for one to dress my hair in different and interesting ways or be able to learn the skill."

Tawna leaned forward and asked, "How will you know she can do that? How will you choose her?"

Kara described the features she desired and what she would look for in the slave. Her voice dimmed in Ziva's attention. Why the quivering in her inner parts? Why the horror at Kara's actions? She was always sensational. These actions were no different. This was a trip to the slave market, but she had not planned that one of them would purchase another person, a slave. Somehow this alarmed her.

Tawna shook her arm. "Ziv? Ziv? What is wrong?"

"Huh? Oh, nothing. Why?" Ziva glanced at her friends.

"You are pale, much more than usual," Kara exclaimed. "Are you certain you are well?"

"Yes. Yes, I'm sure. Just thinking." Ziva cleared her throat. "Are we there yet?"

Tawna looked at Ziva, her eyes saying, "No, you're not." Instead, she gave a half-shrug and leaned back into her seat. "Almost. The carriage is slowing. Kara's driver seems to be seeking a place to leave our carriage."

Ziva nodded as the carriage bounced her from the seat. She grabbed on to a handle with one hand, and Tawna with the other until the rocking of the carriage ended. Soon, Com stood at the door, extending a hand to help her out.

"We are here, Mistress. Wait while I check the area for danger." He did not ask. He expected compliance, and Ziva stood quietly waiting with her friends.

Com returned, a silent danger. Ziva shivered in his presence, happy Com's presence protected them.

"Your hoods are to be over your heads," Com instructed. "You are to remain near us."

"I plan to purchase a slave," Kara's voice filled with petulance as she dragged her hood over her hair.

"Heth shared this information with me. He will choose three women for you to choose from. You will not move closer to inspect them personally."

"How will I choose if I cannot inspect them myself?" Kara's voice became even louder.

Com stayed calm and in control. "You will watch Heth place his hands over each of his chosen women. After you have seen the three he chooses, he will hold his hand above each woman. Nod when his hand is over your choice. If this is not acceptable, we will return home now."

Kara's rage flared, evident to all, but she was intelligent enough to nod in agreement. Heth pushed through the crowd while Com walked just ahead of the girls. Tawna's escort, Keb, followed, watching warily in every direction.

The condition of the market and slaves appalled Ziva. This was nothing like the market surrounding Korm's fabric shop. Naked men, women, and children of all ages, some no bigger than toddlers stood in chains, ankles and wrists worn in running sores. Women struggled vainly to cover personal parts. Their bodies bruised, red stripes crossed backs, chests, and across legs. None, not even the small children, were exempt from the cruel whips. A putrid scent filled the air, causing the girls to pull the edges of their hoods across their noses.

Unshaken, Kara studied the women intently as Heth moved among the younger girls, inspecting them in unseemly ways, prodding and poking in their mouths and private parts. Ziva stared at her feet, no longer desiring to be part of the choosing.

As she turned away, Ziva followed the movements of a young man, tall and confident, accompanied by an older man. Dressed in simple clothing, neither patched or worn. He appeared to be neither a slave nor a merchant. He glanced her way and their eyes met briefly, before the older man touched his arm, drawing his attention to a boy for sale. A strange familiarity touched her heart.

"Which girl is your choice, Tawna, Ziv?" Kara cried. "Heth chose three for me to choose from: the little blond, the red-haired girl, and the dark brown-haired girl. Which would you choose?"

Ziva stared at the choices, strangely disturbed. All the girls were thin, much too young to be sold. She shook her head in dismay.

"The dark one," Tawna said, as though from a distance. "Choose the red-haired girl. Her hair is plaited."

Ziva considered the dark girl. "Yes, the red head seems to know the skill of dressing hair." She turned her back on the slaves, no longer interested.

She felt Kara nod, choosing. She glanced back to see all except the red-haired girl step back in line. Ziva covered her gasp with her hand and glanced at Com.

"Can we leave now that Kara has made her decision?" she asked.

Com turned toward the girls. "Are the others ready?"

"I am." Tawna turned away and nodded.

"My choice is made. Heth will bring the girl when the purchase is complete. Yes, let us leave." Kara turned and began to walk in the direction of the carriage.

The others followed, Keb hurrying to lead the way, while Com followed in the rear, watching all around them. Ziva moved with them, glad to have her back to the depressing sight.

"Orak was right," she said as she settled her skirts around her on the carriage seat. "The slave market is no place for me."

~ ~ ~

"Hurry, boy. We must arrive at the market before the other buyers," Gowdy growled from the kitchen door.

One of the boys employed in turning the meat fell asleep the day before, falling into the fire. He lived but only barely. He would be sold at the market as soon as he healed enough to be purchased by another slave owner. Qinten did not keep injured slaves. The boy continued to be treated only because Qinten knew an injured or sick slave would not bring him as much money.

Nat grabbed his cloak from the peg on the back of the pantry door. "I'm gone," he called to Cook, then turned to Gowdy. "Let's go."

The two strode across the portico and through the gate onto the street. Nat became aware of a freedom he had not experienced in many years. He had not felt this freedom since he had been sold into slavery as a child. He wondered again what had happened to his little sister. To sell a child into slavery should be a crime, but in this city, it was no crime.

"What should the boy be like?" Gowdy startled Nat from his thoughts.

"Boy? Yes, the boy." He glanced at his companion who laughed. "Oh, I was thinking." Nat joined Gowdy in his good-natured laughter.

"Freedom to walk is a pleasure denied me for many years. I savor the opportunity," Nat said.

"Not walked alone before?"

"Not for many years. Always with an escort and wearing chains. Your company, Gowdy, is a pleasure. I don't feel like I'm being guarded."

The two walked on, sharing opinions as to the new boy's requirements, arriving at the plaza near the edge of the city as other men arrived at the slave market. They wended their way toward the docket, intent on choosing one of the middle-aged boys. Nat's skin tingled in awareness. He searched around him to see whose eyes were on him. Briefly, he gazed at the girl, a female version of himself.

Before he could react, Gowdy touched his arm. "Which of these boys do you think is strong enough to withstand the fires? And who will not need to be tamed of his rebellion?"

Nat turned his attention back to the boys, still amazed Gowdy would respect his opinion. Fighting down the stench-caused nausea, he walked along the line of boys, gazing into their eyes, followed by Gowdy. Some boys stared back at him, hatred flaming to the surface. Others' attention focused on their feet, refusing to return his stare. Near the end of the line, a boy of about ten peered up with a hesitancy in his stance.

"Have you the strength to turn a spit?" Nat asked, his voice gentle and sympathetic.

"I can. I am strong. My last master was a rug maker. I carried rugs of every size from the loom to the customer."

"Awkward loads. Spit turning is dangerous. You would replace a boy who fell in the fire. Can you pay attention?"

"Aye. Roasting fires burn. I can pay attention and stay out of the fire, if you let me." Hope sparkled in his eyes.

Nat turned. "Gowdy, what do you think? Is the little man strong enough to turn a spit?"

"Doubt it." Gowdy spat on the ground. "Arms are pretty scrawny."

"I can, sir. Give me a chance." The boy strained against his restraints.

Gowdy spat again. "We'll see."

They had reached the end of the line of boys. None of the others demonstrated anything but submission or anger. Nat trailed behind as Gowdy found the market manager. "What is the price of number twenty-seven, boy?"

The manager scanned his market list. "That 'un is slated for the mines, 'less sum'un offers enough."

"Why? He is scrawny and weak. Probably won't work for us." Gowdy turned as though uninterested. Nat held back his argument, aware of his companion's plan.

"What're ya willin' to pay?" The manager grabbed Gowdy's shoulder.

Gowdy growled and slapped the hand off. "Do not touch me. I asked a price. Name it."

"Paid six silvers for him."

"More like six coppers. Give you a silver," Gowdy retorted. "Boy isn't worth even that much." When the manager didn't respond, Gowdy and Nat turned away.

The manager scratched his dark, bald head and glanced up. "Ya' drive a tough bargain, Gowdy. One silver it is."

Nat struggled to keep his eyebrows from the space near his hair. He should not have been surprised. Gowdy was the buyer for kitchen slaves in Qinten's household. His acquaintance with the slave market manager aided those purchases. Gowdy had purchased Nat almost six years earlier. The market manager was the last of his worries then.

Gowdy fished a silver from the bag inside his waist and handed the coin to the manager. After testing for purity, he signaled a tall assistant.

Less than a hand span of the sun's movement later, the boy followed Nat and Gowdy to his new home. The boy tried chattering his gratitude, but Gowdy grumped and Nat was lost in thought.

The girl was no slave, as he had believed for all the past years. She obviously lived in wealth, her guide was protective. He had never allowed himself to hope to find her comfortable.

Cook eyed Nat suspiciously as they entered the kitchen, new boy in tow. "What pasted a grin on your face?"

"He saved this boy from the mines." Gowdy indicated the boy following them. "Do you have a name, boy?"

Nat almost laughed at the boy's expression. "Me? Of course, I have a name. I am Avram."

"Nat saved Avram, here, from the mines? Boy'd better show appropriate gratitude," Cook grumbled. "Get him some clothing so he can work."

Another cook's assistant ran to the kitchen wardrobe, returning with a short robe and a heavy protective leather apron. Avram donned the clothing and hurried to the spit. Cook nodded to Nat and returned to the meal preparation. Nat smiled. His grin wasn't for Avram or Cook, and Gowdy didn't need to know.

~ ~ ~

Nat lay on his back on his cot, hands laced behind his head, still surprised by his sleeping arrangements. For many years, he had slept on the floor, often with little to pull over him against the cold night air. Sometimes, he had been given a rug to lie upon, most often he slept on the hard-packed earth.

The boys in Qinten's scullery slept together on the floor, little space between them. That had been good, sometimes, for the closeness of the bodies provided warmth. It was a problem, too, like when Kenji decided to surround him with his cronies.

For hours that first night, he had felt poking and prodding from all sides. He had ignored it, knowing a reaction would cause an unwanted battering. Eventually, it ended. This had happened several nights, until the lack of response sent Kenji to plan an assault on Nat.

Since his promotion to Cook's assistant, Nat slept on a cot, with a thin blanket to cover him. Other boys shared the room, but he was off the floor, away from the vermin.

When all the preparations for the next day's meal were complete, Nat was free to do as he pleased. Tonight, he pleased to lie, thinking, on his cot.

His thoughts returned to his trip to the slave market. Avram's boast of strength was correct, so far. He stood for hours turning the spit, his attention on his work. So far. Soon the work would become monotonous. Would he then lose attention and fall into the fire as the boy had before?

Nat hoped not. He liked the boy, Avram. He liked his cheerful willingness to work. Cook noticed, too. He had nodded at him, saying, "Good." For a man as taciturn as Cook, that was a complement. Nat was glad. Avram reminded him of someone. Himself, maybe, with his first owner?

Hoth had not been cruel, though he insisted his slaves work hard in making bricks. Nat had been assigned first to stamp the straw into the clay, mixing clay, straw, and sand to create bricks that would withstand the sun. It was hard work for a boy, but he had done well, moving to filling the molds after three years. By then, his legs and arms were longer and stronger. Filling the molds was more difficult, but Nat soon learned the trick, becoming both fast and accurate.

He had worked hard and long, but he hoped he would not be in the service of the brick maker all his life. He did not anticipate, nor desire, the end to Hoth's service. More than two years after his promotion to filling molds, slaves from his household came to the brick making shed to announce the end. Hoth had losses in his business and started drinking heavily. A fight had ensued at the tavern, and Hoth now lay dying. The slaves in the brickyard would be sold.

Once more, Nat stood naked and chained with the other slaves in the market. Vekt walked the line that day. Many who had previously belonged to Hoth glared angrily into the eyes of those purchasing new slaves. Nat refused to look at his feet or stare in anger. He waited until he saw a man who appeared to be kind, then glanced in his direction, hope filling his heart. Vekt had responded that day much as Nat had responded to Avram.

Nat was purchased, spending much of the next two years lugging lengths of trees and leather to support Vekt in his making of drums.

Had there been a life before slavery? He had almost forgotten the days of being petted and loved by a beautiful mama and a handsome papa. He, and a sister, traveled with them in wagons filled with food and seed. He barely remembered the clean, earthy smell of the seeds. So long ago.

"You comin' to the festivities tonight?" Drak kicked the end of Nat's cot and drew him from his memories.

"Thought I would. Is it time?"

"Yea, but you may want to at least wash your face before you go. Girls prefer a man with a clean face."

"Like you would know? When were you last with a girl?" Nat laughed and headed for the washroom.

Chapter 7

Lost Children

"Can you believe that man?" Kara flounced into the room and dropped into a chair in Ziva's parlor. "Comin' here to search for the lost children of the prophet? How silly. Prophet's children here in Nod?"

Ziva looked up, a bemused smile on her face. "It could happen."

"And camels can fly!" Kara retorted. "Why on earth would anyone look for lost children of the prophet in Nod? Children of a prophet? Here? Humph."

Kara's certainty amused her companions, but her self-importance sometimes frustrated them.

"Nod is known for slaves from across the earth. If a slaver wanted to lose someone forever, this vast city of Nod is the place." Ziva said. She sat with her friends in her favorite white chair.

"Slave markets do a thriving business, here, as you should know." Tawna grinned. "Why not the lost children?"

"We saw no lost children there." Kara poked her lower lip out a bit. "My new maid is no child of the prophet."

Ziva felt annoyance leaking off Tawna and understood it. Kara liked to insist she knew everything.

"What makes you so sure she is not? With that red hair, she could be." Tawna teased.

"She is not. No lost children of the prophet are here."

"And why not lost children here?" Ziva joined in the teasing. She hugged Tigre close, scratching behind his ears.

"What do they look like? Do you know? Are they sons or daughters? Did the man say?" Tawna insisted on pushing the subject.

"He did not have a chance to say. I closed the door on him before he could rant on about the supposed lost children. They would be so … so different," Kara spluttered. "The prophets are so—"

"So … so what? Have you seen a prophet?" Tawna persisted.

Ziva sat quietly listening to her friends argue, enjoying the weight of her sleeping cat.

"Who has seen a prophet in Nod? We have our gods, our priests, and our temples. Why would we need a prophet?" Kara said.

"We are so perfect here in Nod," Tawna taunted. "Do you even know what a prophet would look like? How different would his children be?"

"I have heard stories of prophets. They are wild men from the west. Men who shout about our 'sins.' They must be tanned brown from the sun." Kara flung her hands about as she spoke.

"And their children, they would be? Tanned? Because the children are always out in the sun with their fathers?" Tawna leaned forward to make her point.

"The children would be—" Kara spluttered.

"Light-skinned? And we have no light-skinned children here?" Tawna shook her head.

Kara spluttered a bit more, then laughed with the others. Light-skinned women were among the servants fanning the girls with huge peacock feathers, moving the air just enough to almost cool the air.

The girls sat together in white velvet lounge chairs, deep blue silk drapes quietly swished across the marble floor.

"It's so hot," Kara moaned. "I thought your father's expensive house would be cooler, Ziv."

"Orak is the wealthiest merchant in all of Nod. Surely his home is the coolest." Tawna slipped her tongue between her teeth a bit in Kara's direction.

"He has the thickest walls. If any house in Nod is cooler today, it must belong to the governor." Kara made a face in Tawna's direction.

"Or a priest," Tawna giggled. "Like Qinten?"

Ziva chuckled inside. Everything Kara did was so dramatic. Nothing was merely normal. Her maid had painted her face with bright red lips and cheeks, peacock blue matching her dress, painted above her eyes highlighted her dark brown eyes.

She half expected her to arrive for a visit with black and white spots of color around her eyes, like Tigre sported.

Ziva remembered Tawna saying she had sat as the sun rose a hand span while her face was painted in its artistic, yet subdued manner. A soft red painted her lips and cheeks, while an emerald green paint echoing her green eyes. Even that much color was too much for Ziva.

Her own wealth would allow for the dramatic face paint, and Ana would have painted her face that way if she had asked, yet she had chosen only to allow a light pink lip color and a light brush of blue paint across her eyelids. She had no reason to be so dramatic, especially in her own home.

"I do believe Qinten has thicker walls and more slaves to move the air. Go there, if you want to be cooler." Ziva allowed a measure of sarcasm to leak into her voice as she glanced at Kara.

Qinten's father, the governor of the city, wanted for nothing. His son, a priest of Lorca, similarly had all he needed. Ziva shivered as she remembered his attempts to draw her into a conversation.

"You could be there, could you not, Ziv?" Kara threw the taunt back. "He fancied you."

"He can keep his fancy. I do not fancy him." She stiffened at the thought. How could they suggest such a thing?

The three young women lapsed into quiet, each consumed by their own thoughts.

"It is hot." Ziva listlessly dropped her hand along the floor. "Shall we cool off in the bathing pool?"

Ziva set Tigre on the floor. She looked up at her and softly meowed her annoyance. "You don't want to join us in the pool," Ziva murmured.

The three took little time moving to the pool in the next room. Colorful tiles lined the floor surrounding the pool in the design of a beautiful blue and purple iris. The pool formed the yellow center and a round opening in the roof directly over the pool aided in the cooling of the room.

Cool water filtered through the iris and water lilies planted around the edges. Pools like this cooled many apartments in the house of Orak, each exquisite.

Soon the girls were laughing and gossiping as they sat, nearly naked, in the pool. While the other girls laughed, Ziva listened, making a comment when necessary, her thoughts traveling elsewhere.

Where were those lost children of the prophet? Were they boys or girls or both? How long ago were they lost? How old were they now?

She needed more information.

~ ~ ~

Nat carried a covered tray to Qinten's private chambers. He had drawn the lot to bring the mid-day meal to their master. He quelled an unexpected quiver. The previous three young men who had drawn this lot had not returned to the kitchens. Whispered rumors spread of depravities, acts he chose not to consider. It would not happen to him. He would deliver the meal and leave.

He rapped on the door. A voice from within called out, "Enter."

Nat took a deep breath and opened the door. Qinten sat behind his desk. A pen leaked ink onto a page.

"Set it on the table, there," Qinten ordered paying little attention to Nat.

He set it on the table, bowed, and started to back out.

"Wait here."

Nat froze. Now what? He stood, eyes on his bare feet, waiting. Qinten rose and walked to the facility, closing the door behind him. Nat considered fleeing but knew better. It would only cause him greater problems. He took a deep breath and quietly let it out.

Qinten returned and sat to eat his meal. Nat stood looking at his feet, waiting to be dismissed.

"Can you read?"

Qinten's sudden question startled Nat. "Yes, sir. I can."

"Look at the page on my desk and tell me what you think."

Nat stepped closer to the desk and looked. Only the one ink-spattered paper lay there. He closed his eyes and rolled them upward before plucking it from the desk.

On the paper was written:

Girl	Looks	Father	Problems
Yente	bronze, built, short	Prentz	Sons
Lydia	tall, young, brown	Tubal Cain	Cain
Kara	lovely, tall, elegant	Bram	Brothers & Sisters
Tawna	intelligent, musical voice	Korm	Past problems

A huge spot of ink covered the other names. At the bottom, he found:

Ziva	pale, haughty, exotic	Orak	attitude
Netta	young, tempting	Lyber	Priest of Nimm-old

Nat stared at the names on the list.

"Well? What would you do?" Qinten demanded.

"The splotch of ink in the middle makes it difficult to read. I-I have no idea. I have not been allowed to think of women in the kitchens. What would you have me think?"

"Argh. I should know better than to ask a kitchen slave. Leave."

Nat dropped the page on the desk and walked out the door. He walked down the hall and turned a corner before he stopped to breathe deeply.

A Ziva was on the list. Was it his Ziva?

Chapter 8

Pomegranates and Sacrifice

Nat fingered the pouch containing the coins Cook handed him just before they left the kitchens.

"You are not to waste this, use it only on the items on your list, and get the best price you can. I expect you to bring most of these coins home." Cook had glared at him. "And stay safe."

The last had been almost a whisper.

Now, Nat walked once again free of chains. This time he traveled with Drak and Avram. They had been sent to purchase sufficient produce for the upcoming Growing Festival of Lorca, which was to be celebrated in the priest's home. Qinten sought the honor of High Priest of Lorca. Second in line for this honor, the festival celebration in his home would give him merit in the upcoming election.

Nat knew he must bring only the freshest, only the best fruits and vegetables. Cook required rare fruits, found only in distant lands. He especially desired pomegranates. He hoped to scatter the seeds across the desserts. Nat understood they would be expensive, if they were available.

As they walked through the market, Nat kept his eyes open for danger. Cutpurses and robbers attacked the unwary and unsuspecting and those who shopped alone. He did not want to be their victim. This was no time to jest and play with his companions. He enjoyed this freedom and hoped to be called upon to do it again.

They searched each stall for the needed produce, purchasing beans in one, pears from another, gingerly placing each item in the basket Avram carried. A stall in the middle of the market held the prized pomegranates. Nat signaled Drak to be extra vigilant in his guard duties.

"Pomegranates," Nat said. "How much?"

"I have but three that are not promised to another." The shopkeeper moved the fruit to the top of the pile. "These are a copper each."

"Promised? Promised to whom? I will pay you two coppers for each, if you give me eight. If you give me ten, I will pay twenty-five coppers." Nat fingered the coins in his pouch.

"The High Priest of Lorca has requested them and offered fifty coppers for twenty. I have but twenty-three."

Nat knew he was inflating the value of the fruits. No one would pay so much for so few, even these rare fruits.

He shrugged. "Then, three will have to do." He reached into his pouch and handed the man three coppers.

"You offered me two for each. Now you give me only one?" The shopkeeper moved to draw back the three prized fruits.

"Two if you sell me eight. You have but three, so, three coppers it is." Nat reached for the three pomegranates.

"The High Priest does not need all these. I will sell you ten, for twenty-five coppers, as you offered."

"You are certain the High Priest will not miss them?" Nat reached into his pouch for more coppers as the shopkeeper shook his head. He counted the correct number into the merchant's hand. The coins disappeared below the counter and he handed over seven more large pomegranates. Nat silently handed them to Avram.

"Thank you," Nat said and turned to leave.

"You are welcome. Be careful. They wait for you." The man behind the counter nodded toward the other side of the plaza.

Nat nodded and the three young men crossed the plaza toward the street that would take them home. Suddenly, Kenji appeared in front of Nat, staring into his eyes.

"Hello, Kenji." Drak stepped forward with outstretched hand.

"Drak." Kenji continued to stare at Nat.

"How are you Kenji?" Nat worked to maintain his nonchalance. "Things good with you?"

"Yeah, they are. You got me outta Qinten's place. For that, I owe you thanks." Kenji stretched his hand toward Nat.

Nat did not trust this enemy from years ago, but he reached out and clasped him by the forearm. "Glad you are good, Kenji."

"This is all the thanks you get. Don't come into my market again. You will not get off so easy." Kenji dropped his hand and disappeared into the crowd with his companions.

Nat, Drak, and Avram glanced at each other before continuing across the plaza. They neither rushed nor strolled across the market. Nat did not want to draw attention to their small group, nor did he want the trouble that would follow such attention.

He knew this was not a friendly encounter, regardless of the half-smile on Kenji's face. He had experienced otherwise. He nodded to Drak to stay alert. Drak's grimace told him all he needed. He didn't trust Kenji either and would maintain his watchfulness. Nat scanned the crowd, glad of Avram's quiet sensibility.

No laughter or congratulations passed between the trio as they made their way along the streets to Qinten's home. The tension between them could be plucked by a lute performer by the time they entered the kitchen. Cook's eyebrows climbed high, waiting for them to deposit their purchases in the pantry in silence.

"Was I wrong to send you boys alone to the market?" Cook broke the silence.

"No, Cook," Nat answered. "We were able to purchase everything on the list, including ten pomegranates. Here is the pouch, with money left over." He shook the pouch, making the coins within jingle, then handed it to Cook.

"As it should. Why the tension when you three walked in?"

Nat glanced at Drak and shook his head slightly. "We encountered an old friend on the market plaza. We weren't sure Kenji would allow us to return peacefully."

"Kenji!" Cook spat the name as he would spit out rotten food. "He did not interrupt you?"

"No. He thanked me and left. Strange for him."

"We need those vegetables prepared now, if we are to be ready for the festival tonight." Cook returned to his work.

Nat hung his cloak on the back of the pantry door and retrieved the basket of vegetables. When he returned to the kitchen, Drak had gone back to his duties and Avram sat beside the fire, turning the spit, a smile firmly in place.

Hours later, the food was ready. Nat and Drak returned to their rooms to wash and don fresh livery. They were to help serve the meal and refreshments. The usual servers were not enough for a festival this large. They carried heavy dishes of food to the sideboard, ready to be served to individual diners. Fruits and deserts waited in the cool pantry for the appropriate time to serve.

Drak stationed himself near the slabs of beef and pork, ready to slice off portions. Nat stood behind the table of vegetables, available to dish up portions to the guests. Others were positioned behind the other tables, waiting to serve other dishes. All was ready.

~ ~ ~

Ziva sat in stiff silence beside her father in their carriage. *How could Orak agree to take me to celebrate the Lorcan Growing Festival at Qinten's home? It will be difficult to ignore the man in his own home.* Her fuming made her kick a foot out, just missing Orak's.

Hot embarrassment drove color through her face. She pulled her foot back and forced herself to consider her father's situation. He had little choice. She gazed at her hands, tightly folded in her lap and remembered the conversation.

Orak had called her to his office that morning to share the invitation. "You must attend with me, Ziv. I am sorry. I know I promised you would not be given to Qinten. And you won't."

The flash of anger at those words filled her once more. She tamped them down now, as then. "Then why must I attend? You know he is an evil man."

"Qinten is the priest responsible for the procurement of grains and animals for their sacrifices. You know I provide them with grains and cattle. After the fire in the granary, I must keep the contract."

Ziva grimaced and Orak rushed on. "I must attend to ensure the sales continue. Qinten demanded that I bring you or I will lose the contract. We have no choice, not this time. Please, Ziva. Do not cause me a problem."

Ziva had thought a few breaths, her face drawn. "Yes, Father. I will attend with you. Not happily, but I do understand." She had leaned forward, kissing him on the cheek.

Orak had wrapped his arms around her in gratitude and love. "Thank you, Ziv. I knew you would understand."

Now they sat in their carriage, dressed in Festival finery. She was not comfortable, for attending this festival meant she wore much less than she liked. The skimpy, low-necked top was made of a sheer light-blue fabric the color of a peacock's feather. The skirt hanging low on her hips was equally filmy, though in a darker blue to protect a minuscule portion of her modesty. Tawna's father, Bram, had provided the costume. Ziva still couldn't decide if she should thank him for it.

The carriage came to a jarring halt. They had arrived. The coachman opened the door, holding it as Orak climbed out. Orak turned to take Ziva's hand and help her out.

"You look beautiful," he said, wrapping a cape around her shoulders.

"If only I could keep this cape on." Wistfulness filled her voice. "This 'costume' is not appropriate for a decent young woman."

"I know, Ziv. This festival is not appropriate for decent young women, yet we must attend. We will stay only as long as is required. I promise."

Ziva gave him a weak smile, then squared her shoulders and planted a smile on her face. Together, they walked into Qinten's house and the festival.

The festival overwhelmed Ziva with lurid sights and scents. Participants gorged on the food, pushing and shoving to get the finest tidbits, though there was plenty, and it all tasted wonderful. Ziva stood back, waiting her turn. She received only a small portion, still, more than enough for her.

Sweet incense enticed those in the room to exotic acts. Loud, fast music enticed men and women onto the floor to dance. The men felt free to touch the women and girls wherever they chose, receiving little or no complaint. Ziva sat along the wall, trying to escape the depravity.

Earlier, Qinten roamed through the crowds, speaking to the celebrants. His eyes landed on Orak and Ziva more than once, but before he could reach them through the crowds, they had wandered on, escaping his attention.

The music ended and the dancers moved to their seats, trading ribald jests. Priests moved across the floor, scattering sand.

Thirteen tiny boys, no more than three, dressed in only tiny loin wraps, carried colorful woven bowls, nearly as large as the child, filled with grains. Each boy carried a different variety. A priest stepped forward to accept the bowl from the boys as they drew near the low altar set at the feet of the figure of Lorca. Above them, a human male body with an enormous phallus loomed, his huge eagle head stared past a giant beak toward the low bowl held in his hands, filled with burning coals. The priest raised the bowl of grain to the horrid figure three times, then placed it in the bowl in its hands. Fire licked each bowl, until the fragrance of cooking, then burning grains permeated the room.

Ziva held her face calm, hiding her abhorrence. When the drums exploded into a wild beat, drawing girls and women to the dance floor in preparation for the final rite. She sat near the wall with a smile pasted on her face and her feet firmly planted on the floor, refusing to tap to the enticing music. She sat with folded arms, refusing to participate. Girls spun about the room with hips wiggling and breasts bouncing, tempting the men who followed their every move. She fought to prevent the deep embarrassment she felt for the dancing girls' antics from coloring her light skin that showed every emotion. She moved farther back in the watching crowd until her back touched the wall, trying to hide.

Servants or slaves, probably slaves in Qinten's home, busied themselves removing the remains of the meal the crowd of revelers had consumed. A young man in Qinten's livery caught her eye, the same one she saw at the slave market. His elegant livery showed off the muscles in his legs and arms. The man looked at her, knowingly, then returned to his work.

Ziva did not believe in coincidences. This man must mean something in her life. But what?

She turned back to the spectacle as the music ended. The dancing girls vacated the floor and the musicians left the room. Chairs scraped the tile floor as men made space for the girls, bright with the sheen of sweat, to sit beside them. Orak moved behind Ziva, placing his comforting hands on her shoulders and bent to speak softly in her ear.

"This is the last rite. When it ends, we can leave this foul extravaganza. I tire of the noise."

She looked up at him and a grateful smile flashed through her eyes. She faced forward to observe this last rite, eager to leave. She wondered what the final rite would include. Whatever it was, it would be vulgar and disgusting.

The buzz of activity calmed. Priests moved to the center of the room. Qinten stood at the base of the image of Lorca waiting. Nine prepubescent girls, dressed in tiny white dresses, led a young ewe lamb. The girls proudly paraded their fluffy charges around the circle of festival attendees. One by one, each girl was called to the altar.

The first girl knelt and presented her lamb to Qinten. He took the creature by the feet and raised it in offering to the terrible image. In one swift motion, he lay the lamb on the low altar and sliced its throat, to the roaring approval of the crowd. Lifting the carcass, Qinten allowed the blood to drip on the face and into the mouth of the little shepherdess. Another priest relieved him of the corpse and dripped blood into the waiting mouths of the cheering horde, then dropped it into the fire in the figure's hands.

Each girl repeated the rite. Ziva noticed the sixth little girl kept her precious charge close, trying to protect her lamb. Qinten glared at the girl, until she stepped forward to offer her lamb. When it was her turn to accept the blood offering, Ziva saw the little girls' tears join with the blood.

Orak and Ziva kept to the back of the throng, avoiding the offering of blood. She stared as each lamb was placed in the arms of the huge image to burn. The odor of burnt flesh joined with the acrid bouquet of blood and burning grains, sickening and disgusting her. She tried not to gag.

The drums exploded in wild rhythms and girls, including Kara and Tawna, leapt to dance wildly across the blood on the floor. But not Ziva. The vitality within her cringed away from the appalling vision. She had not shouted in joy nor raised her hands in adulation. She yearned to leave the scene of horror.

Orak appeared in front of her, took her by the arm, and guided her along the outside edges of the room and into the night. Ziva breathed deeply of the clear night air, grateful to have avoided interacting with Qinten. Their carriage stood waiting for Orak to help Ziva into the welcome silence.

Chapter 9

Selection

"Time has come for me to agree to your mating," Orak said. "You are old enough. You will be sixteen soon, old enough to be mated."

Ziva sat in a comfortable chair in Orak's study, invited here only when he had serious things to say to her. She gazed at his desk. His mahogany colored hand lay on top, in contrast to the light birch. She reached over and set her small pink hand on his.

She had been waiting for this day since she was a little girl. She had dreamed of the man Orak would give her to, hoping he would find a kind man who would love her as much as her father did.

Ziva waited for Orak to speak. As the silence extended, she began to fear. If he couldn't bring himself to talk about it, it must be bad.

After several attempts to speak and multiple clearing of his throat, Orak finally managed to speak. "Qinten has asked that I give you to him as his mate."

"Qinten?" she squealed. "I would rather mate with almost any other man."

Orak gazed into her eyes. "I know, Ziva. I'd rather agree to your mating with any other man than Qinten."

"Then, why? Why do you even consider Qinten?"

"Things have … well, things have happened." He pulled his hands back and stared at his fingernails.

"What things have happened? What would force you to expect me to mate with that pond scum?" Ziva's voice raised in both volume and pitch with each word. "Of all men, Qinten. Ugh." She worked to regain control of herself.

"You remember why we went to the festival last week?"

Ziva nodded, beginning to fear for her father.

"He threatened me. If you don't mate with him, he'll—"

"He'll ruin you," she whispered. "You want me to give myself to him to protect you and your business."

"If he ruins me, good men and women will no longer have a means to live. There are many men and women in my employment. If I lose my businesses, if I lose my place, they lose everything, as well. I have little choice." He hung his head, staring at his desk.

"Is there no way out? Can you not argue with him? Is there no other answer?" In her anger and frustration, Ziva wept.

Orak came around the desk to lay a hand on her shoulder. "None that I have been able to find. I have been searching for a way out of this for weeks since he demanded your hand."

"When was that?"

"After the party at Roven's."

"And you agreed I would be his mate?"

"No. Not yet. Yesterday, he gave me a week to decide, after I told him there was no way I would give my daughter to him as his mate."

"Good for you, Father. Show him you have a backbone. How did he threaten you?" Ziva wiped the tears from her face.

Orak returned to his seat behind his desk. "His threat was subtle, hanging between us. If I don't give you to him, he will destroy me."

"Why would he want me? I am different from most women in Nod. None are as pale as me, most have beautiful dark skin. What about me entices him?"

"You are beautiful, my dear. Beautiful and exotic. Your light skin sets you apart from others in Nod. Qinten is looking for someone to help him move up, to become a high priest in his cult. He is seeking a beautiful exotic wife. You." Orak's eyes filled with pride, immediately followed by sorrow.

"Exotic? Me? No." Ziva raised her hands in front of her, palms out, as though to push the thought away.

"You are an exotic beauty. I don't want you to be his mate. I have heard he is an angry, depraved man. He will not care for you as I always have. He may be cruel. I have heard stories. But what can I do? What can we do?"

"He is a vile, wicked man. I want no part of him. Can you put him off, insist he not announce anything for at least — what? —six months, a year?"

"I can try but under what pretext? And for what purpose?"

"To discover a way to escape his trap!" Ziva wanted to shout at her father.

"We must come up with a good excuse, a good reason to ask that we postpone the announcement."

"I am sick? I am not old enough? I desire to be wooed, charmed? There must be a way, a reason to put him off. Maybe he'll grow tired of waiting."

"Even if he does, you will have to mate sometime soon. I grow old. You need a man to protect you." Though Orak shook his head, his face brightened. "I would like to bounce a grandchild on my knee before I leave this life."

"I will agree to another man. I will love someone, but I will not mate that horrible man"

"Remember, Ziva. Most fathers are not as kind. They do not give in to their daughters, as I give in to you. They do not give their daughters a choice. It is the law in Nod. Girls mate the man chosen for them by their father. Girls have no choice."

Ziva bowed her head, then ran around the desk to hug her father. "Thank you, Father! We can solve this problem. We can keep him away."

"We will find a way. Orak patted her on the back. "There must be a way."

~ ~ ~

A moon passed, and another seven-days. Nat spent much of his free time, and some of the time when he worked, thinking of his little sister, who wasn't so little any more. She had grown into a poised, elegant, young woman. How old was she now?

Nat counted back the years. He had now been Qinten's slave for a few moons more than five years, most of them in the cleaning yard, cleaning out kettles, only recently had he been promoted to Cook's helper.

Before that, Vekt owned him. He worked hard for him, carrying leather and long lengths of trees to him. Some days he sat near Vekt as he hollowed out the tree lengths, tapping on them, and listening for the tone. During these days, Nat had become adept at transporting hot coals from the fire to the tree. More often, he stood beside Vekt with a bucket of water, waiting to douse the fire.

It had not been easy nor had he been fed well. Vekt often forgot to eat or feed Nat, and no woman lived with him to help. The lengths of trees strengthened Nat's wiry muscles. He wouldn't have minded staying longer with Vekt. But Vekt fell on hard times, the priests of Lorca stopped buying his drums, and the other cults followed Lorca's lead and stopped purchasing from Vekt. Confronting overwhelming debts, Vekt had reluctantly sold Nat to the slave market not even two years after he had purchased him. Vekt had sobbed on Nat's shoulder that day, but it could not be helped. If he was to avoid total ruin, Nat had to be sold.

That left the five years, and a little bit, he had made bricks for Hoth, as his slave. Five years with Hoth, two with Vekt, and now five more owned by Qinten. Twelve years.

Ziva had been three when they were taken from their parents. Do Mama and Papa still think of us and wonder where we are? He hoped so. He had glimpsed the necklace of beads she still wore, orange, black, and tan. He remembered rolling the clay for those beads.

His papa had told him … told him … He struggled to remember that day so long ago. Yes. That's what Papa had said, "Remember to care for her." He had promised he would. And she had been taken from his arms by a slaver. Silent tears rolled down his face.

"You are wanted by the Master in his apartments," Cook growled. "What did you do?"

Nat quickly wiped the tears from his face and turned to face Cook, shrugging his shoulders. "I thought I was staying out of trouble."

"Well, not well enough. You are wanted. Go."

Nat left the kitchen and walked through the house. He had been to the Master's apartments once before and hesitated to impose his dirty self on his sanctuary. He found Qinten standing near the door to his apartments, giving instructions to another slave.

Nat stood at a respectful distance, far enough to not appear to be listening in, but close enough to know when it was safe to approach.

Though he did not fear Qinten, Nat had a healthy respect for his temper. He had seen the results of others who had not been as respectful as expected. Thus, he waited until the Master signaled for him to approach.

"You desire my presence, Master?" Nat stood with a straight back and bowed head, his eyes on his feet.

"Nat, is it?" Qinten's voice sounded gruff and scratchy. "Cook has given a good report about you. Says you work hard and are resourceful. He told me how you obtained the pomegranates for the Growing Festival."

"Thank you, Master." Nat started to flick his eyes up, then remembered to keep them on his feet.

"I have need of a personal servant, one who is resourceful, hardworking, and unafraid to fight for himself."

Nat flinched. He had not fought anyone except Kenji, who had been ejected from the house almost five years ago.

"You may lift your head, Nat. Let me look into your eyes."

Nat slowly raised his head, keeping his eyes carefully directed away from the Master. Qinten walked around him, sometimes reaching to poke or prod, lifting the brown, curling hair from his neck. After a time, he, again, stood in front of Nat, staring, apparently in deep thought.

"You are different, somehow. I cannot determine what makes you so," he murmured. "Yes. You will do. You are my personal servant." Qinten pulled a note from within his robe and handed it to Nat. "Go to the wardrobe for appropriate clothing. Meet me in my apartments in one span."

Qinten turned, opened his door, and disappeared inside.

Nat felt the eyebrows on his face rise in surprise as he walked back the way he came. What had brought him to the attention of the Master? He had not wanted it and had not sought a change. He was happy in the kitchen with his friends. Would he still sleep with them? How would this affect him? Would he change and become like the Master?

Shaking his head slightly at the mystery, he made his way to the wardrobe. He silently handed the note Qinten had given him to Mott, the slave who supported the head wardrobe attendant. He had been absorbed in his worrying and had not glanced at it. He should have, it was writing, and he had not had an opportunity often to practice his reading. Now, it was too late.

"Who are you dressing today, Nat? Another new foundling kitchen slave?" Mott laughed as he took the note. The laughter died on his lips as he read. "I apologize, great one." He bowed his head. I did not know."

"Know what? I am still Nat. We sleep in cots near to each other. You have no need to bow to me. I am a slave, as you are." Nat looked at his clothing. "Only dirtier."

"You did not read this note" Mott shoved it into his hands.

Provide this slave with the gold clothing of a personal servant of the Master. Treat him with the honor of his station.

"Honor? Me?" Wonder filled his voice. "I am still Nat, slave in the kitchens. You do not need to bow to me."

"You say this now," Mott said, "but you will change. They all do in the presence of the Master."

"I will not," Nat said to Mott's retreating back. "I will not become like him. I will honor my parents," he whispered.

In less than a finger span, Mott returned with a pile of clothing.

"Put these on now, please. You should not be wearing the short tunic of a kitchen slave." Mott voiced the instructions in a distant tone, no longer the friend he had been when Nat had entered the wardrobe.

Nat removed his clothing down to his small clothes, then pulled the light-weight, golden tunic over his head. The fabric was softer, thicker, with a richness to the touch. It was not as long as the Master's, yet it hung to his knees, longer than the short tunic he wore in the kitchen.

Length of tunic was a sign of status in Nod. He had never expected to wear anything so long.

He slipped his arms through the robe of darker gold, just longer than the tunic. These colors were only worn by close servants to the Master. Now he was wearing them? Lastly, he stooped to settle slippers of the darker gold on his feet.

Nat pinched his thigh between his fingers, hoping to waken himself.

"You are awake. This is real." Mott held the kitchen clothing in his hands.

"I hoped it was a dream. I like working in the kitchen."

"You will never work in the kitchen again, at least not here," Mott said.

Nat shook his head as he left the wardrobe and made his way back to the Master's apartments, noting the softness of the fabric against his skin, the gentle bumping against his legs. It was strange to wear slippers over his calloused feet. He had not worn shoes since being taken into slavery so many years ago.

He became aware of the other slaves stopping as he passed. Each bowed as Mott had done. They had taken little thought of him in his earlier travels through these same halls, except those who stopped him to ask why a kitchen servant was wandering in this part of the house.

Now, even these bowed their heads as he passed. It made him feel strange. He wanted to shout at them, tell them he was the same Nat, the same slave who had worked for Cook in the kitchen that very morning.

Something kept him quiet. The last thing Mott said to him. Never work in the kitchen again? Would he be welcome to visit? Probably not, especially dressed like this. He had never seen others in tunics like his in the kitchen.

Nat vowed to himself he would not change. He would not become pompous as other high placed slaves had. He was still his mama's and papa's son. He remembered their faces, their names. He had not changed in all these years as a slave. This elevation would not change him, either.

Chapter 10

Evaluation

"Your father has found a prospective mate for you?" Tawna sat with Ziva in her parlor in the white velvet lounge chairs. "I do enjoy the luxury of your soft chairs and the whisper of the curtains. They tickle when they flow against my back."

The two girls had been visiting and sharing together for almost a hand span as the sun dropped from its zenith.

Ziva leaned back in her chair and grimaced. Her eyes bounced from Tawna to Tigre who languished on the floor in a spot of sunshine. "He has but I will not mate with him."

"No? Why?"

"He has a dark soul. I will die early if I were to mate him." She frowned then thought better of it and allowed her smile to shine again.

"Dark soul? I have heard you say that about someone before. Who was it?" Tawna tapped her long dark finger against her white teeth.

Ziva shook her head and stared at the cat. "I told you. I'm not sharing. I do not want it to happen. I pray it won't. I will not share the name."

"You fear it will happen if you speak the name?"

"No. I do not want my name tangled with his in any way."

Ziva watched her friend think about her words. Although Tawna's face was not as open as Ziva's, Ziva and Tawna had been friends for many years and Ziva could read her friend's face and discern her thoughts. Tawna planned another ploy to trick the answer from her. Ziva wouldn't fall for it.

"Why do you not want to be mated to this man?" Tawna asked. Her finger continued to tap her teeth.

Ziva pondered the response, her foot bouncing fast. She recognized it metered her agitation and set it on the floor.

"Because…" her foot began to bounce once more. "No, I can't say that. He is …" she stared at her bouncing foot. Tigre stood up and jumped on her lap. She stroked his luxurious fur.

"Oh, Tawna, I want nothing to do with this man. His soul is dark. He thinks he is better than everyone else, especially women. His reputation is black. I have heard of women who have been with him describe him as cruel and vicious. Why would I want a man who has been cruel and vicious with other women? Why would I want anything to do with a man like him?"

Tawna lay her hand in her lap. "When you put it that way, I agree. Why would you want to be connected to a man like that? I can think of many men who fit that description. Some of them I danced with at the last festival."

"Exactly. When I think of becoming the mate of one of those men, I quiver. Many times, it feels better to find a way to never be mated. I do not want to be abused by my mate. I want to be loved and cherished by a man, like my mother was cherished by my father. I am blessed to know love. Sadly, many men have never been loved and don't know how to love. How can I agree to mate with a man like that?" Tigre now lay sleeping in her lap.

Tawna stared at her friend. "Cherish? What is cherish? You have such different ideas. My parents love me. They love each other, too. But what is cherish?" Tawna pursed her lips and lowered her eyebrows.

"Cherish?" Ziva stared at Tawna and glanced down at her now still foot. "My father cherishes me. He cares for me and loves me deeply. I love Tigre. He is my confidant. I will be sad if he leaves me," she stopped to swallow, "if he dies. But, I don't cherish him. I want to be admired by someone like my father admires and cares for me. I want to be defended, encouraged, and honored. Isn't that what you want, Tawna?"

Tawna brushed her hair from her face and sat thinking. "Can parents cherish each other and more than one child? I have two sisters and three brothers. Is it possible for my father to cherish all of us? Even when his temper flares?" She shook her head. "I am confused by this word, this idea."

Ziva glanced at her cat and scratched behind his ears. "I have a memory... No. It is gone. I believe a man can cherish his wife and all his children. It must be so."

"To be cherished? Yes, I would like that, if I could be cherished by a wealthy man." Tawna smoothed the front of her dress.

"Wealth?" Ziva raised her eyebrows. "You must have a wealthy man?"

"Of course. Don't you? All you know is the pampered life of your father's house. Don't tell me you think you can be happy with a man of less wealth or even a poor man?"

"No," Ziva answered, stretching out the vowel. "I would like to mate a wealthy man. It would make life easier if he were. I would hope love would make a difference, if he were not."

"Not me," Tawna retorted. "I would settle for someone who treats me well, as long as he is wealthy. I like my life, even if I have to share it with my sisters and brothers. It would be nice to be spoiled, like my sisters."

"And you aren't?" Ziva chuckled. "You always have new dresses. Isn't that one new?"

"Well, yes. But, I'm not spoiled like Giselle. Her lower lip just has to peek out, and Father gives in. Gisselle's tears are unbearable!"

Ziva toyed with her cat's tail until its switching warned her to stop. "Who would you mate with, if you had a choice?"

"Me?" Tawna reached up and rubbed her ear. "If I could be mated to any man I choose? How strange to think of choosing a man! They do all the choosing. We do not even have the right to accept or reject. We do as we are told. Our fathers do all the choosing, accepting, and rejecting. But, if I could choose a man ..." she stopped to think, her finger moved to the side of her mouth, the red paint on her fingernails pointing to her beautiful eyes. "If I could choose, I would choose Qinten, priest to Lorca."

"Qinten? I thought Kara liked Qinten. Do you follow the cult of Lorca?"

"Not really, but the cult is interesting. I don't care if Kara wants him, I can dream, too. I would be a priestess and he is wealthy."

"You would mate for wealth?" Ziva's shock at her friend's choice showed on her face.

"No, silly. He is a handsome man. Everyone knows he is maneuvering to be High Priest in the next elections. I would be his High Priestess." Tawna shivered visibly in excitement. "It would be wonderful."

"Wonderful to slice the throats of little lambs? I hear you would also share your bed with other priestesses, other women, and other priests. You want that?" Ziva's usually calm face twisted and her cat dug his claws into her legs as he jumped off her lap. "Ow, Tigre. That hurt."

Tawna touched the back of her neck and glanced around the sitting room. "No. He would not do that to me. Would he?" A tear slipped down her cheek unnoticed.

Ziva hurried to her friend, wrapping her in her arms.

"You can mate with Qinten, if you choose. It is your dream, not mine."

Tawna wiped the tear from her face and smile a weak smile. "It doesn't matter, Ziv. I do not get to choose. He must choose me."

The discussion moved to the upcoming Harvest Festival and where they would attend, which cult would be more interesting

"Mother will not allow me to attend Harvest Festival at the temple of Lorca. She says I am still too young," Tawna pouted.

"Who would want to attend any festival in Lorca's temples?" Ziva growled. "I certainly do not. I hope I never have to attend another festival led by a priest of Lorca." She knew her words were too blunt, but she could not soften them.

"So where will you go? Everyone has to attend the festival." Tawna twirled a curl around a finger.

"Why does everyone have to attend? I don't know where Orak will take me. Where will you go?"

"We will go to Nimm. Mother has decided. It is milder than Lorca, but closer to what we should expect."

"Perhaps we will meet you there." Ziva stared out her window, hoping she could just stay home. She hated the noise and tension of the festivals

.

~ ~ ~

Nat tapped on the door to the Master's apartments. Another slave walked past. "Do you not know to walk in. That is your right now."

He opened the door and walked into the apartment. He looked around and didn't see Master Qinten, until he heard a sound behind a door. Perhaps there? He rapped softly on the door.

Qinten's voice spoke from the other side. "Come."

Nat opened the door and entered, being certain to keep his eyes down.

"Right on time. Turn around," Qinten ordered.

Nat turned slowly in a circle, the folds of his robe gently flaring with his movement, his slippers making a soft shush on the marble floor. The colors flattered him, the tunic just tight enough to show his muscled arms. He felt better than he had in many years.

"As my personal servant, you may look into my face," Qinten said, "but not in my eyes."

Nat lifted his eyes to Qinten's face, especially careful not to seek the eyes of his master.

"You may speak," Qinten said.

"Thank you, Master." Nat bowed from the waist. "What is wanted of me?"

Surprise flashed across Qinten's face, before he smoothed it from his face.

"You are to be my personal servant. You will help me as I command."

"And now? What do you command of me now?" Nat spoke quietly.

"You read and write?"

Nat worked to smooth away the surprise from his face. "Yes."

"Read through these papers. Tell me which merchant I should use to purchase the animals we need for our next sacrifice. My eyes are tired of looking at them." Qinten handed a stack of papers to Nat.

Nat nodded and glanced around the small study. "Is there some place I may sit?"

"Sit there at my desk for now." Qinten waved an arm in the direction of his desk and chair.

Nat sat in the indicated chair and began to read through the papers. As he read, he saw Qinten sit in the comfortable chair across the room and watch him. Nat read through one page, then another, often referring to an earlier page.

He reached for a pen, then thought better of it. He looked to Qinten. "May I take notes?"

Qinten nodded. Nat retrieved the pen and a blank page of vellum, on which he jotted notes about the things he was reading. He glanced at another page and wrote a note. He became absorbed in the project, happy he had made a point to read everything he saw during his years away from his parents. It made this task easier.

Nat read through all the papers, glancing up at Qinten only once, to see a smile playing about his face. Strange for the things he had heard about the Master. He returned to the project, focusing on the numbers before him and the names of the merchants. He heard a muttering, something about a girl who was intelligent and beautiful, yet different from her father. Nat kept his head down, unwilling to give Qinten an opportunity to dismiss him before he even started.

He focused again on the information in front of him, thinking about the different merchants, when Qinten slammed his fist into his palm. Something, or someone, irritated the man. His determination to avoid such irritation deepened.

He wrote another figure on his page of notes and considered their meaning. Only one merchant had the ability to provide most of the animals for the upcoming sacrifices. Orak, whoever that was.

Nat looked up and waited for Qinten to notice.

"What did you learn?" Qinten asked.

"There are many who can provide the sacrifices needed by Lorca. You can purchase from many or from one. Which is your choice, Master?"

Another small smile crossed the Master's face. "For now, I will continue to purchase from Orak. However, if he displeases, me, I will purchase from others."

Nat returned to the papers, noting how many of each animal they would need to purchase for the next festival.

Chapter 11

A Dance or Three

Nat bent over the figures on his desk. The Harvest Festival preparations were almost complete. He checked and double checked the numbers. As a major holiday in Nod, all celebrations originated in one of the four god cult temples. Nat sighed and stared out the window at the setting sun. It may be easier if some of the celebrations spilled into Qinten's home.

From experience, Nat knew Cook, Baker, and their helpers in the kitchen were busier than ever, preparing foods to be delivered to the temple. Some were to be shared among the celebrants. Some of the sweet treats would be available for purchase, the money going into the coffers of the temple. No wonder Qinten desired to be High Priest. All that money under his control. What man with a greedy nature, like Qinten's, would not crave that much money, and the power that it provided.

Providing grains and animals for the multiple sacrifices had fallen to Qinten and now Nat. The number of sacrifices for the Harvest Festival appeared to be greater than required for the Growing Festival. Fourteen bowls of grain and thirteen ewe lambs would be sacrificed each of the three days of the festival. Three young goats would also be sacrificed on each day of the festival.

Nat added up the actual numbers of needed sacrifices and compared it to those required for the past one day Growing Festival. Extra sacrifices and triple days of sacrifices added up to less than those sacrificed on the one-day festival, replicated in eleven private homes plus the one offered by the High Priest of Lorca in their temple.

He tried not to consider all the blood from the sacrifices. It sickened him. Such a waste of food needed by the masses of poor people who lived in Nod. Some of the food now being prepared by Cook and Baker would feed these poor, binding them to Lorca.

By law, all who resided in Nod were required to attend the celebration at one of the cult god's temples, even slaves. Slaves anxiously waited for these few days of freedom. Many ate until their stomachs swelled and drank until they fell into oblivion. At the end of the festival, these slaves faced beatings or death if they did not return to the homes of their masters. Few tried to escape.

Nat had never followed the practice of overeating or drinking the strong drinks provided. He always stood on the edges of the crowd as required, listening to the shouts and smelling the pungent fragrance of incense and burning flesh. He willingly accepted the offered food, but he often saved some for later, and he never drank the wine or other strong drinks available during festivals.

Memories of earlier days, days with a loving Mama and Papa surfaced. He sat beside Mama, with baby sister in her arms, as Papa helped another recite sacred words and sacrifice one young bull. Only a part of the meat lay on the altar, a simple structure built of rock as tall as he was as a child of four, and wider and longer than him. He could easily lay any direction on the flat rock that topped it, though his mama expressed horror when he when he asked to lie on it. The sacredness of that altar reached out, even now, to fill him with respect. It touched his heart with warmth.

Not the cult gods of Nod. The offerings lay in ornate structures, at the feet or in the hands of the idol gods. Nat felt no holiness in these temples, no joy in the offerings. Only regret and disgust.

He dragged his eyes from the setting sun. The brightness left a shimmer of light, blinding him. He brushed his hands across his eyes and held them there for a breath, washing away the blinding brightness, before returning to his figures and lists. Qinten would soon return, demanding an accounting.

~ ~ ~

The afternoon of the Harvest Festival, Ziva and Tawna strolled through the crowd, nibbling on finger foods served by

103

Nimm's servants. They laughed at clowns and expressed delight in the skill of the jugglers. Everyone celebrated a good harvest.

Along the edges of the hall, tables were set up. Sweets, carvings of Nimm, and other trinkets made by the followers of Nimm filled the tables and were offered for sale to the festival attendees. Both Tawna and Ziva carried a few coppers in the pocket they wore at her waist to purchase a trinket or two.

"These beads remind me of the ones you wear, Ziva," Tawna gushed. She lifted beads from the tray on the table.

Ziva bent to inspect them. Their size and color were similar. She glanced up at the merchant. "Where did you get these? Did you make them?"

"Oh, no, miss. We traded for them far to the west. My brother, he travels to distant lands, trading copper pans for interesting trinkets. Do you like these?"

"I do."

"How did you get beads from far in the west, Ziv?" Tawna held the beads to the sunlight.

Ziva fingered the beads around her neck. "I do not know. I have had these beads for as long as I can remember. These have been important to me for … forever." Ziva turned from the table.

"I want some like yours. I'm buying three."

"If you wish." The sun seemed to have hid behind a cloud. She walked to the next table, her thoughts far away. She didn't really want Tawna to have beads like hers, but what could she say to deter her? Her beads were special.

She bumped into someone. "Oh, I'm sorry."

She glanced up. A young man stepped back.

"It is no trouble, miss. Do I know you?" His eyes took in her hair, her pale skin, her pale pink dress, cinched at the waist with a wide magenta sash, and the soft silk magenta slippers. Memory crossed his face. "You are that girl! I looked for you to dance with at Roven's party."

Ziva blushed. "Crites? Is it you?"

He nodded. "What happened to you?"

"My father needed to leave. He called me away."

"I thought I saw the back of your dress slip out the door."

Ziva dropped her eyes. "I am sorry. I wanted to dance again with you. Only my father ..."

Crites touched her arm. "I understand. But today, you owe me a dance or three because you left without dancing with me."

Ziva allowed her eyes to climb into his eyes, and saw they twinkled with humor. "You are right," she laughed. "I owe you three dances today for leaving before I danced with you again."

"Let's begin now, then." He took her hand and whirled her onto the dance floor.

Few couples danced at this time of day, and they had most of the floor to spin and turn.

Ziva laughed at Crites' jokes. His humor and kindness drew him to her. She understood the whispers she overheard from the other girls. His eyes danced and twinkled as they laughed together. His dark hair gleamed in the sunlight, one lock drooped over his left eye as they spun about the room.

The music ended and they bowed toward each other, smiling.

"You need a drink, Ziva, after all that dancing." Crites' eyes glowed.

"But my friend—"

"She is dancing now, see." He pointed to the floor where Tawna danced.

"You are right. I do need a drink." Ziva put her hand in the crook of his elbow and allowed him to lead her to the refreshment table.

"What would you like to drink? Wine, ale, juice?" Crites asked, sweeping his hand toward the drinks.

Ziva considered the table of drinks. "Apple juice, please."

Crites handed her a glass of apple juice and chose one for himself.

She lifted her eyebrows. "No wine for you?"

"I don't like the flavor or the way it makes me feel the next morning. I'll stick to juice."

Ziva's approval for him rose.

The dance ended and Tawna found them. She smiled knowingly at Ziva. She smiled back.

"Join me at the table. It is time for food." Tawna waltzed toward the tables.

Ziva followed her with Crites hand at her back, warm and protective. The three young people joined Tawna's family. Orak joined them, sitting across from Ziva and Crites.

"I saw you dancing. You looked happy together." Orak smiled at them.

"We had a good time, thank you," Crites said. "Ziva left Roven's party without dancing with me, again. She owes me three dances in return."

"And dinner, as well, it would seem." Ziva laughed.

Other men claimed a dance with her, separating the two, but she danced with Crites twice more and stood with him as the priests of Nimm made offerings to their god. She hid her questions and revulsion. Who could think a carved marble figure of a bull could answer the needs of men and women?

When the priests offered bits of the slaughtered goat to the worshipers, Ziva stepped back. She wanted no part of the offering. She did not follow the cult of Nimm any more than she followed Lorca, or Enid, or Balg. None of their teachings encouraged her worship. They were all created by men. How could she worship a cult god created by men?

Crites, too, melted to the back of the crowd. "You do not follow the cult of Nimm?"

"No. And you do not either?" Ziva leaned against the wall.

Crites leaned next to the wall beside her. "No. The cult of Nimm holds nothing for me. I came here because we must celebrate the Harvest Festival at some temple. This year, for this festival, I chose Nimm. Perhaps, next festival I will go to Enid, or Balg."

"Not Lorca?" Ziva stared into the pecan-brown face that framed his dark brown eyes. A spark of hope filtered through her.

"Never Lorca. His priests are bloodthirsty. Every festival day, they sacrifice more animals. If they could, they would take all the animals to be sacrificed. Men would have no meat to eat, and little grain. No more animals would live to mate and provide for the next festival."

Ziva nodded. Orak had made similar comments.

"Ziva," Orak said. He had managed to move to her side without her noticing. "It is time we leave. We do not want to be forced to commit ourselves to Nimm."

She nodded. "It is time." She glanced at Crites. "Will you be leaving now, as well?"

"I will. Thank you for the dances and dinner. Maybe, … maybe another time." Crites seemed to be suddenly shy.

"Perhaps. I enjoyed dancing with you."

Orak took her by the elbow and led her toward the entrance. She glanced back at Crites, then followed her father.

Chapter 12

Courting Visit

Nat sat at the desk Qinten had ordered to be brought to his study, smaller than Qinten's, but nearly as nice. It had been placed near the Master's desk, crowding the room, so they could work together. Now, he considered the merchants they could choose from to purchase house necessities.

He had earned a place of trust over the few months he had been Qinten's personal assistant. He listened to the Master rant, placated him when he thought to sell a needed slave, and slept in a little room adjoining the Master's with entrances both through the Master's room and into the hall, so he could enter without inconveniencing Qinten.

"My father insists I should be mated." Qinten spoke into the silence.

Nat flinched, surprised at the sudden shattering of the quiet and the content of the Master's comment. "Mated?"

"Yes. He thinks I need a mate to help me move forward with my plans to be the next High Priest."

"How will mating help you?" Caution filled Nat.

"Men wonder why I am not mated, why I still live alone. Some wonder about my virility. Bah! What do they know?"

"Oh?" Nat said in a neutral voice. "And, is there someone you have in mind?"

"Yes. But her father is holding back, finding excuses to delay the announcement."

"And there is nothing you can do?"

"I am working on it. Her father will give her to me, or he will lose everything."

"Oh? Who is the father?"

"Orak." Qinten all but spat the name out.

"The supplier of so many of the sacrifices? That Orak?" Nat's eyes opened wide in surprise. He didn't know Orak had a daughter.

"That Orak. If he allowed me to meet with his daughter, talk with her, get her on my side, there would be no problem—"

"You have not spoken with her?"

"She is always under the protection of her father. When I approach at public gatherings, she slips away."

"That is a problem." Nat allowed sympathy to ooze in his words. "And she is the woman for you?"

"She is the one for me. I carefully analyzed all the available young women. She is the one. She has no brothers or sisters to take all Orak's money."

That Orak?

"Besides, she caught my attention with her beauty. None of the other girls are as exquisite, as delicate, as exotic. Her skin is the color of the moon, her eyes that of the sea, her lips like melons."

"She does sound beautiful, but different from most women in Nod—not like your own mother, I suspect." Nat looked at the papers on his desk. "Most of the wealthy women are dark beauties, with dark eyes. This girl, is she from Nod?"

"She is Orak's daughter. Of course, she is from Nod!"

Nat searched his memory of the young women he served at the festival, months earlier. Only one was a pale beauty. Only one stood out. No! Not her. His mind raced. How could he prevent the mating of his master to her? He could not condemn her to his cruelty.

"I am afflicted of her. So much so that I have not gone to visit others." Qinten's voice became dreamy, then it hardened. "Orak will give her to mate with me. She will be High Priestess, and I, High Priest."

"Can you not be High Priest without a woman at your side?" Nat asked, glad of the shift, but wary of the moods of his master.

"Not now. That will change when I am High Priest. A woman should not have such power over a man. A woman should not have any power."

Nat's fear increased, though he kept his face blank. Who would want to be mated to such a man? How could she?

"Women have no rights, no power? I am but a slave. I do not know?" Nat tried to turn Qinten's thoughts from her.

"None. Men treat women as they please."

"Yet Orak protects his daughter?" Back to her. He must be wary.

"Men protect their women as they protect their cattle or their horses, as possessions. Women are possessions to bring out as baubles on men's arms on festival days."

"I see." Nat now understood his master in a way he preferred not to know. He remembered his papa discussing problems with his mama. She would never be a possession.

"What do you plan? How will you convince Orak to give his daughter to you?"

Qinten stood from his desk chair and paced about the room. "I have asked. I have threatened him. Offered him bribes. He puts me off. I do not want to destroy him. I want his wealth and I want his daughter!"

Nat nodded, thinking. How could he soften his master's approach, and still prevent the mating? What could he do to protect Orak's daughter from this evil?

"Perhaps," he said slowly, thinking as he spoke. "Perhaps you can change your attack? Orak is a proud man. His wealth and property are important to him. I have heard it said you cannot draw a bird to you with a shout and a threat. It must be a song and sweet treats. Perhaps you should visit Orak in his home, whisper sweet words of kindness in his daughter's ear. Draw her to your side." Nat was sickened at the thought. Surely, she was more intelligent than that. Especially if she was who he thought she was.

"You can help me." Qinten stopped pacing in front of Nat and pointed his finger at him. "You can go to Orak, speak kind words, be my song and sweet treat."

"Me? I know next to nothing about women. I—"

"Yes, you. It is your idea."

Qinten dropped into his desk chair, pulled a clean sheet of vellum towards him, and grabbed his pen. He wrote quickly. He rolled the scroll and scrawled a name across the outside, sealed it, and tied it with a gold and white braid. Orak, Nat noticed. What was the Master up to now?

Qinten rang a bell and a slave immediately opened the door.

"Give this to a messenger. It is to be delivered at once."

The slave bowed and took the scroll. The door closed behind him soundlessly. Nat could hear his feet pattering down the hall toward the messengers.

Nat bent to his work, knowing the Master would tell him anything he wanted him to know when he was ready.

Later, there was a knock on the door. Nat stood and stretched, briefly, as he opened it. The slave handed him a scroll with Qinten's name on it. Nat handed it to him and returned to his desk, waiting for the Master to read the note.

"We are to meet with Orak this afternoon," Qinten said. "Make yourself ready."

Nat noted where he was in his work and left the study. It felt good to stretch his legs and walk awhile. He had been cooped up in the study much too long. Swinging his arms and lengthening his stride, he walked down the hall toward his room. He could have entered through the Master's room, but this time he took advantage of the hallway door.

He closed the door behind him and moved to the chest standing beside the wall. He ran his hands across the smooth wood, marveling again that such a thing was his to use, and that the clothing inside was for him to wear. In all the years he had been a slave, he never thought such a thing would be allowed.

Nat opened the chest and withdrew a fresh tunic, a robe, and small clothes. These, he set on the cot, ready to replace those he wore. He stripped, shivering a bit in the cool air, and washed.

He was no longer the small, scrawny boy stolen so long ago. He had grown. The work required of him had built muscles and strength.

The tunic and robe were exactly like the one he dropped at his feet, a uniform designating his place in Qinten's home, only these were clean. Nat sat on a stool to drag soft slippers on his feet, and tucked leather sandals under his arm. He would need thicker sandals on the streets, though they were not allowed in Qinten's home. Amazement filled him, yet again, that he could wear the soft slippers. Until the Master had taken him as a personal servant, his feet were always bare, inside and out.

He opened the door separating his room from the Master's where Qinten sat as a slave placed slippers on his feet. He, too, had been washed and dressed in fresh clothing. His tunic was red, the robe white with red stitching along the edges. Both hung below his knees, almost to his feet, to show his station.

Qinten glanced at Nat. "Good. You are ready. Let us be off."

The two men strode down the halls and out a side door. Nat expected to walk to Orak's home, but a carriage stood on the street, door open and waiting. He helped the Master inside and moved to climb on top with the driver.

"No. Join me inside," Qinten commanded.

~ ~ ~

Ziva paced across the thick, light-blue rug in her parlor. What did Qinten have in mind? Why did he request a personal visit with her and Orak? Something was wrong.

She and Orak had been successful in putting Qinten off, finding reasons to avoid his demand for her to be given to him as his mate. She shuddered again at the thought. Why would he come here today? Why would he want to meet with her? Women had no place in bargaining, it was for men.

She settled on the edge of a chair, then jumped up, unable to sit still. As she paced, Ziva brushed her hair back from her face or dry washed her hands. Why could she not have drawn the attention of Crites? He seemed to be a decent man when she danced with him at Roven's party. No, it had to be the dark Qinten.

Tigre yowled as she tread on his tail. Ziva dropped to the floor and cuddled him. "I am sorry, Tigre. In my agitation, I didn't see you." The cat's long tail twitched under her nose, causing Ziva to sneeze. "Can you believe that awful man is coming here? Here! To visit me. What do I have to say to him?"

She moved to a chair with the cat, petting and sharing her fears. Stroking the silken fur of her beloved cat calmed her.

At last, Ana slipped through the door. "Your father has need of you in his study."

Ziva smoothed her dress and patted her hair.

"You look beautiful, mistress Ziva," Ana said. "You will draw the man's attention."

"Will I, Ana? I don't want to. Perhaps I should put something different on, something less enticing?" She heard the wistfulness in her voice. She growled internally, disliking the man even more.

Ziva followed Ana to Orak's study, though she had been there on her own many times in the past week. With him here, she needed to be announced when she arrived. One more reason to be unhappy with him.

Ana knocked on the door to Orak's study and pushed it open when she heard him call.

"Your daughter, Ziva, sir." Ana made a deep curtsy. Ziva followed her through the door and watched her close it as she left.

Ziva faced three men, not the two she expected. Orak sat behind his desk, while Qinten sat in one of the two comfortable easy chairs. Another man, dressed in the golds signifying a servant of a priest of Lorca, stood behind Qinten, hands clasped behind of his back, unspeaking and alert.

She flashed a smile for her father, held it as she glanced at Qinten, then turned back to Orak. "Hello, Father. You sent for me?"

She knew why Orak sent for her, even knew Qinten would be sitting in the chair on the right. She and Orak had discussed this earlier when Qinten's note arrived earlier. They were surprised by his request to see them, asking to speak with her.

They decided she would wait in her rooms, as though she was not expecting a visitor. She did not change into nicer clothing nor dress her hair for visitors. They hoped to throw him off his guard. They were cautious, unsure of his intent.

Neither Orak nor Ziva expected Qinten to bring a servant, and hadn't planned for Orak or Ziva to have a complementary servant to balance things. Ziva determined to stay in the study with her father. She did not trust Qinten.

"Ah, Ziva." Orak continued the ruse. "We have guests. Qinten and his servant."

Ziva glanced at Qinten, then looked into the servant's eyes.

"Hello," she said. "Welcome to our home."

She dropped her eyes to Qinten's face. He frowned briefly, then composed his face. Good. Maybe she could encourage him to lose his self-confidence.

Qinten took her hand and brushed his lips across the back of it. "Hello, Ziva. We thought it would be helpful if you were able to get to know me."

Ziva fought the desire to wipe his touch from her hand. A chill spread across her back. Instead, she smiled, fighting back her disgust and the desire to rush screaming from the room.

"Sit please, Ziva." Orak indicated the empty chair on the left, much too close to Qinten.

She sat, sighing internally, hoping the interview would not last long.

"Qinten tells me he asked for this meeting because you have not been aware of his interest. He wants you to know more of him. Then he thinks you may encourage me to negotiate your mating with him."

Ziva turned to face Qinten. His dark features highlighted what some girls would consider good looks. His dark brown eyes were just lighter than the almost black hair, he had brushed away from his face, except for a lock hanging over one eye. She could almost understand why other girls swooned when they thought of this priest of Lorca. They didn't feel the darkness emanating from his soul, as she did.

"Tell me about yourself, please. I know you are a priest of Lorca. What else should I know?"

Qinten launched into a description of his place in society, his father's position as city governor, his wealth, his rise through the ranks of the priesthood of Lorca from the time he was a youth, and his schooling in the temple. Ziva listened politely, asking a question or two, all the while trying to prevent her eyes glazing over from boredom. He told her nothing she had not learned from the gossiping of her friends and servants, even less that would cause her to want him.

As Qinten droned on, her eyes were drawn to the silent servant who stood behind his master. His eyes remained downcast; yet, she could tell he watched her.

The servant's face looked familiar, but Ziva couldn't match the face to any in her memory. Another face surfaced but the dress of this man didn't help her make the connection. As she held to her smile and tried to appear to attend to Qinten's words, she struggled to remember where she had seen this servant before.

"You do follow the cult of Lorca?" Qinten's words dragged her back to the present "He is a great god."

"Follow the cult of Lorca?" Ziva closed her eyes briefly. "Father, do we follow any of the cults in Nod?"

Orak started. He glanced at her before answering. "No, Ziva. None of the cults draw me in. I provide sacrifices to all the cults. It is difficult to choose one. It would, um, it would--"

"It would injure your opportunity to sell to the other cults?" Qinten asked.

Orak nodded. "I am careful to prevent offense to any of the gods of Nod. They are important to the people. I have not aligned myself, or Ziva, with any of them. At one time, I thought I followed Enid." He paused and drew a deep breath. "Things happened to change that. I now follow none of the cults."

"Would I be required to follow the cult of Lorca if we were to be connected more closely?" Ziva watched Qinten's face.

"You would become a priestess of Lorca, a great honor for any woman. You would stand beside me as High Priest and you as High Priestess."

If you manage to become the High Priest. "And that would involve?"

"You would participate in the festivals, support the priests in the temple, join me in leading the Planting Festival, and other high responsibilities." Qinten smoothed his hair back. He obviously considered this to be an honor for any woman.

"Planting Festival? I have not attended many of your festivals. How would I lead it? What is involved?"

"The Planting Festival is a fertility festival, one in which we ask Lorca to give us a fertile earth and provide our people with enough grains, fruits, vegetables, and young animals to provide food, meat, and sacrifices, along with other needs."

"Don't all the sacrifices during the year accomplish that?" Ziva asked. "I saw many young animals sacrificed to Lorca at the mid-year festival."

"The ones you saw at the mid-year festival were offered in gratitude for the success of the planting and new birth of plants and animals. We beg Lorca to continue his magnificence we received in the Planting Festival." Qinten took on the face of one instructing a little child.

Ziva lifted an eyebrow in question. "And the priestess? How does she participate in the festival? Does she sacrifice?"

She thought of other possible activities for a priestess, equally revolting, but dared not express them, fearing to give this 'soon-to-be high priest' ideas. Deep within, she doubted the divinity of Lorca, or any of the other cult gods of Nod.

"Boys and girls lead the animals, as always, presenting them to Lorca. Priests always perform the sacrifice. The priestess leads the dancing and celebrations after the sacrifice."

"I will share with Ziva the details of those celebrations," Orak interrupted. "It is not proper for you to share information such as this with a young woman of Ziva's standing."

Qinten spluttered a few heartbeats before falling silent. Ziva watched the frustration play across his face before he managed to smooth it away.

"Come, Nat." Qinten stood. "We will leave Orak to share the events of the Planting Festival with Ziva."

With that, the two men left the room. Nat glanced back, briefly, at Ziva as he left Orak's study.

Chapter 13

Rough Roads

Orak stared at his hands. He found himself doing that more than he liked, lately. How his hands could give him the needed answers, he did not know. His response to that spider, Qinten, had been honest. He did not follow any cult, fearing loss of business with others.

More to the point, after Elin's death, he had no trust or faith in any of them. How could a god made by a man solve his problems? How could any of the cults claim to heal? Or save? Impossible! He slammed a fist into the open palm of the other hand. He would not allow that black thing to hurt his family, again.

Qinten had expertly woven a web around him. Orak could feel the stickiness of it. There must be a way to break out. He would not give his beautiful Ziva to him, or one like him, one who would expect that of her. "Lead the Planting Festivals, indeed not. Not my Ziva."

Com rapped on his office door and poked his head in. "Everything good with you, sir? I saw the spider leave."

"No. He tried to bait his traps, enticing Ziva to be his mate. I hope she continues to see through him."

"She will, sir. Ziv is a smart young woman. I saw her shudder as she left your office."

"You would shudder, too, if you were offered the right to lead the Planting Festival of Lorca."

"No! Ziv would not do that."

Orak took a deep breath. "Not if we can find a way to keep her from Qinten's side as his mate."

Com leaned back, as though retreating from a blow, horror roughening his voice. "Qinten desires our Ziva as his mate?"

"He does. Is there a way I can survive without our sales to Lorca? Qinten threatens to deprive me of those sales if I do not give in. I have been seeking a means to protect Ziva and my household. Lorca purchases more than half our stock and grains."

Com ducked his head. "There must be a way. We must save Ziv."

"I know. I have put him off for weeks, hoping he would tire of it. Today, though, he insisted on visiting Ziva here. He wanted her to get to know him. We have little time. I promised her I would not force her to marry, especially not Qinten. What can I do?"

"Allow me to look into this. I have heard rumors. Perhaps I can enlarge them, cause him to focus his energies on something besides our Ziva."

Orak nodded, fearing his voice would give his feelings away, though he was certain his face had already done that. Com quietly left the office.

What has Com heard? I have heard some, but Qinten has protection as a priest of Lorca, double protection as the son of the city governor. Com is good. He'll find a way.

Orak pulled his ledger toward him on the desk. In the meantime, he would find a way to sell more elsewhere and become less dependent on Lorca. He growled and mumbled aloud, "I know better than to place so much importance on one customer."

~ ~ ~

Nat's thoughts whirled as he rode through the city with Qinten toward home. Would Orak really tell Ziva what happened in the Planting Festival? He need to find a way to thwart Qinten's plans. To be Qinten's mate and to participate in the Planting Festival, or any festival, would be worse for Ziva than anything Qinten could do to him.

Nat served the revelers at the Planting Festival the year before. He stood at the door from the kitchen, horrified by what he saw, and his reactions to it. Much as he tried to control it, his body defied his mind, responding to the music and the wild gyrations of the naked women. He withdrew, embarrassed. Drak had laughed at him and teased him for hiding in the dormitory rather than joining the others. Something deep within him, a memory barely there, prevented Nat from joining in the wild dancing, driving the dancers to acts Nat refused to name.

And now, Orak will be required to share this with my Ziva. Nat shook his head.

"What are you mumbling about?" Qinten demanded.

A bump in the road jolted the carriage, bouncing Qinten into Nat. He pushed himself upright and growled, "Tell the driver to be more careful."

Nat stood enough to hold on the sides and pound on the roof of the wagon and lean out the window. "Master says to drive more carefully."

"Sorry, sir," the driver shouted back. "Unexpected hole."

"Miss those holes. Master is not happy to be thrown about inside. Beware."

The carriage took a sharp turn past another hole, knocking Nat out the window. He grabbed for the edge of it, catching his foot on the bottom of the seat. His body dangled, flailing wildly through the open window.

"Driver! Driver! Slow down!"

Nat grappled for a grip along the top of the door. His hand slipped. He feared he would be thrown out. Wagons and carriages jolted toward them. He felt his foot slip from beneath the seat, and scrabbled for a new grip. He dangled half in and half out the window. The door swung open. Nat could see a large wagon lurching toward them. He beat his legs back and forth trying to drag the door closed. The other vehicle raced closer. Nat shouted in fear and frustration.

The road narrowed and the carriage caromed over a giant rock loosed by the recent rains. Nat knew this would be his end. *How can I protect you if I am gone, Ziva, now that I have found you again?* The door slammed closed, throwing him back inside and onto the seat as the wagon careened past. Qinten shoved him aside with a growl.

"Master," Nat said, "you must choose between your desires to return quickly or travel without this constant jarring. I fear you cannot have both."

"I must speak, again, with father about the deplorable condition of this road," Qinten grumped. "It isn't safe."

Nat nodded. They rode on, lost in thought, holding on to the seat to prevent crashing into the other man, until the carriage slowed and turned toward Qinten's home.

Qinten opened his eyes. "What do you think of Orak's daughter, Ziva?"

"Ziva?"

"Yes. You are not stupid nor am I. I saw you staring at her. What do you think of her?"

"She is a beautiful woman, though her station is much too high for me to consider. Intelligent. She asked good questions. Will it matter that she does not follow the cult of Lorca? Is that a problem?"

"Stupid woman. As my mate, she will have no choice. She will be High Priestess. I am amazed Orak has shielded her so closely from the rites of Lorca or any of the other cults. How can such a man not choose a cult to follow?"

"It is as he said." Nat shrugged. "He follows the cult of business, never openly suggesting interest in a specific cult. Could he sell grain and animals to Lorca if he openly followed, say … Balg?

"Balg." Qinten spat the word out as though it were poison. "Balg is primitive, compared to Lorca. Priests of Balg refuse to join with any woman who is not their mate. Primitive nonsense!"

Qinten stewed and complained more about the Balg cult.

"You would not purchase from Orak then if he openly followed that cult?"

"Never! I could not."

"How, then, could Orak openly follow Lorca? You have put him in a precarious position. Lorca does purchase much of Orak's merchandise for the voracious Lorca, but he does sell to the other three cults. It would ruin him to openly support Lorca."

"It would help him. Lorca is a powerful god, much more so than Nimm or Enid, certainly more powerful than Balg."

"The others would not purchase from him. Will you do this to the father of your mate?"

"He need not openly follow Lorca to give Ziva to me."

Nat saw Qinten's anger raising and stayed silent. He had said too much already. He would be lucky to avoid a beating.

The carriage drew to a stop at Qinten's door. He threw the carriage door open and stomped inside, not waiting for the driver to jump down from his high seat or for Nat to lean forward to open his door. Nat stepped out of the carriage and

followed his master inside, aware the driver may face undeserved punishment.

Nat felt punishments were likely impending. Nearly bouncing Nat from the window was not all the driver's fault. The
roads were terrible after the recent rains. More importantly to
Nat, would the master find a reason to punish him for his rash
questions? If it saved Ziva from his attentions, it would be
worth it.

Chapter 14

Strapped

Ziva held her face still as she walked through the house to her own apartments. The servants could not see her tears nor her fear and loathing. What had she done to attract the attention of that dark man? She ignored all his advances at parties, looking the other way, walking with friends to the women's area, even leaving early. Did he not see she had no interest in him?

She reached her door and hurried into the sanctity of her private apartment. She threw herself onto her couch, at last allowing her tears to fall. "That snake holds no power over me. I will not participate in any of his festivals, especially not the Planting Festival. What man would ask his mate to do such disgusting things? Him. And the other priests of Lorca. What a disgusting cult. I will never follow that cult. I will not mate with him. Ever."

"Who, my lady?" Ana stepped close as if to touch Ziva's shoulder, then thought better of it.

"Qinten." Ziva spat the word out like bad meat. "He thinks he can force me to mate him. Worse yet, he wants to force me to lead the rites of the Planting Festival as his mate."

Ana clapped her hand to her mouth. "Not Qinten. I have heard of him. Rumors spread through the women in the city. You want nothing to do with him."

Ziva jumped from the couch. "I have not heard the rumors, and, no, do not share them with me. I want no more of his filth to soil me." She slipped her dress off her shoulders and let it puddle around her feet. "I must wash. Burn that dress."

"But my lady, … you love this dress." Ana scooped the dress from the floor.

"Not any more. It stinks of him. I will not wear it, ever again."

"But burn it? Will you not change your mind?"

Ziva stared at her maid. "No, do not burn it. Wash his filth from it, then give it away. Find some poor girl in need of a dress. I will not have it in this house."

"I will have it washed. I know a girl in need of a nice dress." Ana held the dress away from her. "After his filth is removed, she will be happy with it."

"Be sure the girl does not work here in my father's house. I do not want that dress to remind me or father of this day."

Ziva stalked, naked, from the room toward her bathing pool. She heard Ana open the door to her apartments and allowed a shudder to shake her. *I can't wear that ever again, but I can't* do that with every dress Qinten sees me in. It would cost father too much to replace my clothing. But he touched me. Ugh!

She sat on the stool and scrubbed her body viciously with a rough brush before stepping into the pool. She sat, immersed to the chin in the warm water. The slow current washed away her anger. If I refuse to marry him, what will Qinten do to father's business? Ziva sat thinking of all the possible consequences of her refusal, shivering in the warmth of the pool.

There must be a way out of this trap. Her father was known as an able businessman who had bested others who had tried to lay traps for him. With Com at his side, surely they could think of something. Ziva paddled to the center of the pool, her long, honey-blond hair trailing. She flipped over to stare into the blue sky through the skylight. Father would find a way. She had to trust him.

Ana came in sometime during her contemplation. She sat beside the pool with a bucket of warm water and a basket of soap. Ziva sighed and flipped over once more to paddle to where Ana sat.

"I can wash my hair."

"I know, my lady, but I wish to comfort you."

Ziva sat with her back to Ana and allowed her to scrub the soap through her hair. Ana's strong fingers massaged her head, soothing the ache Ziva only noticed at the touch.

"How did you know my head aches?" Ziva murmured, her eyes closed to the soap.

"Who would not have a headache after dealing with Qinten"

Ziva relaxed as Ana poured water from the bucket through her hair to rinse away the soap. Ana scrubbed her hair twice more, rinsing between.

"That should wash away his filth." Ana set the empty bucket beside the pool. "Do you feel better, yet?"

"Yes, thank you. I will find a way out of his trap. I will not mate with Qinten."

"Doesn't your friend, Tawna, desire a mating with him?" A tentative fear filled Ana's voice. She rushed on, "I know better than to share the things I hear in your apartments. I heard her share a desire for him."

"Tawna does not know what is good for her. Qinten is too evil for any of my friends. I wouldn't wish him even on an enemy."

"Wouldn't another woman be a better choice than you?"

"It would." Ziva shook her head. "But who? Not one of my friends. How can I encourage his attentions toward one of my friends?"

"There are ways."

Ziva looked at Ana. "How would you know?"

~ ~ ~

"Why did I have to say anything to the Master?" Nat muttered. "I know how to be circumspect. Now, look at me." He spread his arms out and turned to show off the change in his clothing.

"You look good in kitchen clothes," Drak teased. He thought better of the friendly slap on his back a narrow hand width away.

His friends had told him that Drak and Avram had watched the strapping from the kitchen door, waiting for Selib to drop his arm after the required twenty lashes and turn to stride into the house. They had run to untie Nat's hands and to carry him between them from the lashing pole.

Nat's two friends had carried him gently into their sleeping space, washed his back and applied honey to the injuries. For three days, Nat had slept. Avram told him later that Drak had returned to him as often as he could, daubing the honey mixture on his back and forcing down a tea of shepherd's purse. Now, Nat finally felt well enough to return to the kitchen, though he still moved slowly and carefully.

"Cook couldn't let you be his helper anymore," Drak said. "Avram took your place. And, after you were strapped, you could not take a position of honor in the kitchen." Drak led the way into the kitchen.

"I understand that. I could not expect Cook to give me special benefits. I am grateful to have a place in the kitchen." Nat turned the corner to see Cook, Baker, and all the helpers. He stood still, just looking, remembering the good times he had with his friends. Did he have friends now? Drak and Avram were still his friends. There were none among the slaves who worked directly with the Master.

Drak touched Nat's shoulder, returning him to the present. "Cook has agreed to allow you to turn the spit and help peel vegetables. Today you can peel. Tomorrow, you will probably be expected to turn the spit. Cook wants you to be careful."

"No. He wouldn't want me to fall into the fire." Nat grinned to show he understood.

"No, too much trouble for him if you did." Drak chuckled and led his friend into the room.

Cook looked up and nodded a welcome. Other men and boys stared at him for a long breath, then shuddered or shook their heads and returned to work. Not their business who worked in the kitchen. Nat had seen it before. If Cook accepted him, he would be welcomed.

Avram ran from the pantry with a basket of potatoes and set them on the worktable, nodding to Nat who nodded to Drak and walked to the worktable. He opened the drawer with sharp knives, found his favorite for peeling potatoes, and picked up a potato to peel. He was happy to have something to do and to have a place still in the house.

As the day passed, Nat expressed surprise to Avram, who worked nearby, that no one had come to take him to the slave market.

"Qinten sells too many slaves after a lashing. Cook prefers to do what he can to help. It is easier to work with someone who knows what happens here than train a new slave." Avram shrugged a shoulder as he answered in a low voice.

Nat knew he was lucky. "I am happy to be back in kitchen clothing. I'm grateful to be able to work finally. I would much rather be here than washing pots in the yard."

"You are lucky to be in the kitchens." Avram nodded. "Your back would not manage the inside of a pot."

"Nor would it be happy to be waiting to be sold again in the slave market. I appreciate the opportunity to continue in the service of Qinten, even in the kitchen. I was told once I would never serve in the kitchens again."

Avram snorted softly. "Shows you what they knew."

"Yeah, not much." He smiled and picked up a carrot to peel.

Avram smiled and returned to his work, helping Cook. Nat continued to peel vegetables.

Chapter 15

Trapping a Spider

Though his back hurt, then stung and itched as it healed, Nat enjoyed two weeks in the kitchen with his friends, turning the spit and peeling and chopping vegetables. As the injuries on his back healed, he could again wear the tunic of the kitchen slave. He joined in the friendly teasing and Cook began to expect more of him. It surprised him to fall so easily into the rhythm of the work.

Nat wondered if he would be allowed to continue in the comfortableness of the kitchen. Qinten could be capricious in his orders, once banning a slave from the house, other times sending them to work in a dirty job until he was needed again. It took little incitement for a slave to be beaten or sold.

Nat knew his ability to read and do sums would draw the Master's attention back to him. He hoped Qinten would forget about him for a long time.

He would be happy in the kitchen for the rest of his life. Nat could see himself as second to Cook, preparing meals. Only his fears that Orak would give in and force Ziva to mate with Qinten darkened Nat's thoughts and prevented his complete pleasure in his current situation. The only reason he would want to leave the kitchen to return to serve Master Qinten was his concern for his sister.

Did Orak tell her what her responsibilities would be if she mated Qinten? How did Ziva handle the news? I have not heard of a celebration to honor the upcoming mating, yet. We in the kitchen would hear, for we prepare all the foods for the celebrations. Please, Jehovah, Keep my sister safe.

Nat stood still, the potato he was peeling frozen in his hand. Where did that name come from? I have not used it for—for many years. Jehovah. Yes, Jehovah is the God of my papa—my papa, Enos.

"Why the sudden smile?" Avram demanded. "You haven't smiled in all the time you've been back in the kitchen. You'd think you aren't happy to be back with us."

Nat shook himself and continued peeling the potato. "I am happy to be back here in the kitchen. I have been worried about a girl—a girl the Master wants to mate."

"No concern of yours, this girl. Or do you fancy her?" Drak said.

Nat felt his ears grow warm.

"You do fancy her!" Avram crowed. "She is beyond you, if the Master wants her for a mate."

"She is beyond me, but I still fear for her. A young girl should not have to be a part of his depravity."

"True, that," Cook said. "No one should be forced to join in his vile ways."

"You fancy a girl! Imagine that." Drak wasn't willing to let it go.

"I do. What is it to you?" Nat brushed past Drak to reach another potato.

"I'm your best friend. I thought you would have shared all the details with me by now."

"Can't a man have something special, something here," Nat waved in the direction of his heart, "without sharing with others. Who would not keep it to himself? Especially, with friends like you." He glared at his friend until Drak dropped his eyes.

"Well, so what if I have shared other things? I wouldn't have shared this, if you asked."

Nat raised his eyebrows.

"I wouldn't have."

"And you know, now, why I have not shared nor will I share anymore." He tossed the potato into the cold water and grabbed another to peel. For many heartbeats, the sound of his peeling was all that was heard in the kitchen.

"Back to work," Cook growled. "We have a meal to prepare."

The others returned to their tasks, chopping vegetables, mixing sauces, kneading breads, and other tasks necessary to the preparation of a meal for a large household. Nat was glad of the noise. He did not want to share anything about Ziva. Let them think he fancied her. It was safer that way. No one must know. His memory of his papa and Jehovah were sacred, as well, not something to be bantered about the kitchen.

Nat lost himself in thought as he peeled the pile of potatoes. Though aware Gowdy entered the kitchen, he thought nothing of it. Gowdy's responsibility for overseeing the kitchen and kitchen slaves brought him in often. It felt good to be back in his domain.

"Nat!" Gowdy roared. "What are you doing here in the kitchen"

"Where else would I be? The Master sent me to be lashed."

Nat could feel his friends in the kitchen holding their breaths, working silently to hear Gowdy's next words.

"Did no one tell you to return to the Master?"

"No. I have had no word."

Gowdy growled deep in his throat. "Mibiti has been searching for you. The Master is angry you have not returned to your duties. You must hurry to his side."

"Like this?" Nat stretched his arms wide. "Smelling of onion and potatoes?"

Gowdy sniffed Nat's hair. "And garlic, too. No, you must clean yourself and present yourself to the Master as soon as possible."

"In these clothes? As a kitchen slave. Yes. That will be good. Let him know I have been busy in his service."

"No!" Gowdy shouted. "That will never do. Go to Mott. He will provide you with new clothes. Go. Now."

Nat set the half-peeled potato on the table and silently left the kitchen. His friends reached out to touch him, then pulled their hands back as though burned. He was no longer one of them. He was the personal slave to the Master.

"What are you wearing?" Mott croaked when Nat entered the wardrobe.

"Clothing fit for the kitchen."

Mott's eyebrows nearly reached his hair. "Personal slave to the Master in the kitchen?"

Nat dropped his eyes. "He had me strapped. My friends helped heal me. I thought I was no longer needed in the Master's service. I was not forced from the house or returned to the slave markets, so I returned to the kitchen."

"Mibiti has scoured the house for days, searching for you. The Master is in a rage that you are not by his side." Mott sniffed. "You cannot return to him like that. Go to the washing room. I will send for hot water. Wash the odor of the kitchen from your skin and hair. It will not do for you to return to him looking and smelling like the kitchen."

Nat followed the pointing arm into a washing room and stripped off his kitchen tunic. He lifted the tunic to his nose and grimaced. Gowdy and Mott were right. Qinten would never allow him into his presence smelling like onions and garlic. Too bad. Onions and garlic were healthy.

A man entered with a bucket of hot water, which he poured into the large tub. More men carrying buckets of hot water followed him. Nat watched them dump the water into the tub until it was full of steaming water. I'll cook in that!" He touched the water with the tip of a tentative finger, surprised to discover it not as hot as he supposed. He slipped off his small clothes and stepped into the tub. The warmth enticed him to sit and bury himself to the neck in the warmth. This must be how the Master bathes. I remember baths like this, long ago. My mama had a tub almost this big. It held Ziva and me. We splashed and played together while Mama scrubbed us clean.

Nat jerked. He was not here to remember the past but to get clean. He found the rough cloth and soap waiting on a table beside the tub and scrubbed the kitchen from his skin. He sank below the surface to wet hair. He scrubbed his hair with the soap and rinsed, then scrubbed and rinsed again to be certain the stink of garlic was gone.

Such luxury. Nat hated to leave it, but he knew he could not soak in the luxury any longer. The Master was waiting. He stood in the water, allowing it to drip back into the tub and found the large towel. He stepped out and dried himself. Back to the Master.

Nat wrapped the towel around himself before turning to find clean small clothes, a gold tunic, and soft gold slippers on a stool. When had Mott brought these in? He was sure no one had entered the room, but the clothing sat in mute rejection of that belief. Nat slipped on the clean clothing, his skin remembering its softness. He opened the door and returned to the wardrobe.

Mott spun his finger in a circle. Nat complied and turned under Mott's inspection.

"Your hair is a mess. Here. Comb it." Mott handed him a comb and pointed to a small glass on the wall. Nat combed his hair and reached to return the comb.

"Keep it. You will need it to look like the personal slave of the Master."

Nat looked at his tunic, wondering where to put the comb.

"Here. Put this pocket across your shoulder." Mott handed him a pocket on a long cord, both of the same gold as his tunic. "Now, go. The Master waits. We sent a message telling him you have been found, but he will not wait long."

~ ~ ~

Orak looked up from the papers on his desk as Com entered his study. "What did you learn?"

"Much. And none of it good." Com dropped into a chair near Orak's desk. "You will not like the things I have to tell you."

"I knew I would not." Orak leaned back in his chair and laced his fingers together across the front of his chest.

Com shuffled his feet and rearranged his robe.

"Com. Stop stalling. Tell me what you learned." Orak leaned forward, setting his elbows on his desk.

"Qinten is the son of the governor—"

Orak hissed and stared into his assistant's eyes. "This I know."

"And a priest of Lorca." Com hurried on. "I know you know this. He is working to position himself to be the next High Priest of Lorca. He sees himself as powerful and next to the god. As you know, he is responsible to supply the sacrifices for the many festivals."

"This much I know. I supply most of the animals and other sacrifices to Lorca. Qinten keeps our business profitable. His god is ravenous. What can you tell me of the man?"

Com leaned forward, setting his forearms on his knees. "To be a High Priest of Lorca, a man must have a mate. As you know, he and his mate lead the Planting Festival and Harvest Festival. It seems Qinten thought he could get around it—until now."

Orak clenched his jaws. "Why now?"

"Qinten has had little interest in a mate. He takes his pleasure in others, usually women mated to wealthy men, men who must stay silent to continue receiving the gift of his purchases from them." Com bit the side of his lip as he looked at his employer.

"I have heard this," Orak muttered.

Com breathed deeply and went on. "What you may not have heard is what he does to these women." Com chewed on his lip as he stared at his friend.

When Orak shook his head, Com continued with stories of Qinten's sick behaviors.

Orak was sickened by the stories of depravity Com shared. None of it boded well for Ziva. He could not allow her to be his mate. Qinten's open animosity toward women demonstrated to Orak his certainty that he could not allow his daughter to be a part of the Lorcan Priest's life.

At last, he cried out, "Tell me no more! The man has no good in him. I cannot allow him to take my Ziva as his mate."

"You cannot. Not if you love Ziva." Com shook his head and leaned back in his chair.

"I knew he was not a good person, not after what he did to my Elin. What can we do to prevent this? He believes me to be in his trap. I sell much to him for his god, but not as much as he supposes." Orak picked up a pen and doodled on a scrap of vellum.

"Will it destroy you if he stops purchasing?"

"It will be a struggle, but we will survive. It will be more difficult for Qinten and the cult of Lorca. Few other merchants can offer as much as I."

"Is there a way we can turn his trap on him? A way to make him suffer?" Com leaned forward, resting his elbows on his Orak's desk.

"There has to be a way."

The two men bent over the desk, thinking of ways to make Qinten's life difficult. Many ideas were immediately discarded. Others were kept for further consideration. Orak would not write them down, fearing even a shred of evidence would be used against him, rather than Qinten. They spent hours working through the ideas, until they determined one would work. The complex plan must be carried out as quickly as possible. It held many dangers for them and for Orak's business. However, it would be worth it, if they managed to keep Ziva safe from Qinten's clutches.

Late that afternoon, Com left the study, orders and directions set in his mind. Orak knew he would find Keb and get things put into place. His fingertips rubbed circles across his temples. Making plans to ensnare a spider in his own web gave him a headache. The plan had to work. He would not allow Qinten to have Ziva.

Chapter 16

Money. Always Money!

"What is the problem with Qinten? I know. I know. He has a dark soul. You've said that before. He is wealthy. He is in line to be the High Priest of Lorca. What more could you want?"

Ziva shook her head. "We have been friends for years, Tawna. Have I ever been interested in wealth and all its trappings like Kara?"

"Kara would say that is because Orak is wealthy."

Ziva shrugged and turned to pick up a slice of orange from a delicate blue plate on the table beside her white velvet chair. The young women were sitting in Ziva's sitting room. Her father's problems were not something to share with a friend, even a best friend.

"You have always lived a comfortable life, with servants and enough of everything. You have never been hungry, without clothes, or a place to live."

"And you have?" Ziva turned to her friend, eyes wide.

"Well, no. But we have been close. There was a time father struggled. He sold in the marketplace, working to build enough business to support a shop. He did not move into the shop until I was seven. I remember those years, when we did not always have enough."

"I'm sorry. I didn't know. Why is Kara so concerned about wealth? Bram is wealthy. Scholars always have power, and he keeps the city records."

"You know he has not always had a position in the city. Kara's family is new to wealth. She is still impressed by money."

"Money. Always money! Money is not everything. You and Kara still have your mothers. Mine is gone. I would love to share with my mother my challenges."

"I forgot, Ziv. You have so much. I did not remember your loss." Tawna leaped forward to kneel in front of her friend and hugged her. Ziva allowed her to hold her a breath, before pushing her away.

"I'm fine, Tawn. Money is just not all that important."

"So what are you going to do about Qinten?"

"Anything I can to avoid him. I do not wish to help him lead the Planting Festival. Have you heard what happens at that festival?"

"Mama will not let me attend or tell me why." Tawna lowered her voice. "Do you know?"

"Yes. Orak told me." Ziva's response was barely above a whisper.

"Share."

"No. I cannot. It is too … too horrible."

"I cannot believe it can be so horrible. Mother and father participate each year."

Ziva felt her eyebrows raise. "Perhaps this is why they will not tell you about it."

Though Tawna teased and berated her friend, Ziva refused to share the details of the festival. She sighed in relief when Tawna left, still begging for information.

"It is not for me to tell you, even if I could speak the words," Ziva repeated as she closed the door. She leaned against the door and shook her head. "I cannot speak the words."

~ ~ ~

Nat stood outside the door to Qinten's apartment. He straightened his tunic and brushed back his hair. A growl echoed through the door. He took a deep breath and rapped on the door.

Qinten called, "come."

Nat entered and walked to stand in front of his Master. "You wanted me, Master?"

"Yes, Nat." He swallowed and shook his head slightly. He cleared his throat. "Look at the reports on your desk and tell me what is wrong."

Nat moved to his desk and picked up the papers. He glanced toward Qinten, who stared at a copper vase. He wondered at his strange behavior before focusing on the question put to him.

Much later he had an answer. Looking up, he noticed Qinten nodding in his comfortable chair. Now, he wondered whether it was braver to allow him to sleep or wake him with the answer to his questions.

He decided on the latter. "Master?"

Qinten slowly opened his eyes, stretched, and scrubbed his eyes. "What have you found?"

"Something is going on that I cannot quite put my finger on. The levels of grain have dropped, lambs are lost, doves are missing. What has happened?"

"I thought there was a problem. Will there be enough for the New Year Festival? Can you determine the cause of the losses?"

"Yes, there will be enough for the New Year festival, with some left over, but not enough for the Planting Festival unless something changes. As to the cause, I cannot tell."

"Why would there suddenly be losses in all the important sacrifices? Who would be behind this?" Qinten shook his head and reached for his empty wine goblet. Nat hurried over to pour more from the decanter.

"I cannot say, Master. All I have is the numbers. We need reports from those responsible for the sheep, doves, and grain. It may take days to untangle this."

"Are there not explanations with the reports? Surely, they did not send numbers only. I read something about losses …?"

"There are explanations, but they make no sense. I will continue to read the reports and try to find a reason for you."

"Do that." Qinten leaned back in his chair as Nat returned to the reports. After several breaths, he asked, "Why did you not return?"

Nat sat still many heartbeats. Qinten opened his mouth to ask again as Nat answered. "I did not know you wanted me to return."

"Where did you go? I searched everywhere for you."

Nat opened his eyes wider as he looked at Qinten.

"I did not look for you. I sent others to search for you. None could find you."

"I lay on a pallet where my friends from the kitchen carried me. I slept three days on my stomach, the pain eased from the concoctions given to me by my friends, and the honey they daubed on my back. When I could move again, I returned with them to the kitchen. There was no indication I was needed at your side. No one said anything to me that you wanted me back I was grateful to be in your service, still, and in the kitchen, rather than someplace worse."

Qinten stared at Nat, waiting for more.

"Only this morning did Gowdy tell me you were looking for me. I was peeling potatoes."

"Why did it take so long for you to come to me after—was it Gowdy — who told you?" Nat nodded. "After Gowdy informed you I searched for you?"

"I smelled of the kitchen, onions and garlic, and had no appropriate clothing. My tunic was torn from the lashing. I wore the tunic of a kitchen slave. Gowdy sent me to Mott in the wardrobe for a tunic. Mott insisted I bathe away the fragrances of the kitchen. I came as soon as I was dressed."

"I suppose it was necessary." Qinten sniffed. "You no longer smell of the kitchen."

"No. The bath took care of that."

Once more, Nat bent over the reports, making notes as he read. A slave entered the office, lighting the lamps there and throughout the apartment. Nat looked up, surprised to see Qinten prepared for dinner. He had not heard him call the wardrobe slave.

"Do not forget to eat, Nat. I will not have you ill." Qinten stood by the door, ready to leave for a dinner with others.

"Yes, Master Qinten."

The door closed and he returned to the reports, struggling to understand what to make of the losses. Animals and grains were delivered and paid for. He had the receipts to prove sufficient numbers had been ordered and delivered. Now, the actual numbers reflected severely reduced numbers.

Nat became aware of the fragrances of the meal he had been working on that morning. Beside his elbow, on his desk, sat a steaming plate of food. He glanced around, seeking the slave who brought it. The empty room suggested he missed him.

He picked up the fork and absently ate as he read the reports once more. There had to be something more, something they hadn't said, in fear of Qinten. How could he convince those responsible for the care of the sacrifices to reveal the actual causes? He would have to be careful. They would need to be convinced Qinten had no part in the investigation, that his capricious actions would not come to play if they admitted the truth. How would he manage it?

He let his head rest on his hand as he ate the now cold meal. Even cold, it was delicious. He knew Cook knew what he was doing. He allowed himself a few breaths to remember his friends in the kitchen. He would miss them. Would they miss him?

Chapter 17

Extortion

"You want what?" Orak barely contained his desire to reach out and strangle the man in front of him.

"I want five golds. It is not too much for a wealthy man like you." The stranger sat still in his chair, hands folded across his stomach, placidly waiting.

Orak remembered the first time this scum of a man came to his home, demanding payment to keep his knowledge silent. Ziva was still a tiny girl and his beautiful wife, Elin, still lived. That day he demanded payment to stay quiet, not tell Elin where Ziva came from.

Elin was sick, profoundly sick. They lost a daughter to an accident. Their dark little beauty, Liva, had been the delight of their lives. She brought joy to both of them. Her eyes sparkled as she danced down the halls of their home. Her laughter brought smiles to even the grouchiest of his servants.

Orak never owned slaves. The men and women who worked for him were paid, and paid well, to help in his home. His servants were free to leave to find work elsewhere but few did. They were happy in his home, appreciated and respected. They could not be sure it would be the same in other homes. Too many of the wealthy preferred slaves over free servants. Some servants in Orak's home were old men and women who had served in his father's house. They moved to his home when he married Elin.

Orak and Elin took Liva with them to the Shrine of Enid, one of the many shrines to the gods of Nod. The priestesses there fawned over her, wanting her to be brought there to be trained as a priestess. Enid was as good as any of the other gods in Nod. Elin and Orak worshiped there at times of festivals. Planning to send Liva there to train as a priestess seemed right.

The small family spent four happy years together, until the day Liva and Elin went to the market, searching for fabric for a new dress for the little girl. Elin had scoffed at the need to take Com with her, not believing anything bad could happen to them.

Orak worked in his office that day, his door ajar, listening for their return, waiting to hear Liva skip down the hall to show him her new fabric. Orak stood, ready to call Com to go with him to search for them, when Com entered.

"Good. You are ready to go."

"Go? Where?"

"You haven't heard" There has been an accident in the market."

Orak pushed past Com and started down the hall, Com paced beside him. "Accident? Who was involved?"

"Elin and Liva."

Orak picked up his pace and raced out the door. There, he swung into the saddle of the horse kept there for his use. Com mounted his horse and they raced toward the market. They were slowed at the market's edge by the crowd of people surging toward the center.

They slid off the horses and led them into the mass of people. Com and his horse pushed through them, making way for Orak and his horse. Some men grumbled and turned to argue about being shoved. When they saw the horror and fear on Orak's face, they stepped back, taking their neighbors with them.

Orak saw them lying on the ground, covered by swaths of fabric. Elin lay bleeding. He could see wooden shelving laying about near them. He ignored it and knelt between his two girls. He searched Liva for injuries, searching for breath in her body. She looked unhurt, seeming to sleep. He could find only small breaths escaping her mouth. What had happened?

"Breathe, Liva, breathe." He frantically whispered into her ear.

Elin moaned next to him. He turned to her, groaning deep inside. A healer worked to stop the bleeding from her legs, tying a scrap of cloth around the injury.

"Elin. Elin. Stay with me. Please, Elin," he begged.

She moaned, "Liva. Where is Liva?" Her arm flailed about, searching for their child.

"Here, Elin. She is here." Orak had not the heart to tell her how seriously Liva was injured.

"Oh, Enid," he prayed," "save Elin's life. Give me back the life of my precious daughter. Your priestesses say you have power over life and death. Save them! I will give you my daughter if you save her life. Please."

A small gasp escaped from Liva's little lips. He bent near her face, turning his to feel the breath on it. He waited many heartbeats. Then more. No breath came. He kissed her little forehead and sat up.

"Liva," Elin whispered. "Liva. Are you hurt?"

Orak struggled to hide the tears from his mate. He bent over and kissed her on the cheek.

"Liva is hurt, Elin, as you are hurt. You must live."

A healer gently pushed him aside. "Her injuries are severe. We must take her to the Shrine of Enid. There she will receive help from the priestesses and Enid."

"And my Liva? Where will she be taken?" He allowed the tears to flow his cheeks.

"We will take her to Enid, as well. She will take your daughter in her arms to return to her love."

The healers folded his child in the fabric that covered her, covering her face. Then one picked up the small bundle and carried her toward the shrine.

Orak stared mutely as they took away his beautiful daughter. Others had formed a carrier of two long pieces of wood and a length of strong fabric. They lifted Elin onto it. Orak followed them through the market toward the shrine and help. His eyes focused on the men and women in front, in whose care his mate rested. He gripped onto his horse's reins, leading it along.

One healer turned to him. "Go home, Orak. We will care for her. There is nothing you can do for now. Come to the shrine tonight. Give us time to help her.

Orak halted with a nod. The healer hurried to catch up with the others. Orak stared after them.

"Orak? Orak?

A hand took his elbow and shook it a little, then a little harder. He turned a blank face toward the voice.

"Come home with me," Com urged.

"What happened? Orak whispered, feeling anger growing within him. "Why is Liva dead? Elin hurt?"

Orak stomped toward the fabric stall. Scattered lengths of fabric were strewn across the area. Shelving and broken wood tossed about. What could have caused such a disaster?

A small man hurried over to Orak and Com, carefully avoiding their horses.

"Sir? How is your wife and daughter? Are they well? Can they be healed?" He wrung his hands.

As a tall man, Orak often looked down on the men around him. This man shrunk in his terror of his reaction. "What happened here?"

"A boy ran from his tutor, dodging and running through the crowds, pushing things over. There was turmoil and noise, things falling. Then, he pushed past me, behind the shelves of fabrics. He shoved against them as he ran by, trying to escape a beating, I would imagine." The shop owner searched Orak's eyes, begging understanding.

Orak nodded. "And the shelves fell?"

"The little man bowed his head. "Yes. Your mate and daughter were standing there, examining lovely pieces of silk, deciding which to purchase. When the shelves fell, they, ... well, they didn't have time to move. The shelves fell on them. Do they live? Will they heal?"

Orak closed his eyes. Clearly, this man carried no blame for the loss of his daughter, the injury of his mate. "No. My daughter is gone. They take her to give her to Enid. My mate is with the healers, at the Shrine of Enid. Her injuries are serious."

The shop owner gasped. "No! I am sorry. What could I have done?"

No longer able to hold back the tears, great tears dripped off Orak's chin. He shook his head. How could he blame this man?

"Who was the boy? The tutor?"

The shop owner wiped his own dripping nose with a scrap of fabric from the ground and handed another to Orak. "It does not matter. There is nothing you or I can do. It was Qinten, the son of the governor."

Orak roused from his reverie and stared at his visitor. "What would convince me to give you anything?"

~ ~ ~

Ziva made up her mind to ask her father. The question of her identity ran through her head over and over again. It had reached the point she had to know. Since her trip to the slave market, the questions could no longer be pushed away.

She walked through the house toward her father's office, hoping he was there working. Now she had gathered her courage, she needed to follow through, without waiting. She needed to learn the cause of her differences. Why did the slave from Qinten's home look so familiar? She was determined to discover the answers to these, and other similar pressing questions.

As she neared the door, she heard angry voices. She drew back, surprised to hear Orak's voice raised in anger. Even in anger, it's familiarity comforted her. The other voice, though, bothered her. It was strangely familiar. She remembered hearing it before. Where?

Ziva stood thinking of the strange voice, then turned away. She didn't want to intrude on her father's business, especially when he shouted in anger.

Before she walked three steps away, she heard the stranger say her name. How would he know her name? Was this argument about her? Not another suitor, she hoped, at least not one like Qinten. It didn't sound like a suitor. Her father wouldn't shout at a suitor.

"You would tell Ziva? You would tell her?" the stranger shouted, incredulity filling his voice. "Do you really think she will accept it?"

"Yes! Ziva is a strong young woman. She will accept this. There is nothing you can do to hurt her or me anymore. Leave my home and never return!"

"Qinten wants her for his mate. Will he accept her if he learns of this?" The stranger lowered his voice.

Ziva moved closer to the door, hoping to hear her father's answer.

"I care not if he accepts her or not." Orak's voice quieted. "I have not sought to bind my daughter to that man. It would be ..."

"You do not want your only daughter to be married to the man who will be the most important man in Nod? How can you do that to her?" The stranger raised his voice in surprise.

"I have my reasons. They are none of your business. None of this is any of your business. Leave! I will not pay you another copper. You have no more business in my home. Never return!"

Orak's chair scraped against the floor. Before Ziva could turn away, the door flew open and the stranger stepped through.

"You!" he said.

Ziva stared at the man. Long buried memories stirred within her brain. How did this man know her? How did she know his face?

Orak stepped through the doorway and saw Ziva standing beside it. His face paled. "How much of this did you hear?" he demanded.

Ziva lifted her chin and stared into her father's eyes. "I came to discuss something with you and heard my name. You said you would tell me. Tell me what?"

The stranger leered in her direction and reached out to touch her hair. Orak slapped his hand back.

"You will not touch my daughter," he snarled.

"Your daughter? I think not. I will return for my gold."

With that, the stranger marched toward the door and Keb, who held it open for him. The stranger smashed his hat on his head and turned to send Ziva a wicked grin as the door closed on him.

"Who was that, father?" Ziva turned her gaze on Orak. Why is he demanding gold from you?"

Orak heaved a deep sigh, then took another deep, cleansing breath, and let it out before answering. She had seen him do this before after a bout of anger.

"Come into my office. I will explain."

Ziva passed him, reaching out to touch his arm as she entered. Before following her in, Orak turned to Keb.

"Please watch my door, so no one else listens in to my private conversations." He looked at Ziva knowingly. "And be sure to bar that piece of filth from this house. Maybe, later, you should mention to the city guards that he is a problem. That should keep him from entering Nod again."

Ziva couldn't see it, but she felt Keb's nod. This stranger must be horrible.

Orak entered the room and closed the door more gently than Ziva expected. She thought to see his face twisted and angry, still. Was he angry with the man, or with her? She was surprised to see his face calm and a smile play across his lips.

"What did you come to ask that was so important?" he asked as he sat in a chair next to hers.

Ziva turned in her seat to face him, wanting to watch his eyes as she asked her questions. "Father. I know this hurts you for me to ask, but I must know. Who am I? Why am I so different from you? My skin, my hair—?"

"It is time for me to tell you, though it pains me to recount it to you." Orak didn't blink or cast his eyes to other parts of the room. He merely gazed into Ziva's eyes.

He swallowed and closed his eyes. "Where do I begin?" he murmured. Opening his eyes, he cleared his throat and started.

"Do you remember Elin, your mother?"

"I do remember being taken to her, being loved and petted for a while before being returned to my own apartments."

Orak sighed and looked at his hands for a long breath before gazing into Ziva's eyes once more.

"Elin was ill, from before you came to this house. She went shopping with our daughter, Liva, when she was hurt."

Ziva's eyes opened wide. "Your daughter, Liva?"

"Yes. Liva. She was our darling. A dark little beauty who looked like her mother. She was full of life, dancing and singing all day. We loved her dearly."

"Loved? Where is she now?"

"They went shopping that day, planning to purchase fabric for new dresses for both of them. I hugged them goodbye that morning and sat here in my study waiting for them to return. For some reason, I was concerned about them. I waited for what seemed to be spans before I decided to look for them. I stood to leave when Com hurried in, telling me of an accident in the market."

Orak stood and paced around the room as he shared the story. Ziva watched him pace, wondering where she fit into the story. She waited, knowing the answer would come.

When he told her about returning to the market and having the stall owner ask about his family, she wondered if this was how Korm and Orak became friends, and Tawna, hers.

"Did you ever learn who it was? Who was the boy who ran through the market and killed mother and Liva?" She had followed his wandering steps with her eyes, and now looked toward his.

Orak halted and stared at the wall behind her. "Qinten, the governor's son. And, no, I never talked with him or his father about it. What good would it do? The harm was already done."

Ziva felt tears sliding from the corners of her eyes and reached up to brush the tears from Orak's face before brushing hers away.

"Elin did not return to us that day or for many days after. Her injuries prevented it. And, how could I bring her here, with Liva ... with Liva dead?" Orak sank into in his desk chair, propped his elbows on it, and covered his face in his hands. "What could I do? Elin needed Liva, and I needed Elin."

"What did you do? You couldn't bring Liva back for mother. How did I come into your lives?" Ziva searched the backs of his hands, waiting for him to drop them so she could see his face.

Chapter 18

Shared Secrets

At last, Orak lifted his face and stared into this daughter's eyes, fearing her response to the next part of the story. His fear had kept him from sharing all the other times she asked about her differences. Ziva gazed steadily into his eyes. He expected her to flinch from him. Instead, she reached for his hand.

He inhaled, held it, then slowly exhaled. "I went to the slave markets." He rushed on before she could make any exclamation. "I hate them. They are loathsome, but I heard there were little girls there. The stench sickened me, but I endured it, for Elin. The healers had told me she would come home soon, and I needed a daughter for her to love."

Orak paused, searching for a look of hatred on Ziva's face. There was none, yet, so he pushed on. "There were three little girls there that day. Only one was the right size. I carried you home," he glanced into her eyes as she grasped his hand tighter, "and had Ana clean you up. Imagine my surprise when I learned your name, so close to our Liva. It made it easier for you and for Elin."

Ziva nodded, waiting patiently for the rest of the story.

"Once you were clean and dressed, you were a pretty little thing, always have been. You even fit into Liva's clothing. But you were quieter, didn't dance through the house like she did. When Elin asked why you weren't your usual noisy self, I told her it was because of the accident. She came home the day after you arrived. She never noticed the change. She hurt too much."

"That is why she sometimes called me Liva. I wondered about that when I was little. She was good to me, when she felt like seeing me. She treated me well, and I loved her."

"I wondered if you loved Elin. She lived another year after you joined our lives. She loved you." Orak squeezed Ziva's hand. "By then, you were our daughter. I loved you almost much as I loved Liva. My love for you has grown more each day, until now, you are my beautiful daughter."

"I love you, too, father. Your love has shown through each day since mother died. I wondered that day, and have many times since then, how I could have lost a second mother. And, yet, I do not remember my first mother. What has all this to do with that stranger demanding money from you?"

"Mahonri came to see me just weeks after you came into our lives, demanding copper. He said he'd make sure Elin found out about how you came into our lives. She was so sick I didn't want her disturbed." Orak stared into Ziva's eyes, pleading for understanding. Then, he dropped his head to his chest. "So I paid him."

"You didn't? You know men like him will return for more if they are paid once," Ziva cried, shaking her head.

"I did. Elin seemed to be getting well again. I didn't want her to relapse. I knew he'd be back, but I told myself I wouldn't pay him again."

"But you did." Ziva's voice carried no accusations.

"I did. You had become the delight of our lives. Your laughter brought smiles to even the grouchiest of our servants. Even they forgot you were a replacement for Liva. Mahonri, the piece of filth, stayed away many years, until long after Elin succumbed to her injuries. I hoped it would be a one-time event."

Orak lifted his head and relished his daughter's kind and forgiving face and stared into her blue eyes. "You were a part of my life. You brightened this house, making it bearable. When he returned, how could I allow him to whisper into the ears of your friends, or worse yet, into your ears? How could I permit him to cause you such great pain?" Orak lowered his own dark eyes. "I gave him seven silvers that day."

"Seven silvers? That much?" Orak could see horror battling with pleasure in her eyes. At last, she whispered, "I was worth that to you?"

"You still are! He promised to never return, but like all of his kind, he is a liar as well as a thief. He came back today, demanding gold."

"Gold! You didn't give him any, did you?" Ziva grabbed both his hands.

"No. You heard. I told him I would tell you and take away his threat. And now, I have. Do you hate me?" He stared earnestly into her face, searching for revulsion. He could see none, but she was good at hiding her feelings.

"Father, have you thought about what would have happened to me if you hadn't come to the market that day?" Ziva leaped from her chair and rushed to throw her arms around his neck. "I would be a true slave, scrubbing, or cooking, or any of the multitude of other dirty jobs, at the mercy of my master. Instead, I'm your daughter, and you love me. You still love me?"

Orak returned her embrace and thought of the things he heard in whispers about some of the slave owners, men who misused and abused their girl slaves, and even some of their boy slaves, in horrible ways. He shuddered and held her a bit tighter. "I do love you, and I am happy you are here with me, not in some slave owner's home. I hate to think what may have happened to you!"

"The slave market is awful. The stench and conditions those people were in horrified me. The few who were clothed, wore only rags." Ziva quivered and stepped back a step. "I've heard stories from my friends about what happens to female slaves. Thank you for saving me from that!"

She leaned forward and kissed him on the cheek.

She sat back in her chair, leaning forward to gaze into her father's eyes. "But, how did this—Mahonri was it?" Orak nodded and she continued, "this Mahonri know about me? How did he know to threaten you?"

Orak had hoped she would not think to ask this question. He should have known she would; her intelligence would lead her to the next logical question.

"At first, he claimed to have watched me buy you and bring you home. I was so concerned about Elin that I did not think to ask that question."

Ziva's pulled her climbing eyebrows into place and nodded. "I can understand that."

He shook his head and continued. "I thought about it and wondered what you wonder. How could a stranger watching the slave market know to threaten me? How would he know the purpose for which I purchased a little girl slave? I asked around. No one knew this man. I hoped he would not return. If he did not, it wouldn't matter."

"But he came back?" Ziva brushed her hair away from her eyes, then set her hands neatly in her lap.

"Yes. He came back. When I asked, he told the story of seeing the accident in the market. He spent much time in the slave market, for what he never said. When I came for you, he remembered me."

"That sounds plausible, but it stinks. Why would he be watching you? Why would he think to threaten you? How would he know I was not to be another slave for your home?"

"My questions, as well. He wouldn't answer. Com followed him to his rooms in an inn, thinking to find him with partners or owners who direct him. There were none. He comes on his own. Com picked him up, took him to a place in the wilderness, far from the city, and threatened him."

"You told him to do this?" Ziva's voice carried the beginnings of anger.

Orak held up his hands to calm her. "I did. I hoped it would make him stay away."

Ziva breathed in, and let the air out, twice, calming herself. "It did not work."

"No. He is back again, but I found out how he knows enough to threaten me."

"What is his way, his reason? This is something I need to know. Is it not?" She stared intently into his eyes.

Orak blinked and glanced away, then returned his eyes to her. "It is. I hoped to never need to share it with you. Must I?" He gazed into his daughter's eyes, begging her not to ask. For a heartbeat, he thought she would accept his plea.

"You must. I need to know about my life. I love you, father. You have saved me, cared for me, and loved me. I will not repay that love with cruelty. But, I must know. Why does he care?"

"He brought you here. Took you from the men who stole you from your parents. He knows who you are, knows your parents. He can return you to them."

~ ~ ~

Nat stared at the report messengers brought to him only heartbeats before.

"All the sacrificial birds are in disorder. A band of wild dogs raged into the coops. They broke down the walls, freeing some and eating or destroying as many as they could get their snapping jaws around. A few of the birds now roost on the tops of the broken coops. All the others are gone, either flown far away from the dogs, or dying on the ground around the coops. Feathers, beaks, and blood fill the coops. None of those that remain can be coaxed into the damaged coops. Bird handlers work to erect temporary coops to protect these few from the coming storm. Tempting morsels of food have been put out for the escapees, hoping they will return to the protection of the sacred coops."

Nat threw the message to his desk and growled in frustration. This is not what I need just now. Qinten is already upset at the loss of sacrifices. This will not make things better. He reached to his back and absently rubbed a healing scar.

How to present this to Qinten? The bird handlers were doing all they could to retrieve the flown birds. They could not be blamed for a band of wild dogs. What could have stirred the dogs up to such violence—violence against birds? Nat shook his head. He had never heard of wild dogs attacking pens of birds. Other animals? Yes. But not birds. Something or someone had caused this disaster. But what?

Could men cause such a thing? Perhaps, but how? Why would they attack the sanctuary's birds? Birds of all things? Birds were among the least of the sacrifices offered to Lorca. The god preferred larger animals: sheep, goats, and calves. Birds mollified him. What god would not? Feathers would tickle his nose, if it had a nose. Did Lorca have a nose?

Nat wondered about the features of Lorca and his tastes in sacrifices. What would Jehovah desire as sacrifice? Since his plea for his sister's safety, Nat found himself trying to remember the God of his papa, the true God. He remembered going with Grandpapa Adam to offer sacrifice. That had left him feeling good, with his chest burning. He felt a closeness to Jehovah. He could pull few of the words spoken by his Grandpapa Adam to his memory, but the feeling of love and safety in his presence remained strong, along with the burning in his heart when he remembered.

Have I experienced any good during the sacrifices to Lorca? Nat reflected on the many festivals he had observed as a slave in Qinten's house. The excess of blood sickened him. The wild dances of the women were tantalizing, but he had not been enticed. The events of the Planting Festival were things he did not want to remember or participate in.

None of the things demanded by Lorca made him feel good; none caused a burning of joy in his heart. Lorca may be a cult god, but he is a false God.

Nat's eyes fell on the report. "He may be a false god, but I must do all I can to appease Qinten." Birds were demanded. What could he suggest?

He hoped a new report would come in the evening, reporting the numbers of birds returning to the safety and tantalizing morsels of food. The numbers destroyed by the dogs would have to be replaced. Perhaps, men could go to the wilderness and capture enough to replace the destroyed birds. If they were careful with the nets, they would not damage the new birds.

Yes. That would solve the problem of missing birds, but how to explain it? Men? Another jealous god? Which one?

Nat considered each of the gods, wondering which could be considered jealous enough to have set a band of wild dogs on the flocks of Lorca. He would need to suggest one, though Qinten's mind was twisted enough in hatred and anger to choose one without a suggestion. With which of the competing cults was Qinten currently most angry?

Travelers and merchants worshiped Balg, though not all merchants admitted to their worship. Qinten was often angry with the followers and priests of Balg. He constantly grumbled that Balg sought to entice the followers of Lorca into his cult. Balg would not entice by destroying Lorca, not if the characteristics of Lorca were needed as part of the cult. No. It would not be Balg.

A woman's god, worshiped by women and healers, Enid would not instigate destruction. Followers of Enid concerned themselves with healing the injured, not damaging them. She healed the physical injuries of any who came to her. More importantly, women whose hearts and souls had been destroyed by men came to be healed by Enid. Why would such a god be interested in the destruction of Lorca? Beyond the common knowledge that followers of Lorca often abused women? In Enid's softness, her healing ways, she would not seek destruction.

That left Nimm, god of the craftsmen and farmers. Had the priests of Lorca paid the craftsmen for the small images recently created for the past Harvest Festival? Nat searched his records. Qinten kept the records of these payments. Yes, payment had been made. Why else would Nimm concern himself with the destruction of Lorca's sacrificial birds? Did they conflict with Nimm's? Why would a god of craftsmen and farmers want to destroy birds awaiting sacrifice to Lorca? Nat could not think of a reason and eliminated Nimm from his list.

That was all the cult gods with temples in Nod. There were smaller gods, but Qinten wouldn't consider them. Nat couldn't blame them. Perhaps it was Jehovah, the only God who could do such a thing. If a God had caused the damage, it would be Jehovah. No. I will not suggest it. Qinten must not know of Jehovah, nor my belief in Him.

If not a god, then who? Who would do such a thing? Nat continued to puzzle through the problem. Qinten had made enemies of many men, not the least of these were the wealthy men whose mates he visited for his pleasures. Perhaps one of these men? Had one learned of Qinten's visits? This was most probable. How would he take the news? Nat shrugged. He knew—not well.

Nat glanced out the window. The storm neared. It would soon arrive in all its fury. Qinten would not be happy when he returned. He did not like lightning and thunder. Though Nat would never speak the words, he thought Qinten to be frightened by lightning storms.

He walked to the windows and watched the leading edge of the storm rush closer. He stood watching and smelling the storm, thinking. When Qinten returned, soon or late, he'd be angry, though angrier if he had suffered in a thunderstorm. Did any of the birds return? Were any safe in their hastily built new coops? Nat hoped they had returned.

~ ~ ~

Tears leaked, unnoticed, from the corners of Ziva's eyes as she sat thinking in her favorite seat in her parlor with Tigre warming her lap. She now understood her dislike for Qinten. She could never mate with that man. Even as a child, his selfishness and lack of discipline had been disastrous. He had caused the death of her adopted mother. And he had not changed. She saw this reflected in the parties they both attended.

Qinten's age, at least eight years older than her, could not be important to her. Young women were given to older men as mates much more often than to younger men. The darkness of his soul frightened her. How could others not see the blackness there? How could Tawna or Kara consider such an evil man?

Ziva's thoughts wandered, then focused on Qinten's servant. Who was he? She remembered a servant at the Growing Festival, the one who served her food. This servant's eyes were like the servant at the Growing Festival's eyes. Kind. Not hard and cruel like Qinten. She worked to lay the image of that man over the image of this. Change the clothing? Yes. This was the same man, and the same one she saw at the slave market. Each time she saw him, his dress had changed. Had his status?

Was he a servant or a slave? Ziva stood to pace, dropping Tigre to the floor with a yowl.

"Sorry, Tigre." She bent to pet his head once, then stood again.

Pacing sometimes helped her think. Most likely, the man was a slave. Knowledge of Qinten's harshness had spread, even to the women's apartments. His household would include many slaves, not trusted servants like in Orak's house where servants were paid for their help. None were whipped, none purchased. None but her. Only Ziva had been purchased.

She dropped into her seat. "Only me." She knew Orak's love, understood his purposes, and appreciated the difference his purchase made in her life. "No," she whispered, "I cannot fault Orak."

She had not been spared the whispers, the scandalized rumors suggesting the treatment of slave girls. They did not stay lovely. Masters abused them; some wives had them disfigured to prevent their mate using them. Would this have been her life if Orak had not been the one to purchase her? Disfigured to hide her beauty from men?

Ziva dropped into a chair, now lost in her thoughts. The words 'lost children of the prophet' squirmed its way into her thoughts. Who were these lost children? And what was a prophet? Certainly, not someone like Qinten.

How would a prophet lose his children? She had lost her papa. He was not a prophet, was he?

A face filled her memory. A man with sparkling blue eyes, laughing as he lifted her high into the air. She giggled in her memory, sure he would catch her. His brown hair fell across his eyes as he pulled her close.

Papa? This was her papa. Tears flowed freely as she tugged the memory close. Papa. Where did he go? Orak said she had been stolen. Did he search, even now for her?

She yearned for more, more memories of family. "Help me remember," she begged, more in her thoughts than voiced. A woman held her close, her musical voice singing as she rocked her. Ziva peered into her face. Green eyes and wavy, red hair filled her vision.

"Oh, Ziva, my darling, the musical voice said, "you are mama's sweet little girl. How I love you. You and Nat are the joy of my life."

Mama. Mama. I have a mama and a papa. The slimy thief, Mahonri, had been part of stealing her from her parents. Orak had told her he thought her to be too young to remember her family. She hadn't until seeing Mahonri and hearing Orak's story. It had jarred her memory.

Nat? Who is this Nat she heard her mother mention? The name felt familiar, naming someone she should know. She closed her eyes, struggling to remember. Nat must be a brother, to be a joy with her in her mama's life. Had he been stolen from them, too? Was Nat sold in the slave market, as she had been? Where was he?

Her thoughts returned to Qinten's servant. This man was close to her age. His skin coloring was lighter than most in Nod. Like her? Was this her brother? Was this her Nat?

My Nat? Why would I think of him as mine? Memories she considered to be dreams returned, waking in the dark of her room crying for "My Nat," being rocked by her nurse, Ana, until the tears dried, and she relaxed back into sleep. Nat promised he would always be with me. Would always watch over and protect me. He said he would.

Ziva opened her eyes and stared at the wall. Her Nat, her brother, had been stolen with her from her mama and papa. He had promised. Where was he now? Sold as a slave away from her? Would he have been blessed to be purchased by a kind man, as she had? Or had he been required to work hard? Had he been whipped and abused? Tears leaked from her eyes once more.

This man, this servant of Qinten's, could he be Nat? His bright blue eyes and brown hair were familiar. She mentally placed the memory of his face beside the memory of her papa. Yes. This could be her Nat.

How could she be certain? There were no noticeable scars, no bruises on him, or what she could see of him. She had not searched for them. Perhaps he had avoided the lashings she heard others tell of.

"If this is my Nat," she breathed, "let him be safe from beatings. Let him still be my Nat. Oh." She thought of him working closely with the blackened soul of Qinten and her heart skipped a beat. "Preserve him from the darkness. Oh, God of my papa, please keep my Nat safe." She didn't know who she prayed to, only that it wasn't any of the cult gods of Nod.

Chapter 19

Thunder and Lightning

Nat heard the door to the outside slam. Feet stomped up the stairs to his apartment. Qinten was home. Though the door was closed, Nat could hear him shout through it.

"Hot water for my bath immediately."

Not in any mood to be told of the damage to the sacrificial birds. Nat blew the breath from his lungs and composed his face and closed the shutters. The door slammed open and Qinten entered. A slave silently closed the door behind him.

"How did your meetings go, Master Qinten?" Nat asked.

"I am cold and wet. Is my hot water here?"

"It will be soon." Nat grimaced as his master stomped into the washroom.

The door silently opened, allowing a line of nearly naked slaves to enter, carrying buckets of hot water for Qinten's bath. Nat nodded toward the bathing room and returned to the report.

Perhaps Qinten would be in a better mood after warming up. *Dream on, Nat. You know he is never in a good mood, especially after meeting with the other priests or with his father. And today, he met with both. Add that to the storm, and he'll be murderous. And my bruises from the last bad news just healed.* He heaved a huge sigh and steeled himself against his master's rage.

It wasn't unusual to be slapped or slugged when he shared bad news. *He expected worse on this day, the news was worse than any he shared. Would it be easier if Qinten were mated? Not to Ziva.* He stacked the report neatly, then spread others across the top.

The sound of Qinten sneezing echoed through the doors. *Another reason to be prepared for rough treatment.* Later, Nat cringed and stood as his master stomped into the office, a warm golden robe thrown across his dark shoulders. The black hair stood up in places, as though it had been dried quickly and forgotten.

"I would whip that carriage driver if he were not so necessary." Qinten stomped back and forth across the room, fuming and shouting. "He will pay for the loss of that horse."

Nat stood beside his desk, waiting for him to stop raging. When he finally flopped into his comfortable chair, Nat bent to assist him into his warm slippers, searching for something calming to ask.

"The roads are not yet repaired?"

"No! The roads are not yet repaired. They continue to throw carriages around as they skip and bounce through gigantic holes, causing riders within to ricochet from one side to the other. And the cursed lightning hit the horse. I was forced to sit in the depths of the thing, with lightning crashing all about, waiting for the dead beast to be dragged away and another hitched to the carriage. All in the commotion of rain, thunder, and lightning."

Not a calming question. Nat pretended not to notice the unconscious quiver wracking Qinten's body. On another occasion, a slave had been beaten near to death when he laughed at his master's reaction to thunderstorms—out of the Master's hearing, he thought. Nat refused to be beaten again and kept his eyes on the papers on his desk, feeling sorrow for the poor horse, and bad for the carriage driver. It would be difficult for a slave to recompense Qinten for the value of a horse.

Qinten huffed and growled a bit longer, then stared at Nat.

"Did your father offer a time-frame for when they might repair the roads?" Nat attempted to put off the discussion of the destroyed birds.

"No work can be done on the roads this time of year, when the rains pour down. You should know that." Qinten moved from his chair to the chair behind Nat's desk. "What have you been working on?" He shuffled through the scattered papers.

"Bad news, Master Qinten." Nat picked up the damage reports. Better to get it into the open than to wait for him to discover it. "Wild dogs attacked our bird coops this morning, just before the storm arrived. Many birds were damaged and killed in the short time the dogs rampaged through the coops."

Nat picked up the report, turned the page, and dropped it on the desk once more. "The dogs were chased away, one or two were captured, with birds in their teeth. Some of the remaining birds have been coaxed into the coops. The keepers left the empty coops standing open, hoping the birds will return to their safe homes, safe from the oncoming storm. I have not received news of the birds since the storm broke."

Nat stopped speaking and stood still, waiting for Qinten's beating. It did not come. Instead, Qinten set his elbows on the desk and held his head in his hands. Nat softly sucked in his breath. This could be more dangerous than his rages.

"What more will happen?" Qinten spoke barely above a whisper.

Nat drew his eyebrows together. "More, Master?"

"Lorca requires more sacrifices. I am expected to locate and purchase greater numbers of calves, lambs, and goats. Some priests even suggest the need for young swine. Swine." Qinten spat out the word as he would filth. "Next thing you know, they will want asses."

"More of each? Now?" Nat understood his master's struggle. They had purchased extra animals and grain from the other suppliers attempting to squeeze Orak. Now, they would be forced to meet with him and beg for more animals. Soon Lorca would demand all the food for himself, leaving none for the citizens of Nod.

"Now. During the raining season, when animals are big with their young, not delivering them. Lorca's appetite has grown. I do not understand." Qinten shook his head.

"And after other unexplained losses, we lose most of our doves and pigeons. This is not good. I have spent all day trying to determine who would gain from our loss of birds."

Qinten snorted. "That is not hard to figure out. Followers of Balg have done this. They do not like the power Lorca has gained."

"Balg?" Nat inhaled deeply.

"Yes, Balg. Their dove and pigeon supplier, Obike, has breathed threats toward me, recently." Qinten sneezed and wiped his nose with a cloth he pulled from the sleeve of his robe. "His wife is a cow. He should be grateful another man is interested in her. He is not."

Now I see.

"I did not suspect him. I considered many causes but never Obike."

Qinten sneezed three more times and began to shiver. "Oh. I am cold," he moaned.

"The storm chilled you. I will get you a warm blanket and food." Nat went into his master's sleeping room and opened the blanket chest. He dragged out a warm blanket and brought it back to the study, draping it around his master.

He opened the door and gave the command to the boy stationed outside Qinten's door. A messenger stood waiting. Nat raised an eyebrow and held out his hand. The messenger handed him the page.

"Any response for me, sir?" the messenger asked.

Nat opened the message and read it through quickly. "No, not now. I will send word later."

The messenger turned on his heel and left as Nat re-entered Qinten's apartments. He found him doubled over, coughing. "Hot food will be here soon, sir. You do not need this now, sir, but I just received more bad news."

"More? What now?" Qinten growled and lifted a fist, then brought it to his mouth as a deep, wracking cough doubled him over.

Nat pulled the table from beside the wall, pulled out a drawer, and found a mat and silverware, which he placed on the table. "How did you get so wet, Master Qinten. Did you not stay inside the carriage?"

Another deep, rasping cough bent him in half. When he could again speak, he said, "The wind blew rain through the windows, drenching me. Between the holes in the road, the blowing rain, and the thunder and lighting, the ride home was miserable. Curse the storm. Curse the bad roads. Curse—" Another cough overtook him, then he sneezed three times again. When he could squeeze out another sound, he continued, "Curse the weather."

A servant knocked and entered, set a covered tray on the waiting table, and padded out on silent, bare feet. Nat uncovered the food and set it on the table while Qinten shuffled to the comfortable chair beside it.

"What is the bad news?" he demanded.

"A hole has developed in the base of the amaranth silo. Water is pouring in. They are working to staunch the hole, but the amaranth at the base of the silo is ruined." Nat steeled himself, waiting for the punch to his stomach.

"Curses! One more loss." Qinten coughed deeply.

"They could not say if it was natural or man-caused. Who would have dug a hole in the side of the silo? Balg, again?" Nat dared to ask.

"No. That would be Nimm. Stoffle would be behind this. He probably sent a servant to loosen the rocks at the base, enough for this raging flood to break through. His wife is a spirited little thing." Qinten stuffed a bite of the delicious smelling meat into his mouth and chewed. "She didn't like having more than one of us use her, though, nor to watch —" He swallowed.

Nat broke in. "What is it with all these husbands? Are they banding together against you?" He almost flinched away at his audacity to speaking the question.

Qinten coughed deeply before answering. "My father warned me it would happen. I did not believe him." He coughed again and lay back in his chair, his face becoming redder than Nat had ever seen it, even in his frequent rages.

~ ~ ~

Lightning crossed the sky in jagged stripes, followed by pounding thunder, so much of it, the city seemed to rock with the booming. Ziva sat well back from the window as she watched, mindful of Ana's repeated warnings of lightning burning and killing unsuspecting people who sat too close to the window. With all that had been happening in the past few weeks, the last thing Orak needed was for her to be injured because of her inattention. Tigre sat purring in her lap, indifferent to the storm.

Even when she closed her eyes, the flashes glowed through her eyelids. Eventually, the flashes of light receded from her vision. She lay her head against the chair back, thinking of Ana's suggestion. Perhaps it would work. She hated the thought of any girl or woman coming under Qinten's influence. No one deserved that degradation, but Qinten's determination, brought on by his desires to be High Priest of Lorca, would not be denied.

There had to be a way to deny him the "pleasures" of any woman. If he gave up on Ziva, though, he would cast about and choose to mate another girl. In her eyes, no amount of wealth or prestige would ever be worth the degradation of being his mate.

Perhaps some girl really wants the 'honor,' someone whose parents are ardent followers of Lorca. I will ask both Ana and Com if it is possible to find a girl who wants to be mated to Qinten. Something must be done. I am not the girl to be a High Priestess, especially not the High Priestess of Lorca. I want nothing to do with that... that perversion."

Ana entered on soft feet. "Tawna is here ..."

Thunder crashed and Ziva jumped farther away from the window, catching her cat before he fell to the floor. "That was close!"

"You should not—" Ana began.

"I know. I was too close. I thought I was far enough back from the window to be struck by the lightning. I was wrong.

Did you say Tawna is here? She came in the storm? She must be soaked. Bring her in." Ziva strode toward her bathing room and retrieved thick towels for her friend.

The door opened to a drenched Tawna. Her face paint had washed away, much of it now on her soaked dress.

Ziva threw a thick towel around her friend's shoulders and body, another over her head, and drew her into the indoor bathing room. Rain bounced off the window shutters, making it difficult to visit. Tawna shivered while Ana lifted her sodden dress over her head. Ziva toweled more moisture from her friend's hair while Ana found a loose bathing robe for her.

With Tawna finally dried, dressed and tucked into one of the white velvet chairs, a warm, blue blanket securely wrapped about her body, and a brazier near her feet, Ziva could now pull up a stool and sit near her. The wind swirled into the room, accompanied by a rush of rain. Ana dragged the shutters closed.

Ziva waved in the general direction of the kitchen. "Ana, please bring us a pot of warm tea."

"Yes, Miss Ziva." Ana picked up the sodden towels and wrapped them around Tawna's still dripping dress to take with her. "I will have Miss Tawna's dress clean and dry, soon."

The girls chorused their thanks as the door shut behind Ana.

Ziva set her hand on her friend's knee. "What would bring you out in this raging storm? Did you walk all the way from your home?"

"Oh, no, Ziva. I left to visit you before the storm struck. My carriage wheel hit a hole in the road. It threw me forward, causing me to bump my head. Do you see a red mark?" Tawna lifted her damp hair from her forehead and leaned toward Ziva.

"There is one. What did you hit it against? You hit it hard."

"The corner near the door. I was afraid it would bruise."

"It will. Wait here. I'll be right back."

Ziva hurried to the washing room and returned with a cloth, dipped in the cold water of the outdoor pool, and wrung out. Splashes of rain spattered her dress. She brushed at them, then placed the cloth over the darkening bruise over Tawna's left eye. "That should help.

"Ah," Tawna sighed. "That does soothe."

"What happened after you bumped your head? Why did you come here when the storm was so close?" Ziva lowered herself into the nearest chair and gazed at her friend.

"The wheel was broken. I needed to talk to you. It's important. I couldn't wait for the carriage wheel to be repaired. We weren't far from here, so I walked."

"In those slippers?" Ziva glanced at the remnants of her friend's slippers, now tossed into the corner, a wet, filthy, and shredded bundle of silk.

"I didn't expect it to rain so soon." Tawna's lower lip slipped out in a pout.

"Still, not good to walk in those thin slippers. Your feet must hurt."

"Well, they are sore." Tawna pulled her feet up and massaged them. "A hole wore clear through them."

"More than one, it looks like. I'm sure your feet hurt. How far did you walk?"

"From just this side of the market. I hadn't walked far when the dark clouds opened up on me. Then, I ran."

"You didn't dodge the raindrops with any precision," Ziva laughed. "You were drenched."

"No." Tawna giggled. "Hard to dodge raindrops when they fall as heavy and hard as they fall today."

The girls laughed and Ziva settled back into her chair. "Why did you need to see me so desperately?" She crossed her ankles and her foot bounced.

Tawna rubbed her chin. "I have a problem."

"Besides sitting in my apartment with only a robe on?" Ziva laughed.

"Yes. Besides that. I hear you are looking for someone to take Qinten's attention from you."

Ziva sat up straighter and drew her eyebrows together. "I am, but how would you hear about it?"

Tawna shrugged and waved her arm. "That is not important. What is important is …" She stopped to inhale deeply, then rushed on. "I want to be that girl. I want to be his mate."

Ziva opened her mouth and closed it three times, feeling like the fish their cook presented to them for dinner, before she got a sound out. "Why? Don't you know—"

"He has a dark soul? And about Festival days? I do. I nagged mother until she told me. She didn't want to share with me, but I wouldn't let her alone until she told me what happens during Planting Festival." Tawna stared defiantly at Ziva. "Mother and Father are members of the cult of Lorca. They attend all the festivals. They mated only with each other, not others, as so many do during the festival. Even so, mother is not happy that I would desire to be the High Priestess, especially with Qinten."

"Tawna, what mother would be? He is a vile excuse for a man."

"I have heard. For the prestige and power, and the money, I will live with him. I hope he will find affection for me."

Ziva shook her head. "How can you want to be mated to such an evil man?"

"I agree." Ana bustled in with warm peppermint tea and sweet breads for the girls. "Do you realize what you will be expected to do?" Ana's voice lifted an octave.

"Mother told me." Tawna scooted back in her chair and pushed her feet out toward the brazier.

"Not just the Planting Festival. Have you heard of his depravities?"

"Ziv tells me he has a dark soul." Tawna lifted a shoulder in a shrug.

"Ziva is right. He is wicked. Have you heard ...?" Ana leaned close to speak quietly.

Hours later, Ziva escorted her friend to the front door. Korm's repaired carriage had arrived earlier and the driver taken to the kitchen to warm himself with hot soup. Now, wearing her cleaned and dried dress and a pair of slippers borrowed from Ziva, she climbed into the carriage.

After Tawna left, Ziva leaned against the door. "Do you think she understands?"

"Perhaps." Ana took her by the elbow to lead her back up the stairs to her apartments. "What is important is you know better now what you will face if you ever are forced to mate Qinten. For now, however, you must be dressed for dinner."

Chapter 20

Qinten's Silence

Three days later, Nat stood beside Qinten's bed. He wondered if it would matter about missing sacrifices.

Qinten rolled back and forth on the bed, moaning. Healers had been called. They suggested cool cloths on his body to cool the fire in him. One gave Nat something to make into a tea. Another spoke of a new method that may help, using leeches to draw the bad blood from him. Qinten's father, Caomh, stood beside his bed and refused. Nat watched him shiver in horror.

"No way! Not my son!" he had roared and chased the healer out, who gathered up the bits of his healing apparatuses as he ran.

"You will be sorry, sir," he shouted as he ran out the door.

"I will not be sorry to protect him from the likes of you!"

Caomh stared after the healer until he heard the door slam behind him. He glanced at the slaves standing near the bed. "What are you waiting for? Cool cloths, lots of them."

All the slaves moved toward the door. Nat followed them.

"No, not you." Nat and the others turned to see Caomh pointing to him. The others shrugged and left the room to retrieve the desired cool cloths. Nat waited for Caomh to continue.

"You are his personal slave, are you not?"

"I am."

"Good. You know to keep your mouth quiet. Get that tea made, and give it to him. You are not to say a word out of this room about the health of your master. You understand, not a word." Caomh stared into Nat's eyes, waiting.

Nat nodded slowly. "I understand. He is my master. I know better than to share anything about what goes on here."

"Good. You do know what will happen if you forget?"

Nat could imagine—nothing good. "I do."

"Watch over him. Give him the medicine. Keep him cool until the fire cools."

"I will. I would, even if you had not ordered it."

Caomh glared at him many long heartbeats, then relaxed. "My son did one thing right when he brought you into his apartments. See that you do."

Caomh stared at his son a few breaths longer, then turned on his boot heel and left. Nat stared at the closed door until it opened again. Slaves carried in piles of long sheets of cloth and buckets of water. Nat took one bucket before the fabric could be dumped into it and poured it into the pot over the fire.

"Can't give him the medicine without hot water," he shrugged at the slave who had brought it.

"I could have brought a bucket or pot of hot water for you."

"Oh, right. Please do."

The slave took his bucket and scampered out of the apartment. The others dumped the other buckets of cold water into Qinten's bath, followed by all the sheets of fabric. Two men grabbed opposite ends of one sheet and twisted the water from it. They carried it to Qinten in his bed.

Nat followed them to Qinten, where he directed the placement of the cloth. He had them hold the cloth above him, while others removed all his clothing. Qinten had to be cooled off, and quickly.

The cloths picked up Qinten's heat and had to be changed often. When one cloth warmed, men plucked another out of the water and squeezed it until it stopped dripping, then rushed it to Qinten's bed where it replaced the warm one.

Qinten's fire cooled and the water warmed. Nat ordered the others to bring fresh cold water, then sent them off to bed.

Now Nat watched the fire in Qinten's body intensify. He glanced out the window, to see the moon had traversed much of the way across the sky. He returned to the tub and struggled to wring out the sheet alone. It dripped across the floor until he reached the bed. He awkwardly spread it over his master, after pulling the now warm, and nearly dry, sheet off.

Qinten mumbled and groaned, thrashing about in his bed. Nat pulled a stool close to watch him, thinking he needed to know when to change the sheet, again.

"Beautiful. Streaks of light—beautiful." Qinten mumbled, then he shouted. "No. No, I will not leave the window. I want to watch the lightning."

Qinten lay quiet for a time, then screamed. "Ow, ow, ow. It burns. How can something so beautiful hurt so bad?"

Nat stared at his moaning master, glad he had dismissed the other slaves. Qinten lay motionless for a long time, long enough Nat began to nod into sleep.

"Oh, oh, no. I do not choose to lie still any longer. Let me up!" Qinten shouted, before subsiding back into restless quiet.

Nat sat up, wondering what Qinten meant. Why would he be required to stay in bed? It made no sense. Did something happen as he sat by the window watching lightning? If his dreams were any indication, Qinten had been struck by lightning.

Few people lived after being struck by lightning. Qinten had been what? Blessed? Nat doubted it. No, the words of Nod fit his situation. Qinten had been lucky. What god would protect a spoiled brat like Qinten?

The sheet heated again. Once more, Nat struggled with changing it alone. He glanced out the window to see streaks of the rising sun glow above the buildings' rooftops. Qinten survived the night. Would he survive another?

~ ~ ~

Orak paced the distance between the door to his office and his desk several times. His hair stood in curly spikes from brushing his huge hands through it. "What is happening with Qinten? No one has seen him in days. Is our whisper campaign against him working?"

Com sat quietly in his comfortable chair, watching Orak pace. "He met with the Priests of Lorca eight days ago. My informant suggests they demanded greater numbers of sacrifices for the New Year Festival."

"Harvests were adequate this year, not great, just adequate. Perhaps, they believe further sacrifices will entice Lorca to provide greater harvests." Orak ran his hand through his hair again, causing more of it to spike upward.

"He also met with his father, the governor. My informant says he left in a rage, just before the storms hit that day." Com stretched his long legs away from Orak's path. "He was reminded of the need to find a mate, one who will provide him with offspring and act as High Priestess of his cult, when—or should I say, if—he is elected to be High Priest."

"If?" Orak stopped pacing and turned to face his counselor. "If? What makes you say if? Is he not in line to be their next High Priest because of his father's power?"

"Our whisper campaign is making progress. On the day he met last with the Priests of Lorca, wild dogs attacked his bird coops. Later, while it rained, the rushing water of the flood breached his amaranth silo, ruining much of the grain."

Orak stopped pacing and turned to stare at his friend.

Com became animated, moving his hands with his words. "Men who tire of his haughtiness and his taking their wives when and how he chooses, are fighting back. The other Priests grow weary of his posturing."

"Such damage to his resources. Has anyone from his office contacted us about additional supplies?"

Com shook his head.

"He seems to want to do without our supplies. We do not sell doves and pigeons, but we do provide the other animals they sacrifice." Orak dropped into the chair behind his desk and picked up his quill, and stared at it.

"That is the strange thing. I have asked both quietly and openly. No one has been contacted by his office to provide more of the lost and damaged sacrificial offerings, nor more of the usual offerings."

Orak rolled his pen between his hands. "No one has been contacted? Are they keeping it quiet, not sharing? Or is it real?"

"As far as I can determine, it is real. I would expect his personal slave, Nat, would be reaching out for Qinten, at the very least." Com leaned forward and snatched the pen from Orak. "Nothing. It is as if he and his office have disappeared, washed out of Nod in the floods. I have heard murmurs from the Lorcan Priests that Qinten has missed two of the recent required meetings They grumble at his insolence. His silent absence speaks greater of his arrogance than his other acts of disrespect."

A mahogany hand reached up to scratch his head. "Silence? Your informants have heard nothing from his house? Do you have spies inside?"

"The one spy I had was sold two weeks ago. I am in the dark, as is everyone else who desires information from that source." Com set the pen in the middle of the desk.

"Is he hiding in his web, making plans to ensnare us? That is my concern. What is happening with that vile man?" Orak picked up the quill and spun it in his hands.

Com brought his long legs together and folded them next to his chair as he leaned toward his boss. "It doesn't matter. We must continue with our plans."

"We must not be seen to be behind this. Do what you must but do it quietly."

Chapter 21

Of Fathers and Papas

Nine days after Qinten fell ill, he lay in his bed fuming. Nat could hear it through the closed door between the sleeping room and the office. In that time, he had resolved some of the problems.

Men had been sent to the nearby forests with nets to capture doves and pigeons. They had returned with a greater number of birds than the number that had been lost. Some were mating pairs, which the keepers told him had been kept back to increase their flocks.

However, Nat had not been able to find more amaranth to purchase. More than a quarter of the grain had been destroyed by the flood. The men who managed the grain silos had rented a huge empty building and carted all the amaranth above the water line to the empty building. They spread the amaranth out in a thin layer to be certain none had spoiled. Perhaps there would be enough for the upcoming Planting Festivals. Some would be burned to appease Lorca. The rest would be blessed and handed out to men who would grow more for the next festivals.

Nat heaved a great sigh and headed for the sleeping room. When Qinten responded to the rap on his door, he entered. "I see you are feeling better. Is the fire within you gone?"

"The fire is gone, leaving me limp and weak," Qinten growled. "I have been sick near to death these many days, and nothing has been done to resolve my need to increase the numbers of sacrifices available. If extra are not located, I will be pushed to a lower rank in the priesthood, and the responsibility given to another, rather than being lifted to the High Priesthood in the coming election. There are some among the ranks who question my ability, already, Lorca curse them." Qinten pushed himself to sit with his back against his pillows at the top of the bed.

Nat took in the information. If Qinten were pushed down, rather than exalted in the next election, it could bode poorly for him, though it could be good news for Ziva. He didn't know how to feel. To cover his mixed emotions, he nodded to his master.

"Have you made the inquiries?" The question pierced Nat.

Nat straightened his spine to report. "Yes, and I have some results."

Qinten nodded for him to go on.

"I have inquired among the farmers and herdsmen out in the valleys around Nod. I have done this quietly, to keep the attention away from you and any problems you may be having."

Qinten growled under his breath and Nat glanced toward him. He rolled his shoulders back and took a deep breath before continuing.

"Jaivin admits to having a small number of young camels he could sell to us. He has no he-goats, rams, nor bullocks."

"Only camels. Lorca does not receive camels as sacrifice." Qinten lifted his hand and allowed it to fall onto the bed beside him.

"I know, Master, I only tell you what I have learned." Nat lifted his left shoulder.

"Go on. What about the other dealers in animals?"

"Few admit to having any animals available. Most suggest the other cults have purchased their extra animals and are withholding the remainder as food for the people. Some have a few …" Nat read from the list he had prepared earlier. "Kono will sell us ten rams and eight bullocks. Croifan allows he has fifteen he-goats, ten bullocks, and seven rams, and nine ewe sheep. Garr, will be happy to sell you nineteen bullocks, eighteen he-goats, five ewes and twelve rams. Istvan may be able to find fifteen of each for us."

Nat looked up. "I have not contacted Orak, as you required. That gives you…" he checked his notes and looked once more in Qinten's direction, "44 rams, 54 bullocks, 29 ewe sheep, and 48 he-goats. From the looks on the faces of the sellers, I would not trust half of the animals to be worthy of Lorca." He dropped the hand holding the notes to his side and waited.

After breaths of silence, Qinten spoke. "Of course not. The cursed animal merchants seek the best price and will pawn off the worst of the animals if we allow it." Qinten cursed and growled until a deep cough stopped it.

"We will have to visit their herds and choose the best for Lorca, not the culls they will attempt to foist upon us. Call for my carriage and my dresser. We will go now."

"Now, Master Qinten? You are barely able to sit in your bed. Will you be able to command the respect of the merchants in this condition?"

Qinten struggled to sit away from his pillows. "Now. I will go now."

Nat stared at him. "Yes, if you insist."

"Curse you, Nat! I insist." He struggled to throw off the blanket and swing his feet out of the bed. The effort left him coughing and panting for breath.

Nat knew he had said too much. He stood waiting for the blows that would come, sometime. If Qinten couldn't beat him personally, he would send him to be whipped again. He hoped he would be needed more than Qinten wanted him beaten.

Qinten's breathing came fast, shallow, and loud, sounding like the rasp of dull saws. He flopped back onto the bed. "This cursed illness has made me weak. You have mentioned my illness to no one?"

"No, Master Qinten. The healers were sworn to secrecy, on pain of death by your father. No one, beyond the slaves who normally serve you, have entered your apartments. I told everyone else you are away from the house. That way, even those in the kitchens do not wonder why you have not required your normal meals."

Nat waved toward the empty bowl on the table beside his master's bed. "I have requested weak soup in addition to my normal meals to 'bolster my health', so even that will not be seen as caused by your illness. None know how ill you have been. Since the first night, not even the normal slaves have attended you. Only me. None know how ill you have been. None will."

"If I find any know, or even guess, you will forfeit..." Once again, his anger brought on a deep, rumbling cough. "How can you hide the noise of this?"

"Your rooms are well insulated against noise, as you know. None hear your cough, or the shouting and cursing of your fever caused dreams. Only I heard them, and I know nothing of their meanings."

Qinten glared at his slave. "Yes. What of the amaranth, wheat, rye, and oats? Have you obtained replacements for the amaranth and additional amounts of the others?"

"The last harvest brought in only moderate amounts of these grains. All the grain merchants have struggled to provide sufficient that the masses may have bread. Some, including Orak, lost grain laden silos to fire and rain. Your slaves stopped the water and removed the amaranth to an empty, dry barn. Only a quarter of it was lost."

"That is enough to be a problem, especially when Lorca demands more." Qinten filled his voice with sarcasm.

"Yes. Too much was lost. I have found merchants outside Nod who are willing to supply the missing and the required extra grains, for a price."

"For a price! Always for a price," Qinten raged.

Nat waited for the raging to end. At last, Qinten stopped, forced into silence by another nasty, rough cough.

"You are right. You are always right. I am too weak to meet with the merchants today. Make arrangements to meet with them in three days. By then, I should be on my feet again, and rid of this cough. Is there anything the healers left for the cough?"

"There is. I have some herbs for a tea he left for you. You have refused to take it before. Apparently, it tastes nasty."

"Make it into a tea and add some honey. I must get rid of this cough. My sides hurt."

Nat added a portion of the herbs into hot water hanging over the fire and pushed it out of the heat of the fire. "It will have to steep a while. I'll be sure to give you some soon. For now, I will go make arrangements to meet with the merchants."

Nat turned to leave.

"One thing more, Nat. I need you to go meet with Orak. Find out what I can do to break through his stubbornness. I need a mate, soon, and I want that mate to be Ziva."

~ ~ ~

Ziva paced the space between her father's desk and the door. As she walked, she noticed a faint line in the expensive rug. Orak must be doing a lot of pacing here, as well. She shook her head and changed her path to the wood around the rug.

He had said he would return soon after the mid-day meal. She had waited until the sun stood two hands past the apex before coming to find him. He must have run into problems, for he hadn't returned, and she had been here, pacing, for two spans. She had to discuss the problem of Qinten with him. Did he know about Tawna?

The door opened and Ziva swung around, expecting to see her father. Instead, Keb ushered Qinten's tall servant in.

"You?" she said. "What are you doing here? And without Qinten?"

The servant shook his head as though shaking off a fly. "Why are you here? The servant told me I could wait for Orak here."

"He is out. I expect him back within a half a span, or sooner." Ziva glanced around the room, wondering what to do. She had never entertained a man before.

"Could I have a drink of water, please?" the servant asked, his voice barely above a whisper.

"Yes." She could do that. Her father kept glasses and a tall, covered bucket of cold water in the corner near his desk. She nodded to the servant and walked behind the desk.

"You never said why you are here?" She opened the bucket and dipped water into two glasses. She set them on the desk, closed the bucket, and turned to face him.

He stood with a silly grin on his face.

"Well? Are you going to sit down?" Ziva demanded.

"Sit?" the grin fell from his face like a blossom from a plant after a heavy rain. "I never sit in the presence of ... of a ... my betters."

Ziva handed him the glass of water and watched him down half of it. The cold water would give him a headache. She had done the same thing, once, when she had been extra nervous. She watched the man's face to see if it would twist in the pain of a sudden headache. A glimpse of it flashed through his eyes, but he squashed it, smoothing his face and eyes.

Ziva sat in the chair behind Orak's desk. It felt safer there than in the soft, comfortable chair she usually sat in. "So, why are you here without Qinten?" She took a sip of her water and stared into his eyes.

Qinten's servant swallowed. "I was sent to speak with your—er, with Orak."

"My father? About what?" She watched his barely perceptible squirm. Not many could hide their thoughts as well as he could. She crossed her ankles and allowed her foot to bounce.

He took another swallow of the water and sat it on Orak's desk. "Thank you."

She waited, expecting more. As she waited she grew angry. She knew his reasons for coming to her home. He had come to convince Orak to give her to Qinten as his mate. How could he do such a thing?

The more she thought about it, the angrier she became. "Speak to me. Father will not give me away unless I agree."

"Your father will allow you to make the decision?" his voice dripped with sarcasm.

"My father. What does it matter to you? You are a servant, probably Qinten's slave. You have as little say as I do, as a woman," Ziva spat.

"It matters. Qinten sent me here to convince Orak to give you to him."

"As I thought. I will not mate such a man." Her foot bounced faster.

"I am not here to succeed, only to discuss it."

"Why would you care if I am mated to that vile man?" Her foot bumped the underside of the desk. She set both feet firmly on the floor.

"He is vile, as you say. No woman should have to mate with him." A bead of sweat formed at the edge of his blond hair.

"What is with you and my father?" Ziva leaned forward on the desk, her chest heaving. "Do you have an agreement with him?"

"I do. But, not the one you think." The servant held his hands up.

"What does it matter," she said and stared at his smooth hands.

"It matters to me. I worried about you since you were taken from my arms, both of us kicking and screaming, at the slave market. I promised Papa I would care for you ... and I couldn't." He slapped a hand over his mouth, a look of horror crossed his face.

"You promised Papa?" All the anger fled from Ziva, and tears crowded her eyes.

"Yes, Ziva. I promised our Papa I would care for you."

"Our Papa? Our Papa!" Her voice rose.

"Yes, our Papa, and our Heavenly Father." He whispered.

"When?" She forced a tone of anger back into her voice. She had hoped to learn this man was her Nat, but, not like this.

"The day after I gave you those beads you wear around your neck. I made them when you were tiny. When Papa learned I made them for you, he asked me to promise to always watch over you." His voice broke. "I tried. Honest, I did. I fought the men who took you from my arms. All I got was a bruise on my face where he beat me with his stick."

Ziva stood. "Then, it's true. You are —"

"Nat. I'm your brother, Nat."

Ziva slowly moved around the desk. Nat took a step forward. They stood staring at each other.

"Nat. My Nat. I thought it was a dream. I have missed you!"

"And I have missed you. When I saw you at the slave market, dressed like a wealthy woman, it took my breath away. I couldn't be sure you were my Ziva. I had always supposed and feared you lived as a slave, as I have."

"No." Ziva forced the word past frozen lips.

"And when I saw you with Orak at the Festival, I was certain you were my Ziva, my sister." Nat said.

Ziva stepped back. "Sit, please. Tell me more. I need to know." She stepped back and touched a chair with her legs, and dropped into it.

"I am not allowed." He stood with his back straight, staring at Ziva.

"You are here. You are my Nat, my brother."

Nat backed toward the chair, bumped into it, and sat. "Ziva, I don't want you to be Qinten's mate. I have done everything I dared to prevent it. But, I—"

"You can't. You are his slave, are you not?"

His eyes dropped to the floor. "I am. I have no right to be here with you, no right to sit in your presence, ..."

"No right? You are my brother."

"And you live as Orak's daughter. You are not a slave like I am." He surged from his seat and stood straight.

"How does that matter?" She leaped from her seat. "Oh, Nat, what has happened to you?"

"I became a slave, and you became the daughter of a wealthy man," he whispered, carefully keeping his eyes away from hers.

She stepped close. "Aren't you happy to see me, to admit you are my brother?"

Nat allowed his eyes to flick toward hers. "I am but it is dangerous."

"Dangerous? For you do to this?" She flung her arms around him. He stood stiff, his arms at his sides. "Hug me."

"No, for you." Slowly, he brought his arms up and encircled her waist. "I have missed you, Ziva."

"You have missed her? Who are you to put your arms around my daughter?"

Chapter 22

Like an Angry Dog

Orak shrugged his shoulders, trying to relax them after sitting in the carriage for such a long time. It had been a long day, dealing with farm managers. The storms-caused floods filled the fields with a thick, gooey mud. They argued for a need for help in getting the fields ready to plant, though they wouldn't plant for weeks. The she-goats, ewes, and cows were big with young, and miserable in the rain. The managers were harried by the constant effort of trying to keep track of all of them.

Though no rain fell on him, the roads were mucky. Mud clung to the wheels, loading them with the sticky stuff, until the horses struggled to move forward. He lost count of all the times they had been forced to halt while Alrik dug it from the wheels. After the third interruption, he stripped down to his small clothes and joined him. He found a fallen limb and scraped away the nasty stuff.

He shoved through the door into the hall, glad to be home at last. It even stunk. Do I stink? Orak lifted his arm to sniff. Now, all he wanted was a nice hot bath to cleanse the filth from him, and warm food.

"You have a visitor, waiting for you in your office." Keb wrinkled his nose. "I guess the smell won't bother Qinten's slave. If it was anyone else, I'd make him wait for you to get cleaned. But, as it's him ..."

"As it is him, I should clean up, but if I don't see him now, I'll be too tired. Did he say what he wants? He usually doesn't come without Qinten." Orak strode toward the door to his office.

"Something about Ziv. He wasn't really clear. I told him he could wait in your office."

"Yes, well—" Orak shoved the door open, to see his daughter giving the slave of Qinten a kiss.

"I have missed you, Ziva," he said.

"You have missed her? Who are you to put your arms around my daughter?" he roared.

Ziva dropped her arms and stepped back. "It isn't what it looks like, Father—"

"Not what it looks like?" He stood staring at the two young people. "How could it be what it looks like? Do you realize this man is a slave? He is owned by Qinten."

He spun toward the slave. "What do you think you are doing here? Are you attempting to ensure your master achieves his desires by wooing my daughter?"

"No, no sir. There is no attempt for that, not by me!" the slave's face went white. "I know my place, I know better than to get too close to a wealthy man's daughter."

"Father, listen to me. Nat is—" She grabbed him by the arm.

"No, Ziva, I will not listen. Let go." He shook her hands from his arm. "You. Leave." He pointed to the slave.

"I cannot leave, yet, sir. I must give you my message. If I do not, well, it would be bad for me. Please allow me to share my message, then I will leave."

"Share you message?" Ziva stared at him. "And, you didn't think to share it with me?"

"I could not, Ziva. My master insisted that I come and speak only with Orak. If he learns I spoke with you alone, it will not go well with me. If he learns ... if he learns about us, you will be at risk, and I will be ... I will be hurt."

The look on Qinten's slave's face touched Orak. Even in his extreme exhaustion, he could not cause another to be hurt because of him. "I will hear you, but not with Ziva here. Go to your room, Ziva. I will come speak with you later about this. We are not finished."

He stood, pointing to the door, until Ziva dropped her defiant head and pushed past him. She reached out to touch Qinten's slave's hand, before rushing out. He listened to her stamping on the stairs toward her apartment before he closed the door.

"Now, what does Qinten want from me?" Orak stared into the blue eyes of the slave, dressed in the finery of a personal slave.

"Qinten sent me to discuss what must be done for you to accept him as mate for Ziva." He held up his hands in defense. "I am not suggesting I am any more willing for him to mate with her than you are. He is a cruel and vile man, as I well know. Even if Ziva were not ..." He stopped and swallowed, his face coloring. "Even if Ziva were not an, er, intelligent and beautiful girl, I would not encourage you to allow this. I have heard him speak of his conquests. I would not have that for Ziva."

"What does it matter to you? Why do you care?" Orak dropped into the chair behind his desk and sighed. All he really wanted was a hot bath.

The color in the slave's face deepened. "I cannot say, sir. It is ... is," he sucked his bottom lip across his teeth, "personal. Ziva will have to tell you, if she can. What is important, sir, is that we protect her from Qinten."

"You cannot say?" Orak dropped his head into his hands and rubbed his ear. After heartbeats of thought, he lifted his head. "So, how can we protect her?"

The slave stood tall and stared at a spot on Orak's robe. "Qinten is becoming desperate for a mate. He cannot be elected High Priest of Lorca without one, and he is determined to achieve the rank. Others are working to prevent it. The stock of grain and animals has been attacked. And now, the god demands more."

"More? Why has he not come to me? Not that I have many more to sell, especially to a weasel like Qinten."

"His plan is to force you to give her to him. He wants to squeeze you out of the supply line, if he can. It doesn't look possible, you have the largest supply. Without purchasing from you, there will not be enough for the ravenous god."

"It figures. No one has seen him—"

"Please don't ask. For what I have already said, I could be whipped and sold. I wouldn't mind being sold, but Qinten would insist that I go someplace far away and lonely. He has told me too many secrets. He may kill me, instead."

"He is that cruel." Orak stared into the young man's face. "Yes. I can see it is. I will not ask about him. Rather, what can we do to stop him from taking Ziva?"

"For now, refuse to allow it, under any circumstances. He must follow the law, you must agree. I will tell him you yelled at me and threw me out, which you almost did."

Orak studied the man in front of him. He had courage. His status as slave was belied by his stance. Most slaves groveled and stammered when speaking to owners and their peers. Not this one. He stood straight, keeping his eyes lowered, but not on the floor. Orak liked him, though he couldn't figure out why. He reminded him of someone; his exhausted brain couldn't bring up who.

"I can throw you out." Orak began to raise his voice, calling on the rage he felt as he walked into his office and the need for a hot bath. "You insufferable fool. What makes you think you can convince me to allow my Ziva to marry that man? I will not allow it. I will not give in to him. I would rather lose a part of my business than give my daughter to your master. Now, get out! And don't come back!" Orak walked to the door and opened it.

The slave nodded and stepped through the door. Keb escorted him out of the house, banging the door behind him. Orak sighed and headed toward his apartment for that hot bath.

~ ~ ~

The slamming door echoed down the roadway. Nat shuddered at the sound. Was Orak angry at him or was this a show? He felt gratitude for the man who slammed the door. It would lend credence to his report. If Qinten thought to ask the carriage driver, he would support Nat's story of being thrown out.

He slumped in the seat and replayed his time alone with his sister—his sister! She accepted him, she remembered him. Thank Jehovah. He hadn't expected that. He hadn't expected to see her or share with her. He touched his face where she had kissed him. The spot on his face retained the memory of it, warm and loving.

But what will I say to Qinten? I cannot tell him she is my sister. That has to remain hidden.

He breathed a silent prayer to Jehovah, then tried out several stories as he bounced across the width of the carriage. "Something has to be done about these roads. I'd be more comfortable walking."

Nat had settled on the right words by the time the carriage arrived by the door leading to Qinten's private apartments. He sighed and checked his face, ensuring to make it look angry. Angry, although he was ecstatic.

He tromped slowly up the stairs, dreading the discussion with his master. It would not go well; Qinten did not like to be refused.

He breathed deeply and let the air out, then opened the door to the office. Though he hoped to find Qinten in his bed, he sat at his desk with a blanket around him. He glanced up, waiting expectantly.

Nat found the tone of rage he planned. "He kicked me out. Can you believe the man? He kept me waiting for half the afternoon, then he refused your request. Loudly. He shouted at me and kicked me out."

Qinten's face went pale. "Kicked you out? I should have gone. He would not kick me out. I knew I could not trust something so important to a slave."

"I am sorry, Master. I tried. I did as you asked, I did not grovel or beg. He called me an 'insufferable fool.'" Nat raised a hand in righteous anger. "He shouted at me, telling me he would rather lose a part of his business than give his daughter to my master. Then he kicked me out."

"He what?"

"His servant escorted me to the entrance and slammed the door behind me. The sound of the door echoed down the street. I watched the windows, expecting to see faces in the windows."

"That is intolerable! Does he not remember who I am?" A ruddy glow crept up Qinten's neck and up his face. "I am to be the High Priest of Lorca. I can damn him. I can cause him to lose all his contracts with Lorca. Does he not know? Does he not care?" Qinten stopped shouting to cough.

Nat stood still, his eyes focused at Qinten's feet, waiting for the rage to focus on him.

Qinten wiped his mouth and stared at Nat. "It is your fault. What did you say to him that he would throw you out? You must have been disrespectful? Did you look into his face?"

"No, Master Qinten. I am always careful to not look into the faces of my betters."

"What did you say?" Qinten stood and took a stepped around the desk.

Nat steeled himself. "I said the things you instructed. I asked if there was something he wanted to make the bargain for his daughter more agreeable. His eyes bulged almost out of his head." Nat took a breath. "He said there was nothing you could do. The conversation went well, then he changed, raging and shouting like one of the angry dogs, waiting to get to a —."

Nat paused. "He said there was nothing you could do, and he threw me out."

Qinten raised a closed fist, then thought better of it. He turned and walked toward the desk. "He threw you out? I cannot believe he threw you out. You get anything you want."

Suddenly, Qinten spun on his heel to face Nat, again. "You are certain of his words? You were gone most of the afternoon."

"I am certain. I waited for Orak to come home. He was in the country, inspecting his farms, or something like that. His servant did not give me any details, only said Orak was out and would be back soon. I was left to wait in his office."

"Did you look at the papers on his desk?" Qinten sat in his chair, again, and picked up a pen, running his fingers along the feather.

"No, Master!" Nat filled his voice with outrage. "I would never do that. I do not look at yours. I would not want to have him walk in and see me reading his papers. Besides, there were no papers on his desk."

"You looked."

"I glanced at it. What else was I to look at as I stood, waiting?"

Nat watched Qinten stroke the feather. "I do not look at your papers. I would not. I know there are documents there that are not for me to read."

Qinten glanced down at the papers on his desk. "Sit down."

Nat moved to his desk and sat. "What now, Master?"

"Tell me what happened again."

Nat repeated his story several more times that night. Sometimes, after working on other things, Qinten inserted a question about Orak into the conversation. Nat knew he was attempting to cause him to slip up and give a different response, and silently thanked Jehovah for help. He had chosen to speak the truth and could not be trapped in a lie. He had not spoken about the earlier discussion and would not.

"Orak will pay for his insolence. If he feels that way about it, Lorca will no longer purchase sacrifices from him. He will lose the money we spend on him."

"That will show him."

Nat wondered about it. How would they find enough animals to sacrifice without those Orak had promised? They were already short.

~ ~ ~

Ziva stomped into her apartment and slammed the door. How could Orak send her out of the office when discussing her future? She walked into her sleeping room, then paced into the bathing room, and back to the sitting room, fuming and stomping. She stopped to pound her fist into the back of her chair, then stamped in a circuitous route through the apartment, again.

At last, she grew tired of stomping and flopped across the end of her bed. She growled and hit it. "Why is he like that?" Her thoughts turned to Nat. Her dreams of a brother were real. She had a family, a Mama, a Papa, and a brother. A small smile tickled her lips as she drifted into sleep.

"Ziva. Ziva." A hand shook her. "Ziva, wake up. We need to talk."

She rolled over and opened her eyes. "Oh, it's you, Father."

"Yes, it's me. Who else did you expect? That slave?" His voice rasped with the effort to cover hurt feelings.

"No. I was dreaming of my mama and papa. I am happy it is you who woke me, not Ana." Ziva sat up on the edge of her bed and pulled her blanket across her legs.

A genuine smile softened Orak's face. "I thought you'd still be angry with me. I sent you away so roughly. I was tired and needed a bath."

"You did stink." Ziva inhaled carefully. "Not now, though. You must have taken time to bathe before coming here."

"I did. I knew you needed time to calm yourself, and I needed to rest in my bath." Orak sat in a chair beside her bed.

"I was angry. Why could I not have been part of that discussion? It is my life." She heard the petulance in her voice and tried to soften it. "I know, you are the father and I am only the daughter. It is man's discussion."

"It was a discussion for men. The slave—"

"Nat." Ziva added.

"Nat? All right. The slave," she glared at him, "Nat is an interesting and brave man. He is working to keep you from Qinten's clutches. He thinks he has a reason to be concerned with you. He wouldn't say why. Do you know? Why were you in his arms? Is he a secret lover?"

Ziva laughed at the twisted face Orak made. "No, Father. Nat is not my lover, and yes, he does have a reason to be concerned about me."

"A man I know nothing about except that he is slave to the man who is trying to force you to be his mate has a reason to care for you? And he is not your lover?"

Ziva leaped up, throwing her arms around Orak. "I love you, Father. You care so deeply for me, you cherish me. I do not want to hurt you."

"How could you hurt me? Have you been with another man?"

"Oh, no. You know I would not do that." Ziva sat back on her bed so she could look into Orak's eyes. "Do you remember Mahonri?"

"How can I forget? He threatened you."

"And he brought me here. Isn't that right?" Ziva gazed at her hands and her foot started to bounce.

Orak nodded.

"He brought me here from my home far away, far from my mama and my papa."

Orak glanced at Ziva's bouncing foot, then stared at her blue eyes.

"I did not come alone to Nod. Mahonri brought another child with me, a boy—my brother. He was not as lucky as me. No wealthy man sought for a replacement son for a lost child. He was older. Someone purchased him, and he became someone's slave, no longer the free boy he was in our home with our parents. I don't know how it happened, but I will find out. Nat became slave to Qinten. Perhaps he has been his slave since I became your daughter." Ziva focused on the deep brown of his eyes. "Nat is my brother. He made these beads for me when I was tiny." She found the beads around her neck and pulled them out of her dress front for him to see. "He promised our papa he would care for me."

"Your brother? Now I see it. I knew he looked familiar, more than Qinten's silent servant. You have the same coloring, the same tilt to your nose. His hair is darker, but not much. I see the family resemblance."

"Yes. And if my dreams are right, he looks like my papa."

220

"Your papa? From far away? I wonder … No. It couldn't be." Orak's eyes lost their focus.

"Wonder what?" Ziva set both feet on the floor and leaned forward.

"There have been stories. Peddlers who travel across the land return with stories. Most are just that, stories. One they tell is of two children, a boy and a girl, stolen from the prophet Enos. Periodically, they roam through the city, searching for the 'lost children of the prophet.' I wonder." Orak stared at his hands.

"I have heard the same stories. Not long ago, Kara came in a huff because a man had accosted her, asked if she knew where the lost children of the prophet were. She and Tawna had an argument. Kara thought it a silly idea, how would a child of a prophet be hidden in Nod. Tawna disagreed."

"And, perhaps, one of the lost sat among them." He looked up into Ziva's face. "The question now is, what do we do about it. I love you. You are my daughter now. Do you return?"

"How can I leave you?" She reached her pale hand out to take his. Dark against light, the contrast sparked by understanding. "You cherish me. You have protected me." A frown flickered across her face. "You own me."

"No. Not own, you are my daughter. I do not own you. I love you too much."

"I know." Ziva stared at their joined hands. "I love you. I don't even know my mama and papa any more. I wouldn't know where to look for them. And, even if I could leave you, and I can't, I couldn't go without Nat. Nat is still a slave."

"To the vilest man in all Nod. He will never be free."

"I cannot leave you nor can I leave Nat. No, you are stuck with me, bad bargain or not."

Orak tugged gently on Ziva's hand until she moved toward him. He pulled her onto his lap and smoothed her hair, before planting a light kiss on her forehead.

"Ziva, my daughter. I have never been sorry that I brought you home. I will protect you from Qinten."

She wrapped her arms around his neck and hugged him close.

Chapter 23

Mystery Man

Orak sat in his study, considering ways to solve the problems his farm managers brought to his attention the day before. He wanted, he needed, sufficient grains and animals to sell in the coming months, many had already been contracted to the temples. He must find a means to send help to his managers. But how?

Every time he went through the streets of Nod, the poor confronted him, seeking for handouts, begging for work. Would any of these poverty-stricken people be willing to leave the noise of the city for the quiet of the country? Would they be willing to work, and in ways no man in Nod would? Their hands would become roughened and dirty. Their backs would ache. They begged for work. Would they take the opportunity?

He'd send Com through the city to offer them work. Perhaps he would find enough willing to work. Some may be good with animals and could help the managers who struggled there.

That settled, he turned his thoughts to Qinten—and Ziva. Qinten had not asked for an increase in supplies for the Planting Sacrifice. That Nat must know what he was talking about. How could he turn it to his advantage?

Orak picked up a pen, dipped it in the ink, and began to doodle on a scrap of vellum. How to stop Qinten and keep Ziva from him? Could he survive if he reduced his sales to Lorca? He pulled the scroll of his accounts from a shelf behind him and unrolled it.

As he studied the numbers, Keb knocked and entered. "A messenger brought this. Said it was important."

Orak raised his eyebrows. "Who is it from?"

"Not Qinten, at least it wasn't his usual messenger. I don't know this one. He waits in the kitchens for your answer. I sent him there, out of the rain." Keb waved in the general direction of the kitchen. "I'll wait outside for your answer."

At Orak's nod, he left, shutting the door behind him.

Orak examined the outside of the message. He didn't recognize the seal or the braid that tied it. In his many dealings with the merchants, leading houses, and temples of Nod, he recognized most of the braids that identified messages. This was a simple braid of woven flax. No special colors. His curiosity piqued, he untied it, broke the unmarked seal, and unrolled the message.

He scanned through the message, searching for its author. Nothing. Perhaps the message would provide an answer. He read it more closely.

"Most gracious Orak," he read. Unusual for a message. He shook his head and read on.

"You are in the possession a prize worth more than gold. This prize is in jeopardy. I would volunteer to support you in its protection.

"I am an honest man, possessing significant ability to care for such a valuable prize. Perhaps you will agree to meet with me to discuss my assistance.

"I await your response.

"Please send a reply with my messenger. I come at your bidding. Today, if you can. Tomorrow, if you cannot. I wait. I seek only to protect your precious possession."

Orak turned the vellum over. Nothing on the back. No hint of its author. He read it through twice more. No hint of who wrote it, or what possession he proposed to help protect.

"Keb?" he called.

Keb poked his head in the room. "You called?"

"Any idea who sent this? Do you think it was Qinten?"

"No way to be certain, but the messenger comes from the messenger pool. I asked. He does not know who sent him, only that he waits for a reply."

"Strange."

"It is, sir. Why all the secrecy?" Puzzlement filled Keb's stance.

"I do not understand it. I will meet with him. Wait."

Orak sat and unrolled a small sheet of vellum. He dipped his feather pen into the ink and carefully penned a message, inviting the man to come meet him after the mid-day meal. He found one of his braided ties, in distinctive shades of maroon and sky blue, rolled up the message, and tied and sealed it.

"Take this to the messenger and give him a copper for his efforts." Orak dipped into the small money bag at his waist for the copper and handed the message and copper to Keb.

After Keb left, Orak mused about the message for many long breaths, wondering what possession was in danger, and who proposed to help him protect it. He shook his head and returned to his ledgers. As he worked, the mystery tickled the back of his mind. Who knew something he didn't. Was it Mahonri? If so, the dirty dog would be taken to the city guard. He'd be careful.

~ ~ ~

The ride into the country to inspect the available animals with Qinten could never be called pleasant. Still weak from his illness, he growled about the travel and cursed the men who expected him to take less than perfect animals to be sacrificed to Lorca. Nat ached from the jarring ride, understanding his master's bad temper. The roads, if you could call them that, were rough tracks, deep with drying mud near the end of the raining times.

One more farm to visit. They had managed to purchase, and send back to the city with herders, few of the required extra animals. The other cults had culled most of the best from the farms closest to Nod. Lorca demanded more, three more he-goats, two more ewe sheep, three rams, and two more bullocks for each of the five festival days. As the New Year Festival, it would be scattered throughout the city, allowing festival goers the opportunity to wander from place to place, not staying centralized at the temple. Five priests held the honor of conducting the New Year Festival in their courtyards. That multiplied everything by five. Nat wondered how they would manage to find so many. He sighed. Only Orak had sufficient numbers of animals.

"How many animals have we sent back to our barns in Nod?" Qinten roused from his thoughts to demand.

Nat unrolled the scroll and read the notes he made at each of the previous farms. "Jaivin had a small ram, nothing more, as he reported earlier. Of the ten rams and eight bullocks Kono offered, only seven rams and five of the bullocks were satisfactory. Croifan sold us ten he-goats, eight ewe sheep, only three of his ten bullocks were acceptable, and one of the rams. He did have three pigs, in case Lorca chooses to accept them.

Nat looked back at his notes. "We found a new farm, owned by a C. The manager there sold us five bullocks and ten rams. Istvan provided us with fourteen ewes, ten rams, nine he-goats, and five bullocks."

"What does that leave us? The number we need is small, why is it so difficult to find a decent number of animals?" Qinten sounded petulant, a precursor to a full-blown storm of rage.

Nat did a quick tally. "That's 28 of the 75 rams we need, 19 of the 75 he-goats, and 13 of the 50 bullocks. We also have 22 of the 50 needed ewes and three of the possibly ten needed pigs. We will want to have at least five pigs, one for each location."

"Not even half!" Qinten's anger bubbled. "What do the other priests expect of me? Miracles?"

"We have yet to visit Gar. He suggested there might be more available there, for the right price. Of course, his animals may be picked through like all the others." Nat worked to calm the growing storm of rage.

"We shall see. I have yet to see Garr live up to his promises."

"Perhaps this time he will." Nat rolled up his scroll and tucked it into place between his skin and robe.

The carriage rattled on. Nat closed his eyes against the jolting of it against the drying mud. When they last stopped, he saw the craters ahead, caused by previous travelers whose wheels were stuck in the muck. He marveled at Qinten's current level of near calm in his extreme discomfort. It could not last.

The carriage bumped to a halt. Nat glanced out the dusty window. Garr's farm. He hoped all his animals would be of high quality, perhaps they could find enough to make up their numbers without going to Orak. Ha! He dreamed.

As Nat helped Qinten from the carriage and brushed the dust from his cloak and robes, Garr welcomed them.

"You will find all you need here at my farm."

Qinten raised an eyebrow. "All? You told my servant you had only a limited number of unsold animals."

"Things have changed since then. Some of the animals previously claimed by the other cults are now available."

Nat squinted at the man. Because they are not healthy enough to be sacrificed to the other gods. He kept his counsel, Qinten could find out for himself if Garr spoke the truth. He saw hope cross his master's face and held his tongue.

Gar led them to the pens holding the different animals. "See. Many of each animal, and all healthy enough for Lorca."

Nat growled under his breath. "We will see." A herder had jumped from the top of the carriage and now walked through the milling herd of bullocks with a pot of chalk. He marked those acceptable to Lorca with an L.

When he returned to the fence where the others stood he reported. "Twenty, sir."

"Only twenty?" Garr grumbled. "Our animals are the finest."

"Walk through the herd once more. Perhaps you missed a few?" Qinten directed the herder.

The herder grimaced and did as he was commanded. Nat doubted he could find any more. Taj knew Lorca's requirements, and rarely allowed one to slip past his examination that did not pass.

As he passed through the herd, he directed the selected animals toward the gate, where Garr's men pushed them into a separate pen. Three more animals were marked and separated from the rest.

"I found three more, sir," he called.

Qinten nodded to Nat, who recorded the number and raised his arm to signal to him to move to the next pen, he-goats.

Qinten moved with Garr to the edge of the next pen. Taj worked from the back to the front, marking and directing the chosen animals to Garr's men for separation.

Taj stood on the other side of the fence waiting for Qinten to nod.

"There are 35 acceptable he-goats. I have examined the goats with care. No more are acceptable to Lorca."

Qinten nodded as Nat jotted the number on his scroll.

"You may move to the next pen, now, Taj," Nat said.

Taj climbed out of the goat pen and moved to the sheep. First, the rams. He entered the pen through the small gate and began to examine the animals.

"Your man is particular," Garr said.

"He has to be, to work for Lorca. Lorca is a particular god," Qinten growled.

And a bloody one. Nat knew better than to express his thoughts among free men.

"I thought you had all you needed for this festival. What happened?" Garr asked.

"Lorca wants more," Qinten turned away, ending the conversation.

Nat saw Garr lift his hands to the skies behind Qinten's back and shook his head. Who could understand the needs of a god.

Taj separated out 33 rams and fourteen ewes.

"Swine. Do you have any healthy swine?" Qinten managed to say the words without being sick.

"Pigs? Since when does Lorca accept pigs?" Garr stuttered.

"Since now. Do you have swine or not?" Even Garr recognized Qinten's growl and red face as signals of Qinten's growing anger.

"Of course, I do. People eat swine when there are no other animals available. Few gods accept pig as sacrifice." Gar signaled to one of his servants and whispered with him. "It will not be long for my men to bring the acceptable ones herded to an empty pen. Would you like a drink and a chair in the shade while we wait?"

Nat hoped he would rest in the shade. His master sagged with fatigue.

"No chair. A drink would be nice."

Garr signaled to a waiting servant, who brought glasses and wine for the two free men. None was offered to Nat. He did not expect it.

They stood waiting for half a span until the sounds of swine snorting filled the cloud of dust drawing close. At last, the dust settled, and a small herd of swine stood in the pen. The men walked to lean over the fence.

"Your man will have to be careful not to fall down inside the pen. Swine are known to devour whatever they can reach. How many do you want. Perhaps my swineherds can bring them close for his inspection?"

"Ugh." Qinten shivered. "That will work." He signaled to Taj to step closer as he stepped back.

In the end, Taj and two of his men herded the sheep, goats, and bullocks back to Lorca's pens in Nod. Qinten paid an extra bonus for Garr's swineherds to take the eight chosen pigs.

Chapter 24

Powerful Men

At the appointed time, Keb brought news of the visitor.

"Is it someone we know? Is it Qinten?"

Keb shook his head. "No. I don't know this man. He has never been to your house."

"Show him in. Please stay outside the door, until I excuse you. I need a witness."

Keb agreed, then stepped out. Orak stood and moved away from his desk to be ready to meet the stranger. Keb returned. Orak looked up and recognized him from the parties he and Ziva had attended during the heat of the year.

"Crites! Welcome." He reached to grasp his wrist. "I spent most of the morning, after receiving your message, wondering at your cryptic message. Come in. Sit down."

When the men were seated on the comfortable seats in the office, drinks of cold water in their hands, Orak leaned forward. "What precious prize do you mean to help me protect?"

"I like you, Orak. You don't waste time playing games." Crites leaned back, crossed his legs at the knee and lay his slender pecan colored hands in his lap.

"Thank you. What prize?" Orak lay his hands along the sides of his chair, fighting to keep them unclenched.

"You do not know?"

Orak growled and waved his hands.

"It is Ziva, of course. There is not another girl like her in all of Nod. No other girl has such fair complexion, such lustrous, hair the color of honey. Few other girls are willing to admit to their intelligence as she does. I have seen her lead you willingly from parties you were enjoying because she chose not to dance with or be bothered by a man. Your most prized possession is your Ziva."

Orak chuckled. "You saw that, did you? Yes, Ziva knows her mind, and I have taught her to stand up for her beliefs. No. Not taught her. I accepted it from her. How could I not? She has always been one to express her opinion and not back down. But what makes you consider her my most prized possession? And why do I need to protect her."

Crites set his foot on the floor and leaned forward. "I have watched your Ziva for the last two years, on those few times you allowed her to join you at parties and festivals. She stands out from the other girls." He waved his hand at Orak. "Her beauty shines. No other girl in Nod is as fair as she is."

Orak leaned back and sipped his water. "Do all the young men see this in my Ziva?"

"I have not spoken with all of them." Crites lifted his glass and sipped. "I have listened to them discuss her. The words of some you would not want to hear, nor would I desire to repeat such foul things. Some would like to use her, others mate her, while others consider hers a rare beauty. I have worked to keep my thoughts to myself. I do not want them to know, just yet."

Orak roughened his voice and leaned forward, setting his hands on his knees. "And just what are your thoughts about my daughter?"

"She is more than they see. Beyond her beauty, her intelligence and goodness cannot be hid. She is as careful with her face as she is with her modest dress. It impressed me to see her walk away from Qinten at Roven's party. Most girls fall all over his looks, his money, his power. Not your Ziva. She walked away from him. He has never had a girl walk away from him before."

Orak cradled his chin on his hand. "She does not want anything to do with Qinten."

Crites crossed his legs and leaned back. "Though none can prove it, I believe that is why he insists on having her for himself. He doesn't share his plans or desires with other young men, nor does he share with the priests of Lorca. My spies can share no information from there. But I have seen his face when her name is mentioned at Young Men's Society. He desires her. He will not easily be stalled. He believes he deserves everything he wants."

"I have had experience with his stubbornness."

"Then you know he will have his own way."

"He thinks he can have his own way. He has not yet succeeded when it comes to Ziva." Orak clenched a fist.

Crites took a long drink. "I was right. He seeks to make Ziva his."

"Since shortly after the Growing Festival. He has threatened me and done all he can to coerce me into giving Ziva to him as his mate."

"Mate?" Crites dropped his foot to the floor with a bang. "This is more serious than I expected. Ziva is too good for Qinten. He will hurt her in body and mind."

"This I know. Much of my business comes from my sales to Lorca, the blood-thirsty god." Orak gazed at his mahogany hands, wishing they had answers for him.

"He threatens to cut off your sales?"

"He hasn't used the words, but it hangs between us. He even came here, so Ziva could 'get to know him better.' She was polite, but didn't fall for him." Orak picked up his glass and held it between the palms of his hands.

"She is too intelligent for him. Probably, too good for any of us here in Nod." Crites set his glass down and leaned forward. "You and Ziva are in great need of my help."

"How do you plan to help us?" Orak took a sip of water and stood. He paced to the door and back.

"I would be her mate. I love her."

Orak stopped pacing and spun on his heel to face Crites. "You would be her mate? How can you protect her as her mate? Have you not heard how he uses married women?"

"You don't know me or my history, do you?" Crites lounged back in the chair, lacing his fingers behind his head.

"I know your name. I have seen you at the parties and festivals. However, you are a mystery to the other merchants I know and to me." Orak plunked into his chair, splashing a few drops of water from his glass. "Tell me why I should trust my Ziva into your hands."

"My mother took me to live in the country, away from the city, to heal me from a cough. I grew up there, only returning to Nod last year. We raise horses on that particular farm. Long-legged runners. Wealthy young men need something to do, so I started racing mine against others." Crites dropped one arm.

"I heard of those races. Do you own the circus where they race?"

"I do. Between the take from the races and a percentage of the wagers, plus the winnings from my horses, I do quite well."

"Better than the son of the governor?" Orak knuckled his forehead.

"Yes, and I do not depend on the mercy of a cult to support me."

"Nor do you have a cult to back you. Have you more power than Qinten?"

"Tubal-Cain is my grandfather. I have his power, and the power of Cain, if needed. My friends see me as one who plays, riding horses. They do not know my history."

Orak set his glass on his desk and paced around the room once more. "How would you take her away from Qinten? He will rage. I could lose much, though I am willing to lose much."

"We can have the mating ceremony privately and tell Qinten after it is too late." Crites joined Orak in the circuit of his office.

"How can you prevent him coming to your home to take her, as he has so many other married women?" Orak ran a hand through his hair.

"I live in a gated and walled home, guarded by my trusted friends, the elite Reds. We trained together in the country and have fought battles against the men of Alon, to the west. I trust them with my life. I trust Ziva's honor and her life with them." Crites lifted his shoulders and straightened his back. "And no one goes against the wishes of Grandfather Tubal-Cain. Not even the governor."

"Not the governor's son?"

"He will try, but he will not succeed." Crites grimaced.

"There is yet one problem you have not considered." Orak ran his hand through his hair, again. "Regardless of all you can offer, and all the ways you can protect her, Ziva has to agree." Orak held his hands up to stave off the argument. "No, this father will not and cannot force her to mate a man she would refuse. Or she would have been Qinten's mate already. I will trust I can support my people without Lorca's sacrifices. I cannot sacrifice my Ziva to him."

~ ~ ~

Nat and Qinten heaved themselves into the carriage and attempted to settle into something like comfort. Nat listened to his master's snorts and grunts, knowing his frustration and rage would burst soon.

It did not take long.

"What are our numbers? Did we even come close to what Lorca requires?"

Nat knew to be wary. He drew his scroll from its place within his robe, unfurled it and read. "We need 75 he-goats and sent 54 to our pens in Nod. Of the 75 needed rams, we purchased 61. We purchased 36 each of the necessary 50 ewe sheep and bullocks. We did, however, get more pigs than required. With Garr's eight, we have eleven."

"Short on every animal that matters. Only Orak has enough animals to make up the difference, and all his animals are acceptable, always. Curse that man. Curse the other priests of Lorca who would demand an abundance of animals. It cannot be done. It must be done. Lorca curse them all!"

"Yes, master."

"How can we get more animals from Orak, without him knowing it is us? I don't want to beg him."

"There must be a way. Too bad ..."

"Too bad what?" Qinten snapped his head in Nat's direction.

"Well, too bad you are determined to force him to give you his daughter." Nat cringed inside, knowing his blunt words would eventually be his downfall.

Qinten slugged him in the jaw. Nat accepted the punishment without comment or reaction.

They rode in silence. Nat appreciated the quiet.

"His daughter is becoming a problem for me. He refuses. She is pleasant, but not enticed. I grow tired of the battle, yet I cannot have anyone else now."

"Have you spoken to anyone of your desire to have her?" Nat dared to ask. He could not protect his sister if he did not take the chance.

"None, except my father. My search for a mate is no one else's business." Qinten reached up to the handle by the door to aid in his balance.

"And Orak."

"Yes, and Orak and Ziva. I did not believe they would deny me. Women have been drawn to me since my thirteenth year. I have never been denied before, not by any woman. Why would Ziva deny me?"

"She is different from all the other girls. Perhaps that is why?" Nat threw out a hand to stop falling toward the side of the carriage.

"It is the reason I am drawn to her. Ziva is different. She doesn't follow the crowd. She thinks and acts on her thoughts. She is unusual."

Nat grabbed for the edge of the door, barely managing to prevent his head banging against it. "Is that enough reason to desire her? It's like choosing to eat a poison mushroom because it is beautiful."

The two men held on to the walls and handles inside the carriage as it jounced them back and forth across the interior.

"This so-called road is ridiculous. Perhaps I can convince my father to do something about it."

"He hasn't done anything about the roads in Nod. How do you think he can make this road smoother?"

"There should be a way."

Nat and Qinten focused on avoiding bruises until they reached the gates to Nod. A city guardsman, familiar with the carriage and insignia on the horses and the sides of the carriage, waved them through the gate without asking the driver to slow. Both men breathed a sigh of relief as the road smoothed.

"I have to find a way to get Orak's animals and his daughter without begging. I need them both. With her exotic beauty, I would be certain to be elected as High Priest, if I supply enough extra animals for the festivals."

"I am just wondering, and no judgment from me," Nat said, raising his hands, "are you certain a girl so extremely different from the women in Nod would help you? Why not one of the gorgeous girls whose looks imitate the majority of the women here? Have you asked?"

Qinten raised a fist and held it, threatening Nat for a long breath, then dropped it. "Perhaps you are right."

Chapter 25

Not Another Kernel

"Ziva, my dear, I have something I must share with you."

She sat across from her father, feet pulled up beneath her, on her favorite white chair. The blue curtains ruffled the back of her hair in the soft wind from the open window.

"Oh?"

Orak tented his fingers and rested his chin on them. "I have received an intriguing offer. It may solve our problems. But, as always, you may accept or reject it, as it will affect your life as much, or more, than it affects mine."

"Who? What is the offer?" Ziva leaned forward and set her hand on her father's arm.

Orak took her hand in his. The differences in them amazed her, as always.

"Do you remember Crites?"

"We danced together at Harvest Festival. He was pleasant. What is he offering?" She tried to pull away, but Orak held on to her hand.

"Yes, Crites has made an offer. He would like to be your mate. He would like to protect you from Qinten both now and in the future. He has the ability to do that."

"Even keep that vile man from me when he is gone? How?" She grasped his hand tighter.

"He has a private guard, the Reds. He believes they will protect you from Qinten. He thinks he loves you."

"Loves me? We have only been together a short time at a party and a festival. I danced with him four times, total. How can he love me?"

"He has watched you from a distance. He was impressed that you refused Qinten. He liked the times you were together." Orak brushed his fingers across the back of her hand.

"But love me? I know love isn't required for mating here. It would be nice, and it would make life better, like yours and mother's love." Ziva focused on their hands.

"Perhaps you can discover that kind of love together. Elin did not love me at our mating. Her father agreed with mine to the mating. We were young. Over time, I learned to love her, and she learned to love me. After Liva came along, our love deepened. You don't have to love your mate, though it would be nice to like him or be his friend."

"I like Crites. He was kind to me at the Harvest Festival. At least, he does not follow the cult of Lorca." Ziva's foot started bouncing.

She thought about Crites. If his character matched what she learned at the Harvest Festival, maybe she could live with him.

"What do you know about him? What kind of man is he?"

"He recently returned to Nod. His mother took him from the city when he was a sickly child. In the country, his health improved and he became strong. He joined the Reds and went with them to fight in Alon. His farm, the one he grew up on, raises horses and other animals."

"I could spend time in the country?" Ziva glanced from their hands to Orak's face. "I would be safe from Qinten there."

"And far from me. I'm not certain I could live with you so far away." Orak brushed a lock of hair off her face.

"I'm not sure I could be that far from you for long." She stared at their hands again and her foot bounced harder. "It was a thought. Could Crites be the answer to our problem? How do we know?"

Orak cleared his throat. "I have asked Com to investigate. There is little to know about him. He has only been in Nod for just over a year. The important thing is the power he has in the community because of his grandfather, Tubal-Cain. As his only grandson, he has more power in Nod than even the governor, Caomh. More than Qinten will ever have as High Priest. You will be safe with Crites."

Ziva stared into his face. "Safe?"

"I have invited him to a quiet family dinner tomorrow, so we can discuss the matter." Orak shifted in his chair and licked his lips.

"That would be nice." Ziva scooted over and squished her-self between Orak and the arm of the chair, and lay her head on his shoulder. They sat together like that for several quiet breaths.

"Father?" Ziva interrupted the silence. "What about my brother, Nat? Is there something we can do for him?"

"Nat?" Ziva glanced up to see Orak's eyes widen. "What should we do for Nat?"

"He's my brother. Is there a way we can free him from Qin-ten's vile hold on him?" Ziva knew this was not the time to use tears. Even so, a tear dripped down her cheek.

"He is Qinten's slave, his personal slave. If I try to purchase him, Qinten will wonder why. He'll want to know your con-nection to Nat. It isn't safe for you."

"There has to be something to do for him. It isn't right for him to remain a slave."

"No, it isn't." Orak held Ziva on both sides of her face. "But I don't think even Nat would want for your safety to be jeop-ardized."

~ ~ ~

Orak spent the next day inspecting his silos, barns, and ani-mal pens, speaking with his managers about their responsibilities. He worked to know the value of each silo of grain, each pen of animals. They discussed how much had been purchased by the cults for their sacrifices and by city butchers and bakers to feed the masses of people. He counted the extras, the amount available for later purchase. He wanted to be certain there was plenty for the upcoming festivals.

Inside, he counted the costs to his people, to those dependent on him. How much could he depend on the other cults if Lorca stopped its purchases? Who would be let go and who would he find a way to keep? All this buzzed inside Orak's head as he inspected the animals, lifting feet and running a hand across backs, and running his fingers through the grain, bringing some to his nose to smell.

Orak had inspected the sheep and was saying goodbye to the manager, when Qinten suddenly stood beside his horse. He glanced at the man and ran a dirty hand across his sweaty face. "What?" He wanted to say, 'What are you doing here," but caught himself in time. This was his best customer.

He started again. "What brings you to this part of town, Qinten." He reached his hand out to grasp Qinten's wrist, and thought better of it. "I'm dirty from inspecting the animals." He waved toward the pen behind him.

The manager, Mohan, turned to leave.

"I came to speak with you, Orak. Is there somewhere private we can visit?" Qinten wrinkled his nose at the smell.

"Mohan," Orak called. When the man turned back, he continued. "How many men are in the office just now?"

"Three. We make plans for the upcoming shearing."

Orak nodded. "Will you walk with me, then? I will not chase the men from their work."

He saw Qinten's eyes widen slightly and ignored it. It would be good for the man to see what went on here.

245

They walked past the barrel of water with a dipper standing near the door. "I smell rather strong, excuse me." Orak dipped some water into the bowl siting on an upended log beside the barrel and splashed it on his hands and face, cleaning most of the dirt from him. He took a towel from beside the bowl and dried himself.

He waved to Qinten. "Come. We will go look at the sheep. No one is in with them. We won't be bothered there.

Qinten followed him through the maze of barrels of feed for the sheep, and past an open shed with long, loose bags awaiting the next shearing loosely flapping in the breeze. A row of the long knives, cleaned and prepared for the men to cut the wool from the backs of the sheep hung neatly along the back wall. Orak passed by all this, familiar with the barn holding a part of his enterprise. When he glanced back to be certain Qinten followed, Qinten's eyes were wide and his mouth slack. Good.

They reached the sheep pens. Orak stood near the wooden fence and turned to lean his back against it. Qinten stood back a bit, as though afraid to soil his golden tunic.

"What did you want to speak to me about, Qinten?"

Qinten looked up into Orak's face. "I want you to agree now to give Ziva to me to be my mate."

"You want what?" Orak growled.

"I want Ziva to be my mate."

"And if I say no, you cannot have her? Will you stop purchasing sacrifices for your cult from me?"

Qinten stared at his sandaled feet and cleared his throat. "I want to say I will. But not now. No one can add to their numbers for the upcoming festival. Lorca demands more, and though I've tried to find other places to meet our needs, I have not been able to do so without coming to you. I need to purchase more for the upcoming New Year Festival, twenty or twenty-five of each animal you already sell to me. Do you have that many?"

Orak consulted the notes on his animals, taken that day. "As it happens, I can. The question is, will I?"

Qinten's eyes popped open wide. "Will you? What kind of business man are you, to even suggest you won't sell to your biggest account?"

"The kind who loves his daughter. I have heard of your, shall we call them forays, into the homes of other men. I cannot know my daughter will be safe with you. I know you cannot love her. You have not loved anyone except yourself for a long time." Orak pushed away from the fence, folded his arms, and stood tall, looking down on Qinten.

"What do you mean? How would you know if I love your daughter or anyone? What does it matter? Women are things to be admired, not precious jewels, not something to protect. Mates are to be brought out on your arm to bring you favor from your betters, to improve your standing, and to be left home to use when and how you desire." Qinten's face grew ugly with the description, twisting and frowning.

Orak stared down at Qinten until he shuffled his feet. "And that is why you will never have my Ziva as your mate. I cherish her as I did her mother. I seek her happiness, her protection from men like you. She deserves a man who can learn to love her. You only love yourself. I will not allow you to hurt another member of my family."

Qinten opened his mouth to speak, and shut it. "What other member of your family did I hurt?"

Orak spun around and stared at the sheep, angry with himself for bringing it up. It would only endanger Ziva.

Qinten grabbed his arm. He turned slowly to face the man who had caused him so much pain.

"No. It does not matter. You do not need to know. Only know this, I will not allow Ziva to mate with you. If that means you will no longer purchase from me, so be it. I will live with it." Orak stomped away toward his horse.

He had not gone far before Qinten caught up with him, dragging on his arm, once more. "You will not give her to be my mate?"

"Never."

"You will be sorry. I will not purchase from you again. Lorca will not purchase from you again." He raised his voice, sounding like a petulant child.

"I am already sorry I ever sold to you. If my daughter is the price of doing business with Lorca, I will pass." Orak's voice dropped an octave and quieter.

"I could ruin you," Qinten shouted.

"You could try. I sell to others not only to Lorca. As of now, I will not sell another animal or kernel of grain to Lorca. I will deliver what has been paid for, nothing else."

Qinten opened his mouth to shout again. He imitated a beached fish, mouth opening and closing in silence. "You will not sell to Lorca?"

"Not if you are their agent. Why should I? You threaten me, you want to steal my daughter, and you would destroy her. No. I will not sell another item to you. Good day."

Orak strode past the shed with sharp knives, and wondered briefly if Qinten would grab one to threaten him. He touched the belt knife he always carried. He stalked to his horse and untied the reins.

"Orak!"

Orak turned to Qinten's cry.

"But I need more animals."

"Good luck finding them. Go to Lorca. Maybe he can tell you where to purchase them."

Chapter 26

Possibilities

Nat glanced up at a knock at the door to Qinten's office. He wondered who would be knocking. Qinten had left an hour earlier and said he would not be back until late that night after returning earlier from a ride in a rage, worse than any other Nat had observed.

"Orak refuses us any more animals. He insists he will not sell us another kernel of grain or another animal."

Nat knew better than to say anything, though he rejoiced in Orak's decision and courage to stand up to Qinten. He had lifted his eyebrows and sat still, listening to his master rage.

"I will ruin him. Orak won't sell another animal in Nod or another kernel of grain to anyone. I will talk with Father. The audacity of him! Says I love only myself."

"Oh?" Nat dared to say.

"He refuses to give Ziva to me for a mate. Says she deserves better. I will ruin him!" Qinten stormed around the room, raging at Orak.

Nat sat still listening. Although he wanted to cheer at the news, he stayed quiet, listening to Qinten rage and started thinking of alternatives to find the other animals Qinten would need. If he did not find them, he would feel Qinten's wrath on his back again.

Master Qinten stormed into his dressing room and shouted at his dressing slave. Nat heard a violent slap and knew Duhkha would sport redness on his face that evening and a bruise for days. He sat at his desk and hoped Qinten would ignore him. He didn't need another bruise.

Qinten soon marched through the office, dressed in his finery. "I am going out. I will not be home until late. Find enough animals to meet Lorca's needs before I get back."

The door slammed behind him and Nat sighed deeply.

Now, since the master left, Nat had spent the time searching through the records, trying to locate other merchants who might have animals for sale. He found a few, and, he hoped they would still have what they needed.

Then came the knock on the door. He ran his hands through his hair and called out, "Come."

The door opened and someone entered, closed the door, and stood near it.

"What is it?" Nat glanced up, expecting the small boy who spent his days outside Qinten's door, waiting to respond to his commands. Not a small boy, but a young woman, carrying a tray of food.

"The Master will not be in for dinner tonight."

"I know. This is not for him. I brought food for you." The voice sounded familiar. He stared at her more closely. A petite, slim girl with green eyes glowing from a dark face stood waiting for permission. "Set it on the table. Livia, is it?"

She set it on the table and waved for him to come sit there. "No, Liana, from the kitchens. You remember me? Drak said you would, but Cook disagreed."

"I remember you. I have not seen you in months. Did you leave the kitchens? You were not there when I was there last." Nat stood and stretched, then walked to sit at the table.

"I left there for a time. Cook tries to keep me out of Master's view." Liana stood across the table from him.

"With good reason. But when does he enter the kitchen? I thought that was one safe place away from him." Nat sat at the table and indicated for Liana to sit across from him.

Liana shook her head and stood behind the offered chair. "No. He remembers all his slaves. Most of them are men, lovely young men, like you. He likes boys, as well as women. He sometimes comes to the kitchen to inspect, mostly searching for a slave to molest. Cook always hides me behind the beef carcasses in the coolest part of the pantry. It will not suffice much longer. Qinten has asked for me specifically."

"Can you wait for the tray or must you return to the kitchen right away? I miss talking to someone who is in touch with reality. Sit. Share this with me. It is far too much for me to eat alone."

Liana shook her head. "You know I cannot sit or eat with my betters."

"Betters? I came from the kitchen. I am no better than you. I remember when you were kind to me, when Kenji so kindly welcomed me to the kitchen."

Liana laughed. Her voice, a warm, soft sound. "I remember Kenji. He met his match when he met you."

"He did. Here take my spoon and help me eat this. It would be a shame to send it back to the kitchen."

"It would go to the goat, and he would like it." Liana sat down in the chair across from Nat.

"But you should eat it, not the goat." He handed her the spoon.

They laughed and shared memories of the kitchen in the time it took to eat the meal. Nat had never eaten with a woman before. A tickle of pleasure zipped up his back and settled in his chest.

When the meal was eaten and the tray ready to return to the kitchen, Nat covered it and handed it to her. "Stay away from the master. He is particularly angry now, and you are not safe. Is there a place you can go for a while, out of the house?"

Liana shook her head. "I am a slave. I have no right to leave the house without permission from the Master. What can I do?"

"Smear yourself with onion and garlic?"

They giggled together.

"The truth is I don't know, but I will do what I can. I don't want him to hurt you." He cupped her chin in his hand and touched her cheek with his nose. "You are a beautiful woman. Qinten does not need to use you. I will do my best to protect you."

"Why would you do that?" Liana bit her lip. "You have been gone from the kitchen for months. They say you have changed. That you would not even recognize me."

"I have not changed. I work for Master Qinten in his office rather than his kitchen. I do as he bids. I have no choice, no more than you. I would rather be in the kitchen, if I could."

Liana smiled. "You have always been kind. I must go. Cook will be upset."

Nat closed the door behind her and leaned against it. A woman showed an interest in him. He a slave, she a slave, but still, she appeared to be interested. Could he protect her from Master Qinten's attentions?

~ ~ ~

Tigre sat in Ziva's lap, purring. Ziva stared out the window at the brilliant sunset, waiting for time to go down to dinner. Crites had been invited and Ziva didn't know how to feel about it. He told Orak he would marry her and protect her from Qinten's lechery. Would he? Could he?

Ziva absently stroked her cat's luxurious fur, thinking. Crites had been good to her at Rowan's party and even kinder at the Harvest Festival. He hadn't treated her as many young men did. He never touched her inappropriately. Instead, he treated her with kindness and respect. Dancing with him had brought her joy, as had the other experiences they had together.

However, Crites had made no effort to contact Ziva in the months since the Harvest Festival. Though she thought of him occasionally, he had shown no interest in her until now. What had changed for him to offer to mate with her now when Qinten had insisted he wanted her for his mate? Who knew the minds of men?

The sky lost its brilliant maroon, orange, and gold colors and darkened to a velvety purple and black. Dinner would soon be served. Ziva wondered if Crites had arrived.

It did not matter. She gently lifted Tigre from her lap and set him on the seat beside her, then stood, brushing cat hairs from the front of her dress. She washed her face and patted her hair smooth, before leaving her apartment to walk down the stairs.

As she neared the dining room, Orak and Crites strode down the hall from Orak's office. Ziva watched them talking, their heads bent inward, as they walked together. Crites glanced up and smiled when he saw her. The smile warmed Ziva to her toes.

Crites hurried forward, took Ziva by the arm and tucked her hand into his elbow. He escorted her into the dining room, followed closely by Orak. When they were seated, the servants brought in the soup.

Together, they laughed and shared stories. Ziva felt comfortable with Crites.

As they ate the last bites of desert and set their spoons down, Orak leaned forward. "There is something you both must know. Qinten found me at the sheep pens today. He admitted his need for more animals for the upcoming New Year Festival. Almost in the same breath, he demanded that I give Ziva to him as his mate. This time, he did not hide his intentions. If I do not give him Ziva, he will no longer buy from me."

"I will not mate with that filth," Ziva cried. She glanced at her father and lowered her eyes. "I am sorry Father, but I cannot."

Crites stretched his big pecan colored hand across the table and covered Ziva's pale hand with it. "You will not have to mate with him. I will be your mate."

"No, you will not mate with the scum," Orak said. "I told him it would never happen. In fact, I told him I would no longer sell anything to Lorca as long as he is their purchasing agent."

Ziva gasped and covered her mouth with her free hand.

"Nothing?" Crites asked.

"Not a kernel of grain, nor a bleat of a lamb. I will sell nothing more to Lorca."

Ziva allowed her free hand to fall to the table and stared at her father. "You would do this for me? How will your people survive if you do not sell to Lorca?"

"You are more precious to me than all the money I might have made. We will manage. I have searched my ledgers for months. I have provided less to Lorca over the past six months than in year before. Priests of Nimm requested more, as have the priests of Balg. My market has sold more grains and meat to the people." Orak moved his dishes and spoon to the center of the table and leaned his his elbows on it.

"Have they purchased enough to make up the difference?" Crites asked, moving his dishes to the center of the table and leaning on it.

"Enough and more. The loss of sales to Lorca will not hurt me or my people." Orak leaned his chin on a fist.

Crites leaned forward. "Your business may not be hurt, but how will Qinten handle this news? He is not known for accepting it when others hinder him."

Orak sighed. "No. He will not take it well. I fear we must be on our guard. He is a misanthrope and is dangerous."

"You must be wary. Qinten is not one who will gladly suffer such an offense. He will find a way to exact revenge on you," Crites faced Ziva, "and you."

Ziva inhaled deeply and slowly let it out. "What would Qinten do to me? How could he hurt me?"

"He will find a way," Crites and Orak chorused together.

The three of them chortled, glad to have something to break the tension.

Ziva noticed the staff peeking around the corner into the dining room. "We need to go into the sitting room to continue this discussion. The servants are waiting for us to leave so they can clean up this mess and go home to their families." She swept her hands in the direction of the table littered with the remains of deserts and dirty dishes.

Crites helped Ziva pull her chair back as she stood. He tucked her hand in the crook of his arm and escorted her to the sitting room, with Orak on her other side. Ziva enjoyed the strength of the two men in her life — if Crites was to be a part of her life.

The three sat in comfortable, deep green velvet chairs. Crites pulled his close to Ziva's where he could touch her if he chose. She glanced at Orak and raised her eyebrows. Orak shrugged.

"Do we have any idea what Qinten will do? We must be prepared." Crites looked at Orak, then turned to stare at Ziva.

"We must be prepared?" Ziva stared back at Crites. "What is this we?

"Hasn't your father told you? If you agree, you and I will be mated."

Ziva glared at her father. "You said we would talk more about this."

Orak held up his hands in mock protection from her frustration. "Nothing is certain. I told Crites you must agree."

Crites nodded. "And I am here to convince you to agree." He smiled at her and touched her hand. "I would like you to choose to be my mate. I have enjoyed our time together today and in the past."

"Yet, we heard nothing from you in all those weeks since Harvest Festival." She left the question hanging in the air, unasked. She crossed her legs at the ankles.

"I have been busy with my business." Crites leaned back and crossed his legs, though he continued to hold his hand over hers. "Even then, I have listened for news of you. I suspect Qinten would rather his obsession with you and his insistence that you become his mate would go unnoticed. I have heard him say that who he mates, if he mates, is nothing for others to be interested in. Of course, everyone is interested."

"But, but why now?" Ziva's foot bounced gently. "Why do you care if Qinten wants me to be his mate?"

"As I told your father, I am impressed by a young woman who turns her back on a man with wealth and power. You refuse to do what all the other women do, even if it is seen as something important. I am drawn to your intelligence." Crites squeezed her hand gently.

Ziva colored.

"I find it enjoyable to be with you. I enjoyed our time together during the Harvest Festival and I could not stop thinking of you."

Ziva crinkled her eyebrows. "You thought of me?"

"I did."

"And you did nothing about those thoughts?" Ziva's foot jumped up and down faster.

"I did a lot about it, though you would not know. I had a man investigate you. I listened to the young men in the public houses." Crites let go of her hand and laced his fingers together behind his head.

"Oh?" Ziva's eyebrows shot up.

Crites laughed. Ziva turned to see Orak shaking his head in silent laughter.

"What? Why are you two laughing?" She set her feet on the floor and scooted forward in her chair, preparing to stand.

Crites waved her back. "Your father said you would be up-set by my delay and investigation."

"And I am."

Crites nodded. "You are. I am sorry for it. Your beauty is cause for the young men's gossip." He held up a hand. "But never did they say anything that would besmirch your charac-ter. Many would have you as his mate, for nothing more than your distinct pale beauty. None say anything bad of you."

"But why did you laugh about this?" Ziva's stare glanced off Orak and settled on Crites until he answered.

"Your foot. It is springing up and down so fast, I feared it would fly away."

Ziva glanced at her foot, once more twitching up and down. She giggled. "It moves on its own. It's beyond my control."

Everyone laughed.

"You know about me, now tell me more about you," Ziva demanded. "What do you do with all your time?"

"Beyond listening for gossip about you?" Crites chuckled.

"Yes. There must be more to you than that."

"I encourage young men to spend their money on horses." Crites dropped his hands into his lap.

"Such a waste of time," Ziva snorted and shook her head.

"It is, but it provides me with excess coins and puts me in a position to listen to the idle gossip of men." Crites settled his arm close to Ziva's.

Orak leaned forward. "What sort of knowledge do you gain from this idle gossip?"

"Interesting things. They say Qinten has missed important meetings in preparation for the upcoming Festival. The other priests are angry. Most will not be voting for him to be the next High Priest of Lorca."

"That is interesting news." Orak glanced at Ziva.

"And it is said Obike heard Qinten's snide remark about his wife's size and behavior in bed the last time he took her." Crites shrugged and his cheeks reddened. "I believe Qinten called her a cow chewing on her cud. Obike could not openly say or do anything about it. However, they say dogs attacked the Lorcan sacred bird coops later. Many birds escaped. More than half were eaten or destroyed."

"Interesting that he would choose to attack the birds rather than the bullocks." Orak rubbed his chin.

"Isn't it, since Obike sells birds. That is not all. On the same day, in the middle of a storm, a hole developed in the bottom of the amaranth silo, damaging nearly half of the grain."

"Caused by another angry husband, I suspect," Orak said.

Ziva glanced down at her hand, now warmed by Crites' hand covering hers. She allowed a small smile to lift her lips. The men in the room appeared not to notice.

"Yes." Crites nodded.

"And you only listen to the gossip?" Orak asked.

"Well, no. Sometimes I encourage the gossip. I have heard your whisper campaign and seen some of the damage. I support them and you." Crites shot a knowing glance in Orak's direction. Ziva saw him nod.

Something was going on that she didn't know about. Probably better that she didn't.

"And what do you do with this knowledge?" Orak leaned forward.

"Ah, that is the question, is it not?" Crites leaned back, his hand still sitting warmly on Ziva's. "What do I do with the knowledge I gain?"

Orak nodded.

"For now, I keep what I have learned close. I share with you what I have learned about Qinten because you and I share the same objective. We both want to keep Ziva safe and out of the weasel's grasp."

Ziva chuckled. Nice name for him, weasel. She planned to remember that one.

The three of them visited far into the night, sharing stories from their childhoods. When Crites finally left, Ziva thought she could live with a man like him, though she still wondered about the secrets he gathered and kept. What did he plan to do with them? Did he gather secrets about her? Did he know about her past?

Chapter 27

Spies

Nat rubbed his gritty eyes. He stood and stretched. He had discovered three cattle merchants and five grain merchants that Qinten had stopped purchasing from. They may be the source of the missing sacrifices. He hoped they would have enough. He glanced toward the window. The moon had passed into the late half of the night.

As he moved to blow out the extra candles, leaving those the Master required for his return on late nights like these, Nat heard a slamming of a carriage door, followed by the door leading to Qinten's private entrance banging open. He was back.

Nat thought about slipping quietly away to bed. The Master would expect him to be sleeping. But something stopped him. Perhaps it was the sound of the Qinten's heavy steps on the stairs. Nat did not know, but he paused, listening to him climb the stairs slowly. He waited.

Qinten growled at the boy at the door, waking him with a kick. Nat thought better of staying but it was too late. The door swung open to a red-faced and drunk Qinten. Nat stood, eyes lowered, waiting for Qinten to decide whether to say anything to him.

The Master slid his cape from his back and handed it to Nat, then dropped into the nearest chair. Nat hung the cape on the peg behind the door in its place. He could not slip away now. He must wait for the Master to release him.

Nat stood waiting for several finger spans of time while Qinten sat with his elbow on the side of the chair and his head in his hand. Nat wondered if the Master had fallen asleep. Nat waited, thinking he should help Qinten to his bed and get the help of his dressing slave.

Qinten's head bobbed on his hand. Yes, Nat thought, I should help him to bed.

"Cursed Orak," Qinten growled. "What shall I do about that man?"

Nat waited, hoping the question had not been directed to him.

"Well, Nat? What shall I do?"

Nat moved closer to his master and glanced at his disheveled clothing. "Not much tonight, I would think"

"No, not tonight. Tomorrow."

"Why must you do something about Orak? Has something else happened?" Nat dared to ask.

"Everything. Nothing. He refuses to give me his daughter. He swears he will no longer sell anything to Lorca." Qinten shouted.

Nat allowed the echo of the shout to dampen before he spoke. "Has anything changed since you left this evening?"

Qinten lifted a fist, and dropped it, allowing it to hang down beside the chair. "I went to see my father. It did not go well."

Nat knew better than to say anything and stood quietly waiting.

"My father is not impressed." Qinten spoke so quietly Nat had to listen hard to hear. "He called me a crybaby."

Qinten shouted, "He called me a crybaby and told me to stop crying and go do something about it."

Nat silently listening.

"He told me to stop crying and do something about it. Me. Do something about it. Father knows I do things. He sits back and watches his enemies. He waits for them to fail. And he tells me to stop crying and do something about it. No suggestions. Just 'go do something about it.'" Qinten dropped his head into his hands. "What am I supposed to do?"

Once more, Nat stood and waited. He had no interest in helping his master catch his sister in his web. He managed to still the shudder that came when he thought about his sister in Qinten's lair.

"I will have that slut. She will be mine. I do not care what Orak says. I will take her. She will be mine."

Nat raised his eyebrows.

"She will be mine, and she will not like it. I will take her." Qinten mumbled.

Nat hoped his master would forget the things he said the next morning. He certainly did not want his sister taken by his master. It would not be nice, not that any woman's experiences with him were nice.

"I will find a way," Qinten mumbled.

"Yes, sir, you will," Nat soothed. "Now, why don't you go in to bed. It will be better in the morning."

Qinten eased forward and allowed Nat to help him stand. He leaned on Nat's shoulder, mumbling as he stood. "I will show Orak. He will have to let me have Ziva."

"Yes, Master," Nat soothed, hoping nothing would come of all this.

Nat knew better. Qinten had mumbled threats before in his drunken mumbling. He would remember this. Worse yet, he would have determined some vile answer to solve his problem by morning. Nat wished he could erase Qinten's thoughts and soften his response in the morning. He shook his head. It did not seem possible.

Qinten's dressing slave slipped to his other side and put his arm around to hold their master up. He glanced at Nat and nodded.

Nat eased Qinten's weight from his shoulder and shrugged his shoulder in circles to loosen his muscles. He walked through the door into his own sleeping room worried about what Qinten would come up with to take Ziva.

Kneeling beside his bed, Nat prayed to Jehovah, begging for protection for his sister. He could only do a little to save her from Qinten's depraved threat.

"Jehovah, save my sister. Help me know what I can do to prevent Qinten."

~ ~ ~

Orak dragged himself from his sleeping room after pulling on his boots. The night before had been long, listening to Crites tell stories of growing up in the country and sharing stories of Ziva's childhood. They had been careful to keep the stories to the years after she had come to his house. Fortunately, Crites had not asked about Ziva's birth and earliest years. Nor did he ask how she came to have such fair skin.

What will Crites say when he learns of Ziva's parentage and how she came to my home? Will he lose his desire for her when he learns I purchased her at the slave market?

Orak sighed. He would learn later. It could not be kept a secret, not from a man who wanted to be her mate.

He had slept longer than usual, much longer than he wanted. He stopped by the kitchen and grabbed his customary meat stuffed roll and took it with him to his office. He would have to find a way to use the information Crites had shared the night before.

He sat in the chair behind his desk and bit into the roll. Juice dripped between his fingers. He unconsciously licked it away and pulled a sheet of vellum toward him.

Com knocked and entered the office. "I heard a rumor." He sat in the chair.

"Oh? I hope it is something that will help us protect Ziva or help us sell more." Orak set his pen down and finished off the meat roll.

"It is, I think. Do you have water back there?" Com leaned forward to look.

"You know I do. When have I not had water in my bucket?" Orak dipped the ladle into the bucket and filled two glasses and handed one to Com.

Orak watched Com lift the glass to drink. When he sat the cup on the table beside him, Orak lifted his eyebrows.

"The news you have?" Orak asked.

"Kai came to me this morning. He and others from the shanties you saved near our lost amaranth silo listened to the young wealthy men who came to the public house near their homes. They sat near Kai. He chose to stay where he was so he could listen to them talk and brag, sing and share stories." Com leaned back with a grin.

"And Kai brought the news to you?" Orak grinned back.

"He did."

"What did Kai learn? What is the good thing?"

"The priests of Lorca plan a secret meeting today. They plan to set things up to ensure that Qinten is not voted in as High Priest." Com frowned. "That will not make Qinten happy."

"No, but it will give him something else to think about besides Ziva and me." Orak picked up his pen and flipped it between his fingers. "Surely this is not all you have learned?"

"Ah, no. The men whose wives have been taken by Qinten have gathered together, determined to protect their women. They are hiring guards to stand at the entrances to their homes, with instructions to keep Qinten away. He will have no easy targets when their men are gone from their homes."

Orak nodded. "It is time these men found some courage. It is wrong for them to allow a man to take his wife and use her against her will. Once again, it will enrage Qinten. Will he turn his anger toward Ziva and me or toward those husbands?"

"It will divide his attention. Between the priest's plans to vote against him and the husbands refusing him the use of their wives." Com pulled his belt knife from the sheath on his belt to clean his nails.

"It will. I learned last night that two of those husbands have done more than hire guards. They are responsible for a wild dog attack on Lorca's bird cages. They lost many of their birds in the attack." Orak sipped his water, then flipped his pen. "Another husband ensured that a hole in the amaranth silo would open during a rain storm. Almost half the grain was ruined."

"How did we not hear about this before?" Com held his knife up.

"I do not know. Qinten has learned to keep some things well hidden. What else does he have planned for us?" Orak dropped his -pen into the cup in front of him. "There must be something else we can do."

"There must be but what?" Com struck his knife in the desk and left it to quiver in the wood. "You have many people who depend on you, not the least of these is Ziva. How will you protect her and your business?"

"I do not know for sure, yet. Are the poor willing to work for me in the country?"

"Many have taken your coppers. We are to meet tomorrow. We will see how many come." Com shrugged. "I suspect one of three of those with families will show up. Of those men without families, perhaps two of three will come."

"Did you give away all my coins?"

Com nodded. "My men continue to cross the city with your offer and coins. I suspect few of the less honest will try to take more than one coin. With more than one person taking signatures, they may think they can take advantage of you."

"I expected as much. Some of those begging are not truly poor but beg rather than work. I have seen some with more than a little in their collection cups." Orak leaned into his hand.

"And you are not angry? These men are taking advantage of you." Com squinted at his employer.

"It bothers me, but I am not surprised. They will do what they do. I cannot stop their dishonesty. I only hope more are honest about this than not." Orak shrugged.

"It is your bag of coppers we are spreading over the city. At least the poor will know that you are considering them."

"I am hoping they remember me. I suspect there will come a time when this is important. We will want them to remember us." Orak pulled his pen out of the cup and doodled on a scrap of vellum.

Com leaned forward. "What makes you say that?"

LOST CHILDREN OF THE PROPHET

Orak glanced up. "I do not know, for sure. It is a feeling I get, sometimes. I hope I am wrong."

The two men sat silently meditating about the possibilities. Com broke the silence. "All this is good, but what do you plan to do to protect our Ziva from Qinten?"

"That is our other problem. Crites offered to help protect Ziva. He has asked to become her mate and promises his Red Guard to protect her from Qinten. She is beginning to accept him. I do not know Crites. I do not know what is in his past or what his plans are for the future."

"You want me to do a little snooping? Find out more about him?" Com grabbed his knife by the handle and pulled it from the desk.

"Yes, if you would, please. I need to be certain he is what he says to protect Ziva."

"And what does he claim?"

"He claims to be a grandson of Tubal-Cain. He claims to have been sick as a child and was sent with his mother to the country, where he regained his health. If so, he has kept himself apart from the politics of Nod." Orak shuffled the papers on his desk.

"If you are to allow you daughter to be mated to him, you need to be sure of him. I will investigate it for you." Com stood, preparing to leave.

"Thank you, my friend." Orak stood and grasped Com by the forearm and looked into his eyes. As Com strode to the door, Orak added, "One more thing, Com."

Com turned to his friend and employer. "What would that be?"

"Find out what Qinten plans. I do not trust him."

"Nor do I. I will discover his plans before he can do anything to hurt you or Ziva."

Chapter 28

Threats

That next afternoon, Nat sat at his desk listening to Qinten rant. He could do little, beyond listening. Qinten would not take advice from a slave.

"Orak continues to be obtuse. He refuses to even respond to my messages. I know he said he would not allow me to have Ziva, but I must mate Ziva in the next week or I will not be ready for the Priest Forum. I cannot believe he would put me off for so long. What makes his daughter so special?" Qinten paced about the room, picking up papers and setting them down without looking at them, as he ranted.

"Fathers can be like that I have heard," Nat murmured.

"Fathers of daughters. I have never seen a father of a son protect him as Orak protects Ziva. She is not all that special. He may never find her a mate if he does not accept my offer. I may see to it." Qinten shouted.

He dropped his voice almost to a whisper. "That is what I will do. I will start rumors about her how she is not so pure and lily-white as they all think. I know. I'll tell them she is a slave not the true daughter of Orak. How did a man like him get such a fair daughter? I can say he bought her! I'll send him a message, give him one last opportunity."

Qinten sank into his chair, pulled a small piece of vellum toward him, and began to write. When he finished, he sanded his signature, rolled it, and pressed his seal on the outside. He dug in his desk and found a gold and white braid tied it around the rolled message.

"He has until dark tonight to decide."

Qinten handed the message to Nat. "See that this is taken to Orak immediately."

"Do you want the messenger to wait for the answer?"

"No. Give Orak time to stew."

Nat took the scroll. He longed to throw it into the fire. Qinten had no idea how true his threats were. What would Orak do? What would Qinten do if he learned Ziva had been purchased at the slave market? Would Qinten's threats force Orak to allow Ziva to mate this evil man? Nat kept his face carefully smooth.

He handed the scroll to the messenger who always waited outside Qinten's door. "Take this to Orak. Be certain he receives it. Do not wait for an answer."

The messenger turned on his heel to run down the hall and outside.

"It is not my place to ask but what will you do if Orak continues to refuse you, Master?" Nat sat at his desk and lifted his pen. "Is there not another girl who interests you? I saw you dancing with a tiny beauty."

"Who? Oh, yes. Kara. She is a beauty, and she fawns over me. She would not deny me. Perhaps, I will go talk to her father today. See how he would feel about it." Qinten pushed back his chair.

"You would ask him before you receive Orak's answer?" Nat asked.

"Yes. I will." He lifted his gold cloak from the peg near the door, whirled it across his shoulders, and left, shouting for his carriage.

Nat stared at the closed door. Too much was happening too fast.

"Help Orak make the right decision," he prayed.

Jehovah would answer his prayer as He answered his papa's. It happened before. It would happen again.

He left the problem in Jehovah's hands and returned to the work on his desk.

The sun moved three hand spans past mid-day when he glanced up to the messenger bringing a message to Qinten. "From Orak," he said.

Nat took the message scroll and set it on Qinten's desk. Much as he wanted to know Orak's response, he let it lie on top of the other papers on his desk. He sighed and walked around the room, stretching his back and legs. The sun slanted through the west window. He pulled the cover across the window and moved back to his desk. Qinten should return soon. He'd know then.

The room began to grow dark. Nat stood to move the cover from the window. He glanced out to see glorious gold and reds glowing in the high clouds. Slaves entered to light the candles brightening the room. Nearly sundown. Where was Qinten?

Almost on cue, Qinten stomped up the stairs. "Did he respond?" Qinten demanded as he marched into the room.

Nat stood to help remove and hang up his master's cloak and waved toward the scroll on Qinten's desk.

Qinten reached for it. "What did he say?"

"I do not know, Master, I didn't read it."

Qinten raised his eyebrows.

"It is your private message, not mine." Nat pulled the chair out so Qinten could sit.

Qinten pulled the message toward him. He took his time untying the maroon and sky-blue braid. He pulled the knife from his belt and broke the seal.

Nat held his breath. Would Orak give in? How would Qinten react? He watched his Master read the message.

Qinten slammed the message to the desk. "Curse that man."

Nat silently let out his breath and breathed once more. Orak proved to be stronger than Qinten expected once more.

"I will not allow that man to tell me no one more time. It will be more than just rumors. I will have Ziva, with or without her father's permission."

Nat stared at his Master. Was he crazy? What was he planning? Taking a young woman without her father's permission was against the laws of Nod. Even Nat knew that. But, then, Caomh was Qinten's father and governor of the city. He had always done what he wanted, why would now be any different?

Qinten stomped into his dressing room and shouted for his dressing slave to help him change. Nat sat at his desk and stared at the message from Orak. Not now. He would wait to read it when Qinten left.

He sat at his desk once more, studying the messages he received from some of those men who had not sold to Lorca recently. They each had a few animals. One had a full silo of amaranth and other grains he was willing to sell it. He was close to having enough for the New Year Festival.

Qinten would never admit that he had been saved by his slave. He didn't even know yet. He was thinking too much of Ziva to even ask about the sacrifices. Nat sat, considering the tally and waiting for his master to be dressed to leave for the evening.

At last, Qinten stomped past Nat toward the door. Nat jumped to help him with his cloak.

"I don't know how long I will be gone. I know you are waiting to read the message from Orak. Go ahead. Read it." Qinten turned on his slippered heel and left the room.

Nat waited until he heard Qinten's carriage drive out the gate before he sat at his desk and drew Orak's message toward him.

He unrolled it and stared at the words on the page.

Qinten,

You will never have my daughter, Ziva.

Orak

Good for Orak. What was Qinten planning now?

~ ~ ~

Ziva stretched and stroked Tigre. He sat near her, purring loudly. "What do you think, Tigre? Will I be safe with Crites? He seems to be a good man, but ... how will I know for sure?"

Tigre stretched his back into her hand. "I know. You have no idea. What can I do to find out? Does it even matter?"

Ziva sighed and stood to look out the window. The sun sat low against the mountains and dark clouds streamed across the sky. Rain would fall before morning. She hoped it would wait until she woke, so she could watch the lightning.

She walked into her dressing room and brushed her hair. Ana had helped her change into a clean dress for dinner and painted her face, as much as Ziva would allow. Ziva decided she was as ready as she could be and left her room.

During dinner, Orak set his knife and spoon on the table and leaned forward to grasp her hand. "There is something I must tell you, my dear."

Ziva set her knife down and pushed her dishes back to lean forward. "What is it, Father."

"Qinten sent another message."

"Another message? Is that all? He sends messages every day. What this time?" She sniffed and shook her head.

Orak held her hand tighter. "There is more this time, things you must be aware of."

Ziva stared into her father's eyes. "What this time?"

Orak breathed in and let it out loudly. "It is bad this time, Ziva. He threatens to damage your good name. He thinks if he does, you will never find a mate."

"What can he say about me? His time with me is so limited, how can he know?"

"It does not matter if he knows you. He can make it difficult for you. He threatened to tell others you are not pure, as is required at the mating of young women of Nod."

"Would Crites care? Would it matter to him? He knows me better than that. He has watched me. Would he really listen to that weasel?" Ziva brushed her hair back from her face and crossed her legs at the ankles. Her foot began to bounce.

"I doubt Crites will believe any of the rumors the weasel, Qinten, would spread, especially about your purity. I doubt any of the young men will. Crites told me he has listened to them and their foul speech about you. None of it suggested they thought of you as anything but pure. I don't think that is our biggest fear."

Ziva's foot bounced faster. "Why are you telling me about it, if you think no one will believe the lies Qinten threatens to tell about me?"

"That is only one of the lies he threatens you with. The other is more serious. I fear everyone in Nod will believe it."

"What? What does he threaten?" Ziva's foot stopped bouncing.

"He says he will tell everyone you are a slave." Orak stared at Ziva, then dropped his eyes to his plate.

"I am. Or I was a slave. Did you legally free me?"

"I had no reason to believe it would be needed. You are my beloved daughter, not my slave. Why would I need to free you?"

"Could this truth hurt you, Father? How will it affect you?"

"It will not affect me, much. I am known as a man who refuses to purchase slaves. The older servants here know how you came to our home and why. It will be a problem for a while, but I accept it. I will not allow him to take you."

"How can he want me so badly if he thinks I am a slave? Can he mate with a slave?" Ziva's foot began to bounce again.

"Only if he frees you. If he buys you from me, you would be his slave, subject to his degenerate actions with none to stop him. That is what worries me." Orak covered his face with his hands.

"But you would not allow him to purchase me?" Ziva leaned toward her father and grabbed his wrist.

"No, I would not willingly allow it. He could find a way, if he knew the truth. His father is the governor, and he always gets his way." Orak set his other hand on her hand that clasped his wrist.

"Do we have to give in? What will you do?"

"I already responded. He demanded an answer by sundown."

Ziva stared at her father, not daring to ask how he had answered.

"I told him I would never give my daughter to him."

Ziva stood moved around the table to kiss him on the forehead. "Thank you, Father."

After long heartbeats of silence, she sat and they pulled their dishes toward them and started eating once more.

"What will we do?" Ziva asked in a small voice.

"Hope his threat is empty," Orak answered in a voice no larger than hers.

After desert was eaten and cleared away, Orak took Ziva's arm to escort her to the sitting room. She tucked her hand in his elbow and enjoyed his comforting support.

"What about Crites? If I choose to mate him, should he not know my history?"

Orak stopped in the hall and stared at her. "I hoped to put that bit of information until later. I suppose he will need to know sooner now."

"Will it change his interest in me? Will he still want to protect me?" Tears glistened in her eyes. She reached up and dashed them away.

"You want to mate with Crites? Are you willing to accept him?" Orak wiped away her tears with his big thumb.

"If he will still have me after he learns our secret." Ziva tugged her father toward the sitting room.

"I asked Com to nose around, see what he can find out about Crites. He hasn't reported yet, but he has been busy. I sent him into the city with some of his men." Orak stopped beside a soft chair and helped her sit.

"Why did you send Com into the city?"

Orak settled into the chair beside Ziva. "Do you remember I told you about the problems our farm managers are having in the rains this year?"

Ziva nodded. "What does that have to do with Com going into the city?"

"Our managers are in need of assistance. I thought that perhaps some of the poor would tire of begging if given an opportunity to work. I sent Com and his men with a bag of coppers into the city, searching for those willing to work. They were to meet this afternoon at the west gate. Com went to with his men to escort them to the farms. He should be back tomorrow with some information for us. If it is good, we can tell Crites we will accept his offer."

Chapter 29

Attack and Protection

Ziva left for bed and Orak returned to his office to look at the message from Qinten once more. How could he protect Ziva from the snake? He sat at his desk, head in his hands, trying to find a way out of this trap. He knew there had to be an answer.

Two spans later, his office door burst open and Keb entered.

"I am sorry, Orak, but this man insists on speaking with you, now."

"Now?" Orak stood up, pushing his chair back with a loud scraping noise. "Who is it?"

Crites entered the room, followed by a man dressed in a red cape. "I am sorry, my friend. It is too late for visitors, but I have news you must hear."

"Come in, Crites. Sit. Do you need a drink of water?" Orak waved the men to a seat.

"No, not now. I must first give you my news. Then, perhaps I will want a drink of water." Crites sat in the seat, his man stood guard at the door.

"What is it, that you would bring your men into my house?" Orak sat in a chair near Crites and furrowed his eyebrows.

"It is necessary. I was in a public house this evening, listening to the gossip of the young men. Qinten arrived, sober for a change. He sat in a chair staring around the room. At last, he approached a man sitting near my friend. Though they spoke in low voices, my man could hear his words."

Orak leaned toward Crites. "What did he want?"

"He asked the man to help him creep into a house and abduct a woman."

"Who?" Orak gripped Crites wrist as Ziva had gripped his wrist earlier in the evening.

"Ziva. He wants her taken tonight." Crites sat still.

"On a night when Com is gone. Who will protect Ziva?" Orak ran a hand through his hair.

"I brought members of my Red Guard. We will protect Ziva and you. Where is Ziva's apartment?"

Orak found other men dressed in red standing outside his door. He led these men through the house to Ziva's rooms. One of the men in red stationed himself outside her door. Two others stationed themselves in the hall.

"Leo, please be certain all the gates and doors are guarded." The last man in red saluted and went to the door.

"I will take that drink, now, if you don't mind," Crites said with a smile.

"If you are certain Ziva will be safe." Orak looked up in the direction of her rooms.

"My men are the best. No one will get past them."

"If you are certain …" Orak led him back to his office, leaving the door open to hear what was happening. He dipped them each a drink.

"Qinten must be frantic for a mate to want to attempt such a dangerous thing. Even his father cannot protect him from the punishment for this." Crites accepted the water and took a long drink.

"He is selfish. He doesn't like to have anyone say no to him. Though I told him he could never have Ziva, he has sent messages every day, sometimes twice."

"Oh?" Crites set his glass on the table beside his chair.

"Today his message changed. He threatened us. Said he'd share rumors about Ziva." Orak pushed papers around on his desk until he found the message from earlier in the day. "Here, you read it."

Crites took the rolled message and unrolled it. He read through it silently. He laughed quietly once. Orak watched his eyes return to the top of the message, then move slowly down the page.

"This is all lies. Keep this. You can use it against Qinten."

Orak swallowed and took back the message, rolling it and tucking it on a shelf behind him. "There is one problem. I shouldn't tell you now, when you are here with your men to protect Ziva. However, I must be honest with you."

Crites lifted an eyebrow.

"Ziva is not a slave, but when she was tiny …"

Orak told the story of Elin and Liva and their accident in the market. The loss of Liva and the subsequent purchase of Ziva as a substitute. Finally, he told Crites of Elin's death.

"Since the day I brought Ziva to my home, she has been a daughter, never a slave. Though I purchased her at the slave market, she has never been a slave. She is my daughter, whom I dearly love and will protect with my business and my life."

Crites listened with a solemn face during the telling of the story. Orak could not decide if he believed him. It did not matter. Ziva would always be his daughter, regardless of the manner in which she came into his life.

Orak continued, "I have since learned …"

A shout came from somewhere near Ziva's apartments. Orak could hear the clashing of swords and the shouting of men. As one, he and Crites left his office at a run toward the sound of the clash.

When they came in sight of Ziva's door, one of the Red Guard knocked away the sword of a stranger dressed in black. Using the handle of his sword, he banged it across the man's head. The stranger slumped to the floor. The Red pulled a length of hemp from his waist and bent to flip the stranger to his face. He wrapped the hemp around the sleeping stranger's wrists and tied them tightly before kicking him onto his side.

Another of the Red Guard came around the corner with another stranger in black stepping carefully in front and his hands held behind him. The Red shoved the man in black to sit beside the first captive. Orak noticed, then, that this man's hands were bound, as well.

Leo, the captain of the Red Guard pounded up the stairs and slid to a stop in front of Crites. "An attack on the residence gates has been foiled. We captured three men there. The others ran away. I see at least two slipped in."

Crites nodded. "Orak, please check on Ziva. I want to be certain she is safe."

Orak hurried to her door and knocked. When she did not answer, he pushed the door open and trotted through the apartment to Ziva's sleeping room. That door, too, was closed.

Orak knocked again and tried to push the door open. It would not move.

"Ziva! Ziva! Let me in," he called.

He heard heavy furniture scraping against the floor. Good girl. She barricaded herself in. At last, the door opened a slit.

"Is that you, Father?" Ziva's voice trembled.

"It is. Are you well?"

The door opened and Ziva fell into her father's arms.

"I am now, Father. But that man is not." Ziva pointed toward her bed. A man in black lay on the floor at the foot of her bed, blood seeping from his head.

Orak stared at Ziva. "What happened here?"

"What is going on, Father?"

"I will tell you when you are covered. Crites and his men will want to have a discussion with the men who invaded our home."

"There are more?" Ziva's mouth dropped open and she fell into Orak's arms.

"Yes, dear, but I think Crites' men have captured all of them. Put on a wrap and join us in your sitting room. Maybe we can understand together what happened tonight." Orak kissed Ziva on the forehead and released her from within his arms.

His arms chilled without her in them. He missed her presence. He shuddered. Is this how I will feel when she leaves my home for another man's. Can I stand the loss?

~ ~ ~

Ziva sighed and found a wrapper to throw over her night clothes. She carefully avoided looking at the body at the foot of her bed. Who would have thought she could hit a man over the head like that? She pushed her feet into slippers and went to her sitting room.

Orak and Crites both stood when she entered the room. She gave them a half-smile and sat in a chair next to her father. The men returned to their seats, all but the man dressed in red lurking by her window. He nodded to her and turned to gaze outside.

Ziva dropped her slippers off her feet and tucked her feet up beneath her. "What is going on here? Why all the men in my apartment?"

"We've had a rough evening, Ziva," Orak said, and leaned toward her, taking her hand. "Are you all right?"

Ziva stared at the bound men on the floor outside her door. "I guess I am. What happened? Who are those men?"

"Part of our rough evening." Orak glanced at Crites and raised his eyebrows. "Crites brought me news of a problem. Our favorite weasel hired men to come into our home and try to steal you away from me."

"Our favorite weasel?" Ziva glanced at the bound men dressed in black on her floor until it dawned on her. "Oh, Qinten."

"Yes, Qinten," Crites said through clenched teeth. "One of my contacts heard him hire these thugs. He came to me thinking I may be interested. I brought a squad of my Red Guard to help protect you."

"A good thing, too," Orak said, "Com is gone tonight. Tonight, of all nights."

"Where is Com?" Ziva asked, looking around the room for him.

"He is escorting the poor who agreed to work out to our farms. He should return tomorrow. Convenient that he would be gone tonight." Orak rolled his eyes.

"You don't think Com had anything to do with this, did you? Com is loyal to us," Ziva cried.

"No. Com is away, doing what I asked him to do. Just seems convenient that he is gone," Orak said with a growl.

"I doubt Qinten knew Com would be gone. I don't think he even thought about you having someone to protect you." Crites leaned forward and touched her arm.

"The leader of these men may have, however." The man prowling the room spoke at last. "They were surprised to find us waiting when they attacked your gates."

"This is the head of my Red Guard, Leo," Crites said and nodded at the man near the window. "He is responsible for your safety. They stopped five of the men before they could get into your apartment."

Ziva gazed at the tall, muscled man dressed in red. "I'm sorry, but I think your men let some through."

"Two made it past us through. I apologize for that. We stopped them here, though, and you are safe," Leo said with a little bow.

"But they missed one, didn't they?" Ziva shuddered and glanced toward her sleeping room.

"One?" Leo asked.

"Yes. There is one more laying on the floor by my bed." She gripped Orak's comforting hand.

Leo and Crites rushed into Ziva's apartment. They returned soon with the man dragging between them. They deposited him with the others outside her door. Leo bent to tie his hands.

"He still lives?" Ziva asked.

Crites sat beside her. "He does, lucky for him. How did he end up on the floor beside your bed?"

"Carefully?"

Crites and Orak growled.

Ziva giggled as Crites returned to his seat, then became serious. "I heard a commotion outside my apartment. To protect myself, I pushed my dressing table in front of my sleeping room door."

Orak shook his head. "Your dressing table. I thought I heard you move something heavy, but I couldn't think what it would be."

"Yes, it was something heavy I could move. I stood beside it listening to a scratching I heard on the wall outside my bedroom window. Instead of climbing back in bed, I leaned against the wall in the dark shadows beside my table."

Orak nodded his head.

"A man's head appeared in my window. He looked around the room, but he didn't see me in the shadows. I watched him climb in through the window. I think he thought he would be hidden in the dark, dressed in black like he was. He moved to my bed and grabbed for something. He must have snagged some part of Tigre, for Tigre didn't like the man grabbing him that way. He yowled and spit and scratched the man's face."

"Tigre?" Crites asked.

"Her cat," Orak answered. "Good cat, Tigre. Then what, dear?"

"He pulled a knife and tried to stab Tigre. I couldn't let him do that. I grabbed the wash bowl beside me and slammed it over the man's head. He fell to the floor with a grunt and a moan. I left him there. Tigre came to me and I sat beside the wall, shivering. With all the commotion outside, I didn't dare leave, until you knocked on my door."

"Smart girl, Ziva. You did the right thing."

"I am sorry you had to face that man alone. Leo and his Red Guard should have prevented all of them from reaching you." Crites stared at the leader of his guard.

"I am sorry, Mistress. I do not know how he got past us. I will check with my team. We will take these three downstairs and see if they can tell us anything."

"Find out, if you can, who sent them for sure, and how he got past you. He'll be bragging, once his headache recedes." Crites nodded to the man Ziva had hit with her bowl. "Though he won't want to admit a girl outwitted him."

"No, I don't think so," Leo grimaced. He left Ziva's apartment and closed her door.

She heard the men grunt and the rustle of something, then the heavy tread of men on the stairs.

She turned to her father. "Now what? Am I safe?"

"Not as long as you are unmated. Qinten will want to take you for his own until it is certain he cannot." Crites frowned and stared at her.

"Even after I am mated, if what I have heard about him is true. He likes to molest married women, does he not?" Ziva's glance fell on both Crites and Orak in turn.

"He does. The husbands of some of those women are working together, at last, to put a stop to his molestation of their wives," Crites answered, then added under his breath, "It has been more than simple molestation, though, much more."

Orak brushed the hair back from Ziva's face with his free hand and sighed. "We do have a problem, there."

"Is there no way I can be safe from the rat?"

Chapter 30

Messages

The work piled up on Nat's desk as he searched for sufficient animals for the New Year Festival. The Master stalked from the window to his chair, sat briefly, jumped up and traipsed to his desk. He sat and shuffled through the papers, then bounced back to the window.

"Have you found enough animals for the festival, yet? We have only a few days to have them in the pens and waiting for sacrifice."

Nat looked up from his work. "I am working on it now, Master. I may have found sufficient numbers to solve the problems of this festival. I don't know where we will get enough for the next festival."

Qinten meandered around the room, unable to settle. Nat glanced up as he wandered past, then continued to search the records. He felt as restless as his master, though he couldn't express it. What did Qinten do about Ziva?

The Master had returned home late the night before. Nat waited for his return, hoping he would share with him what he had done. He had not. He stomped through the study to his sleeping room with only a nod to Nat. Nat had stood holding his cloak, staring after him.

Quiet filled the study, except for Nat's scratching pen and Qinten's wandering. Neither man spoke.

A knock on the door startled Nat. He glanced at Qinten and saw that he, too, jumped at the sound. Nat scurried to open the door. A messenger handed him a note.

"Is an answer required?" he asked the messenger.

"Yes."

"Wait here, please."

Nat looked at the message. It had not come from one of the wealthy men, as it had not been rolled and tied with a distinctive colored braid. No seal prevented prying eyes from snooping into the Master's business. It was folded and on one side it bore the name: Qinten.

Nat pushed down the desire to read the message. Instead, he handed it to Qinten and returned to his desk. He picked up his pen and watched his master read the message.

All color drained from Qinten's face. "Curse them. Curse them all!"

He strode to his desk and pulled a sheet of vellum toward him. His pen scratched across it in response to the message. He folded and sealed it, and scrawled a name across the page. Rather than handing the message to Nat to return to the messenger, Qinten took it to the door himself.

Nat made a note on a piece of paper and waited for his master to share as he usually did. This time, Qinten did not share. He sat in his chair and drummed his fingers along the arm, obviously frustrated. If it had anything to do with Ziva, Nat didn't mind.

"The Red Guard. Curse them," Qinten mumbled.

Nat shrugged.

"Have you heard of a Red Guard? They are not part of the official guard of Nod. If they were, I would have heard from my father, the governor." Qinten stood and stared out the window.

"I have not, Master. The cults each have a guard. Is one of them known as the Red Guard?"

Qinten shook his head and turned back to face into the room. "No. Each of the cults supports a guard to protect their temple, but none were called by a color. Rather, they are known by the name of the cult. Ours is Lorca's Guard, then there's Nimm's Guard, Balg's Guard, and the Guard of Enid. Even the worthless, tiny cult of Talb has their own guard. However, none are known as the Red Guard."

"Where would it come from, then, sir?" Nat held his pen in the air above the ink pot.

"I wish I knew. They are interfering in my business. Curse them, anyway." Qinten sat heavily in his chair.

"Your business?" Nat raised his eyebrows.

"Yes, my business." Qinten growled and began drumming on the arm of the chair once more.

Nat shrugged and dipped his pen into the ink, wiped it on the side of the pot, and made another note. Qinten seldom kept secrets from Nat. He would speak about the problem, eventually. Until then, he would continue to work.

Nat's heart skipped a beat when another rap on the door interrupted the silence. Once again, he strode to answer the door to a messenger. This one carried a scroll, properly sealed and tied with the familiar sky blue and white braid of the temple of Lorca.

"Will you wait for an answer?"

"I am commanded to wait," the messenger said.

He groaned. What do they want now? He held the message in his fingertips as he carried it to Qinten.

He handed it to the Master. "Are you expecting a message from the temple?"

"What now? Curses." He untied the braid then pulled out his belt knife to break open the seal. "Those priests have too much time on their hands," Qinten grumbled as he unrolled the scroll.

Nat returned to his desk and held his breath. He knew nothing good came from messages like this. It seemed bad things were piling up on the Master.

"Curses!" Qinten exploded. "Those cursed priests. What makes them think they can do such a thing?"

Nat released his breath and stared at his owner.

"I am called to meet with them in a span." Qinten threw the message on Nat's desk. "What more do they want from me? Do you have news of the sacrifices?"

"I have almost enough. I can be certain tomorrow. You can tell them we have enough. It will not be false tomorrow." Nat glanced at the curling message in front of him. "What more can they want?"

"I do not know. Read it and see if you can figure it out." Qinten stomped into his dressing room, shouting for his dressing slave.

Nat noticed that the Master had taken the first message with him, rather than leaving it on his desk. It must contain especially bad news. He smoothed out the message from the temple and read:

Qinten~

You are commanded to meet with the priests of Lorca to discuss issues that have become a problem for our cult. Be prepared to defend yourself against the complaints of those men who have brought the question to our attention.

You are expected to present yourself at the temple within one span.

Astynax,

High Priest of Lorca

Which complaints have been brought to the high priest? Nat wondered. It is not like Qinten had been perfectly behaved. Did Orak complain? The husbands whose wives were taken by him? Are they complaining about the quantity and quality of the sacrifices for the upcoming festival? Or is there something I do not know of?

Nat shook his head. What would be the most realistic problem they would want to discuss with Qinten? If not the problem with sacrifices, the most probable issue would be women complaining to their men about Qinten's use of them. He doubted Orak would go directly to the temple about this. What did Qinten do about Ziva last night?

"Well?" Qinten asked as he rushed through the study in clean priestly robes. "What do you deduce I am to defend myself against?"

Nat cleared his throat to give himself an extra breath to think. "Astynax mentions a need to defend yourself against the complaints of men. I suspect you will be responding to the complaints of those husbands who are angry at you for forcing their wives into your debauchery."

He flinched, waiting for the slap he knew was coming. It did not come.

"You are probably right. Those fools have become more vocal in their protection of their tramp wives."

Nat swung the sky-blue cloak signifying Qinten's status as priest of Lorca around his shoulders and held the door open for him.

After Nat heard Qinten descend the stairs and the door slam, he waited to hear the carriage roll away before he wiped the sweat away from his forehead and breathed a huge sigh of relief.

~ ~ ~

Ziva had yawned and returned to bed after a span of discussion. Crites had not brought up any of the information Orak had shared. Orak breathed a sigh when she suggested a need for sleep.

The men wandered to Orak's office. Leo entered and spoke quietly to Crites.

"Do you have a room below ground in the big home? One that will block any noise?" Crites asked.

Orak had raised his thick eyebrows.

"The man Ziva hit is awake. Leo would like to visit with him."

Orak nodded took a tall candle and walked with the men to a back stairway. He led them down the stairs, lighting other candles along the way to brighten the dark stairway. At the foot of the stairs, he unlocked a door to his wine cellar. He touched the flame of his candle to the candle in a candle holder with a shiny copper shield that reflected the light into the room.

"Will this do?" Orak asked.

"Perfect." Leo said.

"I have but one request. Please do not damage my kegs of wine."

Leo glanced at the kegs in rows along the length of the room. "No need. They will be safe."

The men clambered up the stairs and Orak and Crites returned to the office while Leo went into the back for the man he intended to interrogate. An occasional muffled cry reached them as they discussed what to do. First, however, they needed to be certain it was Qinten who instigated the abduction.

"You will want to threaten him as he threatened you." Crites leaned forward in his chair.

"Yes, I thought it would be best to let him know I know it was him." Orak lifted a sheet of vellum from the stack. "I'd better take notes now. It's late and I'll never remember what I wanted to say."

"Be sure to remind him of the penalty for abducting the daughter of a wealthy man. It is not something his father will be able to rescue him from. Even as Governor, Caomh cannot hide him from this punishment." Crites leaned his elbows on the desk to see what Orak was writing.

"Priest Qinten~" Orak said as he scribbled the draft.

"Good start. No more honorifics than absolutely necessary."

"My home was invaded — no that isn't right." Orak scratched out the words.

"Tonight men attempted to invade my home," Crites suggested.

"Yes, that is good." Orak copied the words onto the vellum and looked into Crites' eyes. "They were repelled, all except the few we took prisoner?"

"Yes, that sounds right. It did not take much interrogation for them to admit to who hired them."

"Have they admitted it yet?" Orak glanced from his writing to Crites' face.

"The ones who spoke admitted they were hired. They did not know who hired them. Their leader is now with Leo. The information should arrive soon."

Orak grimaced as another muffled cry reached him. "Are we certain it was Qinten?"

"We will have the truth. Leo will get it. He is good." Crites stared at the writing on the vellum. "Yes. That is good."

Between them, the two men drafted the letter. Many lines were scratched through. Blots of ink spotted the page.

At last, Orak said as he wrote, "You cannot squirm your way out of this. I will not have another member of my family hurt by you." Orak looked at the sentence. "No. He has no need to know how he has hurt my family." Orak crossed through the last sentence. "You will not hurt my family as you have hurt others." He looked up. "Does that sound better?"

Crites nodded.

"You will not have Ziva as your mate nor will she be a woman you debase and brutalize. She will be—" Orak looked up. "Will she be mated to another? Will you still accept her?"

Crites leaned back in his chair and covered his eyes with his hand. "Tell him she will. I have not yet decided. I must know more before I make my decision, but Qinten need not know."

Orak sighed and wrote the words.

"I need written promise from him, though I do not trust him to follow through. He takes what he wants, always has."

"Suggest that he send you a statement, admitting to the attempted abduction and promising that he will never attempt any lechery on Ziva again."

"That is good." Orak bent to write the words.

As he wrote, Leo entered the room and whispered in Crites' ear.

Crites whispered back and waved Leo out of the room.

When Orak had written the last, he glanced up. "What did Leo learn?"

"Qinten sought out our friend in the cellar. He paid him fifty golds and promised fifty more golds when he returned with Ziva. It was definitely Qinten who is responsible."

"What will you do with your captives? Will you leave our 'friend' in my wine cellar?" Orak waved toward the back stairs.

"No. Leo has brought him out. He and his men will be guests in my home."

Orak started. "You would make them your guests?"

Crites laughed shortly. "They will be guests in locked rooms. Each in a separate room. I will care for them, but they will not go free. Not until we receive a guarantee from Qinten."

"Oh. You will treat them well?"

"Leo has already sent them ahead. My healer will care for their wounds. I will keep them happy and satisfied. Perhaps you can send them and their families to work on your farms when they are strong again. That way, we will always have one to confront Qinten and testify against him, if we need."

Orak leaned back in his chair and steepled his fingers. "That is a good plan. My farms need workers. If they have good jobs, they will no longer need to hire out as thugs and robbers. Or they will be too tired to make plans, especially if they are on different farms."

"It is late. I will return tomorrow. Do not send the message until I return. I may have other things to add to it." Crites yawned and stood.

Orak gripped his forearm. "Thank you for your help, you and your Red Guard. If you had not been here, I would have lost my Ziva. Will you think fondly of her?"

"I will. I must visit with my grandfather. I will be here shortly after mid-day."

Orak had stumbled to bed, and fallen to sleep the short spans of time until the dawning sun shone into his eyes. Orak yawned as he settled in the chair behind his desk. It had been a long night and a longer day.

Com returned before many spans passed.

"How went your night?" Orak asked.

"Much better than I expected. I didn't expect many to show up at the gate. When I arrived with my men, a crowd had gathered. Some were becoming concerned that we would not do as we promised. They cheered when they saw us."

"How many were there?"

"More than a hundred men. Many brought their women and families. They didn't have transportation but willingly walked to the farms. We separated them into five groups and led each group to a farm. Your managers were ecstatic when they saw so many who had arrived to help. They took them to dorms to rest, for it was a long walk. I believe that part of your problems is solved."

"Ah. Wonderful. If only all my problems resolved as easily," Orak said with a sigh.

"All your problems? What has the snake done this time?"

Orak appreciated Com's quick understanding. "You wouldn't believe."

Orak shared with his friend the events of the night before, answering Com's questions.

He fought off a yawn. "And now I hope Crites will choose to make Ziva his mate. He had not decided when he left last … this morning."

"When will he return?"

"He said he would be back just after mid-day." Orak stifled another yawn. "Did you manage to find anything about him?"

"Everything I can find suggests he is honest. He did spend much of his youth in the country, and he is Tubal Cain's grandson. He runs the race track. His organization is well run. I can learn only what he wants me to know."

"Would you trust Ziva with him?"

Com rubbed his eyes. "I don't know. However, I do know he will be better for her than that skunk, Qinten."

"He did protect her last night. I hope he's honest. I cannot wait to learn more."

The men sat together, lost in their own thoughts. Orak yawned again.

"You should lay down and sleep a bit, then. You will need to be awake," Com said.

"I will." Orak leaned his head back against the back of his chair. He lifted a hand to wave goodbye to his friend as he slipped out the door.

Chapter 31

Grand Plans and Demands

Ziva listened to her friends as they cackled and chirped about the upcoming New Year Festival. They looked forward to the festivities. She watched Tigre stretch and move into a spot of sunshine.

"Mother says I may attend the evening sacrifices and the activities after. She says if I am old enough to be mated, I am certainly old enough to attend the festival at the temple of Lorca." Kara set her feet on the floor and folded her hands primly in her lap.

Ziva glanced up at her friend in surprise. "She will allow you to attend the festival at Lorca?"

"Yes. Why not? Are you going to be there?" Kara asked. She looked at each of her friends.

Tawna leaned back in her chair. "We must all attend the festival. It is required by law."

"I know, Tawna. I am attending at the temple of Lorca. Where will you go this year?" Kara twisted a curl around her finger.

"I do not know where father and mother plan to celebrate," Tawna said. "I do not know if I want to go to Lorca."

"I will not be going to the temple of Lorca," Ziva said. Her friends stared at her. "What? Can I not have a choice? I will never choose Lorca. Especially after last night." She spit the words out.

"Last night?" Kara dropped her curl.

"What happened?" Tawna leaned forward.

Ziva sighed and mumbled, "I should not have said anything." She reached down to scoop up Tigre and set him on her lap. She stroked his fur as she sat thinking. Her foot began to wiggle.

"You did, now you must tell us." Tawna and Kara chorused.

Ziva stared at her hands on her cat's yellow and black fur, then spoke in a whisper. "Qinten," she spat, "priest of Lorca sent men to abduct me. That weasel is unable to take no for an answer. Orak would not give me to him to be his mate. He could not stand it. Last night he sent men to take me from my bed. What they planned to do then, I do not know." Her foot bounced faster.

"Oh Ziva," Tawna cried. "He asked for you to be his mate?"

"He wanted you? I would give almost anything to be his mate," Kara gushed.

Ziva shook her head. "You would not be happy." Tigre shook his fur and jumped from her lap. She sighed as she watched him stalk back to the spot of sun and lay down in it.

"Not be happy? How could a girl not be happy as the mate of one of the most powerful men in the city? Qinten has wealth. He will be the high priest of Lorca. What more could a young woman want in a mate?" Kara leaned back in her seat and twirled her curl again.

"She does not know," Tawna said. "Mother told me those things you would not. I thought I wanted to be mated to Qinten. Now ... Now I am not so sure. The wealth ... That would be nice. But ... I do not know."

"What? What is so important about the festival?" Kara leaned forward.

"That is for your mother to tell you, not me." Ziva said. Her foot started to bounce at a quick pace.

Kara gazed at Tawna. "Will you tell me?"

"No. If Ziva's father had to tell her, I certainly will not. She is right. That is something your mother should tell you." Tawna folded her arms and stared at her friend.

Tawna held her gaze on her friend until Kara looked down. "Mother will tell me," she said.

Tension sizzled between the three girls.

Then Tawna laughed. "What does it matter? Ziva, you didn't tell us about last night."

"I retired late last night. Father and I stayed up late discussing things." Ziva leaned back in her chair, her foot stilled for a heartbeat or two.

"What were you discussing?" Tawna asked.

Ziva waved her hand. "It does not matter. We were up late. I crawled in bed and fell asleep quickly."

Kara shook her head and sighed. "Tell us what happened, not this insignificant stuff."

"Let her tell it her way, Kara. It is her story," Tawna swatted her friend on the arm. "So tell us."

"I heard noises in the hall outside my apartment. Men grunting, swords clanging together. I closed the door to my sleeping room and pulled my dressing table in front of it."

Ziva told the story to her friends with more animation than she had the night before when she told her father and Crites. She crunched into her seat to show how she hid in the shadow and waved her hands above her head and brought it down as she told her friend about slamming her copper wash basin onto the intruder's head.

"I looked at my wash basin this morning. There is a dent in it. I hope one of our servants can pound it out." Ziva chuckled.

"Did you kill him?" Kara leaned forward.

"How can you even ask that?" Tawna gasped. She slapped at Kara again.

"Stop that," Kara whined.

"Then think before you ask silly questions." Tawna shook her head and faced Ziva with her eyebrows raised high.

"No. He fell to the floor by my bed. He even bled. It had to be cleaned up this morning. But no, thank all that is good, I did not kill him." Her foot stopped swinging and settled on the floor beside the other.

"Good. You would not want to be responsible for the death of another, not even if he tried to abduct you." Tawna shuddered.

"No," Ziva agreed with a matching shudder. "I do not want to be responsible for that."

The young women sat in silence for a long moment.

"Who was it who came to help your Father? I have never heard of the Red Guard," Kara asked. She leaned forward and set her elbow on the arm of her chair and rested her head in her hand.

"I don't know," Ziva said. Of course she knew, but she wasn't telling her friends about him, yet. She did not know if he still wanted to mate with her. Besides, it was none of their business.

"You don't know? How can that be?" Kara asked.

"He didn't share with me. Father found me in my sleeping room. Red Guardsmen removed my attacker. They didn't stay around for me to chat with."

"Your father didn't share? I have a hard time believing that. He shares everything with you." Tawna chewed on the inside of her lip.

"He does share many things with me but not this. I have not spoken with him today. He has been busy." Ziva shrugged. "I heard Com come in earlier. Father has been discussing things with him for many spans. He must have a difficult problem to solve."

"Your poor father," Tawna said. "He must be tired, after a long night and now dealing with other problems."

"I am sure he is. I hope he joins me for dinner. He may not, as tired as he is."

Ziva's thoughts drifted to Crites. She hoped he would still have her. She did not want anything more to do with Qinten.

"Are you listening to us?" Kara demanded.

Ziva shook her head and glanced at her friend. "Oh, I'm sorry. What did you say?"

"I wish Qinten would come talk with my father. I still would mate with him, if he asks," Kara sighed.

"Even after everything Mother told me would be required of a high priestess, I think I would be happy if he came to Father." Tawna stared out the window, avoiding Ziva's eyes.

"Oh, Tawna. I didn't know. And here I have been blithely jabbering about him, when you…"

"When I hoped it would be me, yes." Tears glistened in Tawna's eyes. "I am sorry to be selfish. I can only dream. Ziva doesn't want him. It should be one of us."

"I haven't won him, yet. He has to speak with my father. I'm dreaming, as well." Kara jumped from her seat and threw her arms around her friend. "I wish we could both have him."

"That would be something!" Tawna laughed. "Best friends and wives of the High Priest. Imagine what the Planting Festival would be like."

"Imagine what our bedding would be like?" Kara laughed.

Ziva stared at her friends as they gossiped and made plans as though it would happen. Her foot bounced faster with each laugh.

"Too bad it won't be a threesome of mates with Ziva," Kara chortled.

"You can have him. I do not want him." Ziva said.

As they laughed and planned, Ziva hoped Crites had decided to mate her.

"How will you make your grand plans happen?" Ziva said, her foot suddenly still.

Tawna and Kara stared at her. Then Kara laughed. We will have our fathers talk to Qinten. Easy."

"If your fathers would agree to such a notion. Imagine, two mates for one vile, dark priest." Ziva's foot began to bounce again.

Kara crossed her arms close to her body. "You don't want him. Why should you care?"

"Because you are my friends. I care about you." Ziva trained her stare on Kara and then Tawna. "Both of you. I don't want to see either of you hurt."

"We won't be. Don't worry." Kara arched her back in a stretch.

Tawna stared at her friend with lips pressed together. Ziva wasn't certain her friends were thinking clearly.

"You know what he does. Tawna, you heard the things Ana told us. Do you really want to be a part of that?"

Tawna hesitated. "I want the wealth and prestige. If we were both his mates, well, it should increase. We could share it all. Huh, Kara?"

"Of course, we would."

"And you would live with all he would expect of you? You would participate in the Planting Festival? Do all that?" Ziva dropped her voice and shook her head.

"Yes. Why not? If not me," Kara leaned forward and grabbed Tawna's hand, "or us, it will be another girl. Why not us?"

Ziva shook her head and gave up. Kara would have her way. Tawna, too. And they'd pay for it in sorrow.

~ ~ ~

Orak leaned his head back against the back of his chair and yawned. Within heartbeats, he slept. It seemed only a few beats later when a knock woke him.

Orak covered a yawn, then wiped away the moisture that slipped from his eyes.

"Long day?" Crites asked as he flopped into a soft chair.

Orak covered another yawn. "Yes, after a late night last night."

"Have you written any more on the letter?"

"No, I haven't," Orak admitted. "I have been taking messages from Com. He escorted some of the poor from the city to my farms. The rains have made it difficult for them to grow crops and help the young animals be born in all that mud. We didn't have enough hands to help through the muck. Now, they have a hundred men, many of them with wives and children."

"That many? I had heard of your men passing out coppers to the poor like molasses drops. I didn't think many would do more than take your coins and drink them away." Crites slapped his riding gloves against the palm of his hand.

"I think many did get drunk. I was surprised, too, when Com told me this morning of the numbers who were escorted to the different farms. We will have enough, and more, for all the contracts we have for next year." Orak pulled his pen from the cup and spun it between his fingers. "I didn't think others would hear of my little foray through the city."

"You forget. I have 'eyes and ears' everywhere. I heard of your search. Most other men have not heard. They don't have 'eyes and ears' to help them know. I know more about most men in Nod than they know about themselves." Crites leaned his elbows on Orak's desk.

"Did you know about Ziva?" Orak whispered, almost afraid to ask.

"No, you had one secret I didn't know. You are very good at hiding that secret."

"How did Qinten land on that particular ploy to attack us?"

"Just a lucky guess, I suppose. I doubt he has any idea how close he came to the truth. He thought he'd scare you with the idea."

"He did but I'm not giving any more of those I love to him. He has destroyed enough of my family." Orak pulled a piece of vellum from a pile on the corner of his desk. "I guess we should look at this again. He needs to know we know what he did last night."

Crites nodded.

Orak read:

Priest Qinten~

"I still like that, not too much honor for the weasel."

Orak grinned and continued reading:

Tonight, men attempted to invade my home.

"No, that isn't right, it was last night." Orak dipped his pen in the ink and crossed through the word and wrote in the corrected version. "They were repelled, all no." He scratched through all, then continued to read. "Except for the few we took as prisoners."

They worked through the letter until they reached the section about mating. "You will not have Ziva as your mate, nor will she be, he scratched through the next words, then added, one of those women you debase and brutalize.

"Yes, that sounds good," Crites said. You have it sounding much clearer" He took a drink of water from the glass of water Orak had given him earlier.

"What about this next sentence? She will be mated to another. Will you still become her mate?" Orak set the pen beside the paper and stared into the eyes across the desk from him.

"I visited with my grandfather, Tubal-Caine. When I told him of my intention to marry a girl whose skin held little or no color, he held up his palms to me, his lips mouthing the words, 'no, no.' I let him think about it as I waited for him to rest and finish his meal."

"And did it help?"

"No. After he thought about it, he pounded a fist on the table and swore he would not allow a son of his to be mated to a daughter of Adam. I did not know what he meant, I had never heard of Adam."

"Who is Adam? I thought he is a myth." Orak shook his head and stared at Crites.

Crites took a deep breath. "Apparently, Adam is no myth. As our first parent, he tried to force his children to believe as he does or so my grandfather says. There was something about a death and our parents left the valley where he lived. Grandfather heard the story from an angry grandfather who fought to gain power and prestige among men."

Orak only dared breathe one word. "And?"

"And I stared at him. 'You would deny me the right to mate with a beautiful, intelligent woman because she may be a descendant of this Adam.' Grandfather's eyes bulged as he screamed at me. I had to wipe away the spittle from my face, when I walked away from him." Crites shrugged.

"So —"

"So I reminded him we must all be descendants of that Adam. He tried to tell me I would have none of his fortune if I mate with your daughter. I reminded him of the things I know about him that he'd rather others not know. Grandfather grew red in the face and very quiet. He knows I do not need his money. Not even his name or prestige, if we are to be honest. I have money enough to live well with a mate."

Crites leaned back in the chair and searched Orak's face. "Grandfather does not want me to share his secrets, and he knows better than to have me killed. He slumped in his chair and nodded. He will support my mating with your Ziva, and no one will ever know her secret."

Orak let out a huge breath and brought his hand to his heart. "I feared you would not want Ziva after you learned how she came into my life. One more thing you must know, before you decide for sure."

Crites rolled his shoulders and bent his neck both ways before answering. "What else is there? Is she one of the fabled 'lost children of the prophet' we hear the traders speak of in hushed tones?" He barked a laugh.

Orak picked up his pen and bounced it in his hands, waiting long breaths before answering. Would Crites still want her? Would he protect her still? He sighed. "Actually, yes."

Crites leaned back in his chair with a bump. "Grandfather will have a fit."

Orak hoped the man in front of him would become his son as Ziva had become his daughter. He watched a variety of emotions cross this man who would have his daughter as his own, and waited.

"He does not need to know. He would have a fit, if I ever share this bit of information with him. No. He does not need to know. I am certain Ziva will win him over." Crites smiled.

"You will still become her mate?" Orak dipped his pen in the ink.

"Yes. Her courage last night impressed me." Crites leaned forward. "How did we end it?"

I expect a written statement, admitting to your attempted abduction and a promise that you will never attempt any further lechery on Ziva. Orak glanced up. "Should I not expect it by a certain time? I thought I should hear by sunset."

"That would be good, but I recommend a shorter term. Don't give him time to run to daddy. Maybe a span of time?" Crites leaned back and laced his hands behind his head.

Orak spoke as he wrote. "'This message of acceptance must be in my hand no later than," he glanced out the window at the sun. The days were still short, and the sun had already moved two spans past zenith, "'a span before sundown. If it does not arrive by then, I will take your employees to the courts and swear out a demand for your arrest.'"

Crites nodded. "How will you end it?"

"With my name. He needs nothing else."

Orak took a clean sheet of vellum from the stack and carefully copied the message to Qinten. He signed it, 'Orak', sanded it, and pushed it across the desk for Crites to read.

As Orak rolled the vellum, affixed his seal, and tied his maroon and sky-blue braid around it, he glanced up at Crites. "Now what?"

"You send it. And then we wait."

Chapter 32

Answers

Nat worked in the quiet study. Tension gnawed at his stomach. What had the Master done to ensure his sister would become his mate? What would he say and do if he discovered she was his sister and his threats of her slavery were not unfounded?

He let out a sigh and walked to the window to stare out toward the mountains. He wondered where their parents were this day. Did they remember him and Ziva? What was happening in Shulon? When had he thought of that place in all these years? Could he find it again, if he ever escaped?

Nat shook himself. There was no way he would escape from the clutches of Qinten. Even if he did, would Ziva leave the luxury of her home to wander in the wilderness seeking their parents? He doubted she would.

As Nat turned back toward the work on his desk, he heard a carriage bolting through the gate toward the Master's private entrance. The carriage driver shouted at the horses and they skidded to a stop. Qinten had returned, and it did not sound like he was happy about his meeting with the priests.

Qinten stomped up the stairs, cursing everyone. Nat steeled himself against Qinten's dark mood and opened the door for him. This would not be pleasant.

Nat took Qinten's cape and hung it on its peg without saying anything.

"Those cursed husbands. Lorca curse them all. They brought charges in the temple against me. If they would protect their wives better, I would not enter their homes to use their wives. Stupid men. Stupid women." Qinten dropped into the chair behind his desk and sat with his head in his hands.

Nat sat in his chair and picked up his pen. He waited for Qinten to say more.

"What more will happen on this cursed day?" Qinten grumbled.

Nat knew better than to answer. He did not want to be punched or slugged.

Qinten pulled the message that had come earlier from the pocket at his waist and reread it. "Curse them. Can they not do one simple thing? What next?"

Nat ducked his head and waited.

After a long pause, Qinten raised his head. "I expected the complaints about my taking other men's wives. It is nothing. They are weak. After they left, though, the priests kept me in their interrogation chair."

Nat raised his eyebrows.

"They asked if I had found a mate. If not, I would not be allowed to put my name forward to be High Priest. I told them I would be mated within the next two or three days."

Nat swallowed the words he wanted to shout. What made him think he would mate with his Ziva? Instead, he asked, "Has Orak changed his mind?"

"Not yet. He will."

Nat glanced at the sun. Not many spans of light left in this day. How would Qinten be mated so soon?

A messenger knocked, breaking the silence. Nat took the message.

"An answer is required," the messenger said.

Nat nodded and took it to Qinten, noting the maroon and sky-blue braid of Orak. He groaned. Was Orak giving in?

Qinten took the scroll, and slid off the braid. "Orak, hmm." He broke the seal and unrolled it.

Nat held his breath. Whatever Orak said would not be good for him.

"Curses. I cannot believe he would say this. How can he demand such a thing?" Qinten threw the message on the desk between the two men. Nat restrained himself, though he desperately wanted to pick it up and read it.

Qinten slammed a fist on his desk. His eyes bulged and the veins along his face and on his neck stood out. Nat ducked as he picked up his cup of pens and threw it. It shattered against the wall. Pens clinked to the floor. The clay jar of ink soon followed it, splattering the wall with blue-black ink.

Nat glanced up to see if anything else would fly past his ear. When nothing else seemed to be forthcoming, he slowly lifted his head.

Qinten sat once more with his head in his hands. "I am lost. Orak foiled my plans. Read it.

Nat gingerly picked up the message and read through it. He growled when he read of the attempted abduction of his sister. He raised his eyebrows as he read of the capture and interrogation of the attackers and their testimony against Qinten. He inwardly cheered when Orak asserted that his daughter was not for sale and would never be given to his master's clutches, nor would he be allowed to molest her.

"Who would mate Ziva, if not you?" Nat dared to ask.

"I don't know. I am lost," Qinten moaned.

Nat finished reading the message, and silently cheered Orak's bravery in demanding a written statement of his culpability and his willingness to comply with his demands.

He glanced to the sun. Qinten had less than a span to write a response and return it to Orak. Would he?

The signature at the bottom of the page simply said "Orak."

No wonder Qinten had thrown things. It would be a problem for him.

"What will you do?" Nat asked after reading the message through once more.

"What can I do? If Orak takes this information to the judges, I will be lost. I will be lucky to be one of the lowliest of the priests. I will never be High Priest, and I could lose all my wealth. Father cannot save me from this." His head fell back into his hands.

"Excuse me, sir. If you do not respond soon, it will be too late." Nat held himself tight, waiting to be hit. Qinten slugged him in the face. Nat sat still, not daring to catch the blood falling from his broken nose.

"Get a towel and clean your face."

Nat went into the bathing room to find a towel and pressed it against his nose. When it stopped bleeding, he dampened the towel and returned to his desk and stooped to clean the drops of blood from the tile.

"Get me a pen and find a new pot of ink. I do not have much time." Qinten ordered.

Nat picked up the fallen pens and set them on the Master's desk, then found a new pot of ink in a closet. He silently handed it to Qinten and returned to his desk and work, waiting for further instructions.

Qinten completed two messages before lifting his head. He rolled the two messages and sealed them, then tied his gold and white braid around each.

"Take this to our messenger. Tell him to take it to Bram. He will be happy to have his daughter mated to me."

Nat raised his eyebrows.

"Yes. Kara will make a good mate for a high priest. She is flamboyant and her parents are definitely followers of Lorca."

"She will be a good mate for you. Will Bram agree?" Nat asked.

"If he knows what is good for him. He has wealth, but not what I have."

"True. And the other message? Shall I give it to the waiting messenger.

"No. I cannot depend on him reaching Orak in time. You go. Take my carriage."

"May I change my clothing first?"

Qinten stared at Nat's blood-stained tunic. "Yes, but be quick about it. Be sure he knows I'm done with his daughter."

~ ~ ~

"What will you do if Orak doesn't respond?" Crites asked Orak. "The sun is near setting and the courts will be closed."

"It will be too late to take a complaint today, but not tomorrow first thing. I will be at the doors when it opens tomorrow." Orak sat in a comfortable chair near the one where Crites sat.

"You will be the first one there?"

"No, I think I will be the last one there before they close tonight. I do not want Qinten to go to his father tonight and figure a way to squirm out of the penalties he deserves." Orak leaned back in his chair and rubbed his tired eyes.

He wanted this over. It had taken too much of his time and energy today. He still feared for Ziva's safety.

Crites had returned with a squad of his Red Guards. Some stood concealed along the borders of Orak's home. Others patrolled the halls inside the house, while a small squad patrolled directly around Ziva's apartment. Neither Orak nor Crites trusted Qinten to respond as they had demanded.

Orak heard a quiet rap at his door, and Keb entered. "You have a visitor."

"Oh? I don't have time for visitors today." Orak spoke without removing his hands from his eyes.

"Sir, I think you want to talk to this one." Keb insisted.

Orak heard Crites sudden intake of breath and his feet slap on the floor. He separated his fingers and turned toward the doorway.

Orak dropped his hands into his lap. "Oh, Nat. It's you. What does your master have to say?"

"You know this man? You know he is Qinten's personal slave?" Crites pulled his feet close to the chair preparing to stand.

Orak stretched his arm out to stop his new friend. "Yes. I know Nat, and I know he is Qinten's personal slave. Keb, would you tell Ziva she may want to come to my office in a half a span?"

Orak watched Keb close the door and heard him tread in the direction of Ziva's room.

"You can stay that long, can't you, Nat?" Nat nodded as he handed the message with the gold and white braid of his master to Orak.

"Sit, son. Your master need not know you sat in my presence."

Nat stared around the room. His eyes fell on Crites.

"Why are you allowing this slave," Crites' voice roughened on the word, "this servant of Qinten, to sit in your presence?" He glared at Nat.

Orak glanced at the hardness on the faces of the men in front of him and softened his voice. "Sit Nat. There is something each of you needs to know about the other."

Nat glanced at Orak then swept his eyes toward Crites before he sat in the chair Orak indicated.

"What is this that we should learn? And is it more important than the message his master sent?" Crites asked. He looked pointedly at the unopened message.

"For now, this is more important. We may not have another opportunity for me to share with each of you the changes in Ziva's life." Orak stared at Crites until his gaze dropped and the stiffness in Nat's posture softened.

"Crites, you should know that Nat holds a special place in our lives."

Crites jerked his head toward Nat. "What? How?"

"I told you I purchased Ziva from the slave market."

Nat's head came up and he stared at Orak.

"Yes, Nat, I told Crites." Orak returned his attention to Crites. "She was stolen from her family far away, from among those who worship Jehovah."

Crites audibly sucked in air.

"She was stolen with her brother and brought here to Nod. I found Ziva in my hour of need, as I shared with you last night. What I did not tell you is that Nat, here," he glanced toward Nat, "is her brother. Nat wasn't as lucky as Ziva. No one bought him to be a replacement for a beloved son. His life has been difficult. Somehow, he was purchased for Qinten's household."

Orak turned to Nat to see him nodding, a brightness in his eyes caused by unshed tears. "You will have to share your story with me sometime, son. I would like to know how you became a part of that household and in this position."

Nat nodded.

"You are her brother?"

"Yes. I promised Papa I would always care for her. It is my sorrow that I could not. She sobbed when she was torn from my arms."

"Oh. I did not know."

"No one important knew. I did not know where she went until recently. Now, I work to keep her from my Master's clutches." Nat stared into Crites' face, knowing he could be beaten for doing so.

"One more thing," Orak added. "As you know, Crites." He stared into Crites' face until he nodded. "Nat and Ziva are the children of the prophet we have heard about."

"They are looking for us? Mama and Papa have not forgotten us? I have not heard." The gleams in Nat's eyes rolled down his face.

"No, son, they have not forgotten about you. No parent would forget their children. I would search until the end of my days for my missing children if I were in your parents' place."

Crites gently touched Nat's shoulder. "It would be wonderful to be loved that way." Orak compared the pink of Nat's arms and hands to the dark pecan of Crites. He looks so much like his sister. Will Crites be good to them?

Nat wiped the tears from his face with his hand. Orak silently handed him a square of white linen. Nat nodded and wiped his eyes and blew his nose.

When Nat set the square of fabric gingerly on the desk, Orak continued. "Nat, there is something you must know about Crites."

"Oh?" Nat's eyebrows rose.

"I have agreed to allow Ziva to become Crites' mate. She agrees, especially after last night."

Nat shrugged. "I read your message. What happened here?"

Orak shared with him the events of the night before. Nat grinned when he learned of Ziva stopping the one who climbed the wall into her room.

"She has always been a feisty independent girl. Even when she was tiny, we knew better than to tease her. She let the boys know she would fight her own battles. It helped that I was behind her, standing up for her."

The men chuckled together, thinking of Ziva as a little girl fighting off the bigger boys.

"Crites questioned him when he woke up, along with the others we captured. They admitted to being paid. The leader admitted it was Qinten who paid them to abduct my daughter." Orak waved a hand toward Crites. "He holds them as his guests, still."

"Guests?" Nat asked.

"Well, unwilling guests, for now." Crites admitted with a shrug.

"I knew he was up to no good last night when he left, but he kept it to himself. Even when he received a message earlier today, he didn't share with me. I suspect one of the abductors sent it to him. It carried no seal or braid."

"It would not. That would mark him, if we take this to the courts," Crites said.

Nat nodded and Orak picked up the message from Qinten. "I suppose we should read his message."

He slipped off the braid, broke the seal, and unrolled it. He made little sounds of approval as he read the message to himself.

"Well?" Crites asked. "Does he capitulate?"

"He does, or at least he says he does. Who can trust the word of that spider?"

Nat surprised Orak, speaking in a quiet voice, "No one."

Chapter 33

Capitulation

Ziva sat in her sitting room on her favorite chair where she could feel the breezes through the window. Tigre jumped up onto her lap, circled three times and stretched, waiting for her to pet him. She ran her hands along the length of his luxurious fur, allowing it to calm her thoughts.

Keb had come to her door to tell her to come to meet with her father in half a span. She wondered what he had to tell her. Perhaps Crites had decided.

The dinner with him two evenings earlier had been pleasant. Crites had treated her with respect and consideration. He had been respectful all the times she had been with him. But, she did not know if she could depend on it to continue.

She listened to rumors of men who treated young women well among others, then when they were alone and the women were mates, the men changed, allowing their true character to show through. Some of the young women were never seen alive again. Others appeared, with bruises and other injuries. The rumors suggested that some men did not hurt their wives physically. However, the women lost their vitality and love of life from the verbal abuse heaped on them daily.

Would Crites be one of these men? How could she know? Ziva was certain Qinten would be one who abused his women, at least verbally. Ana had told her of the women he had taken against their will and the will of their husbands. They sometimes were injured and always feared when their husbands left them alone. She worried for her friends and hoped they failed in their quest.

Crites had come to protect her the night before with his men. That was a point in his favor. Her choice was Qinten or Crites. Between the two, Crites felt safer.

Ziva sighed. What would happen to her? She knew that all men were not wicked and vile. She thought about how she felt around Crites. She had not perceived a blackness about him. His soul did not exude pure light, as had the newborn baby brother of her friend, but he had lived longer.

She would have to depend on Crites and pray he treated her as she had seen her father treat her mother.

Ana entered. "Mistress Ziva?"

Ziva glanced up. "Yes?"

"Your father is ready to talk with you in his office."

Ziva stood, set the cat in her chair, and walked through the house to her father's office.

She knocked softly on the door and entered when her father called out for her to come in. He rolled a message to cover its writing as she entered. What did he not want her to read?

Then, she realized the men in his office were not his employees. She turned and threw her arms around Nat, who barely had time to stand and catch her.

"Nat! I did not think I would see you again. I did not think Qinten would send you back here. Is he still trying to insist I become his mate?" She pushed back from his arms so she could look into his face.

"No, Ziva. He has given up. He finally realized you were too feisty and determined for him." Nat grinned down at her.

"Nat!" she cried.

"Actually, I am here delivering a message from him. He doesn't know just how determined you are. He does know when he has lost, and last night's little ploy lost everything for him."

"He was responsible for the attack on our home and me?" Ziva twirled to stare at her father.

"Yes, it was him. Ask Crites." His eyes flicked toward the other man in the room she had not focused on yet.

"Oh, hello Crites. I am happy to see you. What did those men tell you last night?"

"They admitted to having been paid by Qinten." Crites smiled into her eyes. "They are my guests for now, until we know for sure Qinten has given up."

"Good plan. I do not trust him and his dark soul." Ziva quivered at the thought of him.

"With good reason, sister." Nat squeezed the hand she still held, then handed it to Crites. "You will be safer with Crites."

"Will I?" She stared at her brother a long breath and saw truth in him and turned toward Crites. "Will you still have me?"

Crites pulled her toward him and hugged her gently. "After last night, how can I say no? Even my grandfather cannot stop me from wanting you as my mate. Will you agree?" Crites glanced at Nat. "Will you allow her, Nat, Orak?"

Ziva looked at her brother and father, waiting for their answer. Orak had the right to give her to whomever he chose. As a slave, Nat legally had no say, and no one but the four of them in the room knew he was her brother.

"Crites has proved to me he cares for you and will protect you," Orak said. "What say you, Nat?"

Nat stared at Orak and gulped. Ziva felt his stare on her and looked up into his face. "Ziva, I think you will be safer with Crites than ever with Qinten. I have prayed that Jehovah will bring you a better man and save you from being taken by my master."

Ziva allowed a tear to slip down her face before blinking the others back.

"And you, Crites," Nat continued. "You'd better take good care of my sister. I will find you and hurt you if you don't, even if I am a slave."

Crites extended a hand toward Nat, leaving a cold space on Ziva's side. "Thank you Nat. I promise." He turned his head to stare into Ziva's eyes. "I promise you, too, Ziva," he glanced toward Orak, "and you Orak," he returned his eyes to Ziva's. "I promise I will treat you well."

"That is all I need to know," Nat said. "Welcome to our family." He gripped Crites' forearm and smiled at Ziva and the man beside her.

"Thank you, Nat." Ziva stepped from the warmth of Crites' embrace and threw her arms around her brother once more.

"I am happy you found someone good for you. Qinten is not." Nat gently pushed her back into Crites' arms. "I must go. I have been here much too long. He will be wondering about me. I'll be strapped again."

"Then you must go. Remember I love you, brother." Ziva stretched up to kiss his cheek. "Come see me when you can."

"But don't tell Qinten yet who she is to be mated with. He doesn't need to know about me," Crites added.

"I won't. He will not know anything we said today." Nat stared into Ziva's eyes. "I love you, Ziva."

"I know. I love you, too." Ziva watched him leave the room and leaned against Crites.

"You knew Nat is my brother?" she asked, finally processing what happened.

"When your father told me just now, I was surprised. I did not know you had a brother until today."

"I did not remember him, either, until a few weeks ago."

"Are you willing to be Crites' mate, then, Ziva?" Orak asked.

"Will you have me?" She looked up into his eyes.

"Yes, Ziva. I will have you. We can talk about it later, but your father and I have something more to discuss, about this problem with Qinten. We will talk more about our mating soon."

Ziva glanced to her father.

"Yes. We have to decide what to do about the message Nat brought with him. I'll come get you when we are ready to discuss your mating. Can you do that for us?"

"Yes, Father. I will be in my apartment, waiting for you."

Ziva accepted an embrace from Crites and returned to her apartment, musing about her visit with her brother.

~ ~ ~

"Take the fastest way home, without racing, please," Nat told the carriage driver as he swung inside. As the door closed, the carriage rolled away from the steps in front of Orak's house.

Nat leaned back in the seat and relaxed a breath, thinking about how to tell him about this meeting. It lasted longer than he expected, and longer than Qinten would have expected. He would need a good story to avoid a beating or a lashing.

Nat passed several stories through his mind before deciding the easiest would be to tell the truth, to a point. He had waited to speak to Orak, although not as long as he would tell his master. He had no need to know of his visit with Crites and Ziva.

Nat considered the conversation. If he told Qinten that Orak had kept him to listen to the details of the raid … yes. That would be better than telling a lie. He had been kept longer for the tale. Qinten had no need to know the information Orak had shared with the two young men.

The carriage careened around a corner, throwing Nat to the other side of the carriage. He settled himself when the carriage straightened out and pounded on the roof of the carriage.

"No need to kill us!" he called. "Slow down."

He felt the horses slow and relaxed back into his seat. He wondered if the carriage driver knew he had been rescued from a lashing and an expectation that he pay for the dead horse when the Master had been out in the storm before his illness.

Nat had taken a chance and talked strongly with Qinten as he grew stronger, reminding him that his carriage driver could not drive for him if he was injured from a lashing. He managed to talk him out of forcing the driver to pay the cost of the horse. "Where would the man come up with money?" he had asked. "He is your slave." Eventually, Qinten had listened, and this driver had felt no pain.

It did not matter to Nat, really, if the driver knew of his protection. Nat was grateful to have been a help to him.

As the sun dropped behind the mountains to the west, and sooner than he wanted, the horses slowed to a stop in front of Qinten's private entrance. Nat stepped from the carriage and thanked the driver.

"The Master may need you. Wait until he releases you," Nat said.

"Of course. I know my place." He touched his cap in salute.

Nat smiled and opened the door. As he climbed the stairs to Qinten's apartment and study, the smile slipped from his face. He squared his shoulders and entered the study.

Qinten met Nat with a slug to the jaw and a shout. "Where have you been? I am waiting for my carriage. You have been gone for spans."

"I have been at Orak's, as you commanded." Nat fought to keep his hand at his side and away from the growing lump on his jaw. "He kept me there all this time."

"He kept you this long? Why would Orak keep you, a slave?" Qinten added contempt to his last words. "Were you conspiring with him?"

"You know I would not do that. I do not know his purpose. I was required to wait to take your message to him. He called me in and wearied me with the story of his protecting his daughter." Nat shrugged.

"And did you learn anything of importance to me?"

"I did, sir." Nat stood before his master, eyes focused on his chest, legs spread wide enough to prevent a collapse to the floor if hit again.

"Well?" Qinten snapped.

"Orak continues to have men standing guard around his home and Ziva's apartment. He holds the men he captured as assurance that you will not change your mind."

Qinten stomped to the window and turned on his heel. "You are certain. The men he captured are in his control?"

"I only report what Orak told me. He did not show me the men. I did not ask? Should I have asked?"

"No," Qinten growled. "He would not have shown you. Is that all?"

Nat thought for a few heartbeats. "There is one more thing he told me, perhaps it was for your benefit."

"And that was?" Qinten took a step closer to Nat.

Nat took a quiet breath and braced his legs sturdier against the floor. "He has agreed to a mating for Ziva to another man. Orak did not tell me the day it would happen, but he suggested it would be soon."

Nat waited, expecting a blow, that did not come.

At last Qinten spoke, so quietly Nat had to strain to hear the words. "He said he would mate her to another. I did not think he would."

Nat stayed quiet, knowing that speaking now would earn him another bruise.

"It is good that I just received a message from Bram. He is willing to discuss terms for my mating to Kara. If Orak is willing to allow his spoiled brat to choose who to mate with, perhaps it will benefit Bram and his daughter."

"Excellent, sir. When do you meet with Bram?" Nat asked.

"I am to meet with him a span after sunset." Qinten glanced at the sky. "The horses will have to race to get me there in time. You will tell me about the attempted abduction of Ziva when I return."

Nat hurried to help his master slip into his cloak before he strode out the door and down the stairs to his carriage.

Nat sighed as he sat in his chair, hoping Qinten would forget the request to share the story. *Good thing I told the driver to wait.*

He slumped into the soft chair and rubbed his jaw. It already had a knot on it. It would hurt for days.

Nat could not face another lonely meal in the Master's study. He walked to the bathing room and washed his face, gingerly washing the dirt from around his most recent bruise. When he was certain he was clean, he left the study and sauntered through the house to the kitchen.

Liana met him at the door, a covered tray in her hands. "I was coming to bring your meal to you."

"I did not know you were coming. I did not want to eat alone today."

Liana turned and led him to the table in the corner of the kitchen where Cook often sat to eat. She set the tray down and nodded for him to sit. "Eat here, then. You can absorb some of the fragrance of the kitchen while you eat."

Nat sat and caught her hand to prevent her leaving. "Sit with me. I need company tonight."

Liana glanced around the busy kitchen for approval, then sat in the chair across from him. "I can only stay a short time. Cook will need me again."

"I know. Stay with me as long as you can."

Liana nodded and handed Nat a spoon. "Eat."

Chapter 34

Contracts

"Then it is settled?" Orak set his pen on the desk and sat back in his chair. "Are you satisfied with these terms?"

As Crites nodded, Orak reached into the cold bucket and withdrew a bottle of his finest wine and poured some into two glasses. He handed one to Crites and kept one for himself.

Crites leaned back and sipped from the glass. "Mmm. Nice wine. Yes. I think all the issues are addressed. Where did you get this fine wine?"

"It comes from my own orchards. I don't trust wine from others. Usually we drink water. It is safer."

"You should sell this. It is good."

Orak shook his big head back and forth. "I'm not ready to sell my wine. I keep it for my table for special times."

"I can see that. Special house wine for yourself. Will you share it? It would be a nice addition to the mating celebration?

I am certain my grandfather will be mollified with this excellent wine."

Orak thought about it, his eyes rolling upward, mentally counting the bottles of wine in his cellar. "I think I can supply a few bottles for the celebration."

"Good. Can Ziva be prepared in time?"

"Prepared? She'll want a new dress. Most women do for their mating ceremony. I can ask the seamstress to create a dress quickly. Other than that, she should not take long. Can we safely wait until after the New Year festival, tomorrow?"

"I will meet you at the temple of Balg. Between us and those of my men who will join me, I think Ziva will be safe." Crites set his glass on the table beside his chair.

"Then it is settled, two days after the New Year Festival. You will be able to find a priest to officiate the mating?" Orak sipped his wine and set the glass on his desk.

"I will find one, by tomorrow. All will be prepared on my side." Crites drained the last of the drink from his glass and set it on the desk. "I must go, if I am to have everything prepared in three days. I will meet you at the festival."

The two men stood and clasped wrists. "Until tomorrow, then. Be safe. I do not want to lose her to Qinten after all this."

"And you protect her for me. I will leave my men here. We will take no chances that Qinten will try one more time to abduct her," Crites said as he opened the door. "Until tomorrow."

Orak waved. "Until tomorrow."

Orak picked up his glass, drained it, and sighed. Now to talk with Ziva.

~ ~ ~

Ziva sat with Tigre in her lap, musing about the contract her father was making with Crites. He left her with no feelings of dread. For that, she was grateful.

She wondered if Crites would allow Tigre to join her in his home. He probably would not accept the cat on their bed. Men were funny like that. Would they sleep in the same bed or would she have separate apartments as she did in Orak's home? She would find out.

She had no experience with mated men and women. Elin was ill when she came to Orak's home. She occupied a separate apartment because of her illness. Her friends didn't talk about their parents' sleeping arrangements. Whatever their parents did would be natural for them. Nothing to comment on.

When she searched her memory for her own parents, her mama and papa, there was a vague image of them sleeping together. If she admitted the truth to herself, she was not certain she wanted to sleep with a mate. Not even Crites. Not yet. Not that it mattered. The decision would be his.

Tigre purred and arched his back, bumping his head into her hand to pet him. Ziva complied, enjoying his luxurious fur.

Orak tapped on the door to her apartment and entered.

Ziva jumped up, dumping Tigre on the floor. He yowled and ran under a chair for safety.

Ziva stepped into Orak's arms. "Is it done?"

"Yes. You and I will sign the official papers at the mating ceremony, but it is completed."

"When will the ceremony be?" Ziva looked up into her father's kind eyes.

"In three days. Can you be ready that fast?"

"If Skyla can make a new dress in that time, I will be ready." Ziva glanced about her room, feeling as if she were seeing it for the first time. "Tomorrow is the New Year Festival. She is pretty fast and good. She should have a new dress made by then."

"Then you will be ready?"

Ziva didn't want to answer that question, yet. "Where are we going for the Festival, tomorrow? Certainly not to the Lorcan temple?"

"Never again. I am finished with Lorca," Orak said with a shudder. "Tomorrow we go to Balg. I must spread myself among the different temples that purchase my goods."

"If we must …"

"You know the law. We must attend the celebration at one of the official locations."

Ziva lifted a shoulder in a shrug. "You can't blame me for trying."

"No. If we could, …. But, we cannot. Will you be ready for the mating in three days?"

"If I must. There is not much to do, is there. Prepare to leave your home, the only home I remember, and Father I love dearly. Oh, Father," Ziva threw herself into his arms and allowed the tears to fall. "Will he be good to me? Is this the right man for me?"

Orak pulled the square of linen from his pocket and handed it to her. She wiped the tears and blew her nose. Then, still holding her father's hand, she pulled him to sit beside her.

Orak settled himself comfortably on the seat. "Com has investigated him, talked with everyone he could find who knows Crites. He spoke with the men who work for him at his race track and the men who frequent the Young Men's Society. None can remember a cruel act or an unkind word. Beyond that, he keeps his opinions to himself. That can be good or bad."

"Do you feel safe to give me to him, then?" Ziva sniffed.

"I do, or at least I hope he will be good to you."

~ ~ ~

Qinten's mood improved. It helped that Nat had found all the needed animals for the many ceremonies. Kept busy by last minute preparations for the New Year Festival and his upcoming mating, he did not have time for threats and beatings.

Qinten had returned from his meeting with Bram ecstatic. "Not only did I make an agreement with Bram, Korm joined us, asking that his daughter, too, be included in the agreement. Two mates for me should push me well in the standings for High Priest. Those other jealous priests cannot deny me. Two beautiful High Priestesses to lead the Planting Festival." He leaned back in his comfortable chair with hands laced behind his head. "Imagine. Two mates for me."

"Is it legal?" Nat dared to ask.

"Of course. I will not take a chance, especially now, on something that is not."

Nat let his breath out. "When will the mating rite be held?"

"I woke up the old codger, Astynax, on my way home. He will celebrate the mating two spans after mid-day in three days. Plenty of time for the girls to prepare. Plenty of time for my parents to prepare. They have waited for this day."

Now, the day before the New Year Festival, Qinten rushed around among the corrals, barns, and silos, checking the status of each of the animals and grains. Nat followed behind, making notes of the health of each animal.

Little girls were given animals to bathe and prepare. Older girls prepared the bullocks, while older boys cleaned and prepared the rams and he-goats. The little boys who would carry the bowls of grain were to be scrubbed clean by their mothers.

Two spans after the zenith, dirty and tired, they climbed out of the carriage and mounted the stairs to Qinten's apartments. Slaves ran ahead of them, warned of their coming, carrying buckets of hot water to Qinten's bathing room.

Bram and Korm would arrive in a span to discuss the final details of the mating contract between their daughters, Kara and Tawna, and Qinten. He would need to be clean of the fragrance of beasts' dung. The door to the apartment and the one to the bath stood open, allowing the slaves to carry in the buckets of water.

Qinten's dressing slave met him, leaving Nat free to go to his room. A slave had left a bucket of hot water on the floor near his bed. Good thing, for Nat smelled of dung, too.

He dropped his robe to the floor, and washed himself of the animal smell. Animal fragrance was clean, unlike the odor of sacrifices they would smell of the next day. Now clean, he found clean clothes. Sliding on clean slippers, he hurried down the hall and into Qinten's study.

As he walked in the door, the Master entered from his private rooms. Nat had timed it correctly. He glanced out the window to see if Bram's carriage had arrived. A simple carriage, painted along the borders with dark blue and a thin strip of white, marking the carriage as Bram's turned through the gate.

"Master, Bram comes," Nat said. "Will Korm be with him?"

"He should be. Remember, you are to record the agreement so we can sign it. I expect you to be fast and accurate," Qinten said as he took a seat in a comfort chair.

Nat set a bottle of Qinten's house wine in a bucket of cold water. He wiped out glasses and set them, along with the bucket and wine, near Qinten's seat.

He sat at his desk and straightened the stack of vellum. He checked the nibs of his pens, sharpening those that had become flat during use. He opened his ink and set it near, but not in a place he might accidentally knock it over. He did not want to encourage an occurrence of his master's angry behavior, especially in front of Bram and Korm. That would definitely cause another strapping.

Nat heard steps on the stairs and, at a nod from Qinten, moved to the door and opened it for Bram and Korm.

After the initial greetings in which Nat served them each a glass of wine, the men sat at the table to discuss the terms of the contract. Nat sat at his desk near the table to record the agreed upon conditions.

Nat flinched as Qinten agreed to treat Kara and Tawna well. He knew his Master's temper, short and nasty. As a slave, he had no say and knew that any interruption would result in bruises, at best.

Two spans later after Nat copied the agreement so each man would have one, Bram, Korm and Qinten signed each copy of the pact. Nat poured his master and his guests another glass of wine, then discretely left them to themselves.

The rite to officially mate Qinten and Kara and Tawna would happen three days after the New Year.

Chapter 35

Festival

Ziva walked into the sunshine among the new green of the growing plants in the garden enclosed by high walls. In this place, she could enjoy nature and feel safe from the tensions of the past weeks. Here, she could drink in the warmth of the rising sun and watch the plants grow. She sat on a bench, with an arch above, covered with vines just showing green. Little green shoots poked their heads through the soil, and when they felt the warm sun, stretched upward toward it. She knew she needed to get ready for the festival, later that day, but for now, she sat with the growing plants, absorbing sunlight.

"Mistress Ziva." Ana hurried toward her. "You cannot spend all day in the sun. Your fair skin will redden, and then, how will you look for the festival?"

Ziva lifted a hand and touched her warm face. "Already? I have not been here long, certainly not long enough to burn my skin." She glanced at the sun. It had moved a hand span closer to the apex. "Time moves faster than I want."

"Come in. I will cool your skin to protect it from the redness." Ana stared at the growing plants. "I understand your desire to sit here, but the shade plants that protect you have not leafed out."

"I know but this place is peaceful." She followed Ana toward the house. "Will I be able to enjoy this garden after the mating ceremony?"

"Crites may have a garden lovelier than this one." Ana smiled at her charge. "But, you must be ready for the New Year Festival. It begins at mid-day, and that is not long."

Ziva sighed and turned at the door back toward the garden, absorbing its beauty and hoping it would sustain her through the day ahead.

Much later, when the sun almost reached its midpoint of its travel through the sky, she hurried down the stairs toward the front door and Orak, who waited to travel with her to celebrate the New Year Festival.

Ana had surprised her with a new pale blue dress, the skirt flowed from her waist in frothy gathers. Near the hem, it took on a deeper blue, reminding her of deep waters. The neckline rose to the thin bones below her neck, her beads lay just on top, their orange and black contrasting with the pale blue.

She lifted her arms and felt the delicious softness of the silk against her arm. It was still cool enough to have sleeves fall below the elbow. Ana had taken extra time painting her face with delicate strokes, while acceding to Ziva's demands that it should not be heavy.

Orak held out his arms and she walked into his embrace. He spun her out and she turned to allow him to see all of the dress. "Lovely, my dear. You look like a New Year."

"Thank you, Father. Will Crites be there?" She stepped up into the carriage, accepting Orak's assistance.

"Yes. We discussed it at last night. We agreed to attend the festival at Balg." Orak settled beside her. The carriage driver closed the door and soon they were moving.

Ziva thought back to the intimate dinner. She and Orak had welcomed Crites to their home. He had been as kind and attentive as during the Harvest Festival at the Temple of Nimm. He teased her and made her laugh, insisted on feeding her tidbits of meat and grapes, and complemented her on her beauty. Orak joined in the teasing, supporting her when she felt insecure. The evening had been pleasant. If this was his true character, she could be happy living with him as her mate.

"Do you think he will be as kind to me as his mate as he has been when you are around?"

"No one speaks of cruelty. I hope he will continue to be kind." Orak's voice drifted off.

Ziva glanced out the window. They were nearly there.

"Will the ceremony be bloody?" She shivered. "I did not like the sacrifices at Lorca's Growing Festival."

"Festivals usually are bloody. The priests must show their honor to their god by the amount blood they offer. Balg is nearly as bloody as Lorca." Orak stared out the window. "I have never understood the need for so much blood."

Ziva reached for his hand and squeezed. "Must we stay for it?"

"I don't know how we can avoid it. All citizens of Nod are required to attend the festivals. We can only choose which one." Orak frowned at her. "I wish we had more choice. I would stay away entirely. I would not choose any of these bloody gods."

"Father."

"I know. Blasphemy. But, only this one time, in your presence. I have never uttered my private thoughts aloud before. And never again."

They rode on in silence, until the carriage slowed and halted at the front of the temple.

The door opened and Orak stepped out. "Are you getting out?"

Ziva moved toward the door, surprised to discover Crites' hand reaching out to help her out.

She stepped out, glad of his aid. He tucked her hand into the crook of his elbow and escorted her into the temple, following behind Orak.

"You are beautiful today, my dear," Crites murmured.

Ziva colored a bit. "This will cause gossip," she whispered.

"It will. I want Qinten to know you have a man in your life," Crites murmured.

Ziva giggled.

They entered the temple and gazed at the whirling color of men and women moving across the floor of the temple.

Orak smiled and left them to find his merchant friends. Crites settled Ziva's hand tighter on his elbow. "Shall we?"

She nodded and they moved to the floor. They danced, spinning and whirling to the music. They stopped with the music, and joined the stream of dancers toward the drinks.

"Ziv?"

Ziva turned to the voice. Tawna stood beside her, waiting for a turn to choose a drink.

"Tawna! I did not think to see you here. Don't your parents follow the cult of Lorca?"

"They do. Mother likes to visit each of the temples, ending at Lorca. We came here first. Who is this you are with?"

Ziva pulled Crites close. "This is Crites. Do you remember him from the party at Roven's?"

"Oh, yes. Hello, Crites."

Crites nodded.

"Does this mean …?"

"It means we are together here, with my Father's approval."

Tawna's eyebrows rose. She glowed in a way unusual for Tawna. Before Ziva could ask her about it, the people in front of her moved away and she chose a drink. Ziva turned to choose her own drink. She reached for a glass of plum juice, but Crites slipped a glass of water into her hand.

"You won't be happy with that. They slip a drug into the fruit drinks that takes away your will. Stick to the water, the drug cannot be hidden in water."

"Thank you. I have feared something like this." Ziva took the water and sipped, then swallowed half of it. Crites took a glass of water and guided her to a seat away from the crowds.

They visited, then danced again. When servants announced the meal, Crites led her to a table and seated her next to Orak.

"Are you having a good time?" he asked.

"I am."

Crites sat beside her. He leaned forward to speak to Orak. "What have you discovered?"

"Balg won't do. He requires personal sacrifice."

"I was afraid of that," Crites sat back.

Before Ziva could ask about their cryptic discussion, servants brought them plates of food. Tawna's family joined them at their table, and she joined in their conversation.

"It worked," Tawna whispered to Ziva.

"What?"

"Kara and me. With Qinten."

"When?"

"Soon."

The young women had no chance to say anything more. After the excellent meal, Tawna's family left for another temple and Ziva and Crites strolled past the tables selling crafters' wares and danced. They moved to the back of the crowd when the priests prepared the sacrifices.

Ziva looked at the floor. She had no desire to watch. A girl cried out, a goat bleated. She sucked in her breath and stared at the red and white stripes on the hem of Crites tunic, hanging nearly to his feet. He reached out and took her hand.

"It will be over, soon. Then we can leave," Orak whispered in her ear.

They stood together at the back near the wall, waiting for the rite to end. When the drums began to beat, signaling the end, Crites grasped Ziva's hand and led her toward the door. Orak went ahead to call for their carriage. He had warned the driver they would be leaving as soon as the sacrificial rite ended. He waited with the carriage and Crites shiny black horse tied to the back.

Crites helped Ziva climb inside the carriage, allowed Orak to enter, then stepped inside and closed the door behind him. He knocked on the roof, the signal to leave. The carriage moved away, and Ziva relaxed into the back of her seat, with Crites beside her and her father sitting across from her.

~ ~ ~

Nat stood at the edge of the room, watching the masses of people celebrating at the New Year Festival, hosted by Qinten. Only days before the deadline, he discovered two suppliers who had sufficient numbers of animals to meet Lorca's needs. Qinten had acknowledged his assistance, giving him a silver and time off during the festival.

He dressed in the required tunic and robe of his station as personal assistant to Qinten. His tunic hung to his knees in gold satin. He had carefully washed his body and washed and brushed his hair. He hoped to see Liana serving refreshments.

Everyone in the kitchen would be drafted to help. He did not want her to be seen and desired by the Master.

He drifted toward the entrance to the kitchen. Drak walked out and raised his eyebrows in greeting. Nat nodded and stood still, watching the crowd for the short tunics of the kitchen staff. Avram walked toward him and stopped, holding out his tray. Nat took the last pastry from his tray and smiled.

"How is it in the kitchens, Avram?"

"No worse than usual. Cook keeps us hopping. We've been peeling and cooking for over a week getting ready for this." Avram waved at the crowd.

"I bet you have been busy. This is one of the busier festivals. This and the Growing Festival, where Qinten can be included in all the sacrifices. At least, you will get a break for the Planting Festival."

"Yeah, I look forward to that one. Maybe Cook will take some of us there. I hear it is a festival to see." Avram grinned.

"Nah. You don't want to attend that one, at least not at Lorca. You are too young. For that matter, I am too young, and will always be."

Avram threw his head back and cackled. "Oh, Nat. Always the tease." Avram hurried into the kitchen for another tray.

Nat leaned against the wall eating the pastry and watching the dancing girls. He was happy to see that Ziva and Orak hadn't come here to celebrate. It was good to rest for a time, and not have to worry about anyone. Well, he hoped he didn't have to worry about Liana.

Drak returned, his tray empty.

"Good food, huh?" he asked.

"Must be. It flies off my tray. I haven't tasted it yet."

"When you come out with another tray of it, stop by and let me give it a try. I'll tell you if it's good." Nat winked at his friend.

"And not even share any with me, I bet."

"You know you can't eat while serving."

"Some friend you are." Drak laughed and pushed through the door.

Nat watched the servants come and go, watching for Liana. At last, she exited the kitchen, her arms full of a huge tray laden with fruits. She smiled at Nat and offered him one.

"The green one there," she pointed with her chin, "is called kiwi. It has an interesting flavor. Avram and Drak brought them from the market yesterday."

Nat picked one off the tray and smiled. "I haven't seen you today. Have you been staying in the kitchen?"

Liana smiled and waggled her eyebrows. "You been looking for me?"

"I have."

"Good." She started to leave, then turned, "Yes. Cook has kept me busy in the kitchen. Couldn't keep me back any longer."

"Be careful," he called as she walked away from him, a little extra wiggle in her hips.

He watched her as she offered the tray to men and women along the path to the serving table. She set her half empty tray on the table, backed away, and walked toward the kitchen door.

One of the male guests intercepted Liana, bending close to whisper in her ear and touch her bottom.

Nat knew these free men had the right, but he did not have to like it. He pushed away from the wall and took a step forward. The man laughed and moved away. Liana had handled it on her own. Nat relaxed again.

Another man intercepted Liana, kissing her and putting his hands on her breasts. Nat could hear her, laughing it off, pushing him gently away. He would not listen, and slipped a hand beneath her tunic. Nat found himself striding toward them.

"Excuse me, sir."

The man whipped around to look up at him. "Whaddaya want."

He had been drinking too much of the wine.

"I apologize for interrupting your fun, sir, but Priest Qinten needs all his servants to be helping serve the food, just now. Perhaps, you can resume this little game later?"

"Priest?" Confusion filled his voice and twisted his face. "Wha' priest?"

"Priest Qinten, the owner of this home and temple. I must insist that you let his servant go." Nat took Liana by the arm and tugged her out of the drunk's grasping hands. "Perhaps later?"

He escorted Liana by the elbow back to the kitchen door.

"He has the right. I am a slave, he is a free man," Liana hissed.

Nat saw the brightness of tears in her eyes. "He may have the right, but he does not have my permission. And, no I do not own you, but I would like to be closer to you. Please ask Cook to keep you in the kitchen, safe from these drunks."

"I-I can't do that. I have to what he says." Liana stammered.

Nat walked down the short hallway and entered the kitchen, still holding Liana's elbow.

"What are you doing?" she gasped.

"Keeping you safe. Ah, there you are Cook. Would you be so kind as to keep this slave in the kitchen where she belongs?" Nat took on the tone of his station. "She has no business among the drunks."

Cook glanced up to Nat. "Of course, sir." He took Liana by the arm. "You know you do not go into the serving area. What will you do if Master Qinten sees you?" He turned to Nat and raised his eyebrows.

Nat nodded. Cook understood. He snatched a meat roll on his way from the kitchen.

He resumed his station near the door, watching the crowd, and ensuring that Liana stayed away. She did not return. He was grateful to Cook for understanding.

Master Qinten swept past, dancing with a tiny raisin colored beauty. Her hair shone with red in the black. This must be the girl Kara, he had agreed to mate with in days. She tipped her head back to look into his eyes and laughed. The top of her head barely reached the middle of Qinten's chest.

Poor girl.

Later, Qinten danced past with a tall girl with dusky brown skin and long, dark hair. This must be Tawna. Nat shook his head. Who would have thought he would have two mates?

The music ended. Nat watched the crowd move toward the seating, Qinten escorted the girl to a seat at the front next to the other one. He moved with his assistant priests to stand in the front of the room, the figure of Lorca behind them.

The huge eagle stared past his giant beak at the crowd. His enormous phallus stood up, waiting. Nat cringed and moved through the crowd, purposefully ignoring the touches from both men and women, until he reached the hallway leading to Qinten's private rooms. He would be needed after the sacrifices.

Chapter 36

Preparations

Nat worked alone in the study. The sun rose high in the sky, nearly to its zenith before Qinten stumbled in and slumped into a chair.

"My mating ceremony is in two days. Are you working on the details?"

Nat glanced up. "I have sent messages to the cooks." Nat picked up his list and glanced at it. "Cook will have discussed it with your father's cooks. What else will you need?"

"Did you tell the tailor I will need a new tunic and mating clothing?"

Nat nodded and checked it off his list.

"Have you warned the steward that two mates will come into our home in two days?" Qinten cradled his head in his hands.

"I have. They will have adjoining rooms. Do you want their rooms to adjoin yours, or across the hall? He is waiting on that information."

Qinten lifted his head from his hand. "Adjoining? No, that is too risky."

"Then across the hall?"

"Yes, and down. Have him make certain they have nice apartments. Theirs should be adjoining, but be certain the doors are far from mine. I want some privacy."

Privacy for your reprehensible behavior. Yes, that would be good for your new mates as well. "Yes, sir. I will give the instructions to the steward." Nat made the note on his list of things to be done. "Is there anything else?"

"Not now. When you come back, I will have a list of people to send the invitations. You may need help getting them all written. I am certain there will be other things for you to do. Go talk with the steward. He has only until tomorrow to complete the new apartments. Do not take too much time. I will need you soon."

"Yes, sir." Nat rolled his notes and slipped them inside his robe, thinking which of these needed the information first. Probably the steward.

He found the steward across the hall, leaning across the plans of the building.

"What have you found?"

These rooms were originally apartments. This one, here," the steward pointed to one set of rooms on the plans, "and here."

"Can you open a door between them? The Master wants them to be able to go back and forth." Nat leaned over the plans and stared at them.

"That can be done. Does he want a door opened into his apartment?"

"No. He wants his privacy."

The steward growled deep in his throat, but kept his opinion to himself.

"The Master expects you to create lovely apartments for his mates," Nat waved his arms around the space, "fit for high priestesses and mates of a man of his stature. Make sure their doors don't open close to his."

The steward frowned. "I understand. I expected this, knowing the Master." He shrugged and turned to the workmen and gave them instructions.

Men picked up tools and spread out, each with a task. Nat nodded to the steward and left for the workroom of the tailor. There, he discussed the needed clothing for the mating ceremony.

"Remember to make new small clothes for the Master. He would not want to look bad ..."

"I know how to make mating clothing. I would not forget the small clothes. In gold?"

"Yes, in gold."

The tailor growled. "I'll have to purchase more gold fabric."

"Get it quickly. The mating ceremony is in two days."

"Yes, Nat, it will be done in time."

Nat left the tailor and strode to the kitchen.

Liana met him at the kitchen door. "Your message sure put our kitchen in a stir, especially after the challenges of a festival yesterday. What was in it? Cook won't tell."

Nat wrapped his arms around her. "Nothing much. The Master is to be mated in two days. Has Cook sent messages out to Caomh's cooks, yet?" He kissed her gently on the cheek.

"Yes, just now. Baker and he have their heads together. Drak and Avram have taken over the meals for the household." Liana returned the embrace.

"We will be fed well enough, then. Avram and Drak know better than to feed the Master less than the best food."

Nat and Liana dropped their arms and walked into the kitchen.

"A fine mess you caused, Nat," Drak growled. "Avram and I have to cook for the household. The Master will lash us for sure if we cook."

"No, you will be fine. You have watched Baker and Avram has helped Cook. You will do fine." Nat playfully slugged him in the shoulder.

"You will suffer along with everyone else." Drak laughed.

"Probably so. Where are Cook and Baker?"

Drak nodded his head in the direction of the table in the corner. "Over there, making plans."

"Thanks. You'd better get back to work so the Master doesn't go hungry." Drak and Nat laughed, then separated to complete their assignments.

Nat found Baker and Cook with their heads together and a stack of vellum between them, filled with lists.

"Will you be ready in time?" Nat asked.

"We will need the boys to find some special ingredients at the market, some we don't often use, but, yes. we will be ready. We will need to meet tonight with Caomh's cook and baker tonight to be certain everything is prepared for a crowd." Cook said, looking up at Nat. "I assume there will be a large crowd."

"There should be. The Master is wealthy, the son of the governor, and seeking to be high priest of Lorca. I expect there to be many at the celebration dinner. Is there anything I can do to help this go better for you?"

"Can you go purchase the specialty foods? You know how to barter." Baker asked. "No? I thought not."

"I do not think the Master will allow me to go. I can send others."

"No. We will send Drak and Avram. They will know what we need. You go back to the Master," Cook said. "Keep him happy so we can get our work finished."

Nat slapped the men on the back in parting and left the kitchens. Liana waited for him near the door.

"When will you come back to see me?" she asked.

"As soon as I can. The next days will be busy."

Nat returned to the study to find a list on his desk. Qinten was gone. Nat sat down, breathing a heavy sigh at the long list, dipped his pen in the ink, and started writing the invitations.

~ ~ ~

Ana stood in front of Ziva's wardrobe, pulling dresses from it and throwing them across the bed. Ziva sat in her chair, helping her sort them into piles of dresses to be given away and which were to be kept. Ziva regularly sorted her clothing, giving those she no longer wore or no longer fit to a charity for the poor. Her silks were much too nice for the very poor, but girls whose fathers were moving upward could wear them.

"What about this dress?" Ana held up the filmy top the color of peacock's feathers and the skirt of darker blue she wore to the Growing Festival.

"Ugh. Is that still here? I thought it was gone long ago. I could never wear it again. It doesn't cover me." Ziva shuddered at the memory of the one and only time she wore it.

"It is exciting and sad to see you prepare to leave our house, Ziva. I remember when you came the first day. You were so dirty. We had to scrub you three times before the water ran clear. I have never seen such a dirty little girl." Ana tossed the dress into the give-away pile and reached into the wardrobe for another dress.

"I don't remember that day, Ana. I was three, I think. My first memories were of you dressing me to take me to see Mother." She pointed at the save pile.

"When we got you clean and dressed, you were a pretty little thing, different from Liva, but you brought joy to a sorrow-filled house." Ana retrieved another dress, this one a sea green.

"I forgot about that one. I wonder if it still fits." Ziva took the dress from Ana and stood to hold it in front of her. "I must have grown since I wore it last. Look, it is too short and I doubt it will go around me anymore."

"Into the giveaway pile, then?" Ana took the dress from her. "Too bad, you looked pretty in that. I'm sure some other girl will appreciate it."

"I am certain she will love it, though she cannot look as beautiful in it as you did." Orak said.

"Oh, Father. I did not expect you to be home today." Ziva leaped from her seat and embraced him.

"I wanted to spend time with you, while you are still my little girl." Orak spoke into her hair as he held her close.

"Everything is happening so fast. Is this the way it usually is for a girl? One day she is part of her father's household, loving and content, the next, the mating contract is signed and she is to be mated?"

"No, little Ziva." Orak released the embrace and the two sat down, still holding hands. "For most girls, it is different. If their father loves them—"

"If their father loves them? Don't all father's love their daughters?"

"Not all. Some see their daughters as bargain chips to be traded for wealth."

Ziva covered her exclamation with her free hand.

Orak shook his head. "Those who are loved may have long, drawn out discussions to ensure that the right man is chosen to be her mate. The planning for the mating rite extends over weeks, if not months."

"And for those who are not loved? Does the time extend for them, as well?"

"Not usually. She usually has no knowledge of the discussions until her father informs her that she will be mated and usually that mating occurs within days, if not hours of his telling her."

"Why would it happen so suddenly? I see no reason for a little planning."

"Ah, you would think they would be allowed a day or two to remember their home and family." Orak breathed noisily through his nose. "I have heard that they fear the girl will run away or take her own life. The matches are not always good for the girl."

"So bad she would run or take her life? Why?"

"Men are not always kind to women, and the girls know it. Many times, the man is much older than the girl, and has … well, his desires for a young girl are not honorable."

"And her father still allows the mating?"

Orak touched her cheek. "Remember, I said they were not loved. The fathers not only allow the mating, they sell their daughters to those vile men. It is a contract we sign. Between Crites and myself, it was an agreement that you would mate with him and he would protect and care for you, as I have, in love. Not all girls get that."

"Oh." Ziva lapsed into thought.

"You are lucky to be loved." Orak lifted her hand and kissed it. "And I do love you."

"I am lucky in many ways, to be here, to be loved, and to be given to a man who cares enough for me to want to protect me."

In the silence of their thoughts, Ana continued to pull clothing from Ziva's wardrobe. Ziva flicked her hand toward the pile intended for giving away or the one to be packed for her move to Crites' home the next day.

"Crites is willing to mate with me even though I was purchased from the slave market?" Ziva gazed into Orak's face.

"He is an intelligent man."

"And he still would choose to be my mate?" Ziva nodded and grimaced at once. "Why would he want a girl with my past?"

Orak shook his head. "I have no idea. He seems to be a honorable man, more honorable than Qinten. I trust him."

"I suppose we must trust him." She closed her eyes for a long breath, considering the face of the man she was to mate. "At least, I feel no blackness when I am with him."

Orak stood. "Our time alone is nearly past. Crites is here. There are things we need to discuss about your mating to him. Can you come now?" Orak offered Ziva his hand.

She sighed deeply and nodded. "Yes, I am ready. I will miss these visits, Father." She turned to the older woman, "Ana, can you take care of these?"

"Of course."

Chapter 37

Tangles

Nat sat at working at his desk. He had given other slaves who could write the responsibility to write out the invitations for Qinten's mating ceremony. The worked in a room down the hall from Qinten's study.

A messenger arrived from the kitchen for Nat. He opened it and read the contents.

He dropped the scrap of vellum and stared ahead. How soon before the Master returns? Qinten left to check the fitting on his wedding clothing just breaths before. If he knew about this, his friends would be sold from his house.

Nat had a few minutes. He rushed from the study to the kitchen.

"Where are they?"

Cook glanced up from his work and bent his head toward the cool room.

Nat rushed into the cool room and found Avram and Drak lying on the floor. Blood and bruises covered their faces, their short robes were torn. He bent beside them.

"What happened? I thought you could go to the market and back safely."

"Kenji," Drak moaned. "Caught us by surprise. Leaving the market." He stopped and held his ribs.

"They beat us," Avram moaned holding his stomach. "Didn't do anything."

"You didn't have to do anything. You were seen with me," Nat brought his hand close to Avram's face and decided not to touch him.

"Once," Avram said.

"That is all it takes. Kenji has hated me from the first time he saw me."

"What will we do? Will the Master sell us?" Drak moaned.

"Not if I can help it. He is busy preparing for his mating. I'll have them help you to the dorm when they can. Get well as soon as you can."

"Will Cook agree? He and Baker need helpers?" Avram asked.

"I'll talk to him. He sent the message to me. Did you manage to bring back the anise and pomegranates?" Nat sat back on his heels.

"Most of it. We knew Cook needed them." Avram turned his head away and a tear leaked from his eyes. "It hurts, but I don't want to leave here."

"You won't. Get well. I'll go talk with Cook."

Nat left the cool room and found Cook. He stood back, careful to keep flour and other bits of kitchen refuse from his clothes. He didn't need the Master to know he'd been in the kitchen again.

"Can you manage a day or two without them?"

Cook lifted his head and stared at Nat. "One day. With this celebration, I need them."

"Have someone take them to the dorm and wash the blood from their faces. They are tough. They will be back tomorrow."

"They will have to be," Cook growled.

"Kenji attacked them because of me…" Nat said.

"No. Kenji knew they came from Qinten's kitchen. He hates Qinten. I'll help them." Cook waved his spoon toward Nat's face. "Don't take the blame for this."

"Thanks, Cook. I have to get back to Qinten, or he'll know something is happening. Take care of them."

Nat waited just as long as it took for Cook to nod, then turned on his slippered heel and rushed back to the study. He sat in his chair and picked up his pen as Qinten walked into the room.

"I should fire that tailor," Qinten roared. "His measurements were off and has to take half of it apart."

"He is the only one you have. Who else would you get in the time you have?" Nat dropped a sheet of vellum over the message from Cook.

"No one. That is the only reason he isn't sold this afternoon." Qinten dropped into his soft chair. "Will the messages inviting people to my mating be ready soon?"

"I have not checked on them in a span. I'll check on them. They should be ready, soon." Nat stood.

"Good." Qinten leaned his head back and covered his eyes. "Too much to do just to take mates."

"It only happens once," Nat said.

"For most men," Qinten sighed. "I won't go through this again."

Nat left the room and then sighed deeply, glad that the girls Qinten would be mating were not Ziva.

He opened the door to the room the slave scribes worked in and checked on their work. A stack of velum sat in the center of the table. Nat picked up the stack thumbed through it, spot checking their work. "Looks good. How close are you to being finished?"

One looked up, "Nearly."

"Good." Nat picked up the stack of vellum up from the table. "Bring the last ones to me as soon as they are finished."

He took the stack back to Qinten's study and dropped it on his desk. "They have nearly completed the task. I'll start the rolling them."

"The seal is on my desk," Qinten waved his hand. "You know where and the braids. I've put together a list of where to send them when you are finished."

"Yes, sir."

Nat found the wax and seal on Qinten's desk, and pulled out a handful of braids. He worked rolling, sealing and tying braids around each invitation, then set them into a messenger bag. A scribe brought him the last of the invitations and slipped out the door as he worked. A span after he started, he set the last message into the bag.

"They are ready."

Qinten lifted his head. "Give them to the messenger with the list. Be sure he knows to deliver one to each person on the list."

"Of course, sir. I'll go check on the apartments for your mates."

"No. I'll do it." Qinten pushed himself up from his seat. You take care of those messages." Nat took the bag of messages and the list to the messenger and sent him on his way.

When he returned, Qinten was gone. Nat found the message from Cook and tucked it under his robe where Qinten would not find it.

~ ~ ~

Orak walked with Ziva to his office, where Crites waited. When they entered, he stood and smiled.

"You would mate me even knowing my history?" Ziva asked.

Orak moved to his favorite chair and sat down, watching his beloved daughter, listening to her and Crites.

Crites took Ziva in his arms. "Because of your history. You are special. I have heard those who come looking for the lost children of the prophet."

Crites guided Ziva to the other two chairs. She sat in the one close to Orak, and he smiled. Crites pulled the other chair next to hers and took her hand in his.

"Mahonri came to me last night seeking a way to steal money from me."

"How did he connect you with Ziva," Orak asked with a growl deep in his throat. "We have been careful to keep the knowledge of this close."

"I don't know. Perhaps he heard of my search for a priest to perform the rite. He came to me and admitted to taking her from the men who stole her," Crites turned his gaze from Orak to Ziva, "and bringing you here to Nod. He has heard your papa's plea for his lost children."

"My Papa is searching for us? Who is he?" Ziva put her hand over her mouth and looked at her father, who sat in his desk chair.

She sat in one of the comfortable chairs. Crites held her hand and sat in the other.

"Enos, grandson of Adam. They send messages, when they can, searching for you and your brother."

"I don't understand. You are a grandson of Cain. I am a daughter of the prophets. How can we mate? Doesn't your family hate mine?" She pulled her brows together.

"My fathers do, I don't." He pushed a lock of dark hair out of his eyes, then leaned toward Ziva and gently brushed a lock of her honey blond hair behind an ear.

"My mother was taken against her will from a village near Home Valley where Adam lives by raiders. My father saw her fair beauty, much like yours, and became her mate. I am the only child of that mating. Because I was sickly and weak, after my father died in a battle, she convinced Tubal-Cain to allow her to take me to his country home."

Ziva glanced up into Crites' searching gaze.

"I grew up there, growing ever stronger in the fresh air and eating the healthy food. Seth and a young son, perhaps it was your father, stopped at our home during a heavy rain. Mother gave them refuge from the storms, and listened to the words he taught. I sat at their feet listening and learning. I follow no cult in Nod, though I attend the festivals as required. Secretly, I honor Jehovah."

"Jehovah?" The name rolled off her tongue and felt right.

"Yes. Jehovah, God of your fathers."

Ziva glanced at Orak. "Is this why we honor none of the cult gods? Did you know?"

"Mahonri did mention Jehovah, and after Elin's death, I could no longer follow the cult of Enid. None of the other cults entice me. You know this." Pain stabbed Orak in the stomach. "How can I believe a god of so much blood can help us?"

"Not even Jehovah?" Ziva asked.

"Jehovah isn't allowed in all of Canaan. You should know this," he growled.

"How can I know about a God I have never heard of?"

"Jehovah has been banned since the beginning of Nod. The priests no longer preach against him, thinking no one knows enough of him to be a problem." Crites smiled and squeezed her hand. "No reason for you to know, since you have lived in Nod for so long."

Orak watched Ziva take in this information and wondered if it would change her love for him. The things he told her before had not. He would have to trust her love.

"Have you determined who can perform the ceremony if you don't want any of the cult's priests to do it?" Orak asked.

Ziva had not considered this to be a problem. How could they mate, without a priest? She turned to gaze into Crites' dark eyes, waiting to hear how this would happen.

"I will not go before the major cults." Crites quivered briefly. "There are some small cults, so small they are forgotten. They have no temple, but they are recognized by the government. We have two choices." Crites glanced to Orak's face, then back at Ziva. "We can accept the assistance of one of these or we can speak the words of mating in front of a few guests. What do you choose?"

Orak felt her gaze, as she waited for his answer. This would always be important to her. He could not choose.

"You must make the choice, Ziv. This is your life. You must decide," he said.

"I am your daughter in every way. What do you recommend?"

Her answer sent a thrill through him. "It would be better, in your battle against Qinten, to have an official mating. Speaking on your own in front of others is legal, but having a priest bless it gives you greater power against Qinten and his rumors."

"And it will soothe the ruffled rooster feathers of my grandfather," Crites added.

"Then it is settled, we go to the priest of a smaller cult." Ziva glanced at Orak and then to Crites. Any idea who?"

"Actually, I do. Cotta of Talb has agreed to perform the ceremony tonight, at dusk."

"Today?" She looked toward Orak. "I thought we planned it would be tomorrow? Skyla hasn't finished my dress yet."

"Yes, she has," Orak pulled a box from behind his desk. "I had her deliver it to me, rather than you. I wanted it to be a surprise."

He held it out for her. She let go of Crites hand to take it. She lifted out a beautiful cream-colored satin dress and pulled it to her chest. "Oh, it's beautiful," she breathed. "But why not wait until tomorrow?"

"Because I do not trust Qinten. Even though he signed a contract to leave you alone..." Orak's voice trailed off.

"Oh. I understand. I don't trust him, either." Ziva turned her gaze from Orak to Crites. "Will that work?"

"It will for me. Anything else we need?" Crites asked.

"Can my friends attend? Tawna and Kara would be hurt if I didn't include them."

"I purchased the fabric from Korm. He plans to be there." Orak winked at Ziva. "We will need to send them a message to invite them. Where, Crites?"

"My house. Everything will be ready."

"We will be there." Orak held his hand out for Ziva's. "You will need to get ready. Go on upstairs."

Ziva hugged Crites, then leaned over to kiss Orak on the cheek. "Thank you. I love you."

She turned, grabbed the box, and ran out of Orak's office to ask Ana to help her get ready.

Orak felt the brightness of tears dampen his eyes.

"She is my jewel. You will take good care of her?" He glared at the man who would soon be his son.

"I love her, too, Orak. I will treat her well."

Chapter 38

Love Mates

Orak climbed into his carriage and leaned back in the seat as they moved down the road toward his home. It felt strange to leave Ziv behind. She had been a part of his life for years. They would celebrate her 16th year in a couple months, 13 years in his home. And now, she was gone.

He missed her already. She was the light of his life, the reason to keep going. After Elin and Liva's accident, only Ziva's cheerful presence had prompted him to wake up in the mornings and keep moving forward. Now … Well, now she was in another man's home, mated to him. She would be responsible to keep another man happy.

Orak put his hand over his eyes, working to prevent the tears from falling. Ziva had not returned to Home Valley and her other family. She lived across the city, he could reach her in less than a half a hand span. She belonged to another family.

Perhaps, soon, she would bring children of her own into her home.

And, still, he missed her.

He scrubbed the tears from his face and smiled at the memory of her mating.

Ziva had come from her apartment floating in the satiny beauty of her new dress. Ana had convinced her that now, as a woman to be mated, it was appropriate for her to wear more face paint. She had not used too much, just enough more to emphasize her vivid eyes and shy, sweet smile.

They rode together through the streets of Nod, discussing the upcoming rite. Ziva had been justifiably nervous. She told him she had been thinking of mating for months, and considering this particular mating with Crites for a only a week. The actual day of mating had been sprung on her.

Orak remembered his pride in her, as she stood straight, barely resting her arm on his as she walked gracefully toward the front of the room, where Crites waited for her. He watched her focus on Crites, unaware of the room full of people there to witness the ceremony.

Orak saw them, felt their eyes on him and his beautiful daughter. Crites' mother, Lilah, was the only other guest with fair skin, and hers was shaded a darker brown the Ziva's. She sat with Tubal-Cain and his mate, Cili, Crites' grandparents, in the front seats. Kara and Tawna, and their parents, filled in the seats behind. Ana, Com, Keb, and others of his servants filled in the back of the room. Members of the Red Guard stood around the room, at the doors, and at the entrance to the house. Orak suspected they stood watch all around the house.

He placed Ziva's tiny, white hand in Crites' huge, dark one, and stepped back to observe the ritual of mating Ziva to Crites. Unlike many of the large, elaborate ceremonies in the temples to the gods, Cotta spoke a few words and suggested that Ziva surrender her will to Crites, with honor and respect. A slight shiver had stirred her dress. He understood her fears.

After Cotta completed his words, and declared them mated, Crites had swept Ziva into his arms and kissed her deeply. The crowd applauded, though kisses were not a normal part of the rite.

When the pair turned to face their well-wishers, Ziva's face colored a garnet red. Orak stepped forward to congratulate the pair, when a disturbance at the door drew his attention away from them.

Qinten growled and shouted as he pushed his way past Crites' Reds. Crites must have signaled them, for they allowed him to pass. He stumbled as they released him, then pulled himself to his moderate height and stalked toward the couple.

"So, this is why you refused me?" he spat. "You wanted another. My wealth, my power, and my standing were not good enough for you." He turned on Orak. "What did he promise you? Did he give you gold? A contract to purchase all your cattle? You will not sell one more animal to Lorca!"

Qinten had stood so close to Orak that he felt his shouting as wind upon his face. Rather than step back, as he knew Qinten desired, he stepped forward, bringing his nose next to the angry priest's face.

"I agreed to allow Crites to mate Ziva to ensure you could not," he growled in a low voice. "You have destroyed my family in more ways than you will ever know. You. Will. Not. Destroy. My. Daughter. I told you already. My goods, my animals, and my grains will never again cross the gates of the Lorca temple or any of its priests as long as you are associated with it."

Orak stared into Qinten's hate-twisted face until Qinten backed away. He glanced back to see Nat near the door. "Take your master from this place. He wasn't invited and is unwanted."

Orak returned his stare to Qinten who continued to stared at him, eyes shining black with hatred. Nat came forward and gently took his master by the arm.

"Master Qinten. Come with me."

Qinten grudgingly allowed himself to be led away, all the while casting hateful stares at Orak. Orak returned his stare until the door closed behind the man and his slave. Even then, he stood, staring at the door until he heard the shout of the carriage driver and the rattle of wheels pass the entrance to Crites' walled home. Only then did he slowly turn to face his daughter, whose fear-filled face stared at the door.

Crites pulled her to him. "That is the last time you will ever be confronted by that man. He has no power over you. I am your mate. I will care for you."

Orak closed the distance between them. "Do not fear, my dear Ziv, Qinten has no power over me or you. We are free from him."

"I know, Father. But what about Nat?" Ziva whispered. "He still must face Qinten's wrath."

Crites hugged her close. "He is strong. He can manage it. I will see what I can do, tomorrow. This is your mating day. Smile and greet our guests."

Ziva glanced with fear on her face at Orak, who smiled at her. She then placed a smile on her face and turned to greet Crites' mother and grandparents and the other guests who waited for a turn to congratulate the pair. Orak saw Ziva's friends hang back, waiting until all the others moved away from the pair and on to find seats in the dining room for the feast his cook had helped to prepare. He walked toward the door and waited for them to greet Ziva in low tones.

He couldn't hear the conversation, but he could see Tawna's and Kara's faces. Tears washed away carefully painted faces. They shook their heads almost in unison. A servant appeared at their side, Crites had managed to signal one, offering them large squares of white linen. The girls took the squares and dabbed the tears away, before taking turns to hug her.

Kara and Tawna did not stay for the dinner. They took Kara's family carriage home and sent it back for her parents, who stayed, as Orak's guests.

Qinten's appearance dampened the joy of the occasion briefly. The guests wondered at his words and behavior. Then, the food was served and he was forgotten. For his sake, Orak hoped they wouldn't remember it later.

Orak ensured that his and Ziva's special guests, his servants, were seated in a side room and provided with a portion of the feast before taking his own seat next to Ziva. He didn't know when she would return to his home and he chose to spend the last of the evening near her.

The party had lasted long into the night until Tubal-Cain announced it well beyond the time for Crites to take his new mate to the mating bed. Ziva blushed and Crites laughed. Orak joined Crites' grandfather in escorting him to the sleeping room. Lilah and Cili escorted Ziva, whispering words of encouragement in her ears.

The men undressed Crites, leaving him only his small clothes and stood behind him. Lilah and Cili entered through another door, with Ziva dressed in a filmy nightdress. They took her to Crites and set her hand in his.

"Fill her womb with a child that our family not end," the women recited and stepped back.

"May you be open to him and bring honor to our line," the men intoned.

They withdrew from the room. Ziva and Crites would have to do the rest, and the maid and groom who changed the sheets the next morning would announce the fulfillment of the mating.

Orak joined Tubal-Cain in bidding the guests a goodnight.

He stirred in the carriage. Cool air flowed across his face.

"We are home, sir," Keb announced from the doorway of the carriage.

Orak climbed out and walked inside. He moved through the halls toward his apartment. The house felt as cold and lonely as it did that night so long ago when Elin and Liva were hurt. Would it ever be warm for him again?

Tigre strolled around a corner and rubbed his fur against Orak's legs. He bent and brought the cat close to his face. "You miss her already, too, don't you."

The cat purred and settled into his arms.

~ ~ ~

Nat had been sitting, as usual, at his desk, when a message arrived for Qinten. It had no identifying braid or seal. Only Qinten's name. Nat had silently handed it to his master at his desk across from him.

Qinten had read the note and dropped it with a roar. "That cursed Orak! Call my carriage and get ready to go with me."

Qinten had rushed toward his dressing room and Nat stepped out the door and told the slave to call the carriage. He had then rushed to his own room and changed into clean clothing. He still had no idea where they were going.

Qinten had ranted about Orak as they rode through the city. "Crites. Who is this Crites? I don't know a Crites."

They had arrived as the priest began his words to join Ziva and Crites as mates. Qinten had growled throughout while Nat breathed a sigh of relief. If Tubal-Cain was involved, Ziva was safe.

He tried to ignore his Master's rantings as he watched Crites look at his sister. The look of love in Crites' eyes warmed him. With that look, she would be safe.

He saw Tubal-Cain on the front row, an honored guest. Was he related to Crites? Tubal-Cain? He was more important than Qinten's father, the governor. Was Qinten crazy?

And then, Qinten had exploded from his side and shouted at Orak. Nat's face warmed with embarrassment. Even though he was a slave, he struggled to be connected to the man.

Now, Nat escorted his raging Master from Crites' house and helped him into the carriage.

"Take us home," he directed the driver before seating himself.

The door closed and they were soon moving past the gates and onto the streets of Nod. Qinten cursed and growled at Crites, at Orak, and at Nat. Nat knew he would be beaten, and waited for the rain of blows to fall on him. He had no right to touch Qinten, especially during one of his rages, and especially not in public.

Crites' home may not have been public, but enough people had seen his master lose control and heard Orak's blunt statement. The Master did not like to be in a position of weakness.

"The other priests will hear of this. I will never be High Priest. Curse that man!" Qinten raged.

"Who will tell them? Does Tubal-Cain worship Lorca? I have never seen them there."

"No, but Kara's and Tawna's parents do. They were there. Will Bram and Korm still allow my mating with their daughters?" Qinten lowered his head into his hands.

"Of course, they will. You signed contracts. It takes more than this to nullify a contract. You still hold power in the cult of Lorca. Your wealth and power brought them to you and worked in your favor in the negotiations. They will not change their minds."

Nat worked to think of other things to mollify Qinten. "I doubt they will say anything to the other priests. They want their daughters to have the prestige of high priestess. They are contracted to you. Your mating with their daughters is certain and will take place the day after tomorrow. You will stand in a stronger position at the Priest Forum next week. Your mating to two beautiful women will overshadow any rumors of today's actions."

Qinten slumped into his seat across from Nat with a vacant stare. Nat feared for the health of his mind. He sat back in his seat, grateful to have avoided a beating, so far. As they rode, he went over the plans for the coming mating in his mind.

The ride ended before Nat wanted. He followed his master up the stairs and into the office attached to his apartment, breathing deeply and preparing for the blows. They did not fall. Qinten sat in his comfortable chair and stared out the window.

Nat opened the door and ordered hot water for Qinten. A bath always seemed to help him. When enough water filled the bath, Nat assisted him toward the bathing room.

Qinten glanced up, his eyes unglazed for a heartbeat. "Don't think I will forget your insolence."

"Of course not, Master."

He left him in the bath to steam and returned to the never ending papers and problems awaiting his attention. The bathing slave attended Qinten, for now.

His thoughts returned to Ziva, safely mated to another man, who appeared to have enough power to protect her from Qinten. Nat hoped Crites would protect her. Even mated to two women, Qinten would carry his mortification like a badge of office. He would seek revenge on Ziva and her mate. Nat would have to protect her.

He considered the strapping he would most assuredly receive. Even then, he would have to return to Qinten's apartment, to soothe his moods, and to protect his sister.

He heard a tiny rap at the door. Who would knock so timidly? The slaves at the door would never knock. Understanding the results of disturbing the Master in this mood, he strode to the door, half angry at the intrusion, and flung it open.

"What?"

"We are sorry. We need to see Qinten." The tiny girl with midnight black hair, contracted to mate Qinten, spoke in a tiny voice. She drew herself tall, waiting.

"You two? What are you doing here? Do you know of my Master's rages?"

"We have heard of them," the tall girl said. "We need to talk with him."

"Talk?" He stepped back and allowed them to enter the office. "He is in his bath. Now is not a good time. Perhaps you would like to wait?"

"No," the tiny girl said. "I think not. Which way to the bathing room?"

"Are you certain?" the tall girl lowered her eyebrows and stared at her friend.

Nat stared at them for several heartbeats.

"Of course. What better time? He can't ignore us. Which way to the bath?"

Nat shook his head. "You can't go back there. It would be—"

"Yes, it would but who will know? Unless, you should say something?" The small girl looked up at Nat.

He shrugged and started to lead the way.

"No. Just point the way. We can find it on our own." Her voice indicated she had experience ordering servants around.

With a mental shrug, Nat pointed her toward the bathing room and stood at the end of the hall, waiting for the shouting. It didn't take long. Qinten's voice raged for only a few heartbeats, then the bathing slave opened the door and shut it. With a glance toward Nat, he left.

Nat heard voices but no shouts or screams. After waiting for a few breaths, he turned on his heel and returned to his papers. The girls had put themselves in with his master. They could leave, when they were ready.

Chapter 39

An Invitation

Stretching her arms over her head, Ziva took in her new surroundings. The bed she lay in was bigger than the one she used at home. It had to be bigger, to hold two people, she mused. She remembered the night before with Crites and lay her hand over her stomach with a smile.

Curtains hung from a frame above the bed. Strange. They were a light fabric, allowing the breeze to move them gently. She looked at them more closely. Unusual patterns were painted on them, scenes of men hunting animals, arrows flying, and extending from the backs and necks of animals. Men stabbed with spears and swords. Streaks of red blood splashed across the green of the forest and tans of the animals.

Ziva shivered in disgust and rose out of the bed. She would have to talk with Crites about those curtains. Where was he, anyway.

After relieving herself and washing away the sleep in the bathing room, she glanced around the room where she woke, looking for clothing. She didn't want to wear the beautiful dress she wore the night before, not today.

A dress lay on a chest, one of her favorites. Its blue brought out the blue in her eyes. She slipped it on and struggled with the ties. Dressing was much easier with Ana. Who would help her now?

When she finally managed the ties, she dragged a brush she found through her hair, pulled on her slippers and walked out the door, intent on exploring. Her stomach growled. In her explorations, she'd better find food, she laughed to herself.

Ziva didn't go far before Crites found her.

"You live!" he teased. "I thought you would sleep all day."

"Is it late?" She glanced through a window looking for the sun.

"Past mid-day. I bet you are hungry."

"Not much," she said. Her stomach rumbled again. "Well, I guess more than that."

They laughed together. Crites showed her the way to the dining room, where a meal waited for them. After eating, he showed her around the house and into the gardens.

"Oh, I love the gardens. It's peaceful here." Ziva bent to smell a large bloom and jumped back when a bee buzzed out of it, almost into her nose.

"Peaceful, if you stay away from the bees," Crites teased.

Suddenly shy, Ziva looked up into his eyes. "Can you love me the way my parents loved each other?"

Crites took her hands in his. "I love you, already. I would not take a mate for the riches her father could provide, nor just because my family insist on it, and, yes, they have been insisting." He kissed her knuckles. "I would not take a mate I do not love. I watched you from a distance after we danced at Roven's party. I liked what I saw and what I heard. When I saw you again at the temple of Nimm, during the Growing Festival, and you danced and ate with me and laughed at my silly jokes, I knew you were the one for me."

They sat on a bench in a little gazebo, with morning glories and roses climbing up the outside, providing shade. Crites kissed her gently.

"I think I loved you then, too. I had dreams of a kind man rescuing me," she said.

"And I did."

"You did. Are you not afraid of what Qinten may do to you for taking me away from him?"

"He can do nothing. He didn't threaten me last night His threats were directed at Orak. He knows he cannot hurt me."

"Why? Isn't his power as priest of Lorca great?"

"He would like you to think it is. Even if he is elected to be High Priest next week, his reach is not as great as mine."

"Not even as High Priest? How can that be? His father is governor."

"Given that right by my grandfather, Tubal-Cain, and his father, Cain. He can lose the position any time grandfather chooses."

"And you can protect me from his forays? I have heard he enters men's homes and uses their wives."

"You are safe here. Even if he dared to attempt that, the Reds would not allow him entrance. He enters unguarded homes. Ours is walled and well protected from thieves and men like Qinten."

Ziva gripped Crites' hand. "You are certain?"

"I am."

She responded as he tenderly kissed her, putting her arms around him.

"Excuse me, sir."

They looked up to see a Red guard standing outside their little gazebo.

"The lady has visitors."

"Today? It is our first day together. Send her away." Crites flapped his hand toward the guard.

"Wait. Who would visit me today?" Ziva asked.

"They say they are your friends, Kara and Tawna."

"Oh." She hoped Orak would visit, but he wouldn't today.

"Go see what they want," Crites encouraged, "then get rid of them. We have things to do." He waggled his eyebrows at Ziva until she laughed.

"I will." She turned to the guard. "Lead the way. Someday I will be able to find my way around here."

Crites laughed.

~ ~ ~

The guard stopped at the door to a small parlor. Inside, Tawna and Kara sat. Kara scanned her surroundings, taking in the tables with gold dishes and elegant oil lamps sitting on them, the decorations on the walls, the curtains, covered in needlework, and the trinkets on the chests. At last, her eyes found Ziva's.

Ziva closed the door behind her and found a seat across from her friends.

"Welcome to my home."

"This is beautiful," Kara breathed.

Ziva glanced around. "Yes, it is. I have never been in this room."

"Never?" Tawna asked.

"No. Today is my first day here, remember. I only mated with Crites last night." She exaggerated a sigh and glanced around the room.

"We are sorry," Tawna said. "I know we shouldn't be here today. We should have sent a message."

Kara rolled her eyes.

"What can I do for you?"

"We don't have much time," Kara said. "We should be home preparing for our mating tomorrow."

"Oh?" Ziva leaned back in her chair. "You are being mated tomorrow? Who will you be mating?"

"Qinten," her friends chorused together.

"Both of you?" Her gaze bounced between her friends.

Kara giggled. "The look on your face is choice. Yes, we are to be mated with Qinten tomorrow. We will have the power and prestige of high priestesses of Lorca. We are here to invite you to the ceremony."

"Oh. That should be … nice." Ziva struggled to show interest. She wanted to be back with her new mate.

"It's at the temple of Lorca, tomorrow at mid-day. We'd love to have you there." Tawna reached out for her hand, then pulled it back.

Ziva blinked back her surprise. "What happened? How did you both manage this?" Though her feet sat on the floor, they began to tap a rhythm.

"Qinten spoke with my father while we were visiting with you. You didn't share everything that day, did you. You knew you were to be mated to Crites soon." Kara leaned back and laced her fingers behind her head.

"I didn't know when. And I wanted to keep it from Qinten. I feared he would ruin the celebration. He almost did."

"I don't know why Qinten raged as he did yesterday. He has asked for me. Our fathers discussed our mating father and signed the papers before the New Year. They set the mating rite for tomorrow. You have to come." Kara's lip extended in a little pout. "We came to yours."

"And so did Qinten." Ziva folded her arms. "This is the time for Crites and me to get to know one another, a time to be alone …" she glanced out the window, wondering where if he still waited for her in the garden.

"I am sorry to have interrupted your mating time." Tawna gave Ziva a little hug.

"I am sorry, too." The sparkle in Kara's eye belied her words as she stood.

"We wanted to be the ones tell you." Tawna shrugged.

"We wanted to invite you. It will be fun." Kara's effervescent character shone through.

Ziva walked with Tawna and Kara to the door and gave them each a quick hug.

"Come if you can, Ziva," Tawna whispered in her ear.

And they were gone.

Ziva stood many heartbeats by the door staring after them.

"Here you are. I thought you were lost." Crites' arms surrounded her. "What did your friends want?"

"No, not lost yet. I almost know where I am." Ziva mumbled into his chest. "They had news."

He moved his hands to her shoulders and stepped back a step. "What did they want? I hear a problem."

"Perhaps. They will be mated tomorrow at mid-day."

"To?" Crites' voice rose a pitch.

"To Qinten. Apparently, he contracted with their fathers before the New Year."

Crites stared at her for a long breath then began to shake. He let go of Ziva's arms and turned slightly, covering his mouth. Soon, sounds escaped from beneath his hands.

Ziva touched his shoulder. "Are you well?"

He nodded. A roaring guffaw escaped. "I'm fine," he managed between laughs. He held his stomach and shouted with laughter.

"He roared and threatened Orak in front of his new fathers. And, now, he will be mating not one, but two girls."

Ziva stared at him for three breaths, then saw the humor, tittered, then joined in full, stomach-shaking, laughs. "He will deserve what he gets."

They whooped and laughed. A guard peeped in, causing them to laugh even harder. At last they sat together on a long seat, exhausted.

"I wonder if Qinten will ever know the joy he brought us today?" Crites wiped tears from his eyes with a linen cloth.

"I doubt it. I, for one, will never share." Ziva accepted the cloth and wiped her face.

"Come with me. We have a garden to explore and a house to examine."

Arm in arm, they left the small parlor and walked down the long hall, occasional giggles erupting along the way.

~ ~ ~

That night, as Ziva brushed her hair before bed, she thought about the invitation. Qinten had spent time and effort in his attempt to lure her into his bed. His actions the night before gave away his desperation to have her. Taking her friends as his mates so soon after her own mating to Crites indicated an impatient need and a determination to be mated.

She sighed.

"What is it?" Crites took her brush and brushed the long tresses down her back.

"I fear for my friends. Do they really know what they're getting themselves into?"

"How could they? They are young girls, with no knowledge of the world, especially the world Qinten represents as a priest of Lorca."

"That is my concern. I have heard of what happens during the Planting Festival at the Temple of Lorca." She shuddered. "Kara thinks they will be fine, with her outgoing personality and desire to be the center of attention. But I don't know about Tawna and having to share? Especially, if Qinten manages to be elected High Priest. I fear they will not be so joyful after that festival."

Crites leaned forward, wrapping his arm around her. "Their mothers must have warned them. It is too late, now. They will have to manage."

"She invited me to attend tomorrow." Ziva's frown caused wrinkles in her forehead.

"You want me to approve?"

"No. Not really. I'd like your opinion. I'd really rather not be anywhere close to Qinten. Even thinking of him makes my skin squirm and my stomach threaten to empty. They are my friends." Ziva rubbed her arms then grabbed her stomach.

"Don't!" Crites pulled back in mock horror, laughing. "Don't go, then."

She stuck her tongue out.

"It isn't good to be sick just thinking of someone. Besides we are in seclusion. This is our mating time, not time to party with others."

Ziva turned on her stool and touched his cheek. "You are right. This is our time. I can visit with them later. They can tell me all about it … or not. I think I'd rather not."

Crites wrapped his arms around Ziva and lifted her from the stool. "I'd rather you do not, as well. There are other things for us to do together."

Ziva giggled.

No, she would not attend her friends' mating. She needed time to be with Crites.

Chapter 40

Lorcan Mating

Something startled Nat awake earlier than usual that morning. He stared around his little chamber, wondering what would cause his heart to beat so rapidly.

A noise? If a noise woke him, it no longer sounded. He sat up, sniffing the air.

Smoke, perhaps? No, nothing out of the ordinary.

Movement? Someone or something watching him. Not much to see. He sighed. If someone did lurk behind his wardrobe, more power to him. He would have to be thin to fit there. With a laugh, he settled back into the bed.

He thought of all the beds he had slept on in his life. Most were a blanket on the ground, or on the floor, if he was lucky. Only after he had been raised to Cook's helper did he earn a cot in a room with fewer others beside him. If only his friends from his life as a brick maker could see him now, if they dared to venture into Qinten's home. Good food, a real bed, off the floor and away from the rats, with clean blankets.

Clean bedding. What a treat. He remembered the grime filled blankets of his early days as a slave. He often felt he'd be better off without a blanket—except for the rats. Nat shivered unexpectedly at the thought.

He spoke aloud to drive the memory away. "Not now, Nat."

What was now? Why wake before the sun? What would happen today?

The mating ceremony. He remembered. Today Master Qinten would be mated, not with his sister but with her friends. Did Qinten know Tawna and Kara were Ziva's friend? He saw them there, at Crites, on the day of Ziva's mating — only two days previous? — while Qinten had made himself to look a fool. Somehow, they still chose to be his mates. Did they have a choice? The contract was signed.

Nat shook his head. Who would have thought this would happen?

The last two days had been busy, following Qinten's instructions in preparation. Cook had been extra busy. Avram and Drak had returned to work earlier than they probably should have, but, like Nat, they knew Cook would need their assistance. No one else could do it right.

He had stopped by the evening before to see how they were doing. They were doing well enough and Nat had other things to attend. He tapped Drak's shoulder and shrugged, then waved to Avram before leaving.

He stopped by the tailor's rooms, who had asked rapid questions about time and place, then shooed him from his workplace. Qinten had returned to ensure the costume had been repaired to meet his demands.

He had spent more time with the steward, Mibiti. The apartments were nearly completed, without the private connections to Qinten's apartment.

The steward mumbled as Nat returned to Qinten. He shouted for slaves to clean the apartments and dress them appropriately for mates of the Master. Nat left him to it.

After recovering from Ziva's mating and the visit of his future mates, Qinten gave him multiple tasks, sending him, along with multiple messengers, out to resolve challenges and gather necessary items from the market, from the temple, and from Qinten's father's home. He spent much of the day in a carriage, carrying messages and gathering supplies. Among his travels were a trip to the temple sacrificial pens. There he arranged for the sacrifices for the mating rite. Exhausted, he fell into bed the night before, after a small, cold dinner.

Perhaps hunger had brought him to wakefulness. His stomach growled even now as he flopped to his other side. Cook would already be in the kitchens. On a day like this, he doubted Cook went to bed. Nat threw off the blankets and pulled his tunic over his head and padded toward the kitchen.

"What are you doing here so early?" Drak cackled. "Searching for crumbs?"

"If that is all that is available. I woke with my stomach growling." Nat's stomach gurgled. The two men laughed.

Drak escorted him to the porridge pot and scooped up a bowl for his friend. Nat sat down at the table in the corner of the room and absorbed the comfort and friendliness of the kitchen.

Liana poured him a glass of milk and ran her hand across his back on her way to the pantry. "The sun rises. Do you have places to be?"

He glanced out the window at the red tinged clouds. "I do. May I see you later tonight?"

"If you can get away." She touched her fingertips to her lips and touched his.

Nat swallowed the milk, scraped back his stool, and strode back to his chamber. He quickly washed, dressed, and hurried to Qinten's apartment.

There he found Qinten in the process of rising. "You are here. Is all in readiness?"

"I just came from the kitchen. Cook has his part of the dinner prepared and ready to transport to your father's house. The steward reported last night that the apartments are prepared."

The tailor entered after knocking, bringing with him the new ceremonial finery and a thin robe to wear that night, with his new mates. Qinten accepted the new clothing and handed the tailor a gold coin.

Nat escorted Qinten to the bath. A man from the kitchen brought Qinten's morning meal, and Nat brought it to him before helping the dressing slave place the new tunic and robe on his master.

The sun stood but two hands above the horizon, slowly moving toward its zenith, when Nat opened the door to the carriage for Qinten. He stepped back to close the door, when Qinten called to him. "Ride inside with me."

Nat had changed into his own best tunic, to observe the rite from the edges, as was befit a personal slave. However, he expected to ride with the driver today. He stepped up into the carriage, pulled the door behind him, and sat across from his Master.

They rode in silence. Nat waited for Qinten to speak.

At last, he spoke. "Have you observed a mating ceremony in the Temple of Lorca?"

"No, sir."

"I will need you to stay close, ensure Astynax remembers to sacrifice two lambs and two doves before the ceremony. I will show you where to stand when we arrive. Watch for him to switch the animals. He will not want to use those you sent, rather he will want to choose to use imperfect animals, unacceptable to Lorca, or to sacrifice only one. I want Lorca to bless my mating with these women, not curse it. It is your responsibility to ensure this."

"Yes, Master Qinten." Nat nodded.

"Watch for those who might interrupt the rite." Qinten waved his hands toward the window.

"Who would want to interrupt it?"

"Orak, for one." Qinten spat. "Or Balg's priests or Nimm's. Perhaps Obike, or Stoffle. Be alert."

"I will. Anything else you want me to do?" Nat grabbed for a handle as the carriage bounced through a hole in the road.

"Cursed road." Qinten growled. "No. That will keep you plenty busy."

"Oh, ride on top when we go to Father's house. You don't need to be in here with me and my new mates."

~ ~ ~

"Were there any problems?" Liana stared into Nat's eyes from across the small table in the kitchen.

"The priest did try to exchange animals. I suspect he wanted to keep ours for his dinner table. I stood with them, pushing the correct ones forward, ahead of his. He had no choice but to use our lambs and doves.

"It was sad to see the beautiful things offered up to that bloody god. Their blood dripped from the bowl onto his phallus. Perhaps that was the plan, to cover it with blood to bless the mating." Nat shivered at the memory. "I hope no creature will have to be sacrificed to bless my mating."

Liana leaned forward and gathered Nat's hands into hers. "You do not believe Lorca can bless a mating?"

"No. How can he? His figure is made by craftsmen in Nod. From the finest basalt and marble, I agree, but he is created by man."

"Are not all the gods created by man? Are they not all metal, stone, or wood?"

"No, not all." Nat curled his lips inward, holding in the words that tried to spill out.

Liana's eyebrows rose skyward as she clutched his hands. "I have heard of another…a god of those who live in the west. He needs no icons, no statues to honor him. Is this who you mean?"

Nat stared at her for a long heartbeat. "Yes," he breathed the word so softly he could not be certain she heard. "Jehovah, the God of my papa."

"Then, you are—"

Nat set a finger on her lips. "Don't say it."

Liana formed the words without speaking: 'A lost child of the prophet.'

Nat nodded. The two were silent for a long breath.

Nat picked up the long metal spike and prodded the fire near them into life.

"No one tried to prevent the mating. The old priest, Astynax, became confused when calling upon both Kara and Tawna to accept the obligation to serve and honor Qinten. Even some in the crowd tittered at his mistake. But he managed to complete the rite. It is no wonder they seek a new high priest."

"No one attempted to sabotage it, then?" Liana lay her hands on the table between them again.

Nat stared at them, longing to take them in his. Not yet, he dared not.

"I did not see Orak there. Why would he want to ruin Qinten's mating?"

"Because Qinten tried to ruin his daughter's ceremony."

Nat stared at her. "You must not speak of this. Where did you hear such a thing?"

"The bath slave came into the kitchen blathering about girls in the Master's bath. His tongue ran amok, telling of Qinten's tears, crying that he had ruined his chances to be High Priest. Everyone in the kitchen heard it."

"That stupid slave. Doesn't he know his life is forfeit if Qinten ever learns of it ... and mine will be if he learns I knew and did not speak of it." Nat dropped his head into his hands. "That stupid man."

Liana ran her hands through his hair. "Better him than you."

Nat shook his head, then lifted his eyes toward Liana. "Perhaps. Or, perhaps I can catch him in a good mood, after his mating with his new mates, and convince him a to apply a lesser punishment." Nat sat up straight and looked all around the kitchen. "You must not repeat this. Tell the others."

"Of course, we won't. We are smarter than that, after living in Qinten's house all these years. I will have a word with Cook." Liana stroked Nat's hand.

He relaxed a bit and stared into the fire.

"Nat, what happened after the mating?"

Nat turned his gaze on Liana. "Qinten turned to walk his new mates from the altar. Confusion crossed his face. He took one new mate on his right and the other on his left and walked down the path between the crowd toward the waiting carriage."

He grinned. "Those in attendance tossed tiny seeds over their heads and birds from all over swarmed to eat it." He giggled a bit. "Not a pretty site, all the bird guano across the temple floor and out the door to the street. I think they missed Qinten and his guests, mostly."

Liana joined in laughing. "And you? How did you get to the Governor's home?"

"I jogged around the outside of the crowd, away from all the birds pecking up the seed, arriving in time to open the door for Qinten and his mates. After he helped them in, he climbed in and sat between them. I climbed on top and rode with the driver."

"It must have been a beautiful day to ride on top of a carriage. I stood outside in the kitchen garden for a long time, enjoying the warm sun on my face." Liana turned her face up, in memory of facing the sun.

"I thought so. Your face has a glow." Nat trapped her hands in his, enjoying the feel of their warmth.

Liana gazed at him, a warmth touching her small smile.

"Was the mating party grand? Cook worried that their cooks would not prepare enough. He took huge roasted beef, along with all the pies, cakes, and puddings with him. It took ten wagons to cart it all there and nearly all our kitchen help. He even took along the scullery boys to help clean pots."

"That is why it is quiet here. They should be along soon. The food was grand. It is a good thing Cook brought the extra beef. I saw a look of fear cross one of the carver's face when asked for more beef. Drak wheeled out the beef just then. I thought it had been arranged between the two cooks."

Liana shook her head. "No. Cook took it over without being asked. Avram returned for more pastries, and told of the

Governor's cook shouting at them for their insolence. 'Did they not believe he could plan for a big party?' It looks like he did not."

"He must have miscalculated, for much of the carcass was bare before they moved in to dance. I watched from the edge, as I always do, waiting for instructions from the Master. The party was going loud and happily when Qinten gave me permission to leave. I guess he can bring his mates home and ... well, on his own." Nat felt the red creep up his neck.

"And bed them without your help? I would hope so." Liana laughed.

Nat joined her, though the joke was on him.

"One of the carts was returning home, rather empty. The driver allowed me to ride with him."

"Allowed? I doubt he had a choice." Liana said.

"Not really, I guess. I did ask, not order it."

"And now, you are home, sharing with me."

"And now I am home." Nat leaned across the table and kissed Liana. She did not pull away but returned his kiss.

When they separated, Nat stared at her. Fear tickled his heart. "What will we do? Qinten will not allow us to mate."

"We will find a way."

Chapter 41

Mated Before Jehovah

A message arrived for Ziva. Tawna and Kara wanted to see her. They could not come to Crites' house, and Ziva was not welcome in Qinten's, as if she would go into that spider web. Tawna suggested a visit to her father's fabric shop at the market.

Ziva had taken on responsibilities of supervising portions of the household. She met with the steward about the cleaning and decoration of the rooms. She visited in the kitchen, conferring with the cook about meals. In spite of all this busyness, Crites felt her loneliness.

He had responsibilities to his businesses that kept him occupied and busy. She had books and the household responsibilities she had taken on for herself, along with quiet sewing, alone in the parlor of the apartment she shared with Crites.

Crites had employed the daughter of Ana's sister, Dinah, to help her dress and paint her face, but servants were not sufficient company. Ziva had lived like this with Orak, with a few female servants. However, her friends had been welcome and visited frequently.

The message from Tawna sparked a desire in Ziva to visit with her friends. She had not been out of her new home since the mating ceremony, not even to visit with Orak.

Ziva took the message to Crites, seeking his support and aid in meeting with Tawna. He was concerned for her safety. The market continued to be filled with cut-purses, thieves, and robbers. Thieves had no problem with stealing wealthy men and women to force their families to pay for their return.

Crites conferred with Leo, the head of his Red Guard, about the safest way to escort Ziva to meet her friends. He understood her sadness at her separation from her friends and her desire to see Tawna.

On the appointed day, Ziva dressed carefully with Dinah's assistance, then searched for Crites. He took her by the hand and spun her around.

"Beautiful, my dear. You look lovely."

Ziva smiled and felt the warmth of a blush rush into her cheeks. "Thank you. Are the preparations made so I can go? Will I be able to go safely?"

"You will go in an unmarked carriage. It will take you as close as it can get you to Korm's shop. Here." Crites handed her a little pouch.

The weight of it surprised her, and she shook it gently.

"A few coins for you to purchase fabric for new dresses, and, perhaps purchase a treat for yourself and your friends." Crites grinned at her confusion. "You are my mate. I will have you act and dress in a way that those who see you know of your new status."

He pulled her close and embraced her. "I would keep you safely here in the house where I can protect you. However, I know you need to see your friends. I will have you protected."

Ziva rode in the carriage, nicer than the one Orak owned, to the entrance to Korm's shop. She was escorted by four Red Guards, their swords in their hands, frightening away any customers, as well as cut purses or body thieves.

The bell above the door tinkled as the leading guard entered Korm's shop. The others kept her back, until he had entered and examined it, to be certain she would be safe. At last, they allowed Ziva to enter. Two guards stationed themselves outside the front door. The other two stood inside, eyes sweeping across the room. Korm came from the back, a measuring tape in his hand.

"Ah, it is you, Ziva. Crites is an intelligent man to protect you so carefully."

"Hello, Korm. Is Tawna —"

Tawna peeked from the back room. "There you are! I was afraid you would not come."

Ziva ran to her friend and touched her face. Tawna kissed Korm on the cheek. He made an excuse and returned to the back.

"I am here. I wanted to see you. I worry about you and Kara in … In Qinten's house.."

"It has been … interesting. So far, Qinten has been kind to us. I think he is liking the prestige of two mates."

"I hope he continues to be kind. I brought coins to purchase fabric for a new dress."

"Good," Tawna said, then pulled Ziva into an alcove near the back. "Your guards can watch you here, and not listen in."

Kara came from the back of the house and joined the other two in the alcove.

"How is it, really? You two don't look as happy as I expected you would." Ziva stared at her friends.

"We are as happy as we can be." Kara stared at her hands for a long breath. "We each have our own apartments. I took my maid with me. She takes care of my every need." She stopped to wind a curl around her finger.

"We are treated well. You must admit that, Kara," Tawna said.

"Do you have everything you thought you would get from a wealthy man?" Ziva felt the weight of the purse Crites gave her before she left.

"I suppose." Kara glanced up. "Oh, Ziva. You were right. Qinten has a dark soul. He expects us to do horrible things. I should have listened to you. Now, it is too late. The Planting Festival is next week. We are here to be fitted for our costumes. You should see the fabric."

"I am certain they are beautiful. Tawna's father sells beautiful fabric." Ziva became aware of her foot bouncing and set it on the floor.

"It is beautiful, a lovely dark amber. It matches my eyes. But, well, come." Kara grabbed her hand to drag her to the back room.

One of the guards followed.

Korm looked up and smiled. "You have come to see Kara's and Tawna's new costume? Qinten said to spare no expense." He held up a beautiful amber colored fabric. "This is Kara's," he lifted a beautiful yellow, "and this is Taawna's."

"Oh, they are beautiful." Ziva reached for Tawna's. "May I?"

Korm handed it to her. She lifted it up to hold it in front of her friend. The sheerness of the fabric clearly revealed Ziva's hand. "Will you be wearing another dress beneath this?"

"No. And look at it." Tawna encouraged Ziva to lift up the short, slender skirt and tiny top, a shade lighter, that covered little.

"This is it? Why would he have you wear anything?" Ziva gasped.

"Exactly." Tawna sighed.

"Does this mean Qinten is—"

"Yes. He was elected High Priest the week after our mating. You should see him strut and brag." Kara tittered a few heartbeats.

"Will you be attending the festival at the Temple of Lorca?" Tawna asked.

Ziva shook her head. "No. We are not followers of Lorca. I do not know where we will celebrate the Planting Festival, but it will not be with any of the Lorcan priests."

"Oh. I had hoped you would be there to see us." Kara's shoulders slumped and she dropped her head.

"I am sorry."

"I'm not." Tawna said.

"Mistress Kara, Mistress Tawna, we are to return shortly. Are you ready?"

Ziva's eyebrows shot up. "Nat?"

"Yes, Mistress Ziva." Nat spoke stiffly. "I escorted Mistress Kara and Mistress Tawna to this fabric shop to have their costumes for the festival fitted."

"I have coins to buy material for a new dress. Help me choose, if you have time, Kara, Tawna?"

"I want to spend some time with my father. You go," Tawna said.

Kara and Ziva returned to the front of the shop, with her guard, where fabric was jammed close together. Some flowed out in display.

"How am I ever going to choose among all these?" Ziva waved her hands around the room.

"Your eyes are blue. You can look for a blue like them. Or choose a color you love, like pink, or a soft green. I'll be back," Kara said. "Tawna's father wants me to put the costume on one last time to be certain it 'fits'. How can it fit? There is not much of it."

Kara hurried to the back of the shop and Ziva wandered around. She discovered the colors were stacked together, mostly. She touched several pieces, caressed by their softness. She was drawn to an orange, and held it to her face.

"How does this look on me?" She glanced around. The guards were staring past her. She turned to see Nat standing near her. "How does this look against my face?"

"I've seen other colors that look nicer." Nat spoke barely above a whisper.

"Which would you choose for me, then?"

Nat glanced at the guards who took a step toward them.

Ziva waved at them. "Don't worry about Nat. He won't hurt me." She looked back at him. "Will you?"

"No. I promised I would care for you, a long time ago. I could not hurt you, even if my Master demanded it." Nat reached out to touch the orange and brown beads at Ziva's neck. "I'm glad you still wear these. I feared your new mate wouldn't understand."

"He does. I'm glad you met." Ziva dropped her voice.

"Let's look at some other fabric then." Nat glanced at the guards.

They walked around the shop discussing the fabrics, and exchanging little bits of information."

"I have a woman I would mate, if Qinten would allow." Nat glanced down into Ziva's eyes.

"He will not allow it? Why?"

"I am his property, as is Liana, my woman. We would mate. Do you think our papa would understand if we do not and act as if we had?"

"How can he know or think bad of you? He is far away."

"I have seen Mama in my dreams—"

"A beautiful woman?"

Nat nodded.

"I saw her months ago, in my dreams." Ziva whispered.

"Papa believes in Jehovah. They have … other laws." Nat lifted a blue fabric and shook his head.

"And we are in Nod, and you are a slave. Do what you can to be happy, Nat. How are we going to get you out of Qinten's home?"

Nat dropped the fabric. "I do not know. Qinten is jealous and fearful. I know too much of what is going on in his life. I fear he will never allow me to leave. What about this?" He held up a maroon fabric. "It looks nice against your skin."

Ziva touched the fabric. There was a checked design, layering gold through the material. "Yes. This will work."

"But, what about you? And, what about Tawna and Kara?"

"For now, they only know of me as Qinten's personal slave. Kara will be upset if she thinks I am still trying to get you for Qinten."

"True. You'd better check on her."

Nat touched her cheek and marched toward the doorway as Tawna breezed out. "Did you find something? I had to try on my costume again. I'm sorry."

"Yes, this." Ziva held up the bolt of maroon checked fabric. "What do you think?"

"I love it. Your hair will look beautiful against it." She turned toward the doorway. "Father. Father. Ziva wants to make a purchase."

~ ~ ~

Qinten entered Kara's apartment, calling her and Tawna to come to him. He had given Nat the rest of the night to rest and be ready for the morning and the Planting Festival.

Nat knew, from previous nights, that he would have time to himself. He felt a twinge of sadness for Kara and Tawna but their fathers had agreed to the mating.

He waited a time, ensuring the Master would not remember something for him to do. When no call came, he opened the door to his chamber and sauntered toward the kitchen.

He had no reason to hide his movement within the house, as the Master's personal slave. Still, he walked quietly, wanting to meet no one on this trek through the big house. He avoided the board that squeaked, not willing to talk to anyone along the way.

Liana waited for him in the warmth of the kitchen. Although the days grew longer and warmer each day, the kitchen still held a welcome warmth. The darkness within provided a protection from outside eyes.

Nat and Liana embraced and kissed. The two young lovers stood in front of the fire, enveloped in its warmth and the strength of the other's arms. They stood with foreheads touching.

"What shall we do, my love?" Nat asked. "This is not going to last. Someone will learn of our love and share it with the Master. I have nothing to give to silence them nor do you." He silenced her offer with a kiss.

"I could only offer any nosy man or woman an extra plate of pastries," Liana whispered.

"For how long?" Nat stared into her eyes.

"Not long. Cook would notice."

"Exactly my point. What will we do?"

"I do not know."

Nat dropped his arms and paced around the table, remembering the times he worked here, when things were simple. "I will not give you up, nor will I have you thrust into the attention of Qinten. I will not allow you to be used, as he uses the other women of this household. I do not know how you have avoided it so long."

"Cook protects me. I do not understand why. He will not speak of it. He has hidden me from the Master since I was but a tiny girl, barely big enough to stand on a stool and wash vegetables."

"You have been here that long?" Nat stopped pacing and caught Liana up in his arms.

"I can remember no other home, no other existence."

"There has to be a way for us to be together, to be mated, without him knowing." Nat gripped her arms.

"We can't be mated without a priest, without the blessing of one of the gods. That would expose us." Liana touched Nat's cheek. "We can —"

"No. We have discussed this before. I will not be with you, will not pretend to be mated, unless we are. I would not stand before one of those priests, regardless of the danger. My papa would be sad to hear that I bowed before the idol of another god." Nat lifted a loose strand of hair and tucked it behind her ear.

"Then we have no hope. Qinten will never let us go free."

"No, there is always hope. We will find a way." Nat pulled her close and held her, a memory of his mama and papa flitted past his vision. They stood just like this.

"Liana, I have something to ask you. Sit with me."

They moved the bench beside the table and sat with their backs to the table. Nat turned so he could look at Liana's face.

"I have never heard you talk of the gods. Do you believe any of the gods of Nod can help you?"

She pulled her eyebrows together until they bent into little squiggles across her face. "We watch the rites here, when the Master performs them during the festivals. Some of the women here have little goddess idols they pray to. I never have."

"I was but a child when we were taken from my parents. My memories of Jehovah are vague. But, when I call upon Him, my heart burns. I cannot bow before another. Not when I feel the life and love of Jehovah. Can you understand?"

Liana lay her hand on Nat's chest. "I have felt a warmth when you speak of your Jehovah that I have never felt around the many figures of gods in the women's rooms."

Nat took her by the hands. "Kneel with me. Let us pray to Jehovah. If any god can solve our problem, He can."

Liana gazed into his eyes, her face softening. She slipped from the bench to kneel beside him. He held his hands up and closed his eyes, as he remembered seeing his papa do when he prayed.

"Oh, Jehovah. We come before you searching for solutions to our problems. We are slaves, property of Qinten, whose heart is black. We desire to be mates, husband and wife, as my papa and mama are. How can this be without the blessing of a priest? Will you bless us? Bless our mating and make it honorable?"

A warmth enveloped Nat, filling him with joy. He opened his eyes and glanced at Liana. Tears flowed down her cheeks as she gazed at him, then nodded.

Nat bowed his head. "Thank you, Jehovah."

He dropped his hands and leaned toward Liana, joining her in a tender kiss. "We must remember this time and pray often."

Liana nodded.

The darkness began to lighten when Nat slipped back into his chamber. A grin played across his face. The night of sleeplessness had been worth it. He would need to be on guard with Qinten. He could not allow his joy to show. Slaves were not allowed joy, especially Qinten's slaves.

Nat fell to his knees and lifted his hands in prayer. He intoned softly. "Lord Jehovah. I thank you for the gift of Liana and our mating. Bless us, that we may find a way to freely express our love. Help us to be free of Qinten. His soul is dark, his god repelling, and his ownership of our bodies confining. Help us be free of him.

"I thank you that I have found my sister, Ziva. I am grateful she avoided the trap of mating with Qinten. May she find joy with Crites. May their union be blessed.

"Bless our papa and mama. Let them know we have found a measure of joy in our lives. I pray, Lord Jehovah. Keep us all safe."

Tears soaked his shirt as he pulled it off and lay in his bed for the short part of the night left to him. All would be well. He and Liana would find a way.

~ ~ ~

After visiting with her friends, Ziva ran to their apartment looking for Crites, though she knew he may not be there. She left her package containing the dress fabric and the purse with the extra coins on a table and wandered out into the garden. She hoped he would find her there.

The plants had grown. The sunshine warmed the earth and where once there were tiny leaves and buds, Ziva saw big, open blossoms on full plants. She inhaled the fragrances, allowing the beauty to settle her mind as she walked.

She found the seat in the gazebo she and Crites occupied that first day after their mating and sat in it, wishing he would find her and sit beside her once more. Where the sun had shone brightly on them, the morning glories and roses now completed the shading. She leaned back on the seat, warm from the heat of the day, and closed her eyes, remembering Crites' attentions of the night before.

"Hello, lovely lady. May I join you?"

Ziva smiled and kept her eyes closed. "Mmmm. Perhaps."

Crites sat beside her and drew her into his arms. "I missed you today. I don't like it when you are gone, and I can't find you." He kissed her gently.

Ziva opened her eyes and gazed into his. "I hoped you would find me here. You were busy somewhere when I returned."

"Yes, business. But when Leo reported that you returned, I came looking for you. I saw the package in the apartment. Did you find fabric you like?"

"I did, a lovely maroon. It is so hard to choose just one."

"You had enough coins for more, didn't you?" Crites lifted his eyebrows.

"I did."

"Then you should have purchased more. Or was it a ploy to have a reason to visit Tawna again?" Crites pulled his eyebrows low together.

"No. I would not do that," Ziva cried and waved her hand toward him as though to hit his arm.

Crites caught it with a laugh. "I know."

"You know?" She heard his laugh. "Oh. You were teasing."

They laughed together.

"It is nice to go out and see my friends, occasionally. And Nat escorted them to the shop to try on their costumes for the festival. We spent a short time together alone." She set her hands in her lap and crossed her ankles.

"Ah. That is who the mysterious man you were with."

"I didn't think to introduce him to the guard." Ziva's foot bounced up and down.

"No need. He behaved."

"Of course, he's my brother." Ziva set her feet on the ground and stared at her mate.

"I know that. They didn't. Better they don't for a bit longer. It will be safer for you both." Crites brushed back a lock of her hair from her face.

"I didn't think of that. We were alone in the shop, except for the Red Guards. I'll be more careful. It will be hard to see him now." She set her hand on Crites' arm.

Crites kissed Ziva once more.

"Um. I like that. Thank you for taking me as your mate," she said.

"I like it, too." Crites took her hand in his. "I do love you, Ziva."

She lifted his hand to her lips and kissed his knuckles. "I know, Crites. I love you, too. I just worry for my brother."

"And you should. He is in a dangerous place. We will find a way to get him away from Qinten."

"Can we?"

"We are smart, we will find a way." Crites kissed her on the forehead. "You will have to go back to visit your friends again." His voice became sterner. "But next time —"

"Be more careful?" She stared back into his eyes.

"Yes, that, but purchase more than one piece of fabric."

Their laughter sounded through the garden.

Back Matter

Acknowledgements:

Once more, there are many people to thank in the creation of this book.

First, and foremost, thanks go to my beloved husband, Jack, who patiently helps me remember words I forget and supports me in my writing journey. He has spent hours and headaches proofreading my manuscripts to be sure they have fewer mistakes. Though I probably didn't catch them all, he helped to catch most of them.

I must also thank my sister, Tina Gilger, whose encouragement in the very beginning pushed me to start writing when I had no idea I could. Together, we share ideas, challenges, courses, and conferences. It is because of her that I even tried to write.

Thanks to my editor, Danica Page, whose thoughtful comments have added to my ability to write a story. I appreciate her editing skills. Also, thanks to Dar Albert, my cover artist, whose skills make it possible for you, the reader to find my book among all the hundreds of thousands of other books available to you.

Thanks go to my parents, as well. They continue to love and support me. My nearly-90-year-old father assists in the final proofreading. He helps to make this book, and every other book better for you. Their love gives me an example of the love I hope to share in my stories.

Last, but never least, I am grateful to you, my readers. Without you, my stories would never be shared. Thank you!

Did You Enjoy This Book?

If you did, will you do something for me?

I'm and independent author, publishing my books without the backing of a major publisher. That means no six-figure advances and no advertising budget. This makes it difficult to promote my novels and put them in places new readers can find them. But you can help me.

Honest reviews and genuine "word-of-mouth" advertising makes all the difference. I'm not asking for one of those awful book reports I used to try not to sleep through, that you did in school. What will help me is if you would leave an honest star rating and a couple of sentences on Amazon or Goodreads. Or a short review on your blog. Or tell your friends about it on Facebook or Twitter.

Let people know what you liked about this book and why they might like it, too, maybe even buy a few books for your friends to read. And, if there was something you didn't like, you can say that, as well. Constructive criticism helps me write a better book next time. Send those to me at Angelique@AngeliqueCongerAuthor.com. I look forward to your email.

But, please. No spoilers!

Thanks for reading.

Other Books by Angelique Conger:

Ancient Matriarchs:
Eve, First Matriarch

Into the Storms:
Ganet, Wife of Seth

Finding Peace:
Rebecca, Wife of Enoch

Moving into Light:
Zehira, Wife of Enoch

Coming Soon:

Captured Freedom
Lost Children of the Prophets,
Book 2
(Look for it in Spring 2018)

ABOUT THE AUTHOR

Angelique Conger discovered the wonders of writing books later in her life. For years, the stories of ancient women enticed her, challenging her to tell their stories. No one knows or tells the stories of these women, unknown in history, not even most of their names. Many of the stories of their husbands are unknown. Angelique tells their stories as though they sat beside her, whispering their stories into her ear in her series **Ancient Matriarchs**.

Angelique is currently working on the next books of this *Lost Children of the Prophet* series. She says the only way to discover the answers to certain questions is to write the story. This book was written to answer one of those questions.

Angelique lives in southern Nevada with her husband, a bird, and two turtles. She looks forward to visits from her grandchildren, and their parents.